PATRICIA BRIGGS' ™
MERCY THOMPSON
moon called
VOLUME ONE

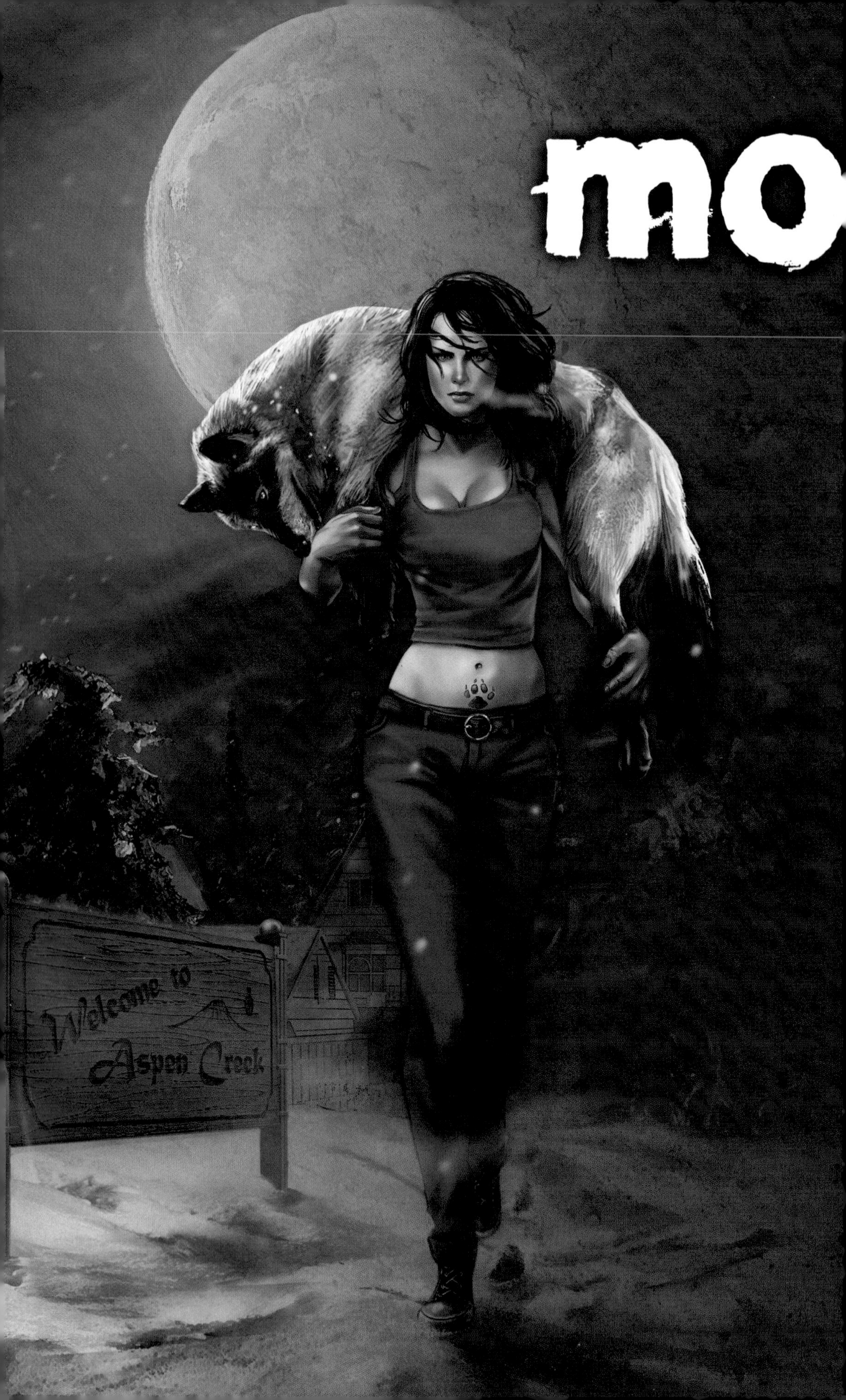
mo
Welcome to
Aspen Creek

n called

VOLUME ONE

WRITTEN BY:
PATRICIA BRIGGS
& DAVID LAWRENCE

ARTWORK & COLLECTION COVER BY:
AMELIA WOO

LETTERS BY:
ZACH MATHENY

THEMATIC CONSULTANTS:
LINDA CAMPBELL, JENIFER LINTHWAITE & DEBRA LENTZ

CONSULTATION: **LES DABEL & ERNST DABEL**

COLLECTION DESIGN BY: **BILL TORTOLINI**

DYNAMITE
ENTERTAINMENT

ISBN10: 1-60690-203-2
ISBN13: 978-1-60690-203-5

10 9 8 7 6 5 4 3 2 1

namite Entertainment:

CK BARRUCCI	•	PRESIDENT
AN COLLADO	•	CHIEF OPERATING OFFICER
SEPH RYBANDT	•	EDITOR
SH JOHNSON	•	CREATIVE DIRECTOR
H YOUNG	•	BUSINESS DEVELOPMENT
ON ULLMEYER	•	GRAPHIC DESIGNER

w.dynamite.net

Dear Reader,

Most authors are control freaks. Why else would we sit for day after day building stories if not to find people who will listen to us at last and do what we tell them to do -- or at least suffer horribly when they don't? Imaginary people, but still, it satisfies some yearning desire to have someone, someone who understands that we are the ones in charge.

Mercy has been my imaginary friend for a long time. I worried a little about how I'd feel letting someone else play in my sandbox for a while. I expected to be traumatized -- not delighted. Watching Mercy and her friends come to the visual world of graphic novels and comics has been an amazing journey full of talented and terrific people. It hasn't been a journey without perils and setbacks -- but any journey worth taking has those. And for me, this has truly been worthwhile. I've discovered new friends-- and had my breath taken away by the results of their efforts.

These are not the comic books I grew up with. The artistry and the availability of new printing techniques have drastically improved the final product. But the dedication and the talent are the same. I'm ecstatic about the new paths the world of graphic novels has opened for Mercy. I hope you enjoy the adventure as much as I do.

Best wishes,

Patricia Briggs

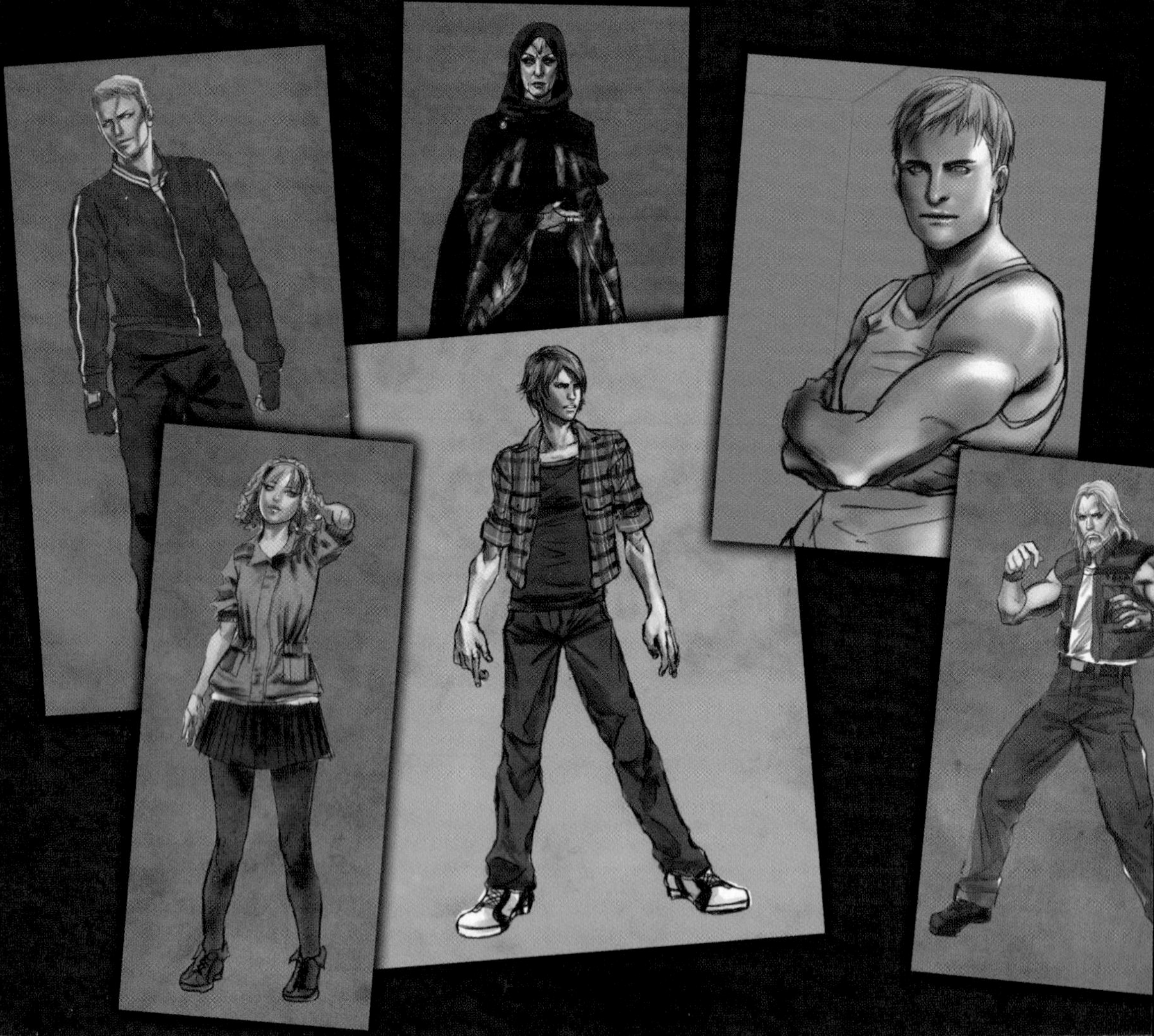

Mercy Thompson inhabits two worlds without truly belonging to either.

To the human inhabitants of Washington's Tri-Cities she's a bit of an oddity, a fiercely independent woman who repairs cars for a living.

To the town's darker residents, werewolves, vampires, and fae, she's a walker, a last-of-her-kind magical being with the power to become a coyote.

Always an outsider, Mercy warily straddles the twilight line dividing our everyday world from that darker, inhuman dimension.

But now her two worlds are about to collide. Outnumbered and outmuscled, can Mercy possibly survive?

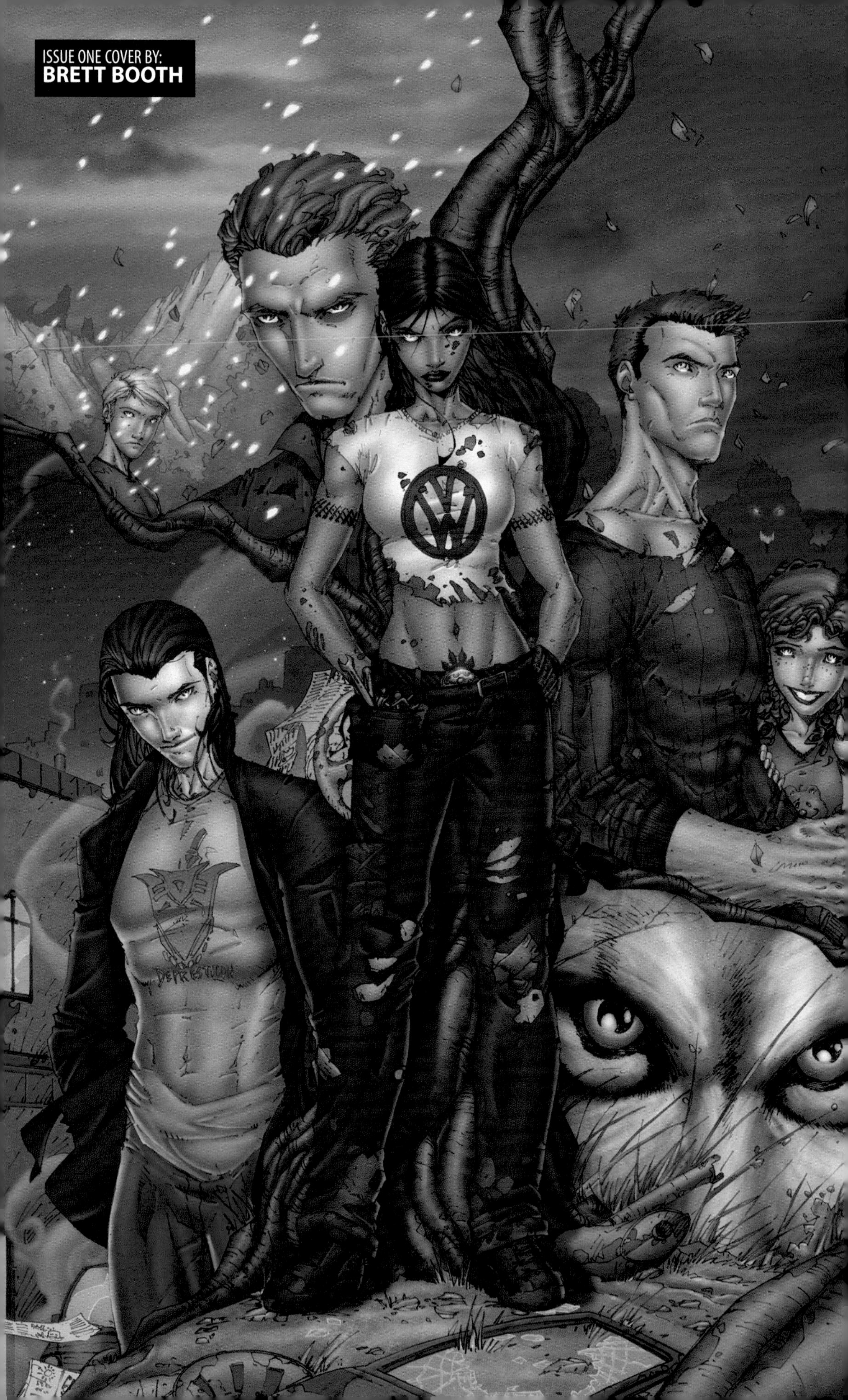
DEPRESSION

ISSUE ONE COVER BY:
BRETT BOOTH

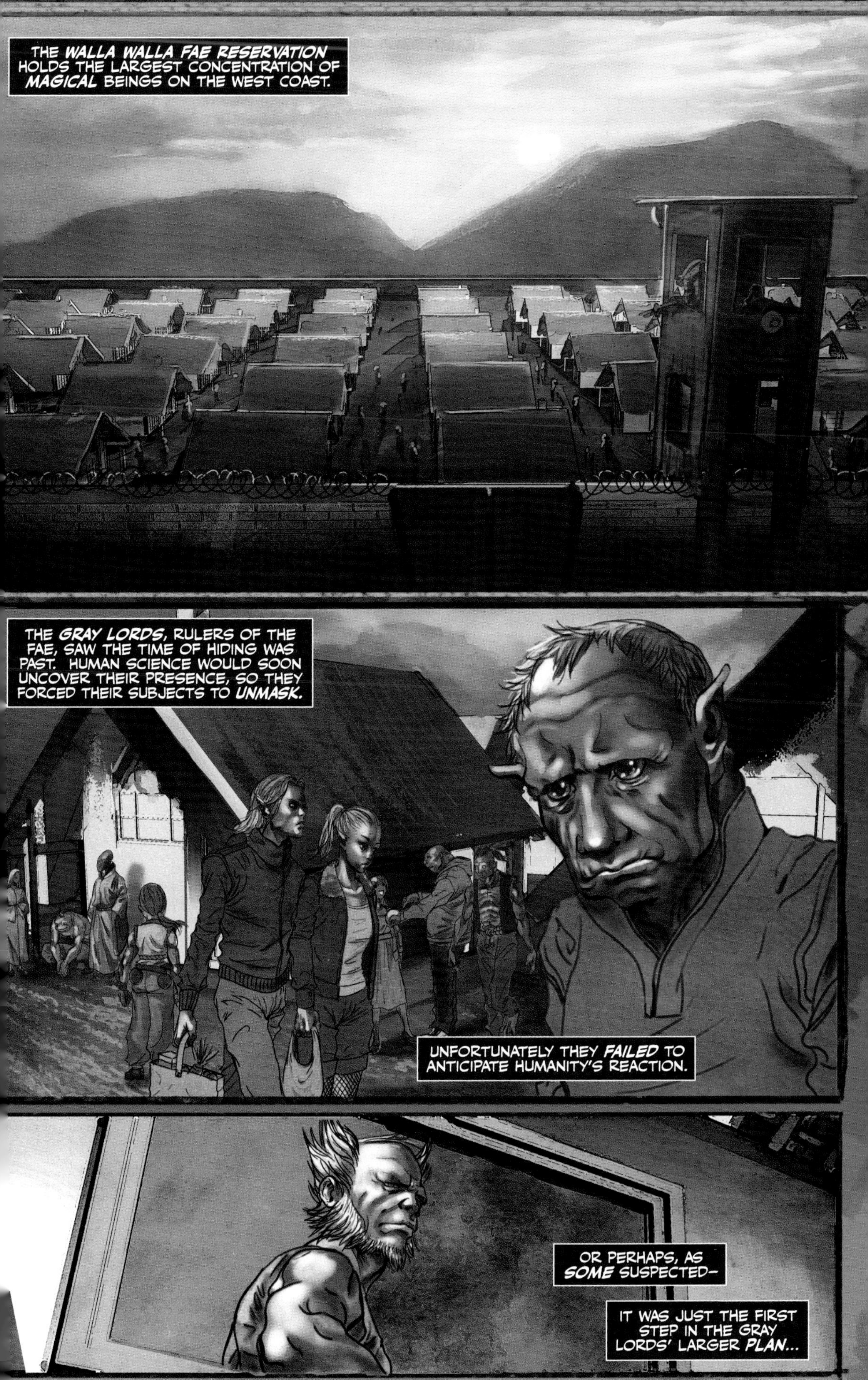
THE WALLA WALLA FAE RESERVATION HOLDS THE LARGEST CONCENTRATION OF MAGICAL BEINGS ON THE WEST COAST.
THE GRAY LORDS, RULERS OF THE FAE, SAW THE TIME OF HIDING WAS PAST. HUMAN SCIENCE WOULD SOON UNCOVER THEIR PRESENCE, SO THEY FORCED THEIR SUBJECTS TO UNMASK.
UNFORTUNATELY THEY FAILED TO ANTICIPATE HUMANITY'S REACTION.
OR PERHAPS, AS SOME SUSPECTED–
IT WAS JUST THE FIRST STEP IN THE GRAY LORDS' LARGER PLAN...

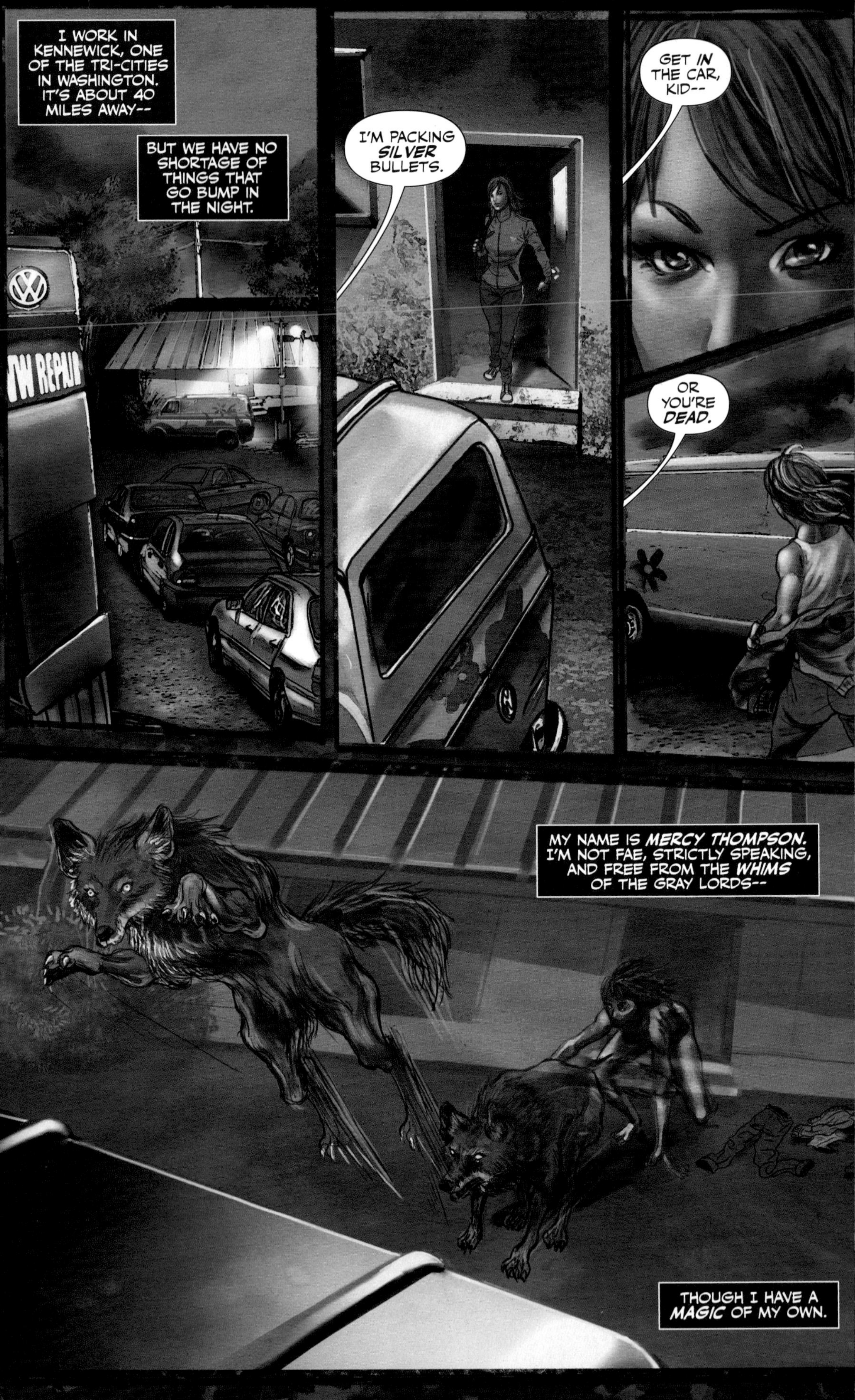
I WORK IN KENNEWICK, ONE OF THE TRI-CITIES IN WASHINGTON. IT'S ABOUT 40 MILES AWAY--
BUT WE HAVE NO SHORTAGE OF THINGS THAT GO BUMP IN THE NIGHT.
VW REPAIR
I'M PACKING *SILVER* BULLETS.
GET *IN* THE CAR, KID--
OR YOU'RE *DEAD.*
MY NAME IS *MERCY THOMPSON.* I'M NOT FAE, STRICTLY SPEAKING, AND FREE FROM THE *WHIMS* OF THE GRAY LORDS--
THOUGH I HAVE A *MAGIC* OF MY OWN.

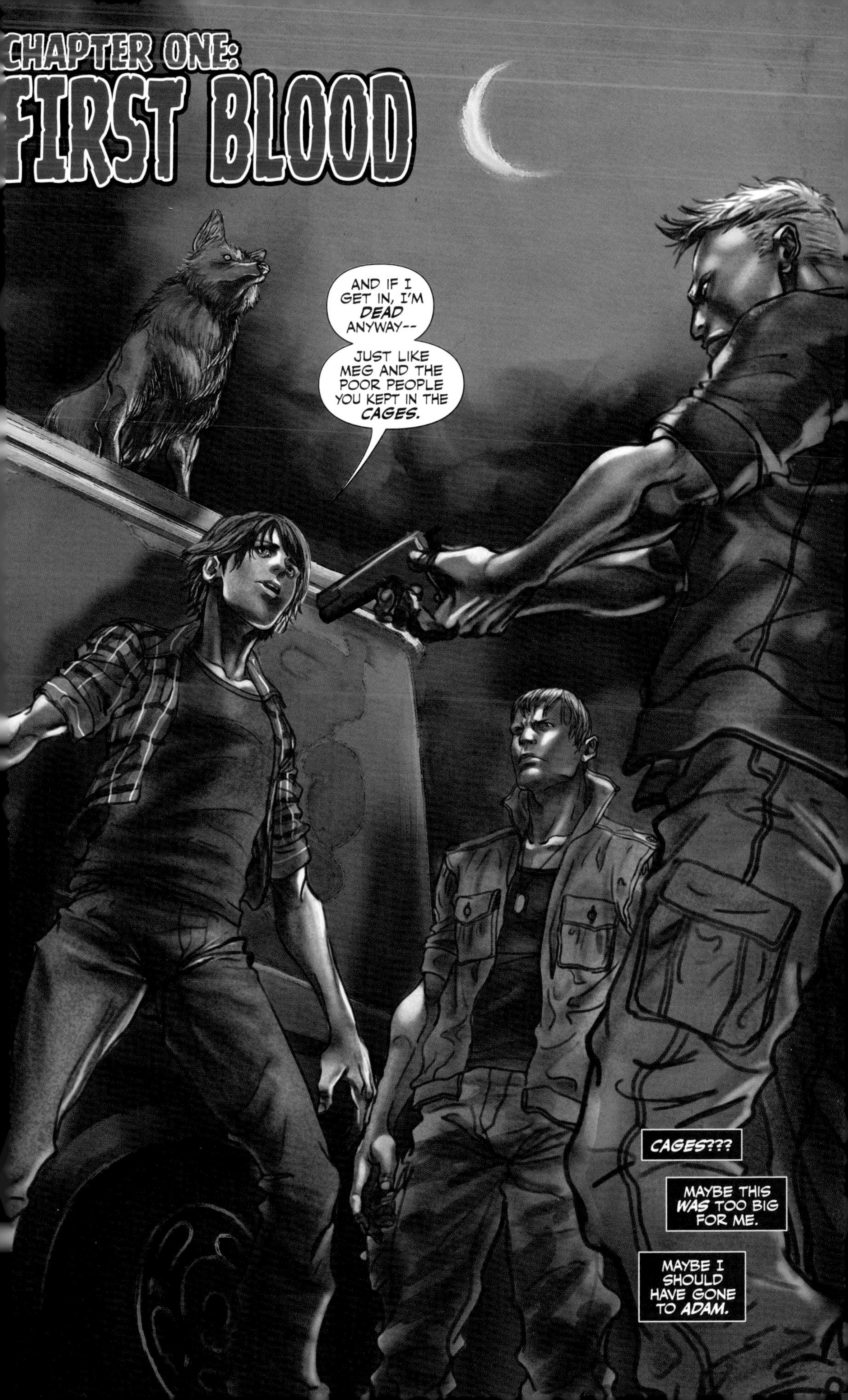
CHAPTER ONE:
FIRST BLOOD
AND IF I GET IN, I'M DEAD ANYWAY--
JUST LIKE MEG AND THE POOR PEOPLE YOU KEPT IN THE CAGES.
CAGES???
MAYBE THIS WAS TOO BIG FOR ME.
MAYBE I SHOULD HAVE GONE TO ADAM.

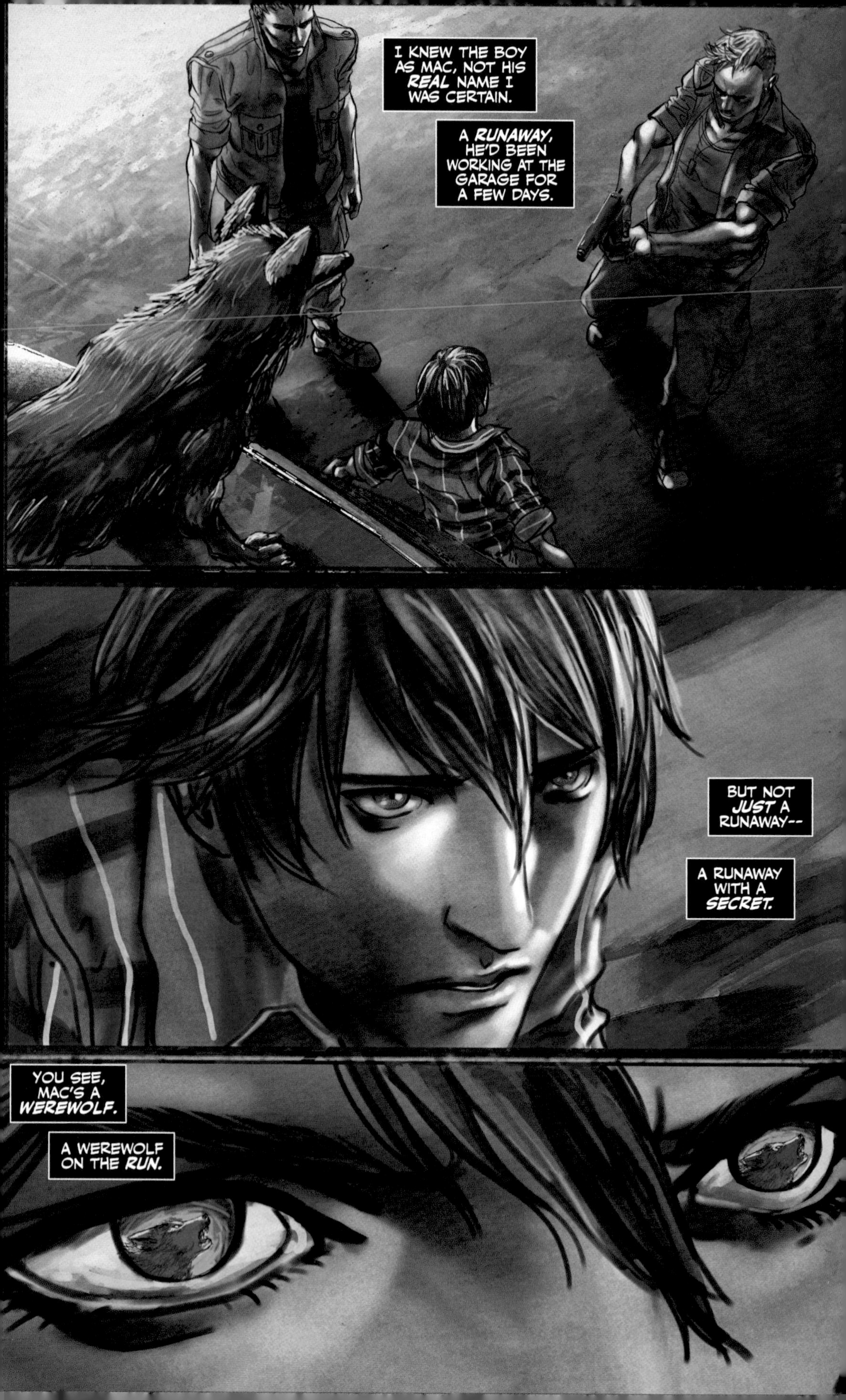
I KNEW THE BOY AS MAC, NOT HIS REAL NAME I WAS CERTAIN.
A RUNAWAY, HE'D BEEN WORKING AT THE GARAGE FOR A FEW DAYS.
BUT NOT JUST A RUNAWAY--
A RUNAWAY WITH A SECRET.
YOU SEE, MAC'S A WEREWOLF.
A WEREWOLF ON THE RUN.

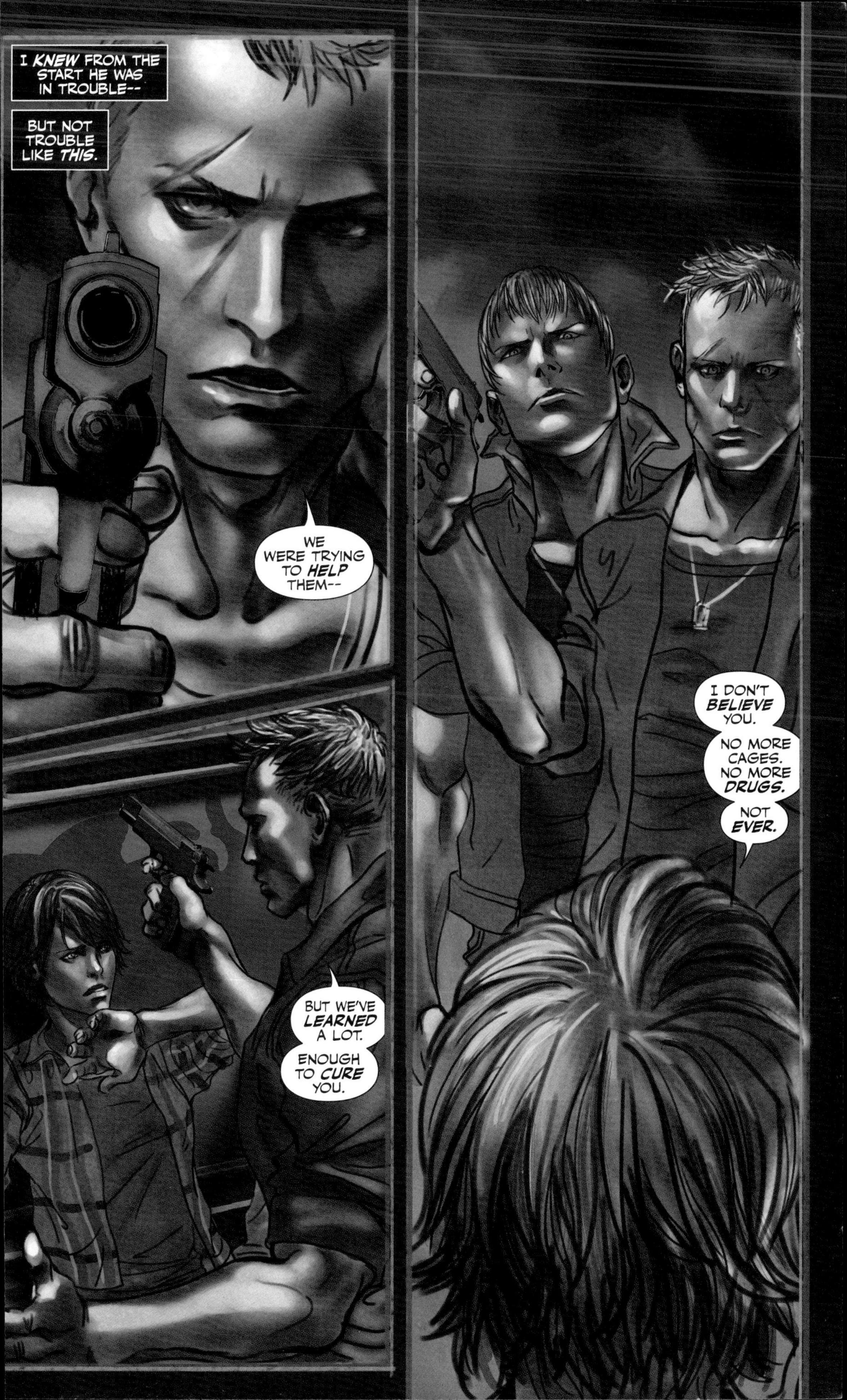
I KNEW FROM THE START HE WAS IN TROUBLE--
BUT NOT TROUBLE LIKE THIS.
WE WERE TRYING TO HELP THEM--
BUT WE'VE LEARNED A LOT.
ENOUGH TO CURE YOU.
I DON'T BELIEVE YOU.
NO MORE CAGES. NO MORE DRUGS.
NOT EVER.

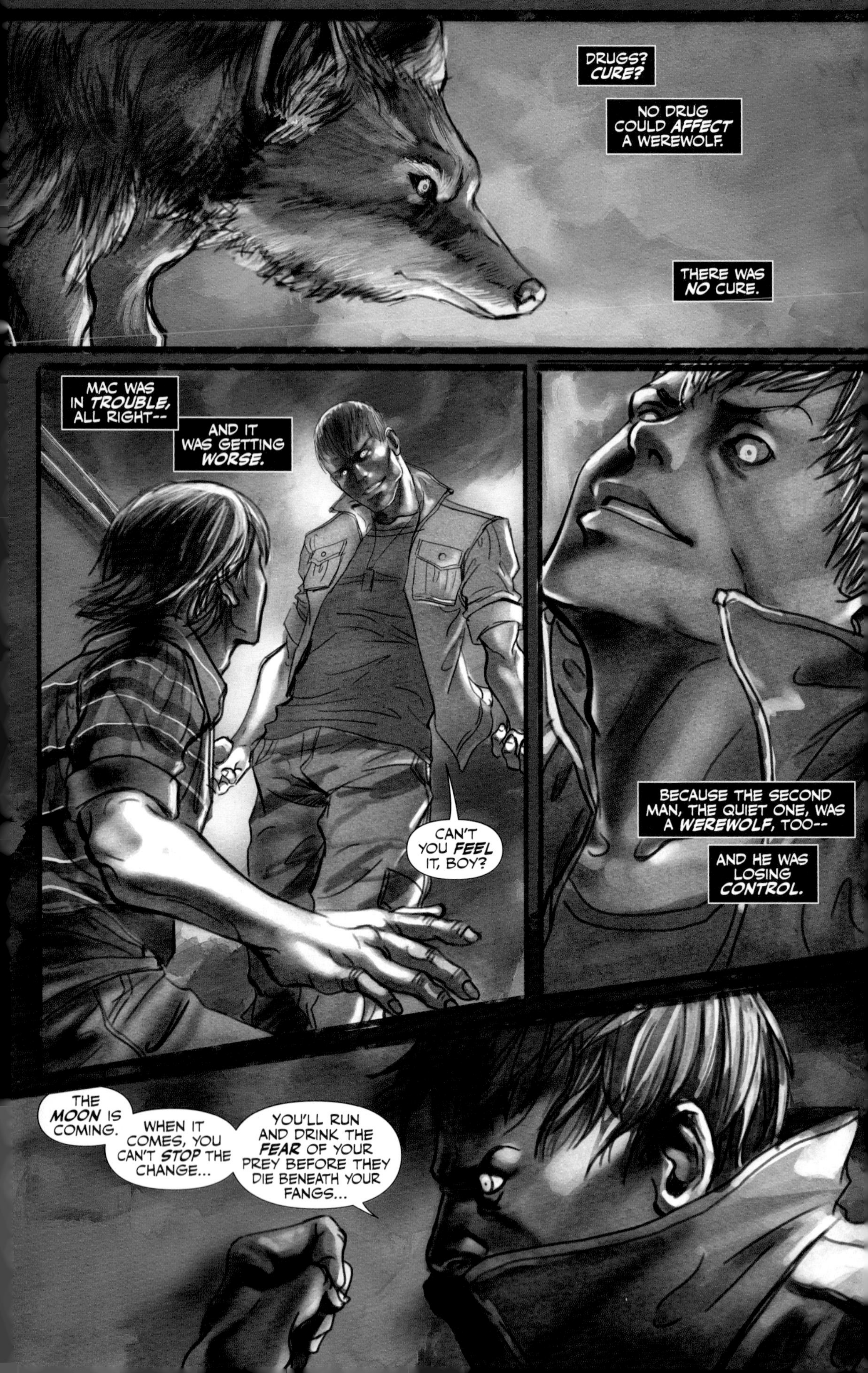
DRUGS? CURE?
NO DRUG COULD AFFECT A WEREWOLF.
THERE WAS NO CURE.
MAC WAS IN TROUBLE, ALL RIGHT--
AND IT WAS GETTING WORSE.
CAN'T YOU FEEL IT, BOY?
BECAUSE THE SECOND MAN, THE QUIET ONE, WAS A WEREWOLF, TOO--
AND HE WAS LOSING CONTROL.
THE MOON IS COMING.
WHEN IT COMES, YOU CAN'T STOP THE CHANGE...
YOU'LL RUN AND DRINK THE FEAR OF YOUR PREY BEFORE THEY DIE BENEATH YOUR FANGS...

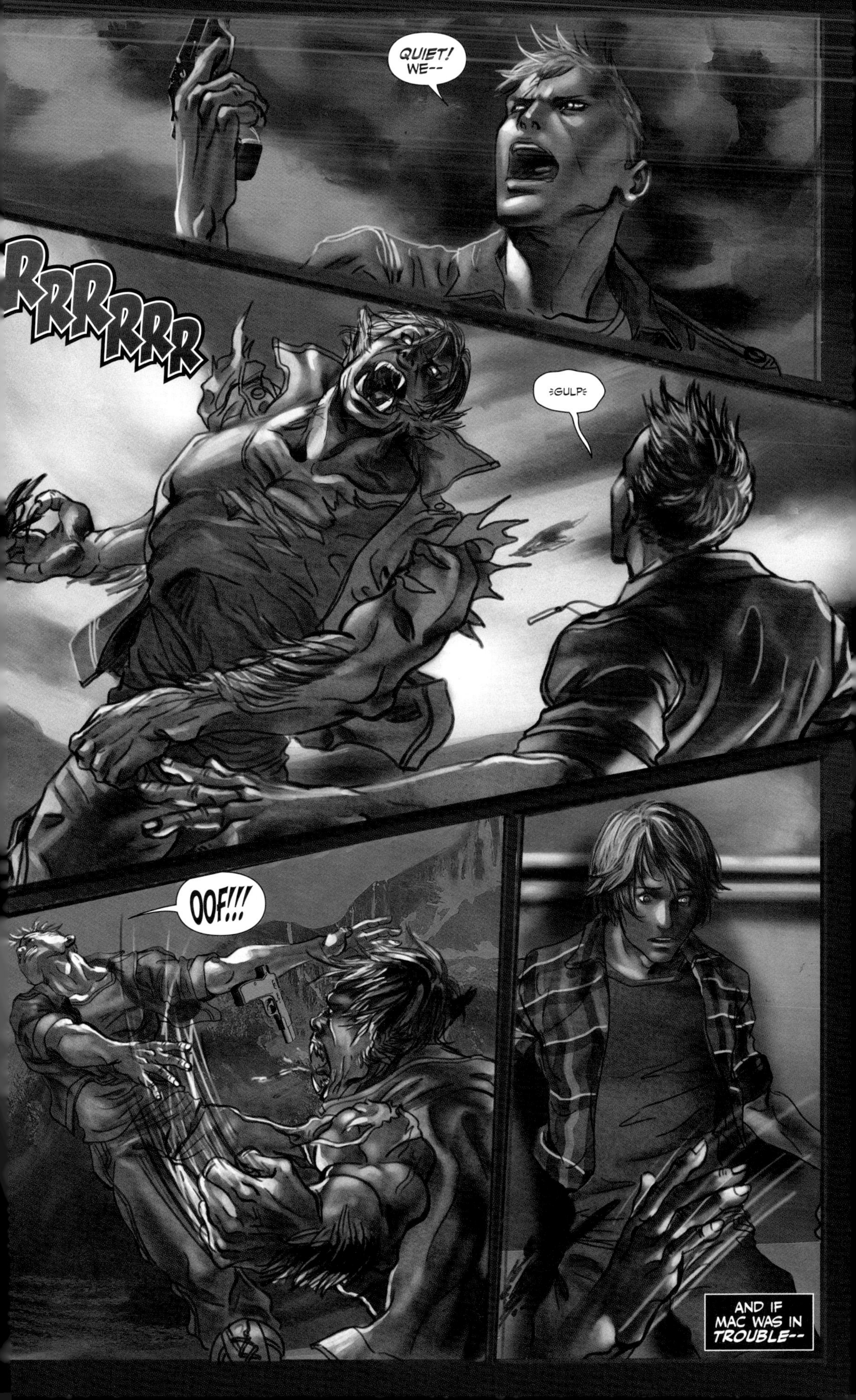
QUIET! WE--
RRRRRRR
GULP
OOF!!!
AND IF MAC WAS IN *TROUBLE--*

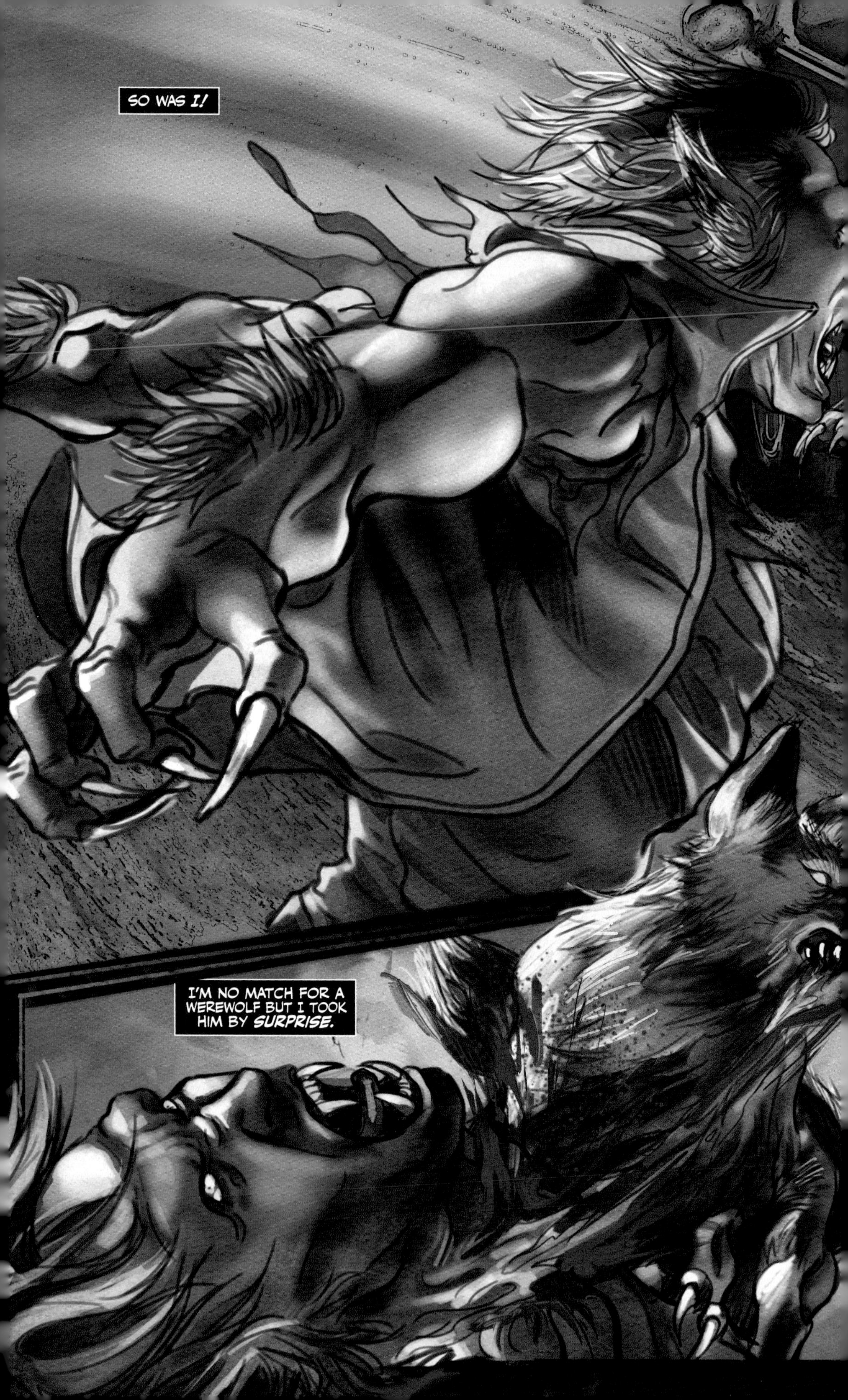
SO WAS I!
I'M NO MATCH FOR A WEREWOLF BUT I TOOK HIM BY SURPRISE.

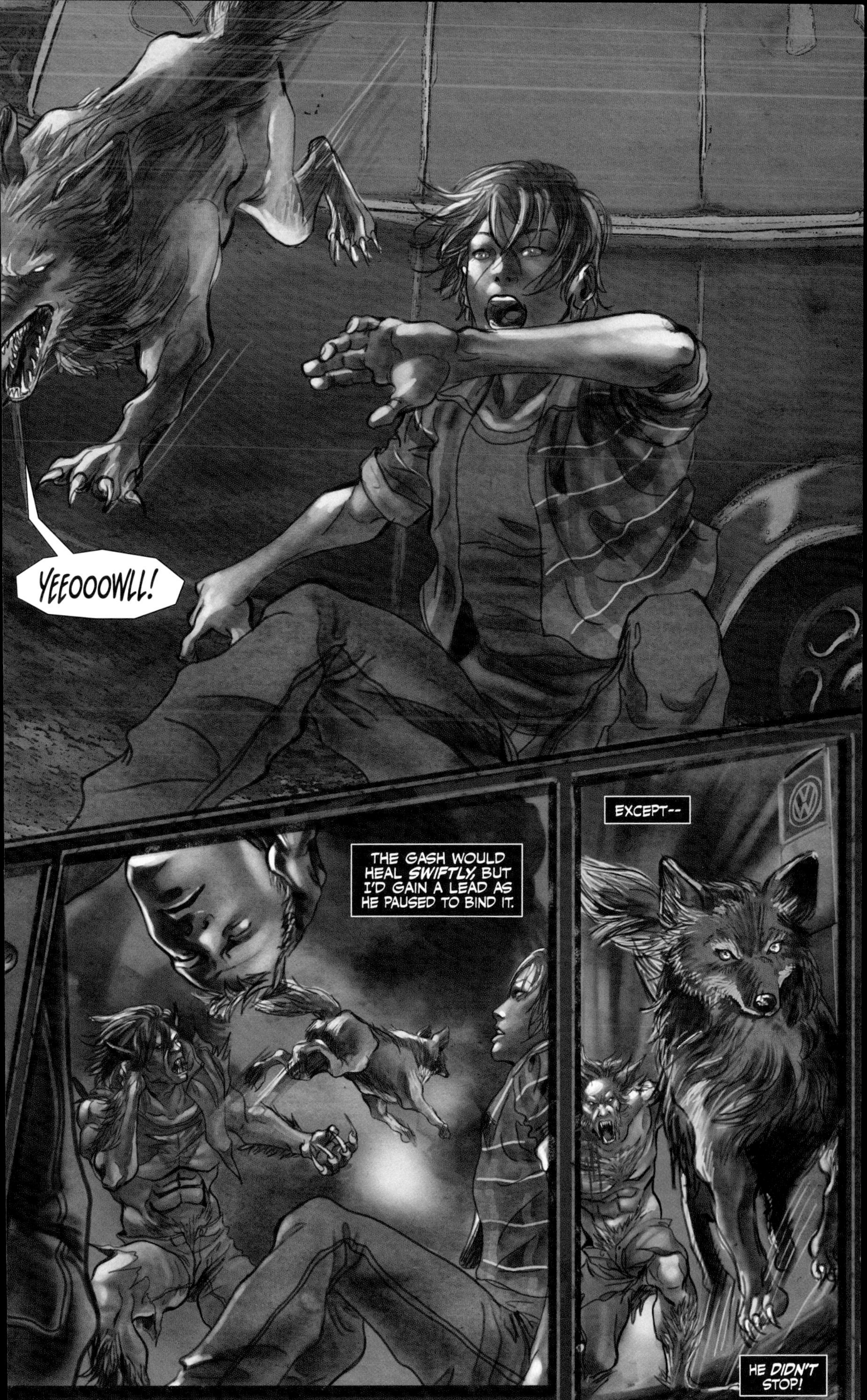
YEEOOOWLL!
THE GASH WOULD HEAL *SWIFTLY,* BUT I'D GAIN A LEAD AS HE PAUSED TO BIND IT.
EXCEPT--
HE *DIDN'T* STOP!

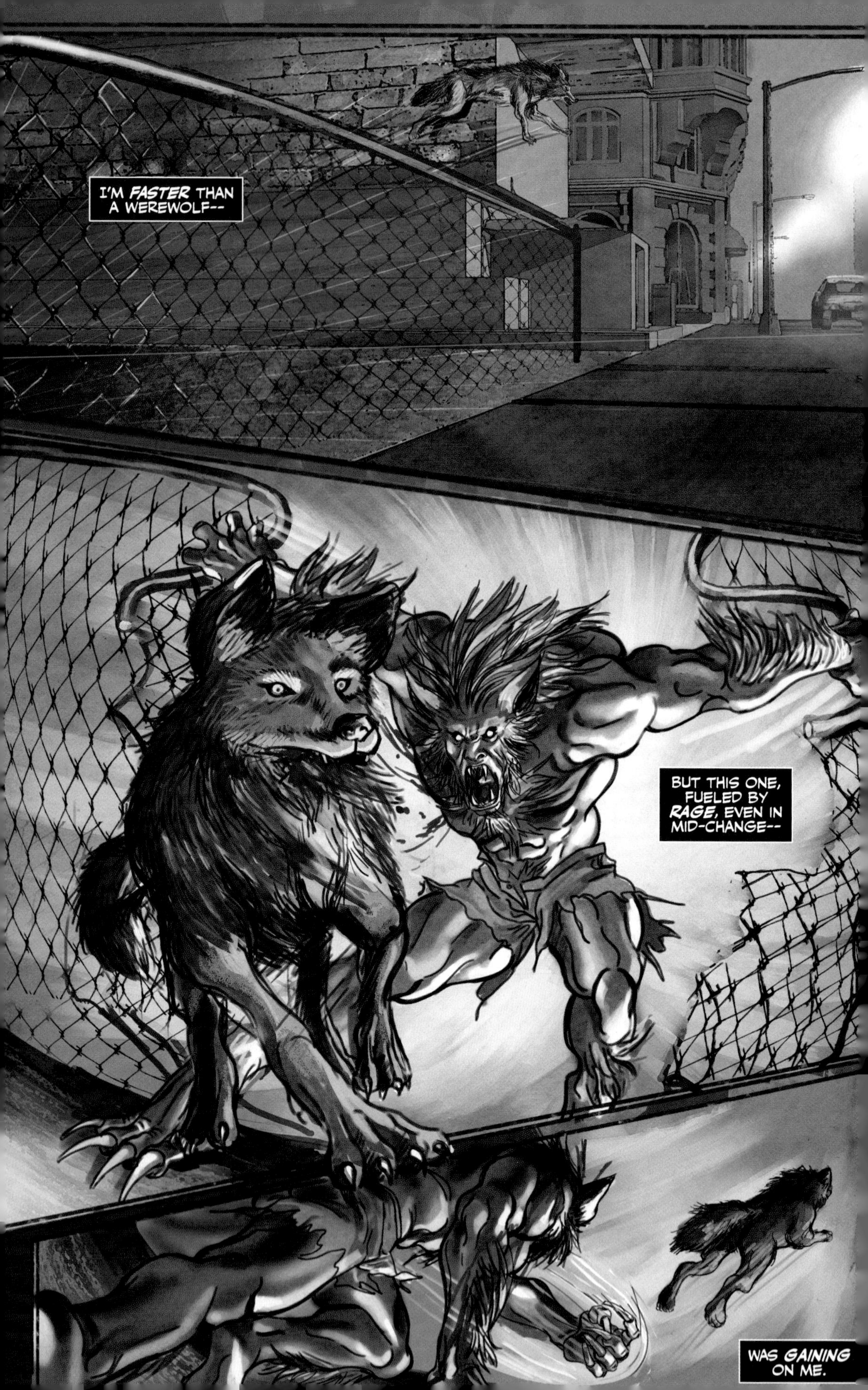
I'M FASTER THAN A WEREWOLF--
BUT THIS ONE, FUELED BY RAGE, EVEN IN MID-CHANGE--
WAS GAINING ON ME.

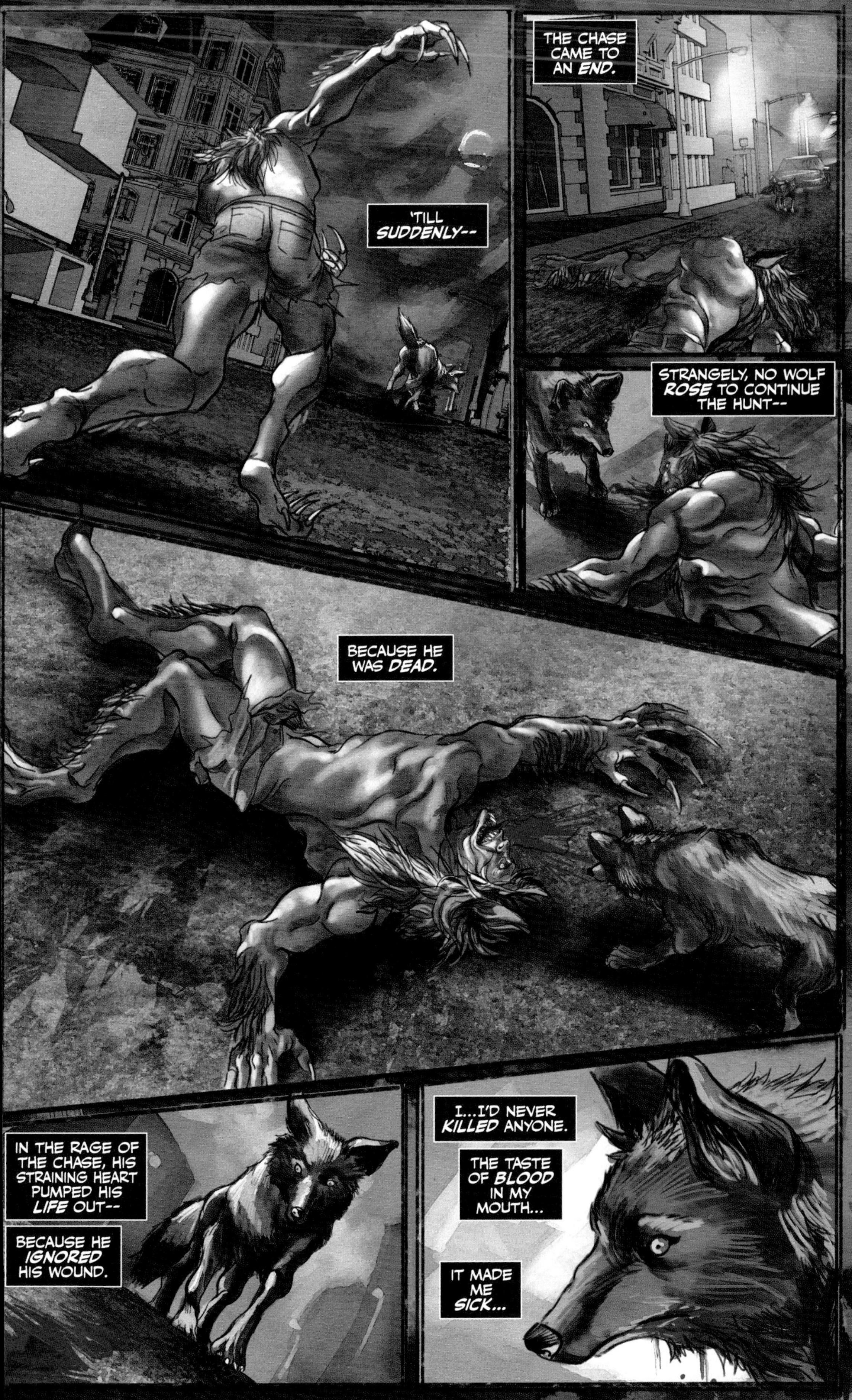

'TILL SUDDENLY--
THE CHASE CAME TO AN END.
STRANGELY, NO WOLF ROSE TO CONTINUE THE HUNT--
BECAUSE HE WAS DEAD.
IN THE RAGE OF THE CHASE, HIS STRAINING HEART PUMPED HIS LIFE OUT--
BECAUSE HE IGNORED HIS WOUND.
I...I'D NEVER KILLED ANYONE.
THE TASTE OF BLOOD IN MY MOUTH...
IT MADE ME SICK...

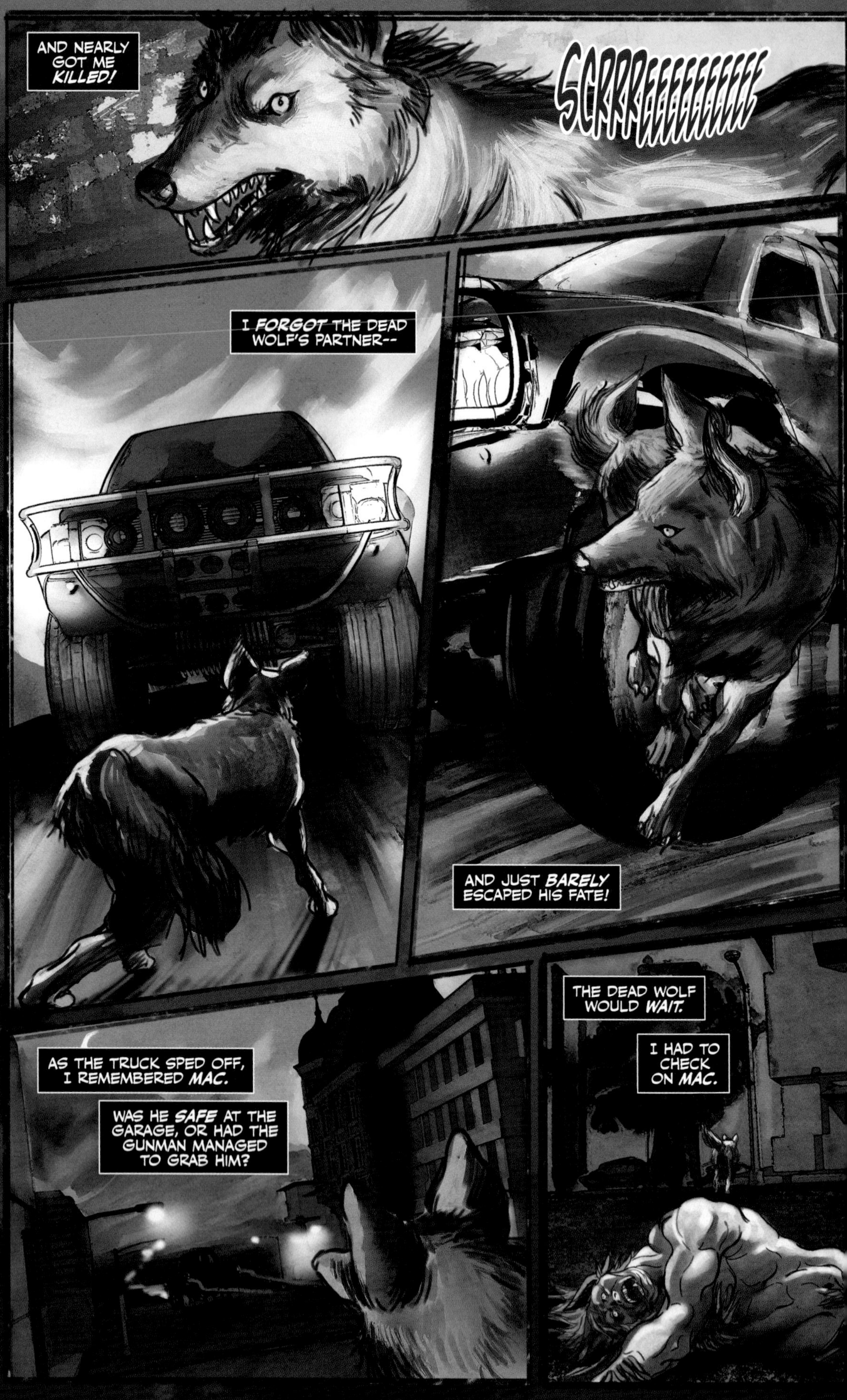
AND NEARLY GOT ME KILLED!
SCRREEEEEEEEEE
I FORGOT THE DEAD WOLF'S PARTNER--
AND JUST BARELY ESCAPED HIS FATE!
AS THE TRUCK SPED OFF, I REMEMBERED MAC.
WAS HE SAFE AT THE GARAGE, OR HAD THE GUNMAN MANAGED TO GRAB HIM?
THE DEAD WOLF WOULD WAIT.
I HAD TO CHECK ON MAC.

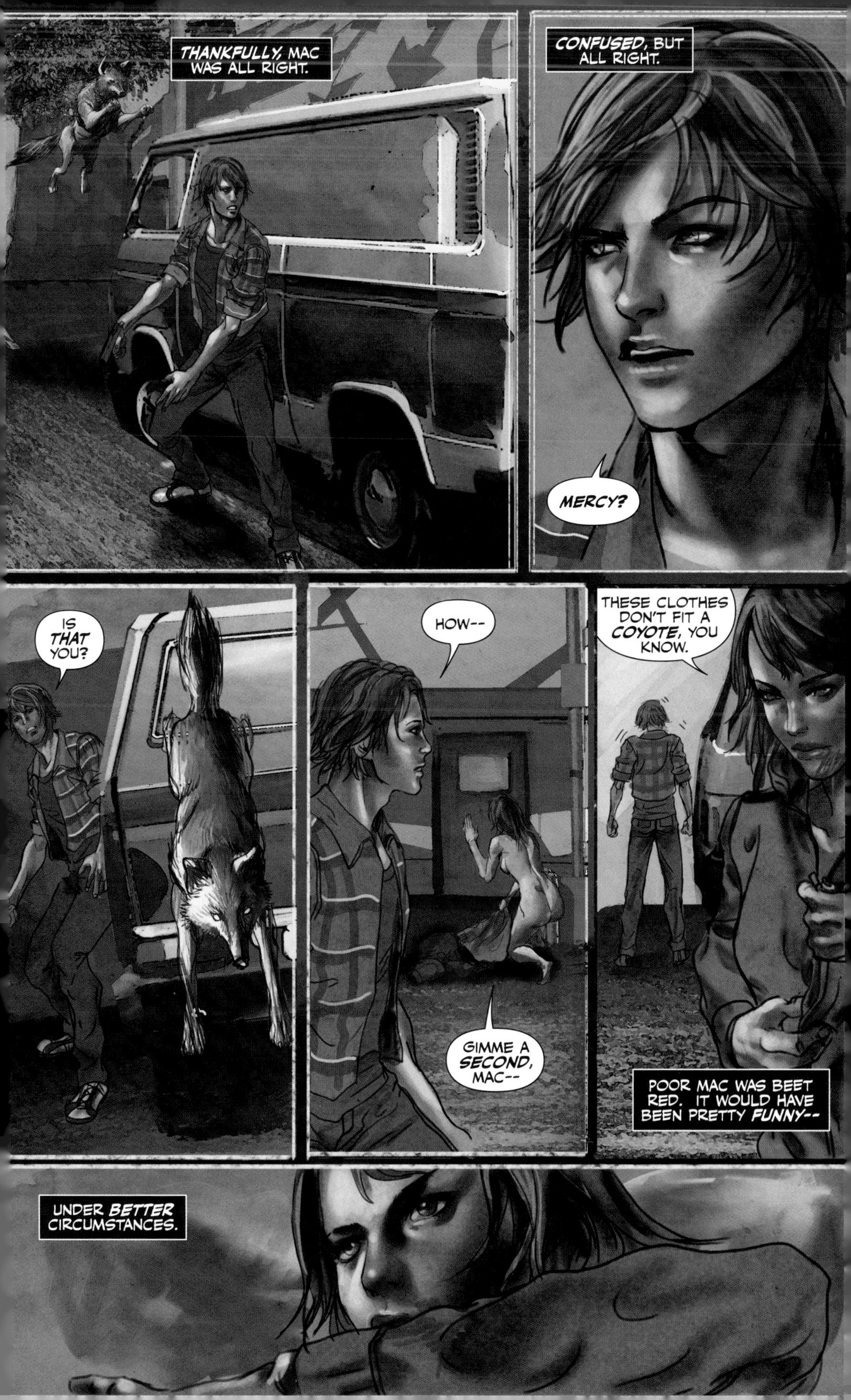

THANKFULLY, MAC WAS ALL RIGHT.
CONFUSED, BUT ALL RIGHT.
MERCY?
IS THAT YOU?
HOW--
GIMME A SECOND, MAC--
THESE CLOTHES DON'T FIT A COYOTE, YOU KNOW.
POOR MAC WAS BEET RED. IT WOULD HAVE BEEN PRETTY FUNNY--
UNDER BETTER CIRCUMSTANCES.

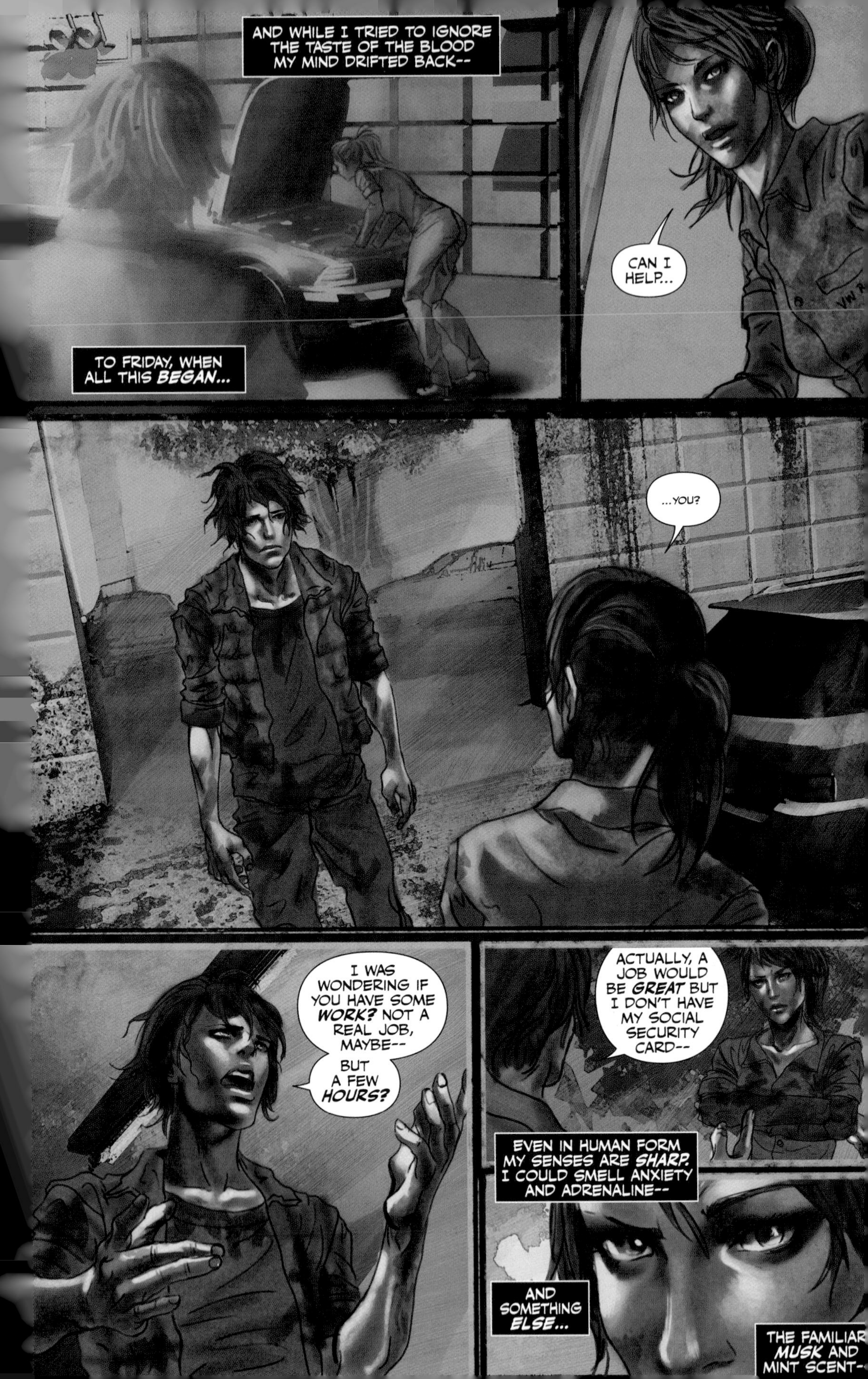
AND WHILE I TRIED TO IGNORE THE TASTE OF THE BLOOD MY MIND DRIFTED BACK--
TO FRIDAY, WHEN ALL THIS *BEGAN...*
CAN I HELP...
...YOU?
I WAS WONDERING IF YOU HAVE SOME *WORK?* NOT A REAL JOB, MAYBE--
BUT A FEW *HOURS?*
ACTUALLY, A JOB WOULD BE *GREAT* BUT I DON'T HAVE MY SOCIAL SECURITY CARD--
EVEN IN HUMAN FORM MY SENSES ARE *SHARP.* I COULD SMELL ANXIETY AND ADRENALINE--
AND SOMETHING *ELSE...*
THE FAMILIAR *MUSK* AND MINT SCENT--

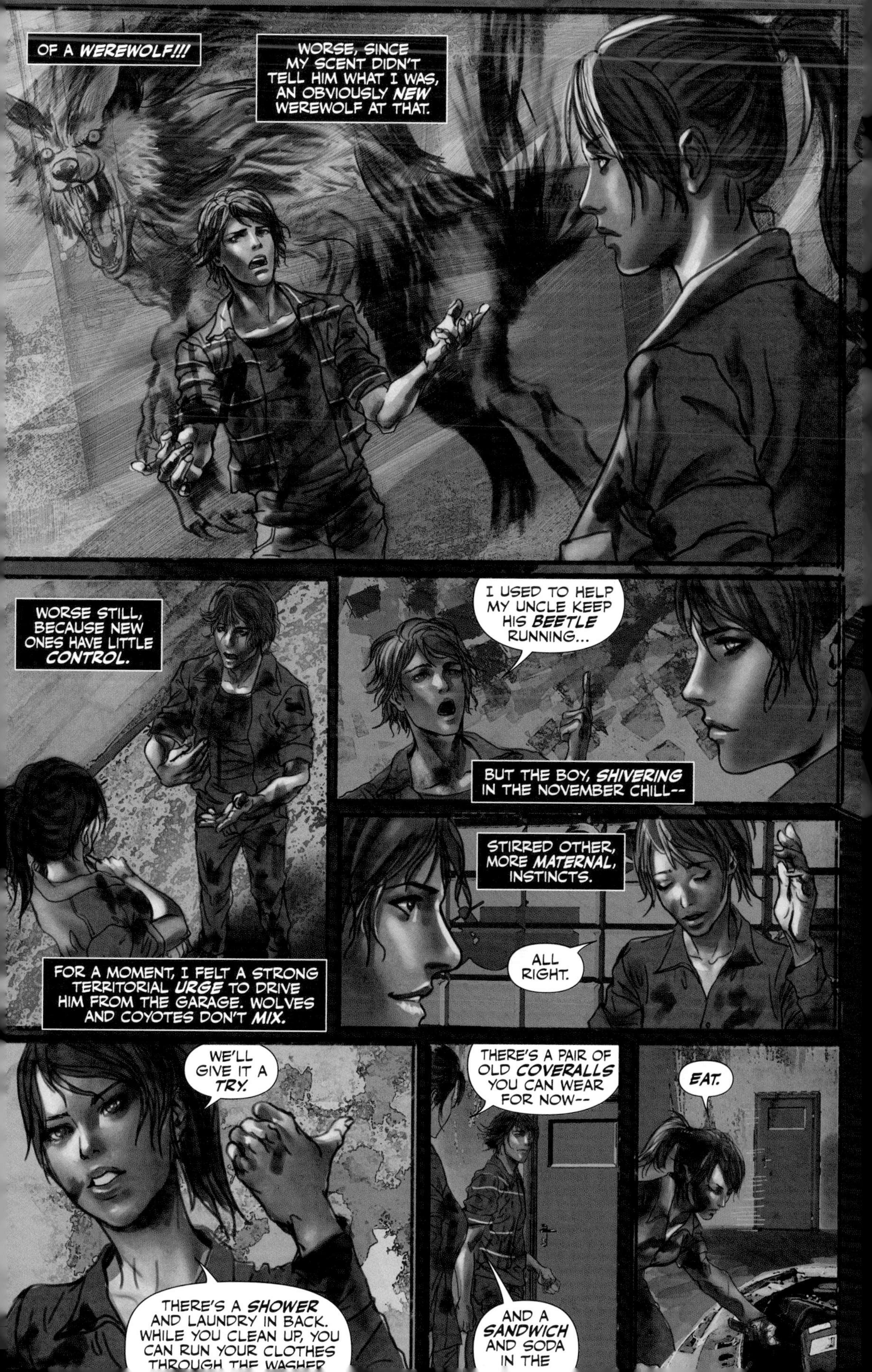
OF A WEREWOLF!!!
WORSE, SINCE MY SCENT DIDN'T TELL HIM WHAT I WAS, AN OBVIOUSLY NEW WEREWOLF AT THAT.
WORSE STILL, BECAUSE NEW ONES HAVE LITTLE CONTROL.
FOR A MOMENT, I FELT A STRONG TERRITORIAL URGE TO DRIVE HIM FROM THE GARAGE. WOLVES AND COYOTES DON'T MIX.
I USED TO HELP MY UNCLE KEEP HIS BEETLE RUNNING...
BUT THE BOY, SHIVERING IN THE NOVEMBER CHILL--
STIRRED OTHER, MORE MATERNAL, INSTINCTS.
ALL RIGHT.
WE'LL GIVE IT A TRY.
THERE'S A SHOWER AND LAUNDRY IN BACK. WHILE YOU CLEAN UP, YOU CAN RUN YOUR CLOTHES THROUGH THE WASHER
THERE'S A PAIR OF OLD COVERALLS YOU CAN WEAR FOR NOW--
AND A SANDWICH AND SODA IN THE
EAT.

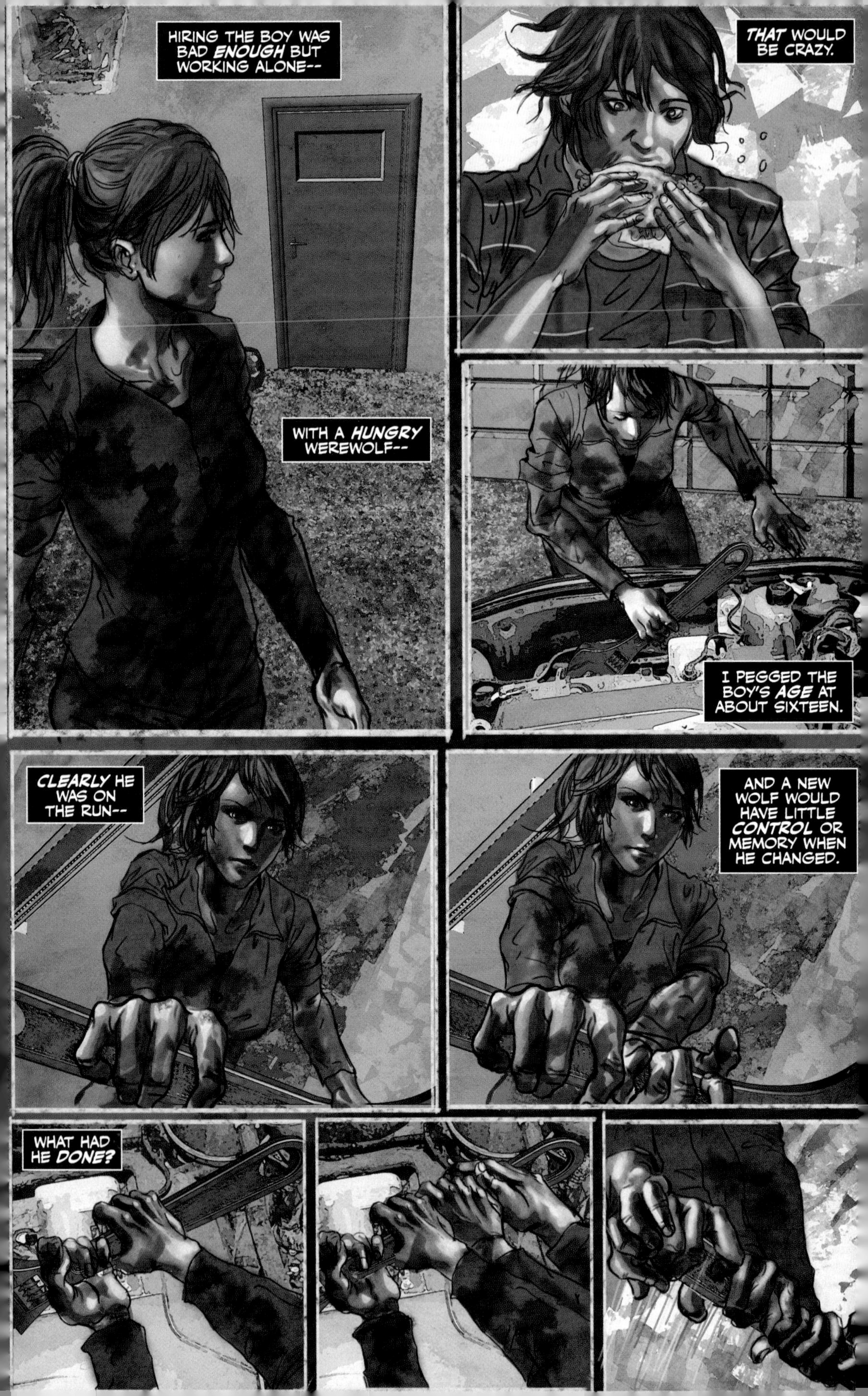
HIRING THE BOY WAS BAD ENOUGH BUT WORKING ALONE--
THAT WOULD BE CRAZY.
WITH A HUNGRY WEREWOLF--
I PEGGED THE BOY'S AGE AT ABOUT SIXTEEN.
CLEARLY HE WAS ON THE RUN--
AND A NEW WOLF WOULD HAVE LITTLE CONTROL OR MEMORY WHEN HE CHANGED.
WHAT HAD HE DONE?

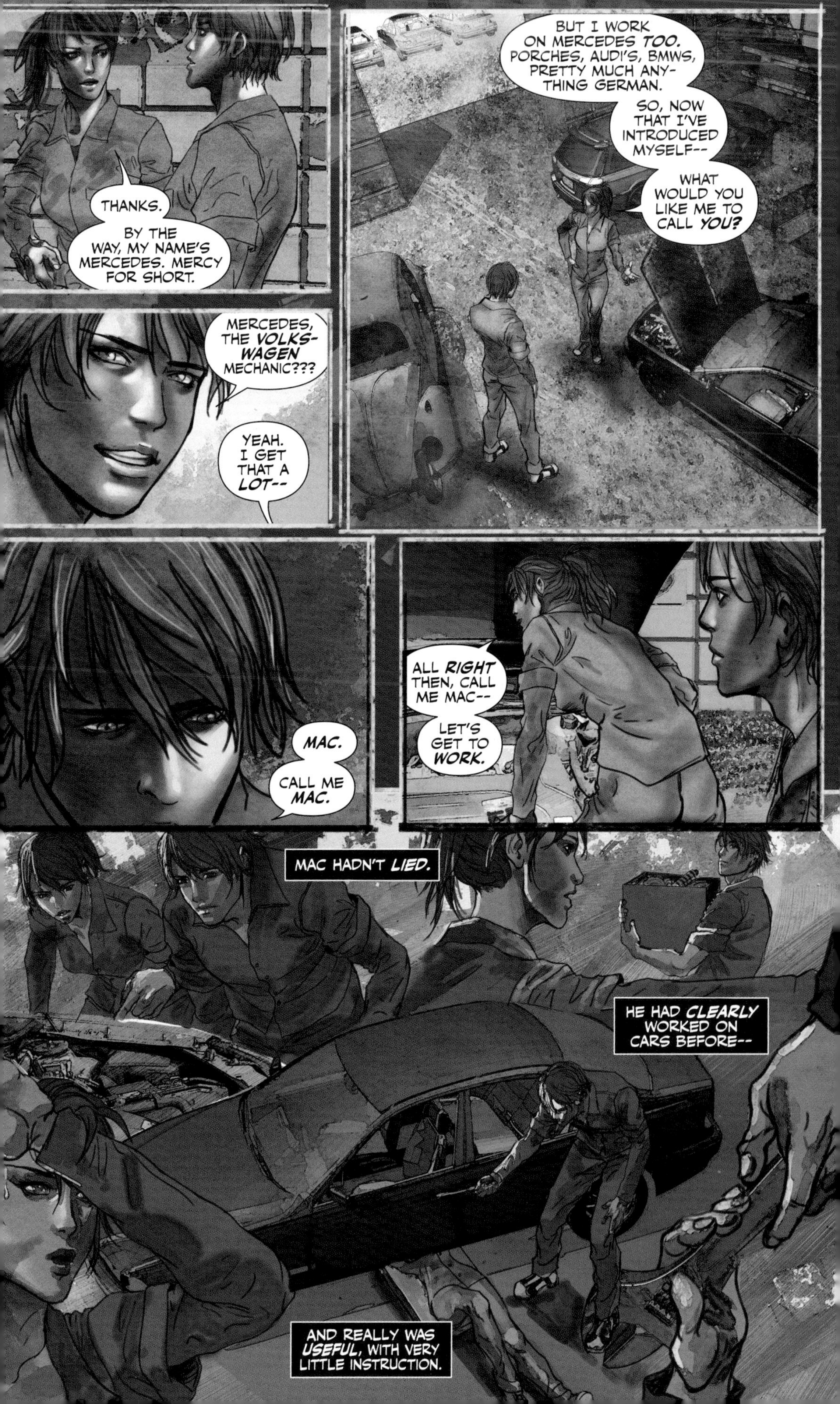
THANKS.
BY THE WAY, MY NAME'S MERCEDES. MERCY FOR SHORT.
MERCEDES, THE VOLKS-WAGEN MECHANIC???
YEAH. I GET THAT A LOT--
BUT I WORK ON MERCEDES TOO. PORCHES, AUDI'S, BMWS, PRETTY MUCH ANY-THING GERMAN.
SO, NOW THAT I'VE INTRODUCED MYSELF--
WHAT WOULD YOU LIKE ME TO CALL YOU?
MAC.
CALL ME MAC.
ALL RIGHT THEN, CALL ME MAC--
LET'S GET TO WORK.
MAC HADN'T LIED.
HE HAD CLEARLY WORKED ON CARS BEFORE--
AND REALLY WAS USEFUL, WITH VERY LITTLE INSTRUCTION.

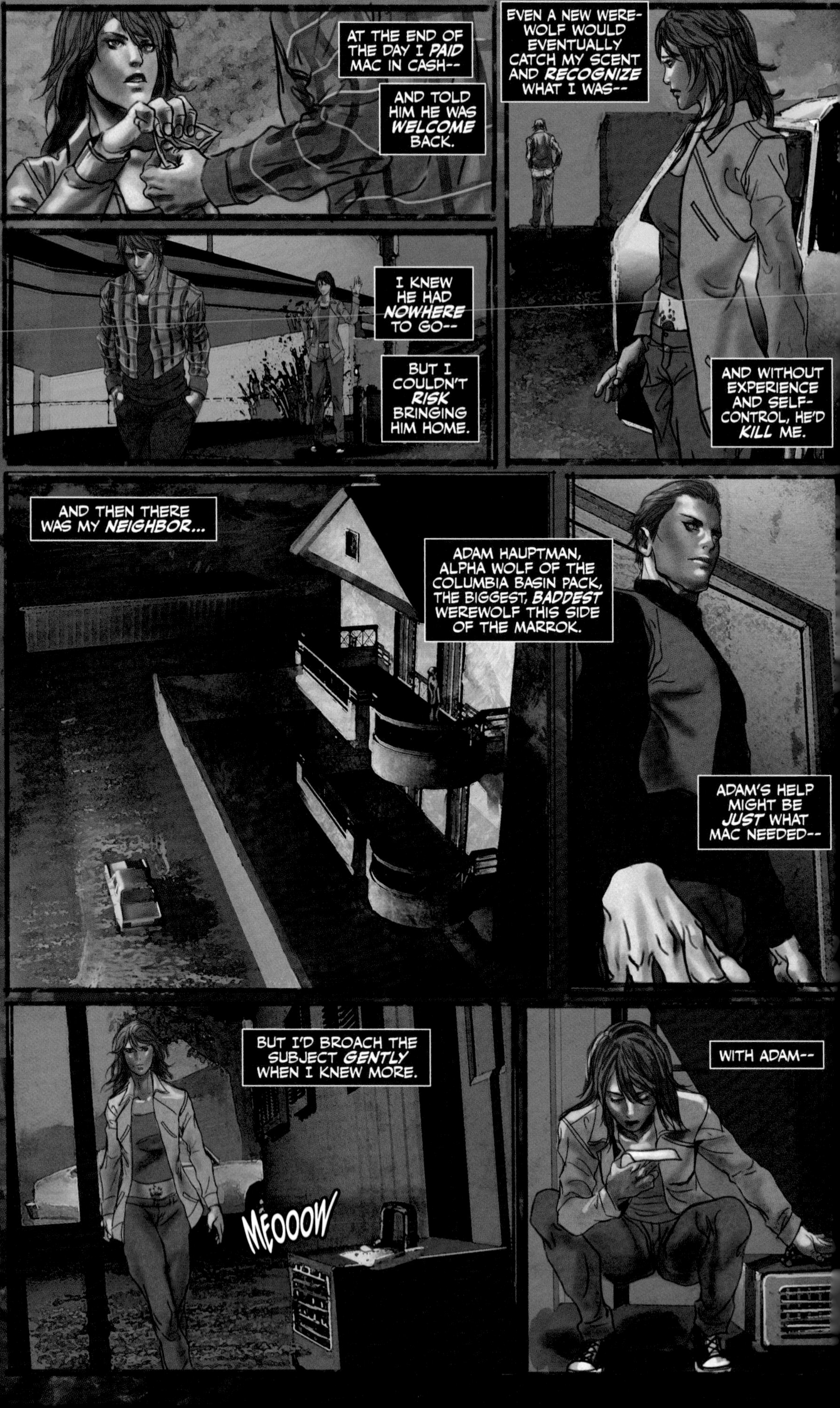

AT THE END OF THE DAY I PAID MAC IN CASH--
AND TOLD HIM HE WAS WELCOME BACK.
EVEN A NEW WERE-WOLF WOULD EVENTUALLY CATCH MY SCENT AND RECOGNIZE WHAT I WAS--
I KNEW HE HAD NOWHERE TO GO--
BUT I COULDN'T RISK BRINGING HIM HOME.
AND WITHOUT EXPERIENCE AND SELF-CONTROL, HE'D KILL ME.
AND THEN THERE WAS MY NEIGHBOR...
ADAM HAUPTMAN, ALPHA WOLF OF THE COLUMBIA BASIN PACK, THE BIGGEST, BADDEST WEREWOLF THIS SIDE OF THE MARROK.
ADAM'S HELP MIGHT BE JUST WHAT MAC NEEDED--
BUT I'D BROACH THE SUBJECT GENTLY WHEN I KNEW MORE.
MEOOOW
WITH ADAM--

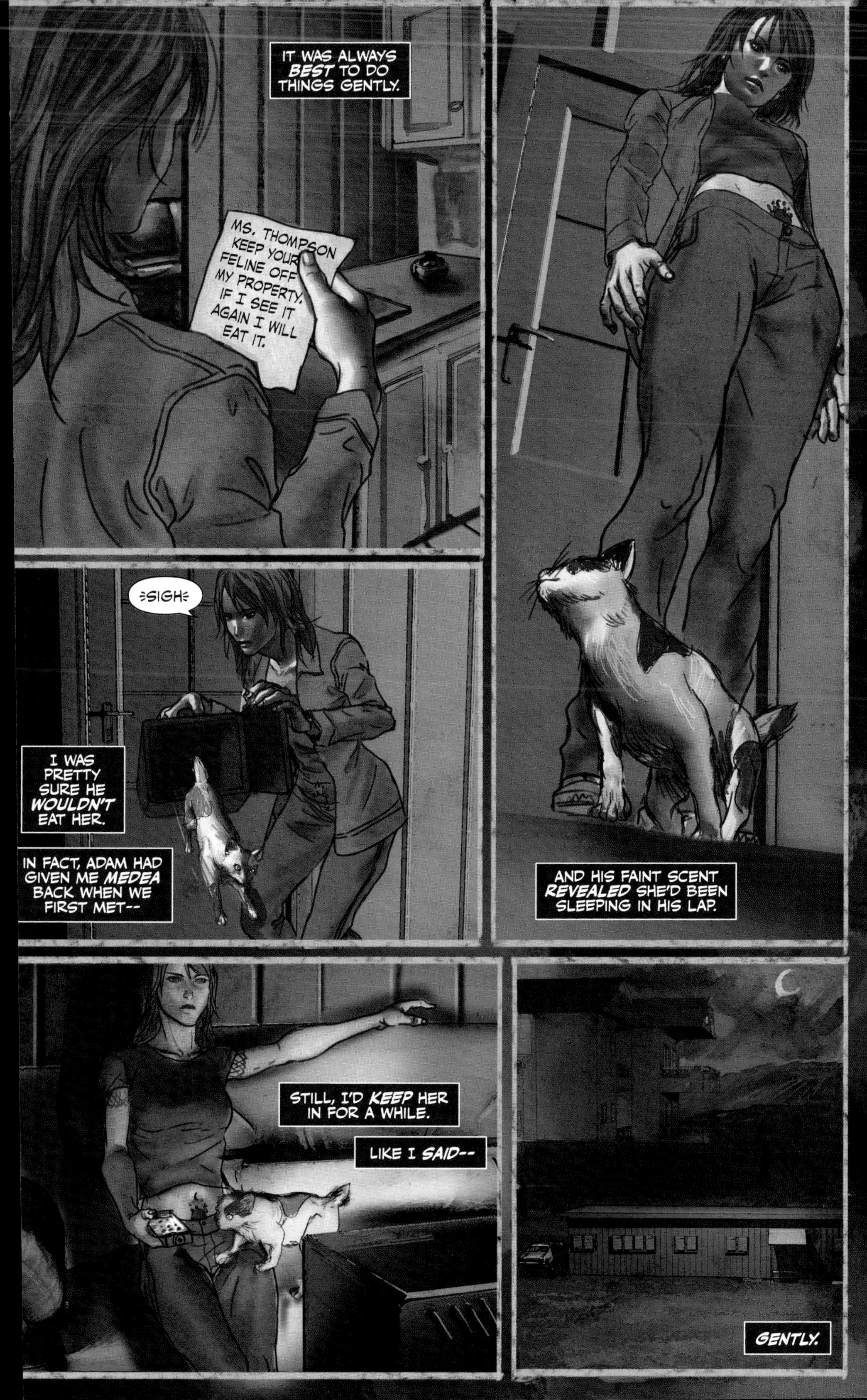
IT WAS ALWAYS BEST TO DO THINGS GENTLY.
MS. THOMPSON KEEP YOUR FELINE OFF MY PROPERTY. IF I SEE IT AGAIN I WILL EAT IT.
SIGH
I WAS PRETTY SURE HE WOULDN'T EAT HER.
IN FACT, ADAM HAD GIVEN ME MEDEA BACK WHEN WE FIRST MET--
AND HIS FAINT SCENT REVEALED SHE'D BEEN SLEEPING IN HIS LAP.
STILL, I'D KEEP HER IN FOR A WHILE.
LIKE I SAID--
GENTLY.

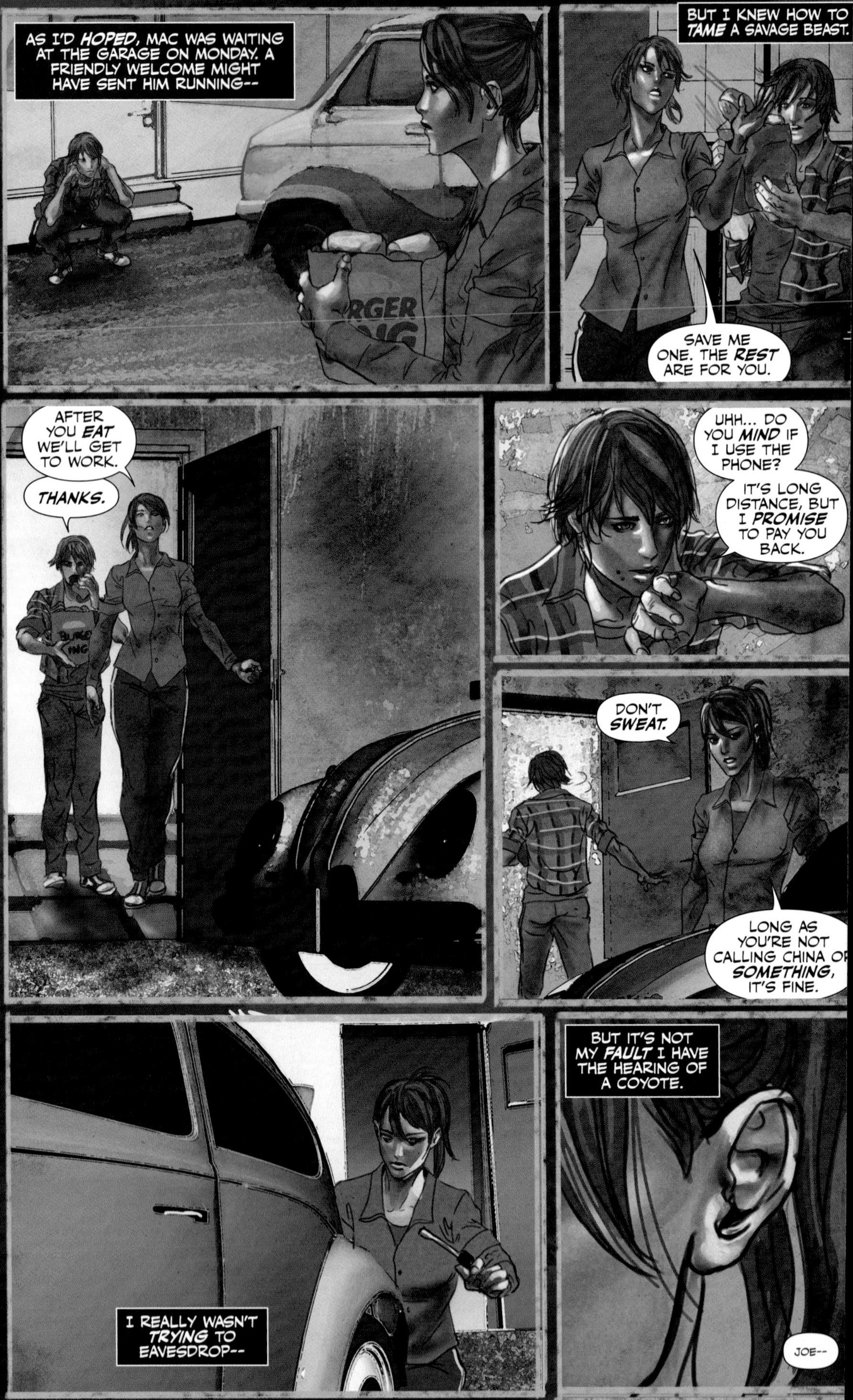
AS I'D HOPED, MAC WAS WAITING AT THE GARAGE ON MONDAY. A FRIENDLY WELCOME MIGHT HAVE SENT HIM RUNNING--
BUT I KNEW HOW TO TAME A SAVAGE BEAST.
SAVE ME ONE. THE REST ARE FOR YOU.
AFTER YOU EAT WE'LL GET TO WORK.
THANKS.
UHH... DO YOU MIND IF I USE THE PHONE?
IT'S LONG DISTANCE, BUT I PROMISE TO PAY YOU BACK.
DON'T SWEAT.
LONG AS YOU'RE NOT CALLING CHINA OR SOMETHING, IT'S FINE.
I REALLY WASN'T TRYING TO EAVESDROP--
BUT IT'S NOT MY FAULT I HAVE THE HEARING OF A COYOTE.
JOE--

I'M *FINE*--

BUT I *CAN'T* TALK LONG.

I DON'T REMEMBER *ANYTHING* AFTER THE DANCE.

I DON'T KNOW *WHAT* KILLED HER--

OR *WHY* IT DIDN'T KILL ME.

TELL MOM AND DAD I *LOVE* THEM.

YOU *TOO*, JOE.

CLICK

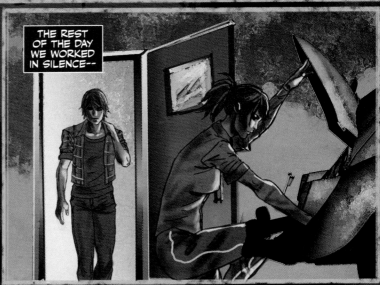

THE REST OF THE DAY WE WORKED IN SILENCE--

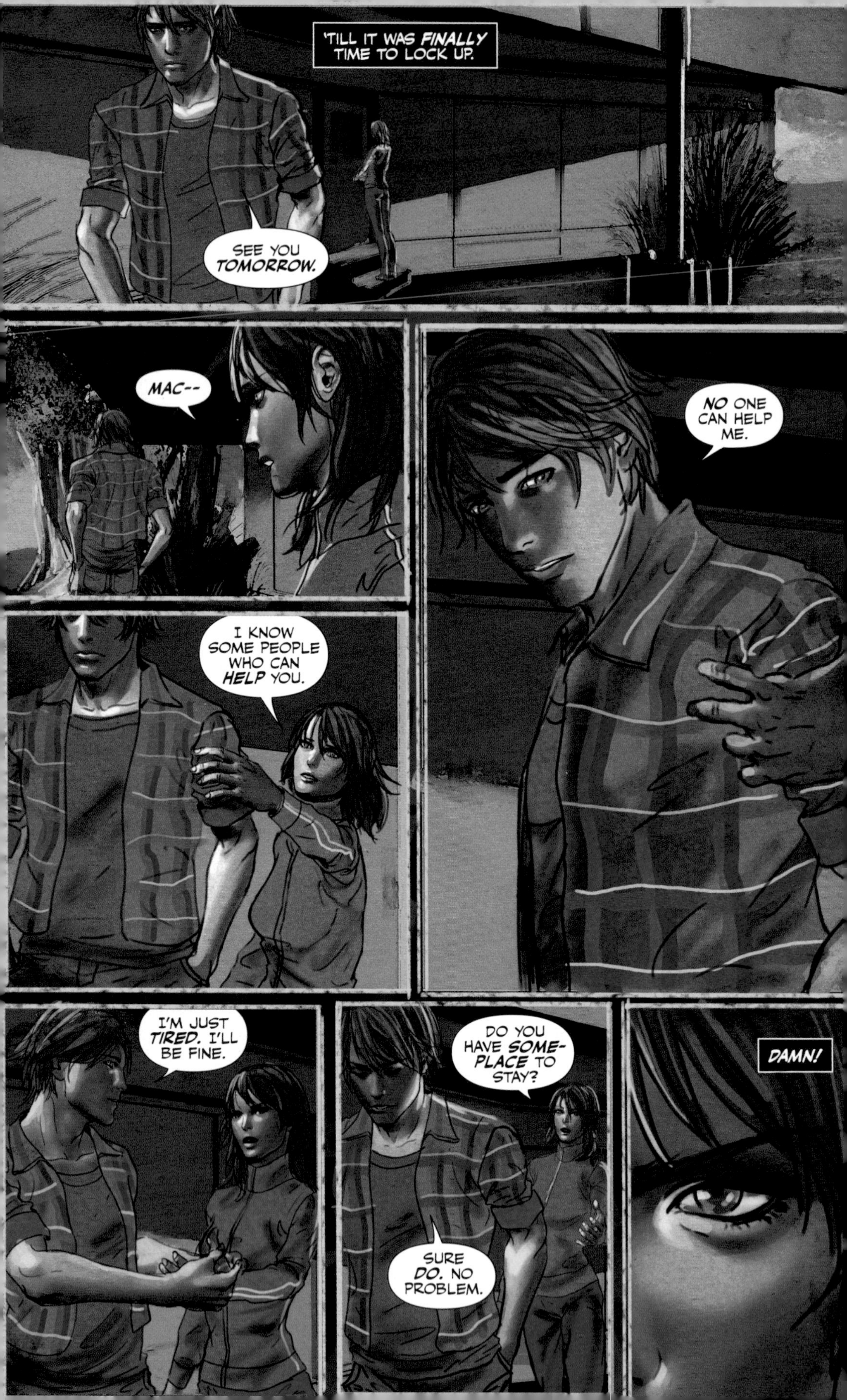
'TILL IT WAS FINALLY TIME TO LOCK UP.
SEE YOU TOMORROW.
MAC--
NO ONE CAN HELP ME.
I KNOW SOME PEOPLE WHO CAN HELP YOU.
I'M JUST TIRED. I'LL BE FINE.
DO YOU HAVE SOME-PLACE TO STAY?
SURE DO. NO PROBLEM.
DAMN!

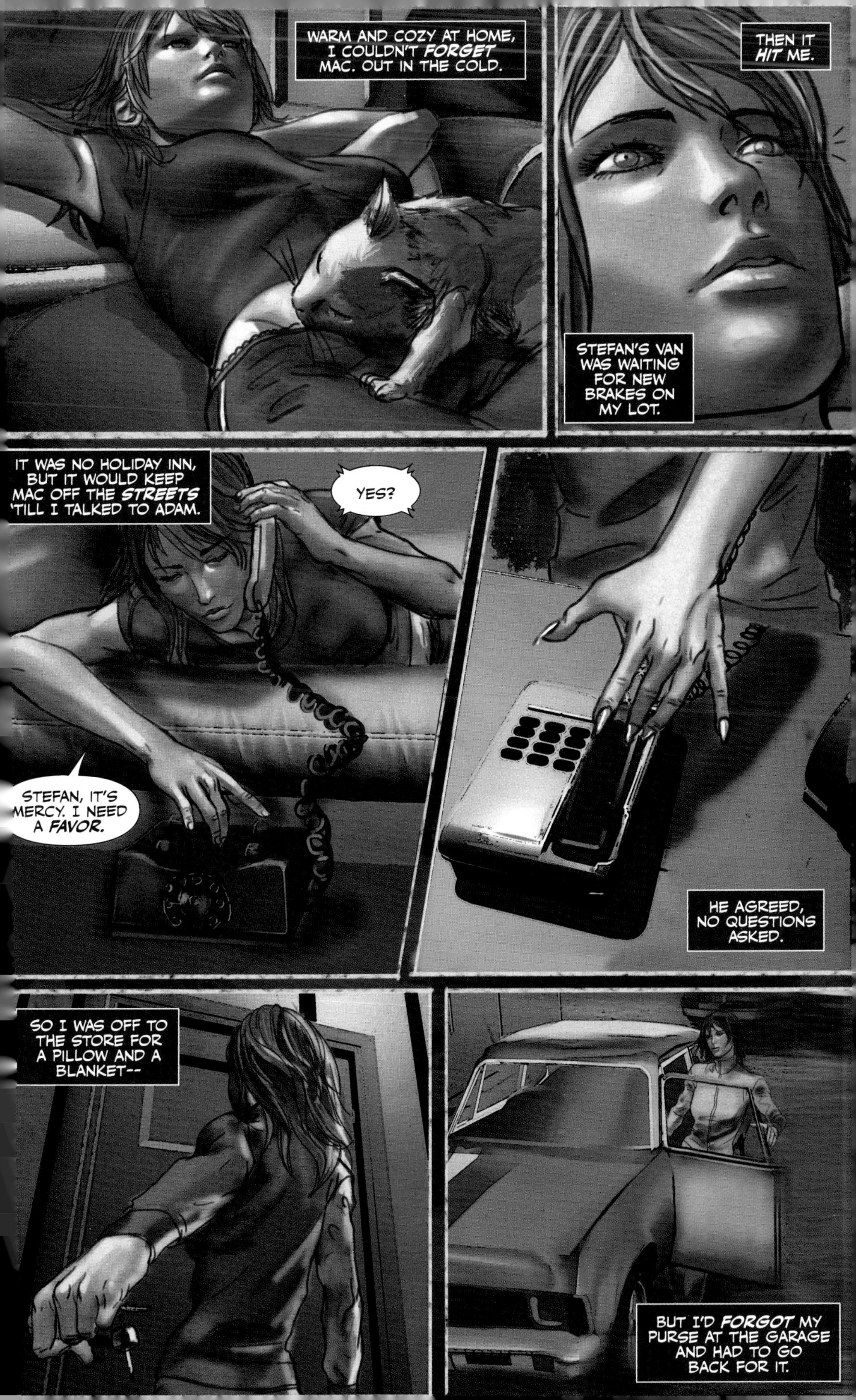
WARM AND COZY AT HOME, I COULDN'T FORGET MAC. OUT IN THE COLD.
THEN IT HIT ME.
STEFAN'S VAN WAS WAITING FOR NEW BRAKES ON MY LOT.
IT WAS NO HOLIDAY INN, BUT IT WOULD KEEP MAC OFF THE STREETS 'TILL I TALKED TO ADAM.
YES?
STEFAN, IT'S MERCY. I NEED A FAVOR.
HE AGREED, NO QUESTIONS ASKED.
SO I WAS OFF TO THE STORE FOR A PILLOW AND A BLANKET--
BUT I'D FORGOT MY PURSE AT THE GARAGE AND HAD TO GO BACK FOR IT.

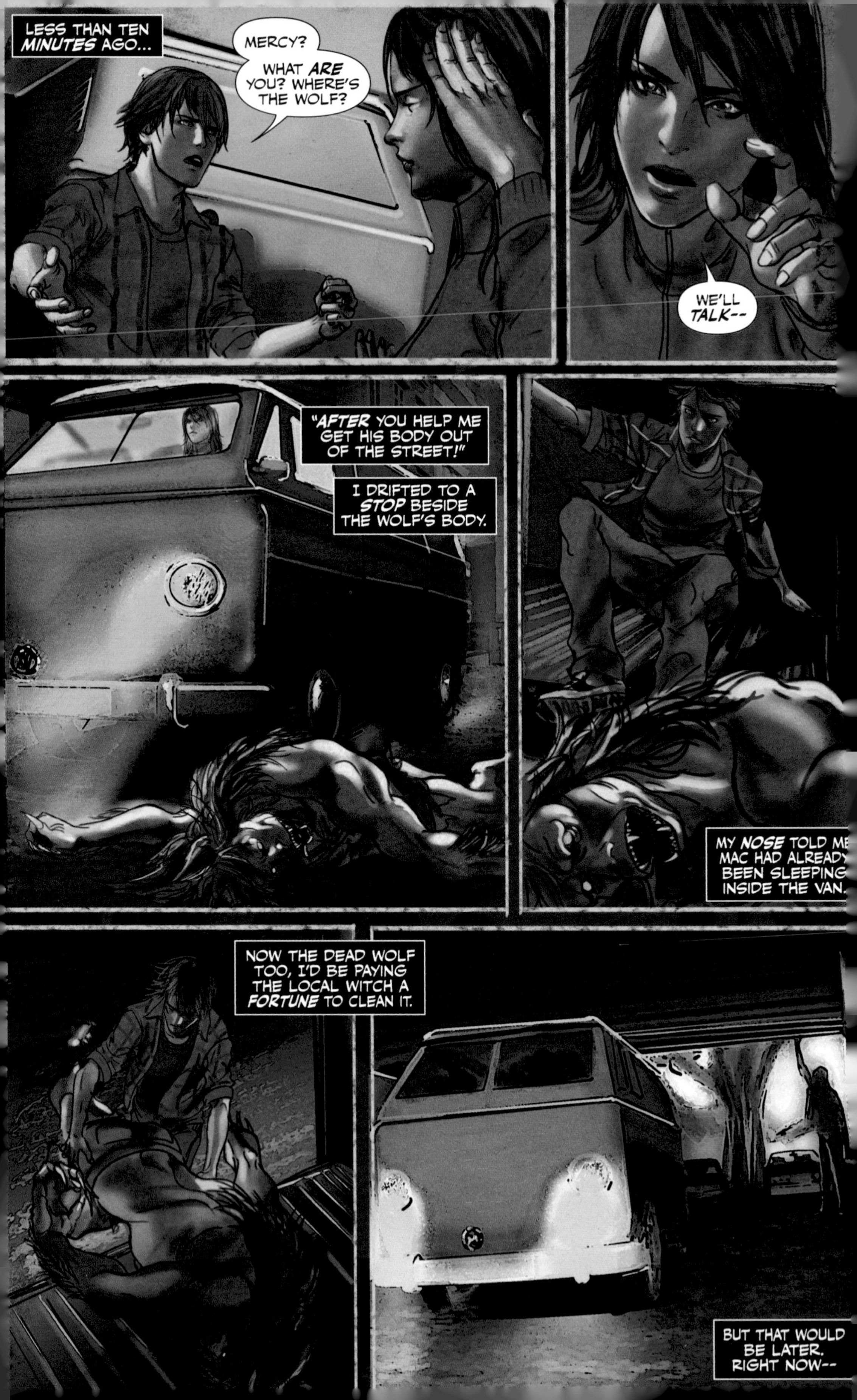
LESS THAN TEN MINUTES AGO...
MERCY?
WHAT ARE YOU? WHERE'S THE WOLF?
WE'LL TALK--
"AFTER YOU HELP ME GET HIS BODY OUT OF THE STREET!"
I DRIFTED TO A STOP BESIDE THE WOLF'S BODY.
MY NOSE TOLD ME MAC HAD ALREADY BEEN SLEEPING INSIDE THE VAN.
NOW THE DEAD WOLF TOO, I'D BE PAYING THE LOCAL WITCH A FORTUNE TO CLEAN IT.
BUT THAT WOULD BE LATER. RIGHT NOW--

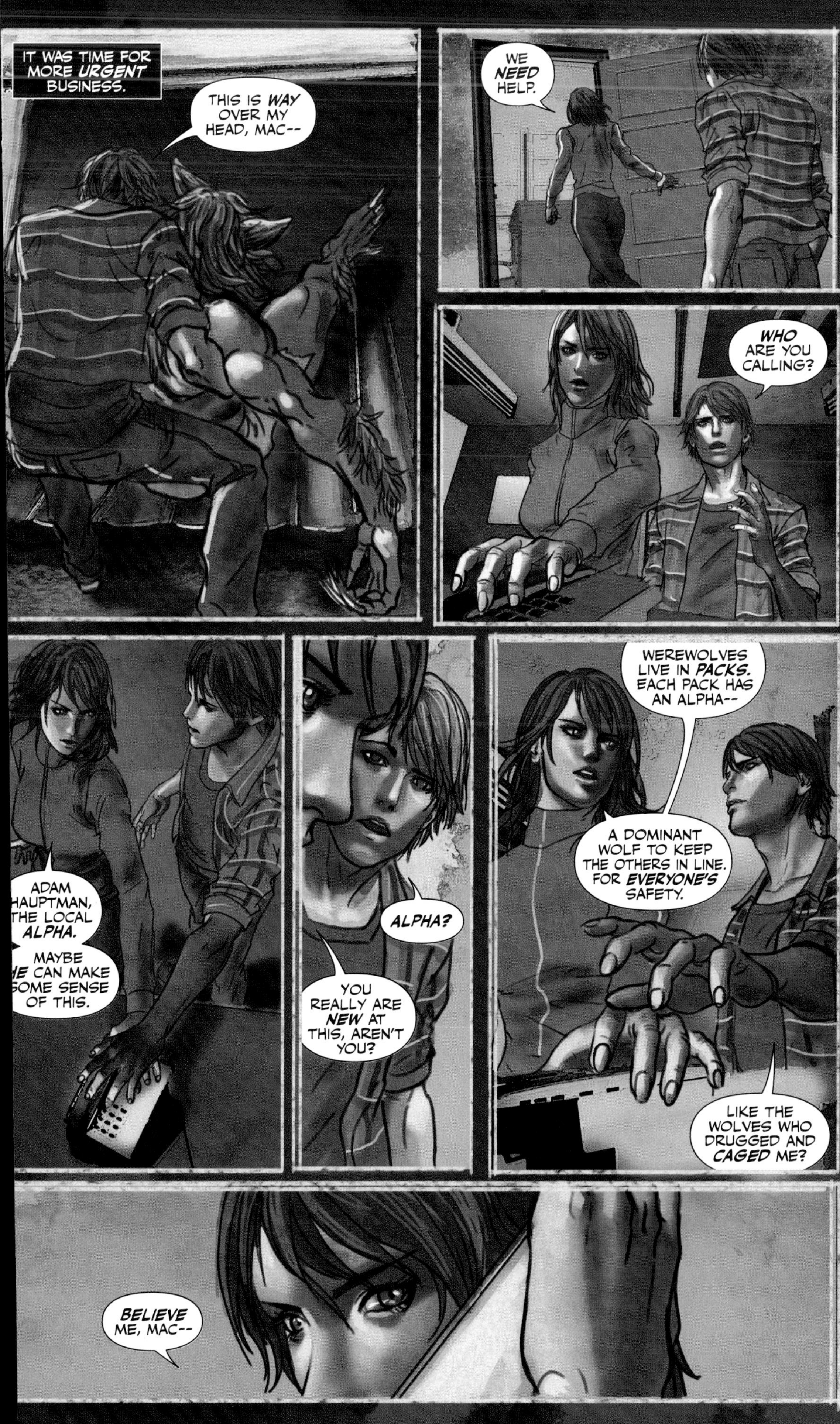
IT WAS TIME FOR MORE URGENT BUSINESS.
THIS IS WAY OVER MY HEAD, MAC--
WE NEED HELP.
WHO ARE YOU CALLING?
ADAM HAUPTMAN, THE LOCAL ALPHA.
MAYBE HE CAN MAKE SOME SENSE OF THIS.
ALPHA?
YOU REALLY ARE NEW AT THIS, AREN'T YOU?
WEREWOLVES LIVE IN PACKS. EACH PACK HAS AN ALPHA--
A DOMINANT WOLF TO KEEP THE OTHERS IN LINE. FOR EVERYONE'S SAFETY.
LIKE THE WOLVES WHO DRUGGED AND CAGED ME?
BELIEVE ME, MAC--

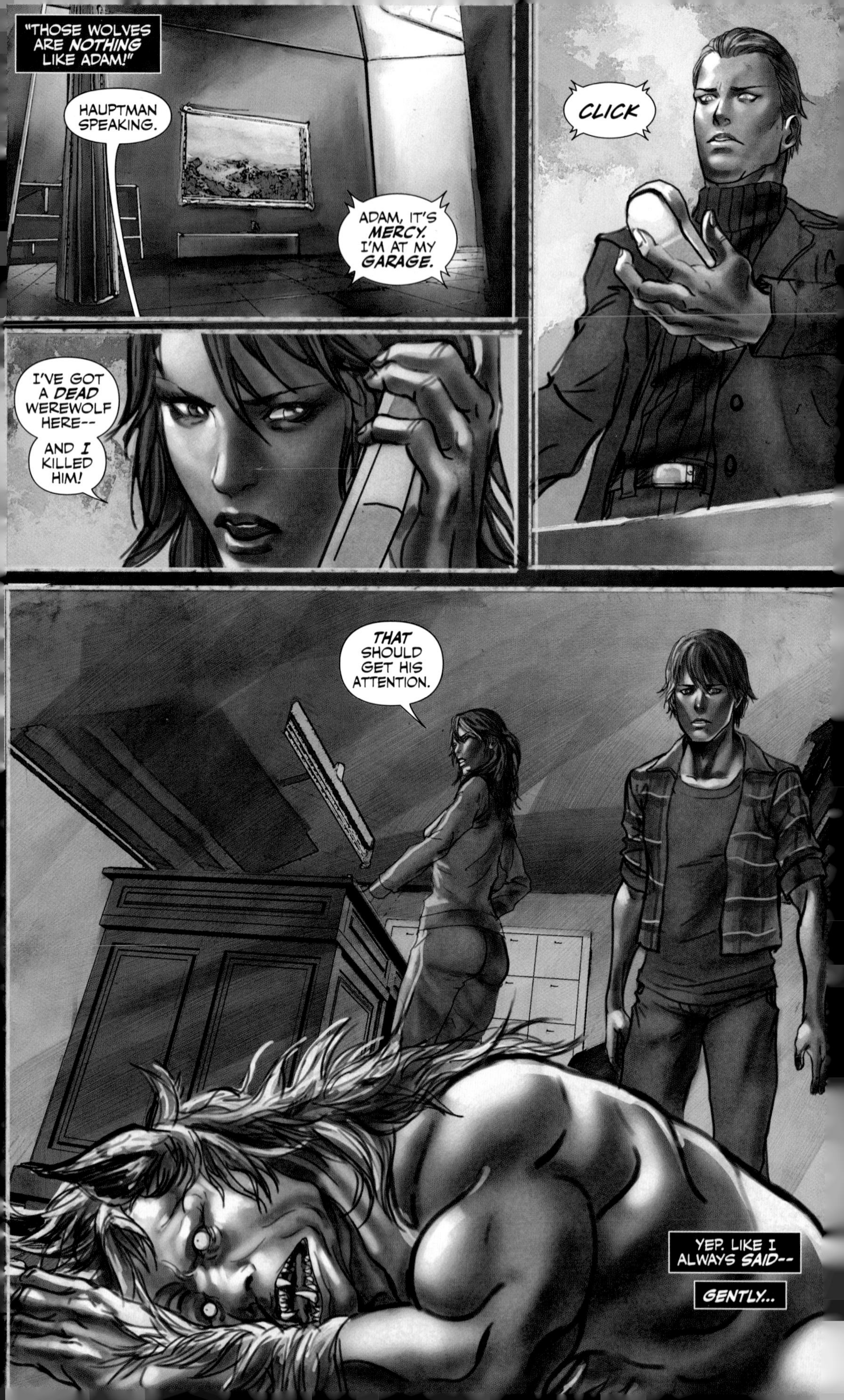
"THOSE WOLVES ARE NOTHING LIKE ADAM!"
HAUPTMAN SPEAKING.
ADAM, IT'S MERCY. I'M AT MY GARAGE.
CLICK
I'VE GOT A DEAD WEREWOLF HERE--
AND I KILLED HIM!
THAT SHOULD GET HIS ATTENTION.
YEP. LIKE I ALWAYS SAID--
GENTLY...

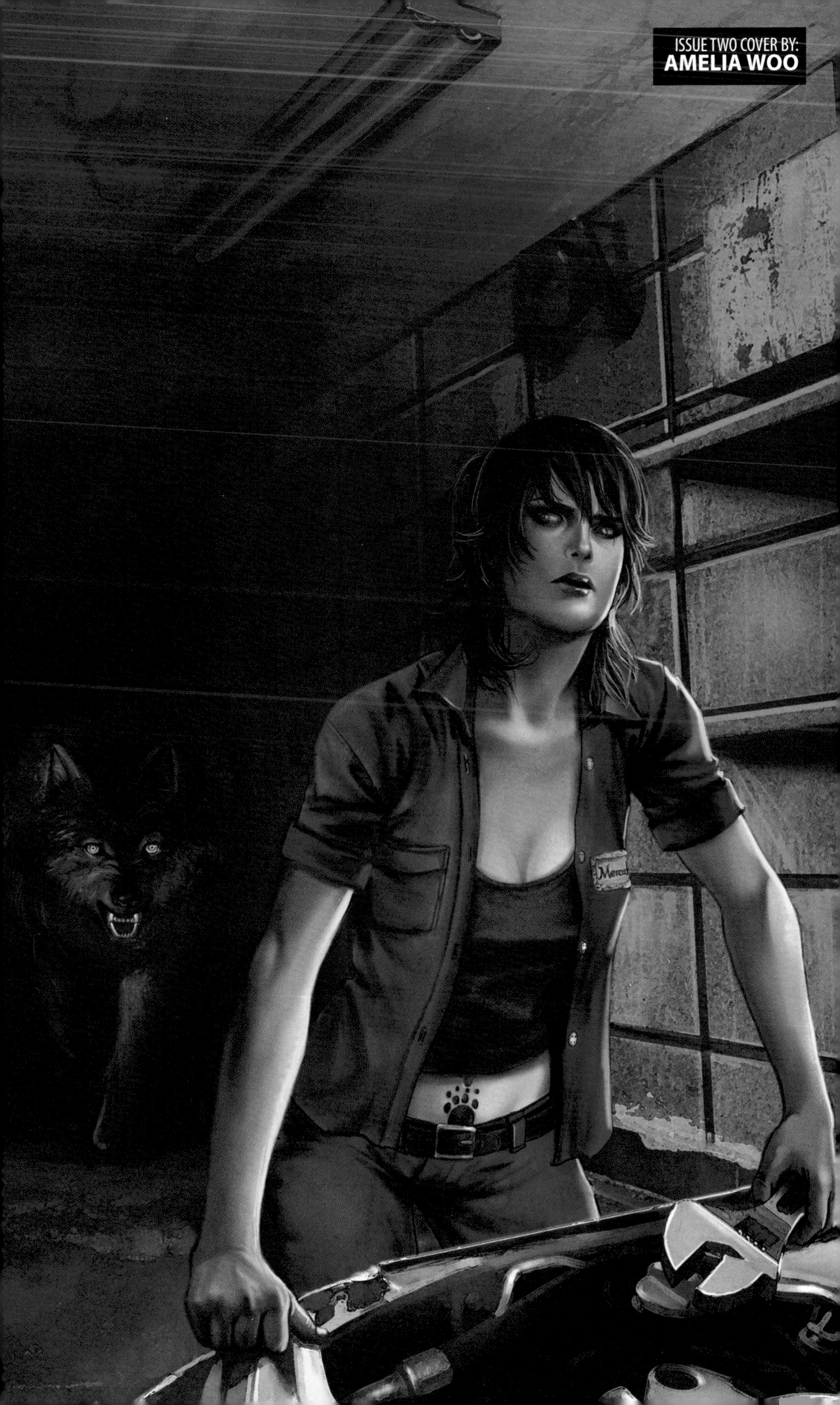

ISSUE TWO COVER BY:
AMELIA WOO

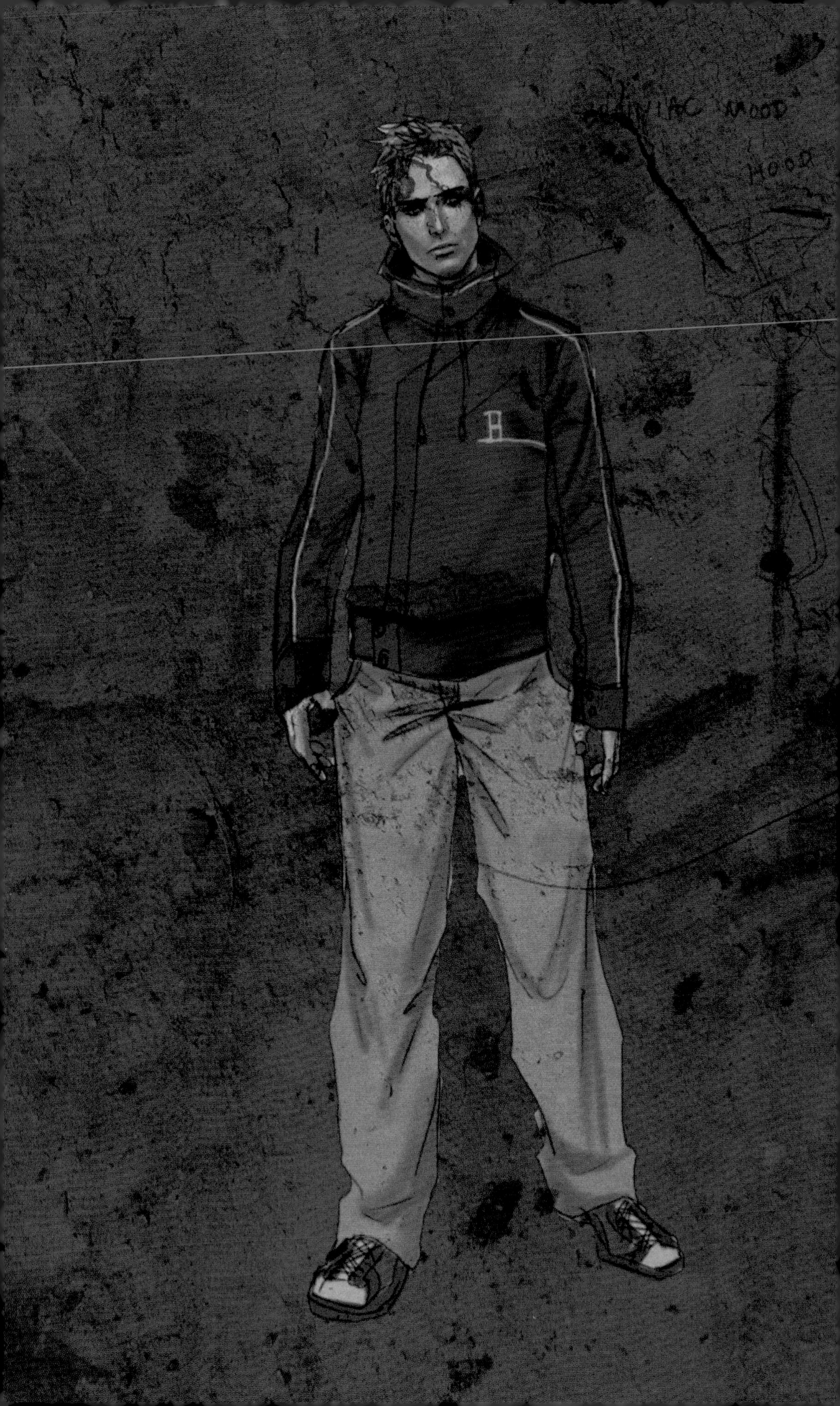
MOOD
HOOD

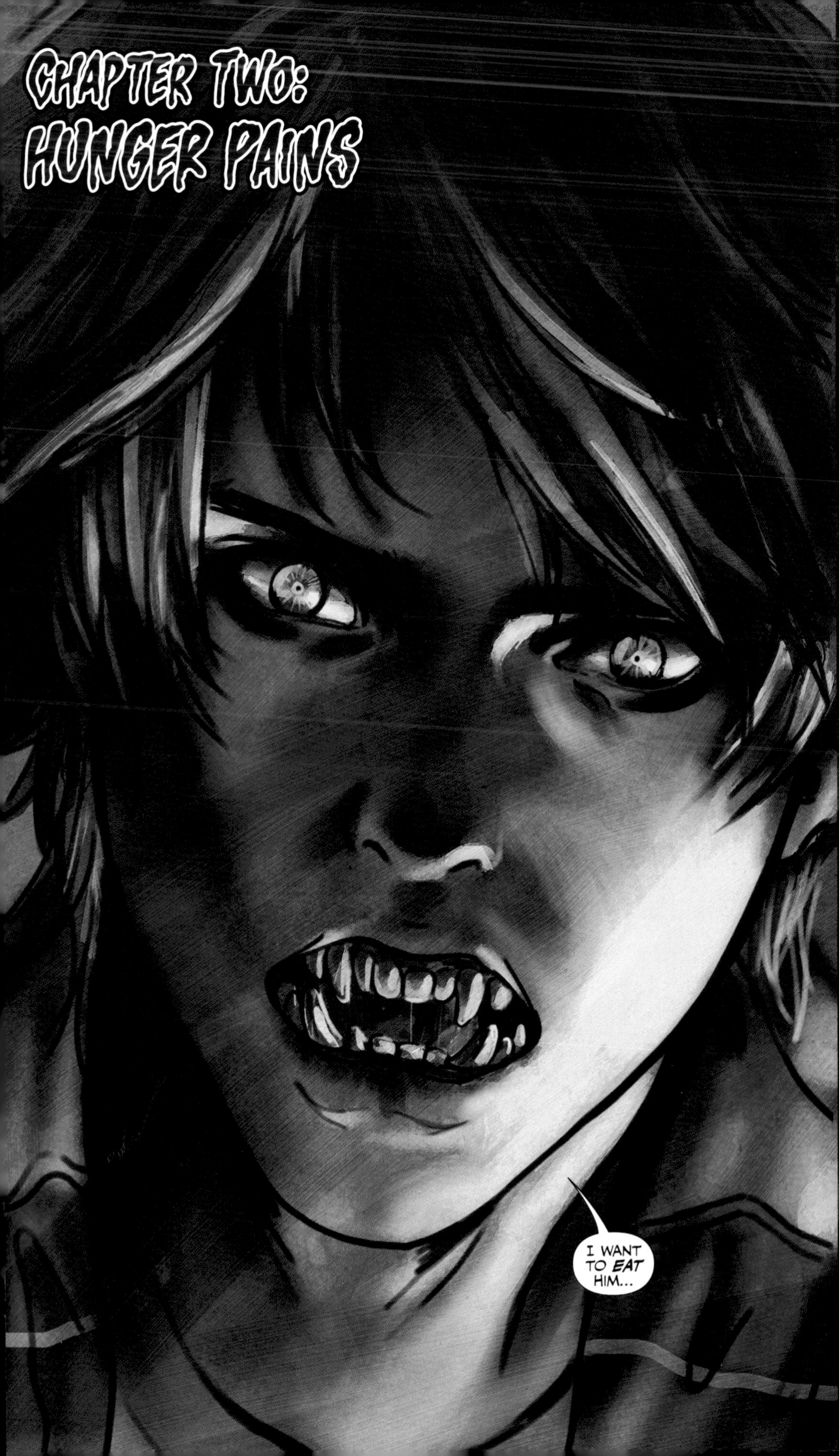
CHAPTER TWO:
HUNGER PAINS
I WANT TO EAT HIM...

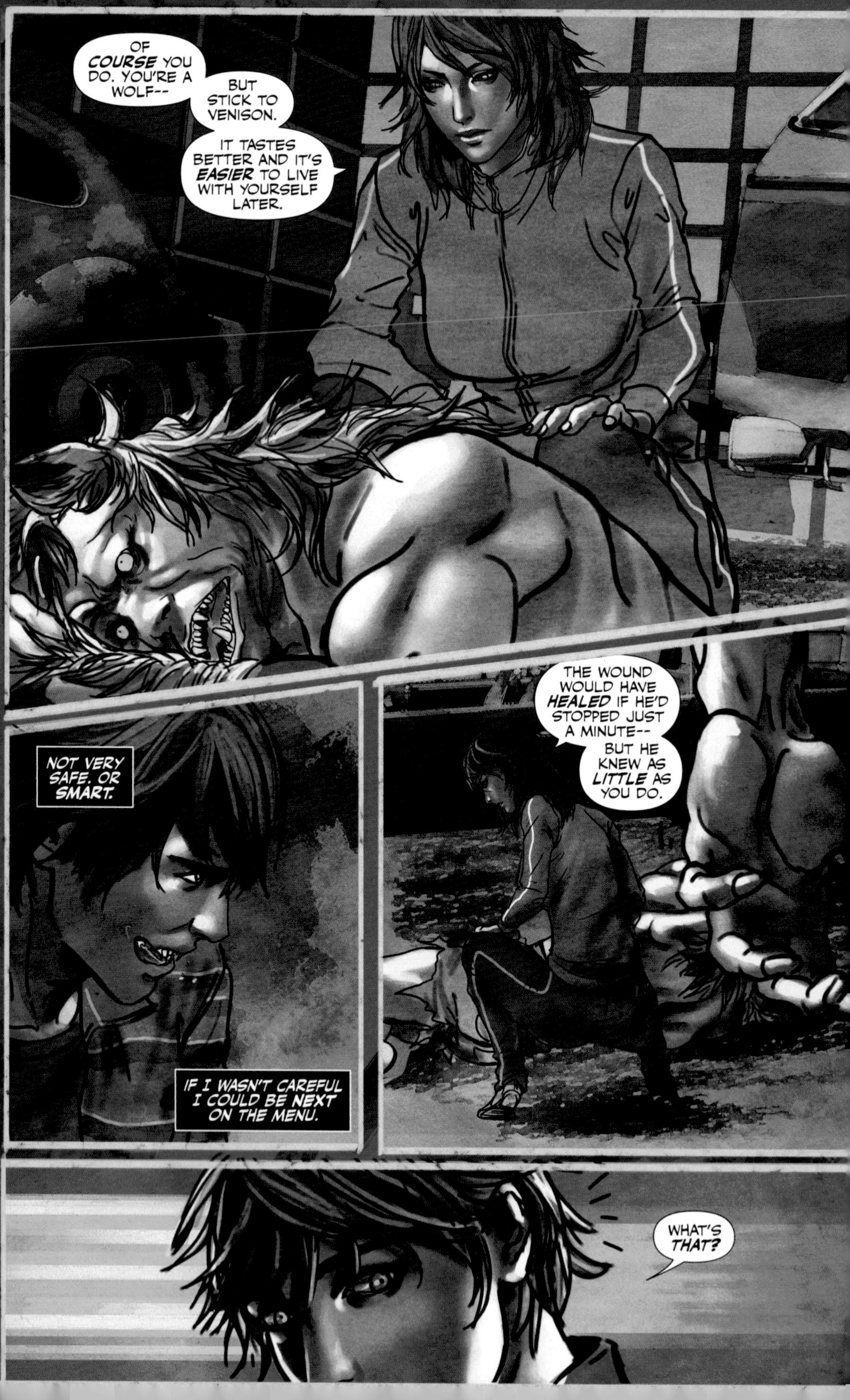
OF COURSE YOU DO. YOU'RE A WOLF--
BUT STICK TO VENISON.
IT TASTES BETTER AND IT'S EASIER TO LIVE WITH YOURSELF LATER.
NOT VERY SAFE. OR SMART.
IF I WASN'T CAREFUL I COULD BE NEXT ON THE MENU.
THE WOUND WOULD HAVE HEALED IF HE'D STOPPED JUST A MINUTE--
BUT HE KNEW AS LITTLE AS YOU DO.
WHAT'S THAT?

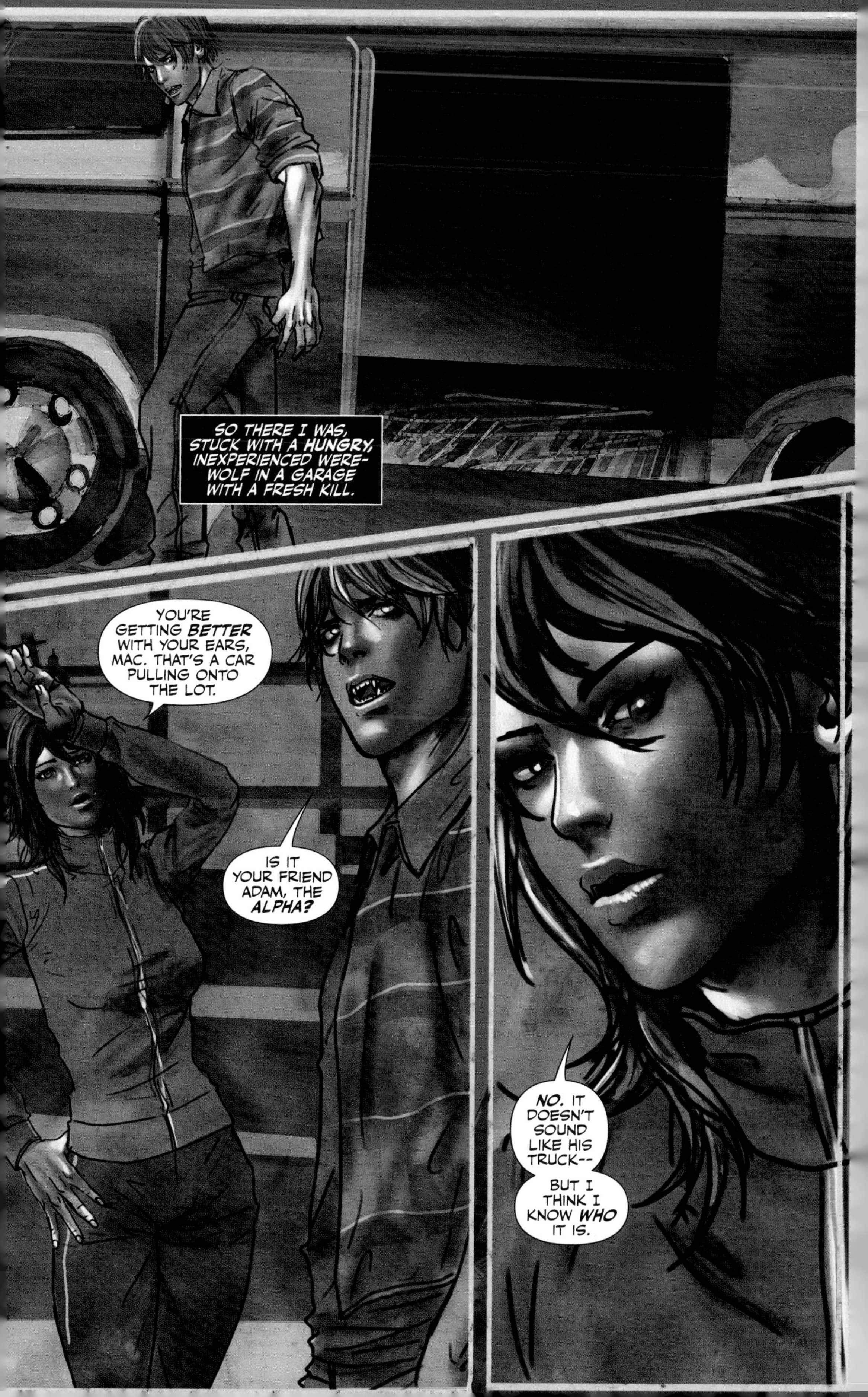

SO THERE I WAS, STUCK WITH A HUNGRY, INEXPERIENCED WERE-WOLF IN A GARAGE WITH A FRESH KILL.
YOU'RE GETTING BETTER WITH YOUR EARS, MAC. THAT'S A CAR PULLING ONTO THE LOT.
IS IT YOUR FRIEND ADAM, THE ALPHA?
NO. IT DOESN'T SOUND LIKE HIS TRUCK--
BUT I THINK I KNOW WHO IT IS.

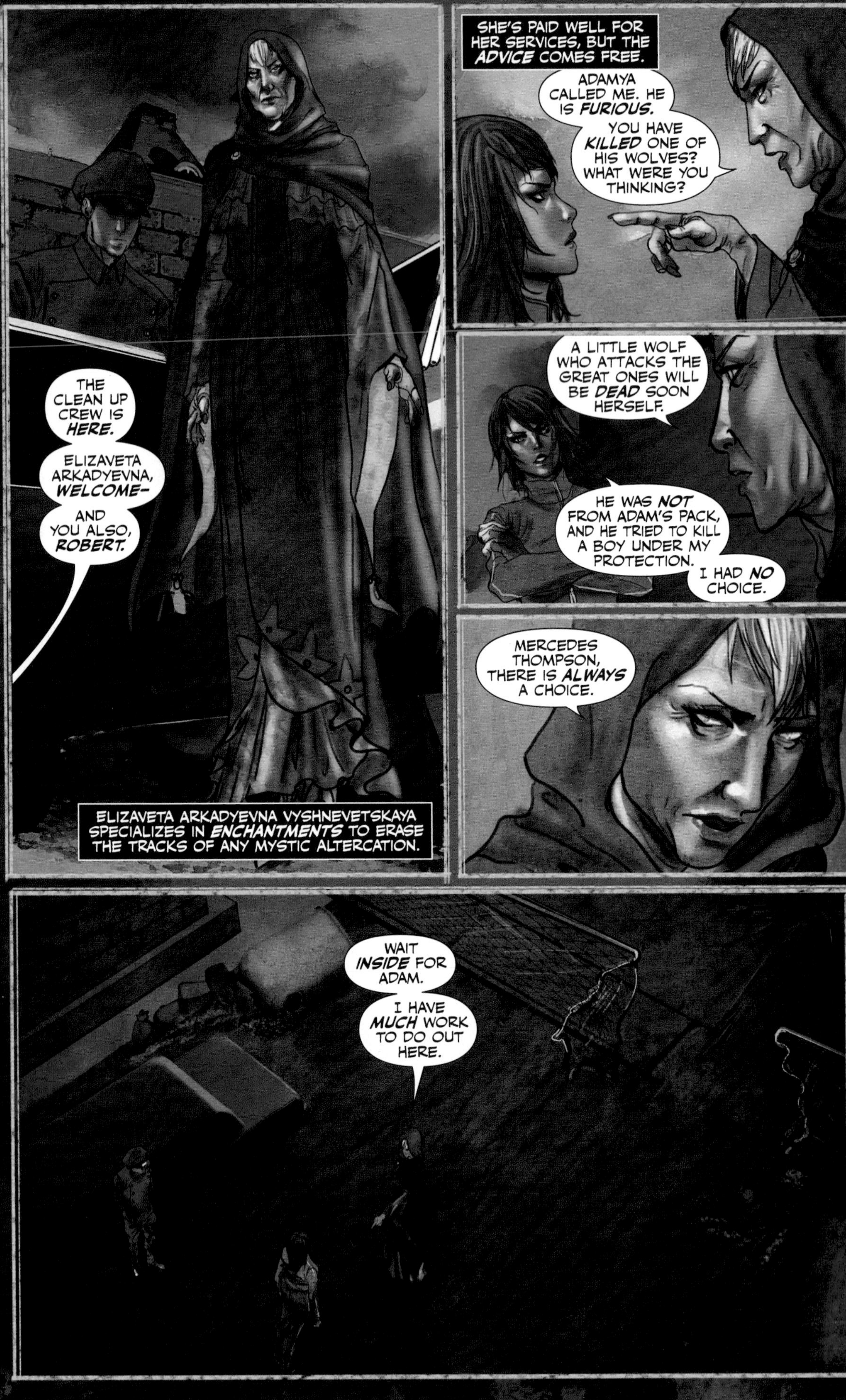
THE CLEAN UP CREW IS HERE.
ELIZAVETA ARKADYEVNA, WELCOME–
AND YOU ALSO, ROBERT.
ELIZAVETA ARKADYEVNA VYSHNEVETSKAYA SPECIALIZES IN ENCHANTMENTS TO ERASE THE TRACKS OF ANY MYSTIC ALTERCATION.
SHE'S PAID WELL FOR HER SERVICES, BUT THE ADVICE COMES FREE.
ADAMYA CALLED ME. HE IS FURIOUS.
YOU HAVE KILLED ONE OF HIS WOLVES? WHAT WERE YOU THINKING?
A LITTLE WOLF WHO ATTACKS THE GREAT ONES WILL BE DEAD SOON HERSELF.
HE WAS NOT FROM ADAM'S PACK, AND HE TRIED TO KILL A BOY UNDER MY PROTECTION.
I HAD NO CHOICE.
MERCEDES THOMPSON, THERE IS ALWAYS A CHOICE.
WAIT INSIDE FOR ADAM.
I HAVE MUCH WORK TO DO OUT HERE.

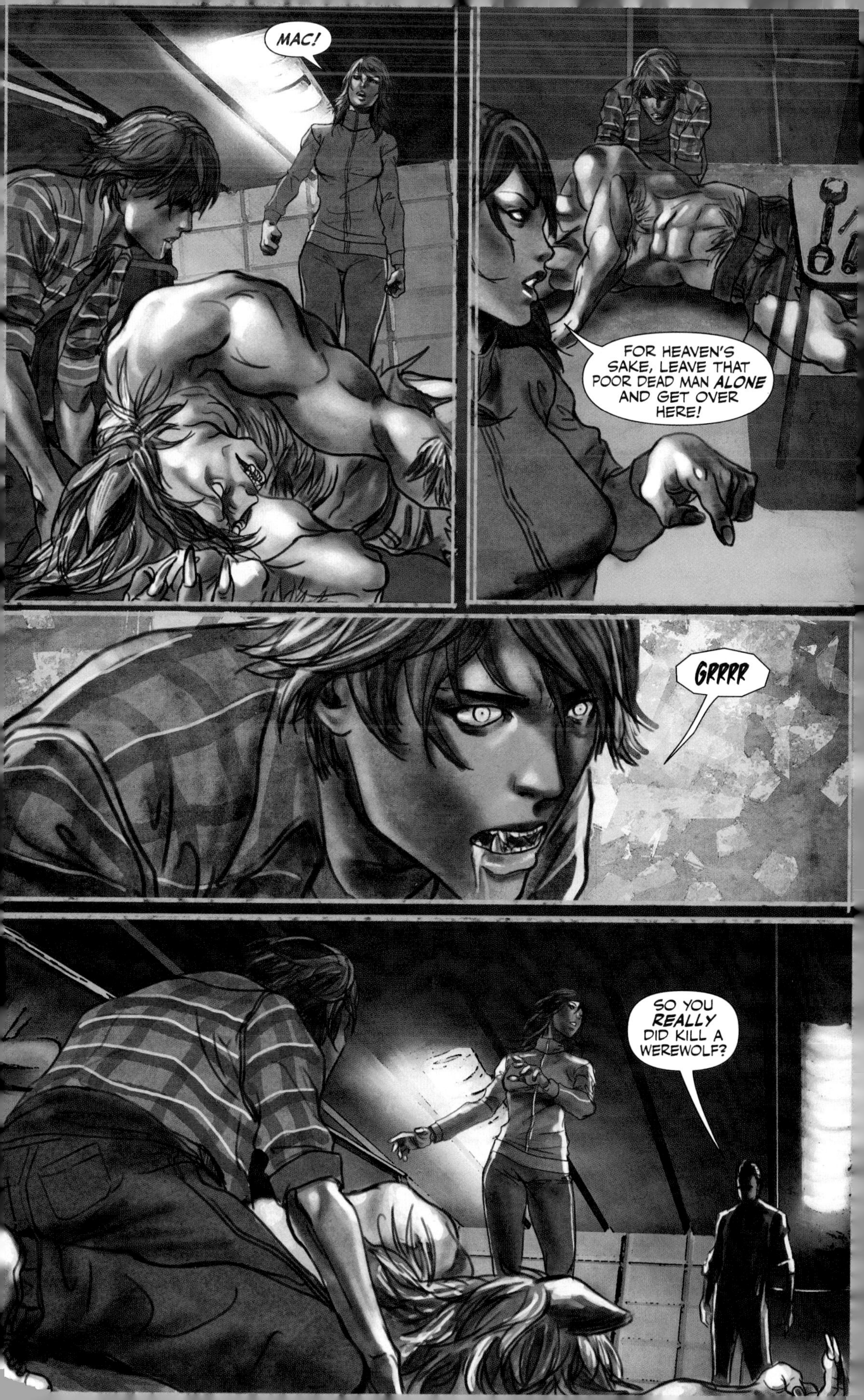
MAC!
FOR HEAVEN'S SAKE, LEAVE THAT POOR DEAD MAN ALONE AND GET OVER HERE!
GRRRR
SO YOU REALLY DID KILL A WEREWOLF?

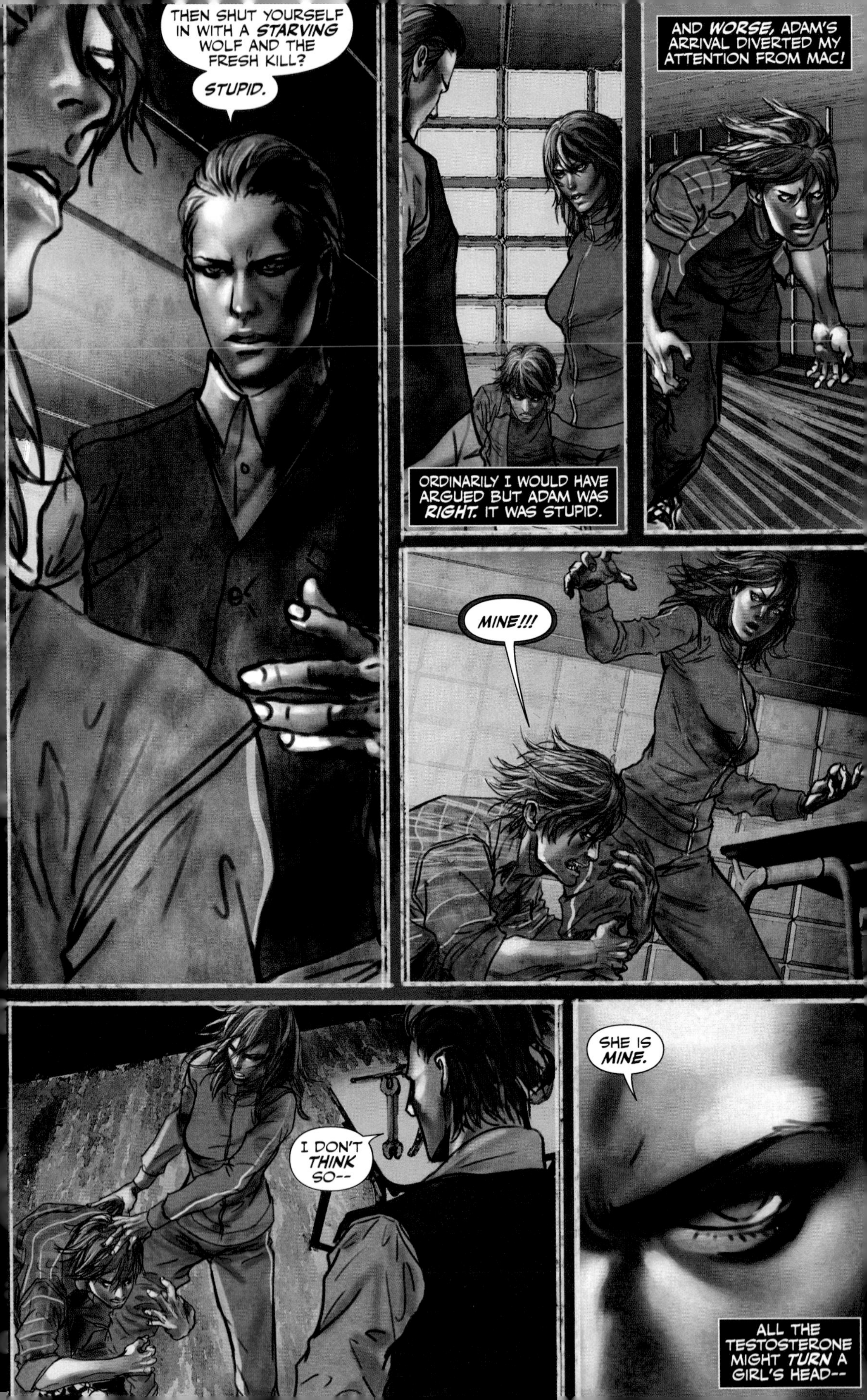
THEN SHUT YOURSELF IN WITH A STARVING WOLF AND THE FRESH KILL?
STUPID.
ORDINARILY I WOULD HAVE ARGUED BUT ADAM WAS RIGHT. IT WAS STUPID.
AND WORSE, ADAM'S ARRIVAL DIVERTED MY ATTENTION FROM MAC!
MINE!!!
I DON'T THINK SO--
SHE IS MINE.
ALL THE TESTOSTERONE MIGHT TURN A GIRL'S HEAD--

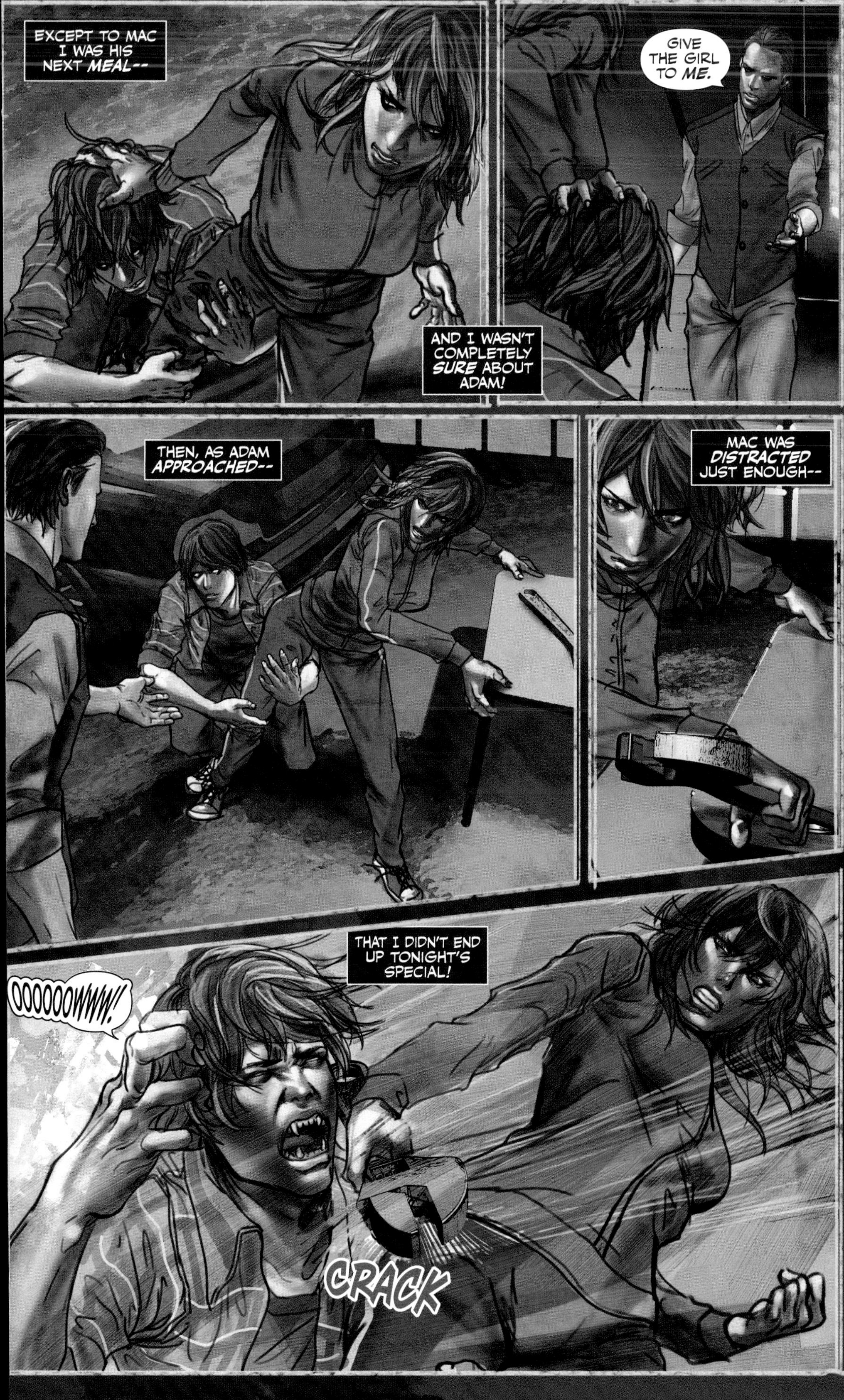
EXCEPT TO MAC I WAS HIS NEXT MEAL--
AND I WASN'T COMPLETELY SURE ABOUT ADAM!
GIVE THE GIRL TO ME.
THEN, AS ADAM APPROACHED--
MAC WAS DISTRACTED JUST ENOUGH--
THAT I DIDN'T END UP TONIGHT'S SPECIAL!
OOOOOOWWW!
CRACK

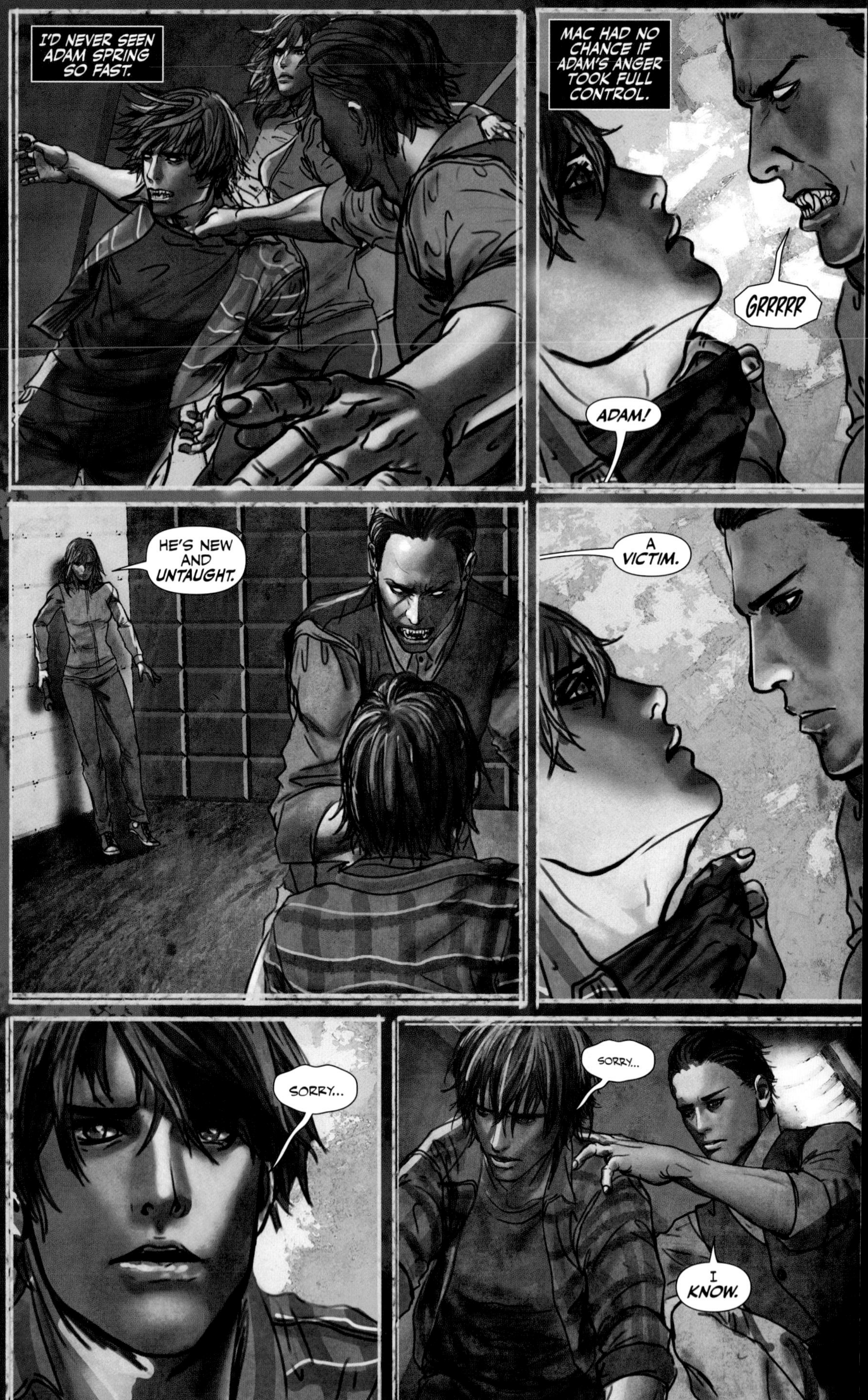
I'D NEVER SEEN ADAM SPRING SO FAST.
MAC HAD NO CHANCE IF ADAM'S ANGER TOOK FULL CONTROL.
GRRRRR
ADAM!
HE'S NEW AND UNTAUGHT.
A VICTIM.
SORRY...
SORRY...
I KNOW.

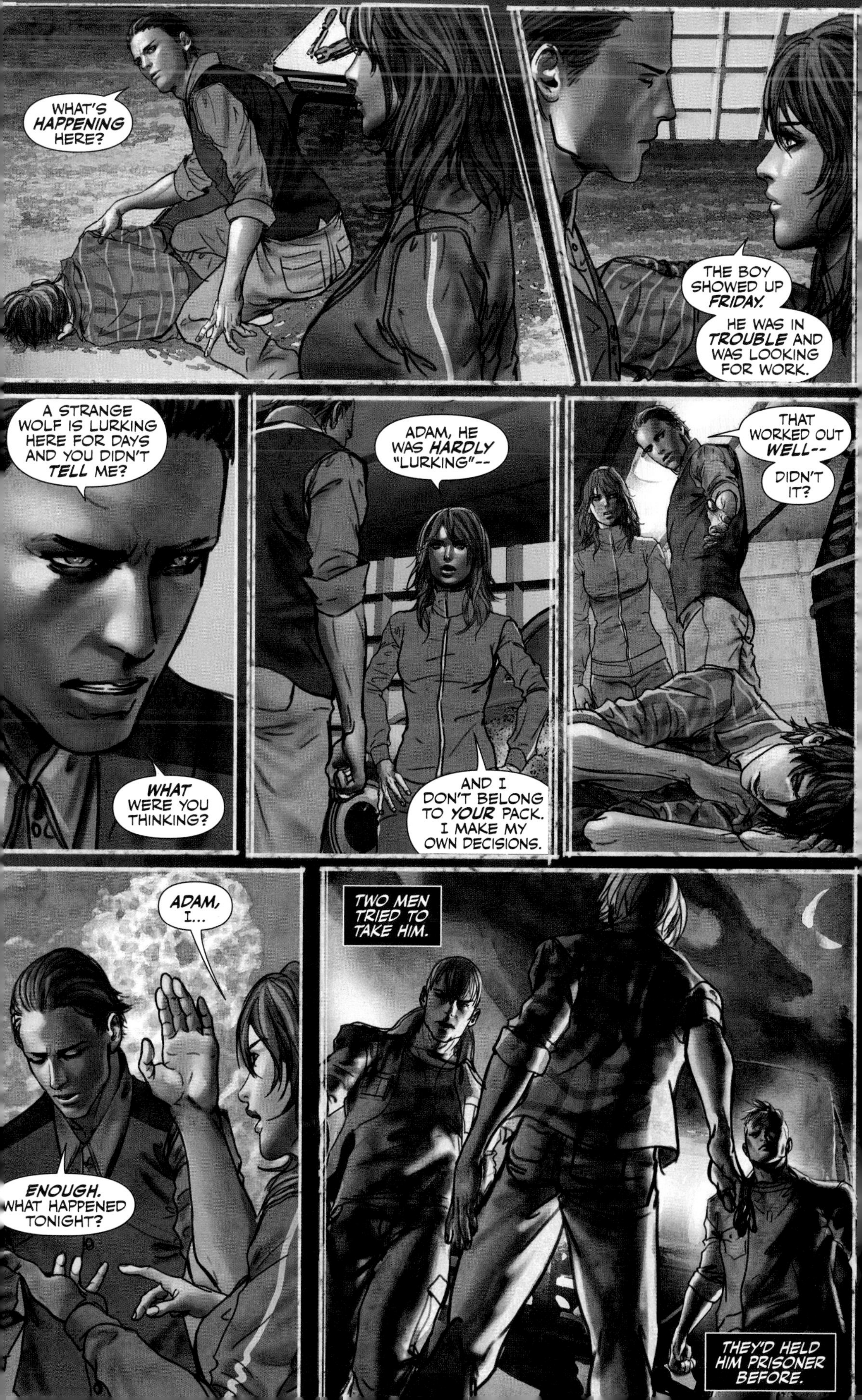
WHAT'S HAPPENING HERE?
THE BOY SHOWED UP FRIDAY.
HE WAS IN TROUBLE AND WAS LOOKING FOR WORK.
A STRANGE WOLF IS LURKING HERE FOR DAYS AND YOU DIDN'T TELL ME?
WHAT WERE YOU THINKING?
ADAM, HE WAS HARDLY "LURKING"--
AND I DON'T BELONG TO YOUR PACK. I MAKE MY OWN DECISIONS.
THAT WORKED OUT WELL--
DIDN'T IT?
ADAM, I...
ENOUGH. WHAT HAPPENED TONIGHT?
TWO MEN TRIED TO TAKE HIM.
THEY'D HELD HIM PRISONER BEFORE.

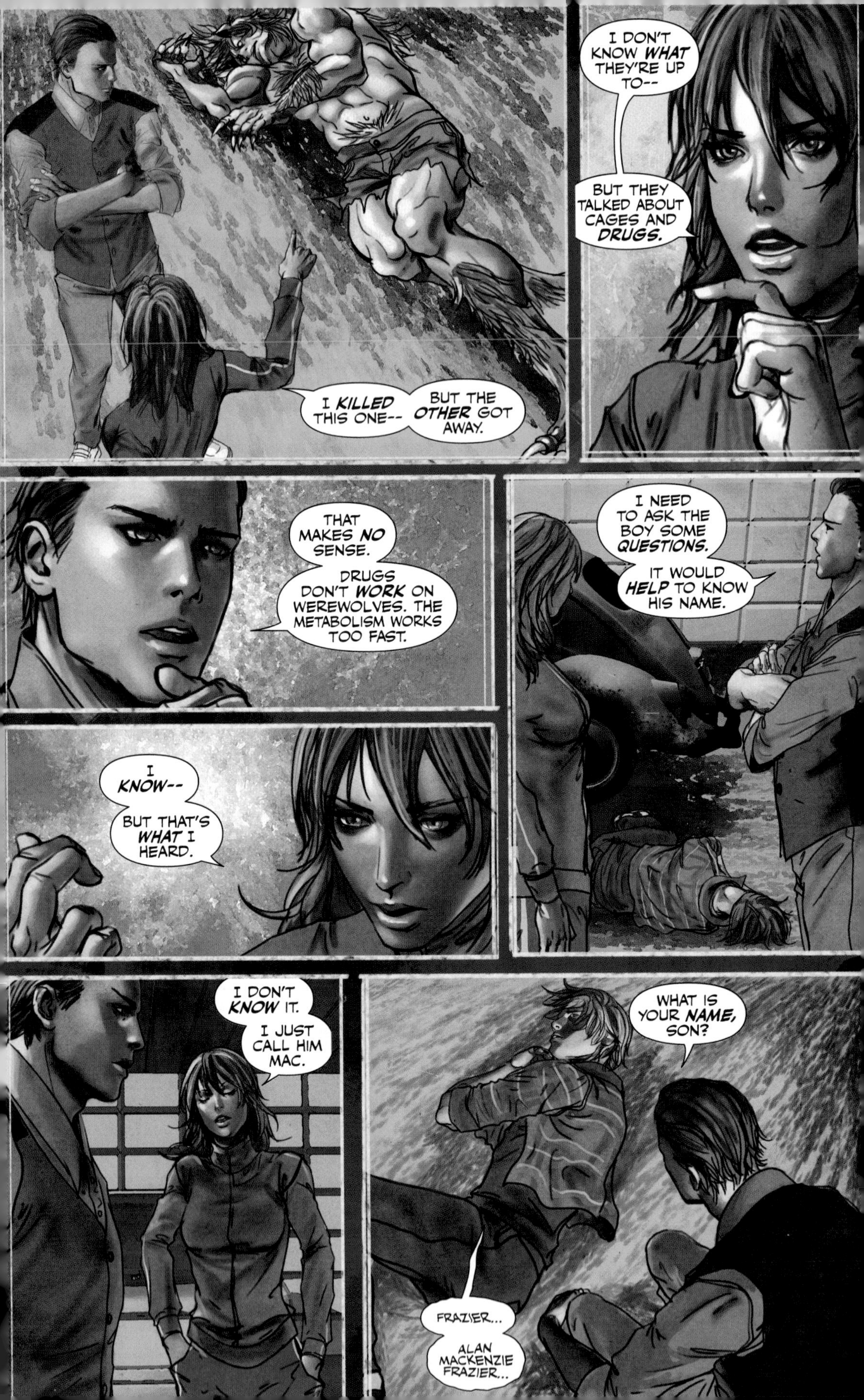
I KILLED THIS ONE--
BUT THE OTHER GOT AWAY.
I DON'T KNOW WHAT THEY'RE UP TO--
BUT THEY TALKED ABOUT CAGES AND DRUGS.
THAT MAKES NO SENSE.
DRUGS DON'T WORK ON WEREWOLVES. THE METABOLISM WORKS TOO FAST.
I KNOW--
BUT THAT'S WHAT I HEARD.
I NEED TO ASK THE BOY SOME QUESTIONS.
IT WOULD HELP TO KNOW HIS NAME.
I DON'T KNOW IT.
I JUST CALL HIM MAC.
WHAT IS YOUR NAME, SON?
FRAZIER...
ALAN MACKENZIE FRAZIER...

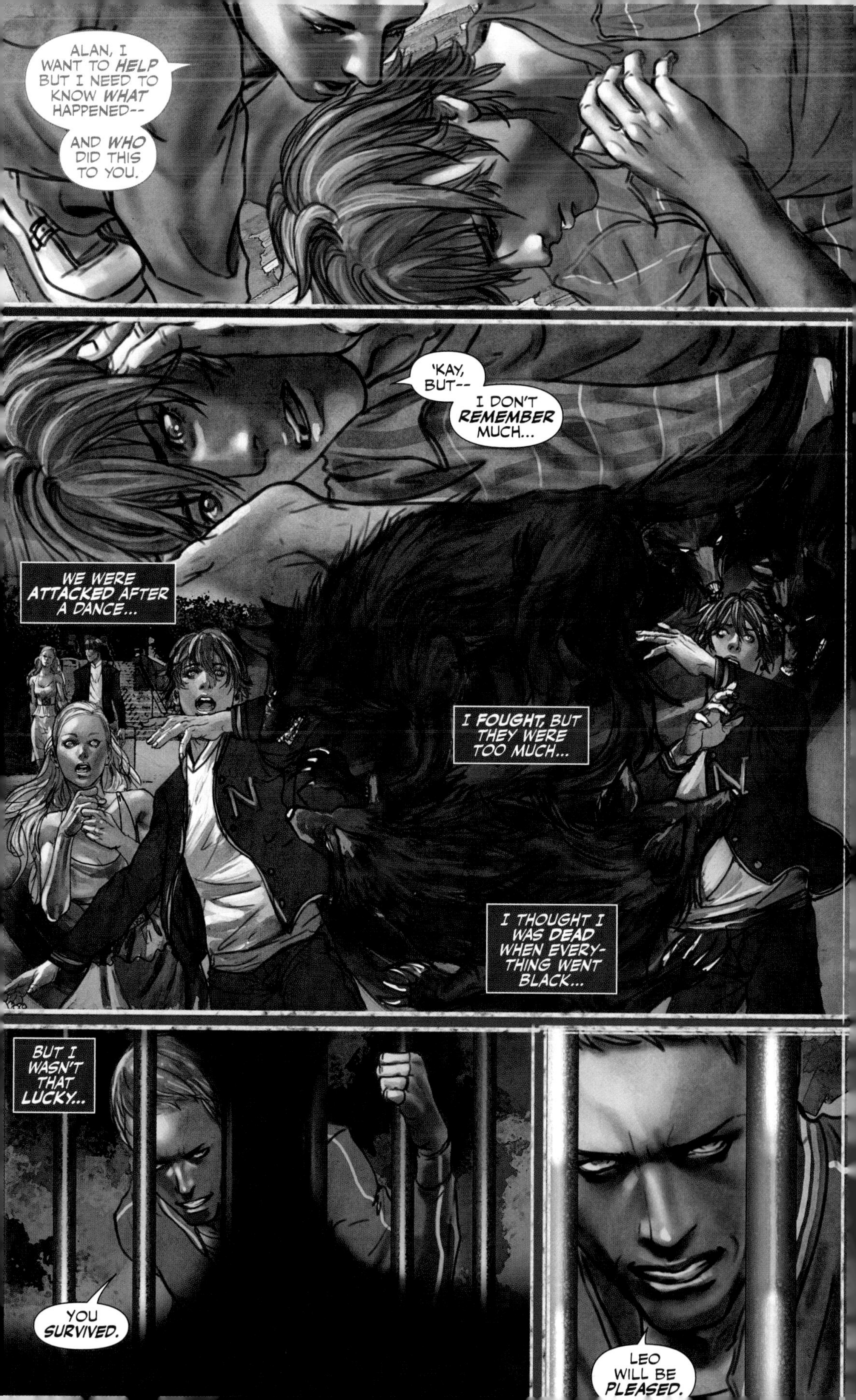

ALAN, I WANT TO HELP BUT I NEED TO KNOW WHAT HAPPENED--
AND WHO DID THIS TO YOU.
'KAY, BUT--
I DON'T REMEMBER MUCH...
WE WERE ATTACKED AFTER A DANCE...
I FOUGHT, BUT THEY WERE TOO MUCH...
I THOUGHT I WAS DEAD WHEN EVERY-THING WENT BLACK...
BUT I WASN'T THAT LUCKY...
YOU SURVIVED.
LEO WILL BE PLEASED.

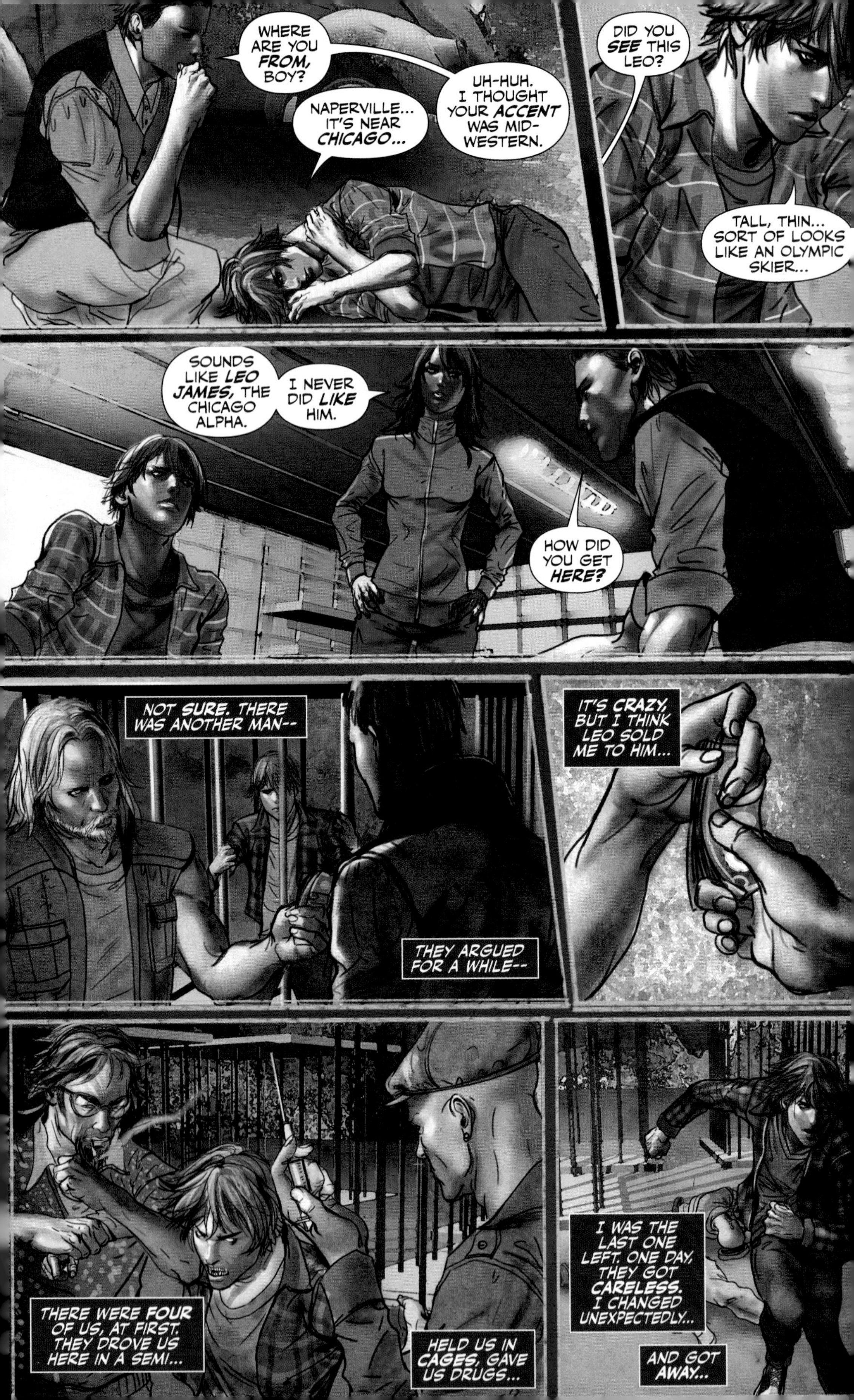
WHERE ARE YOU FROM, BOY?
NAPERVILLE... IT'S NEAR CHICAGO...
UH-HUH. I THOUGHT YOUR ACCENT WAS MID-WESTERN.
DID YOU SEE THIS LEO?
TALL, THIN... SORT OF LOOKS LIKE AN OLYMPIC SKIER...
SOUNDS LIKE LEO JAMES, THE CHICAGO ALPHA.
I NEVER DID LIKE HIM.
HOW DID YOU GET HERE?
NOT SURE. THERE WAS ANOTHER MAN--
THEY ARGUED FOR A WHILE--
IT'S CRAZY, BUT I THINK LEO SOLD ME TO HIM...
THERE WERE FOUR OF US, AT FIRST. THEY DROVE US HERE IN A SEMI...
HELD US IN CAGES, GAVE US DRUGS...
I WAS THE LAST ONE LEFT. ONE DAY, THEY GOT CARELESS. I CHANGED UNEXPECTEDLY...
AND GOT AWAY...

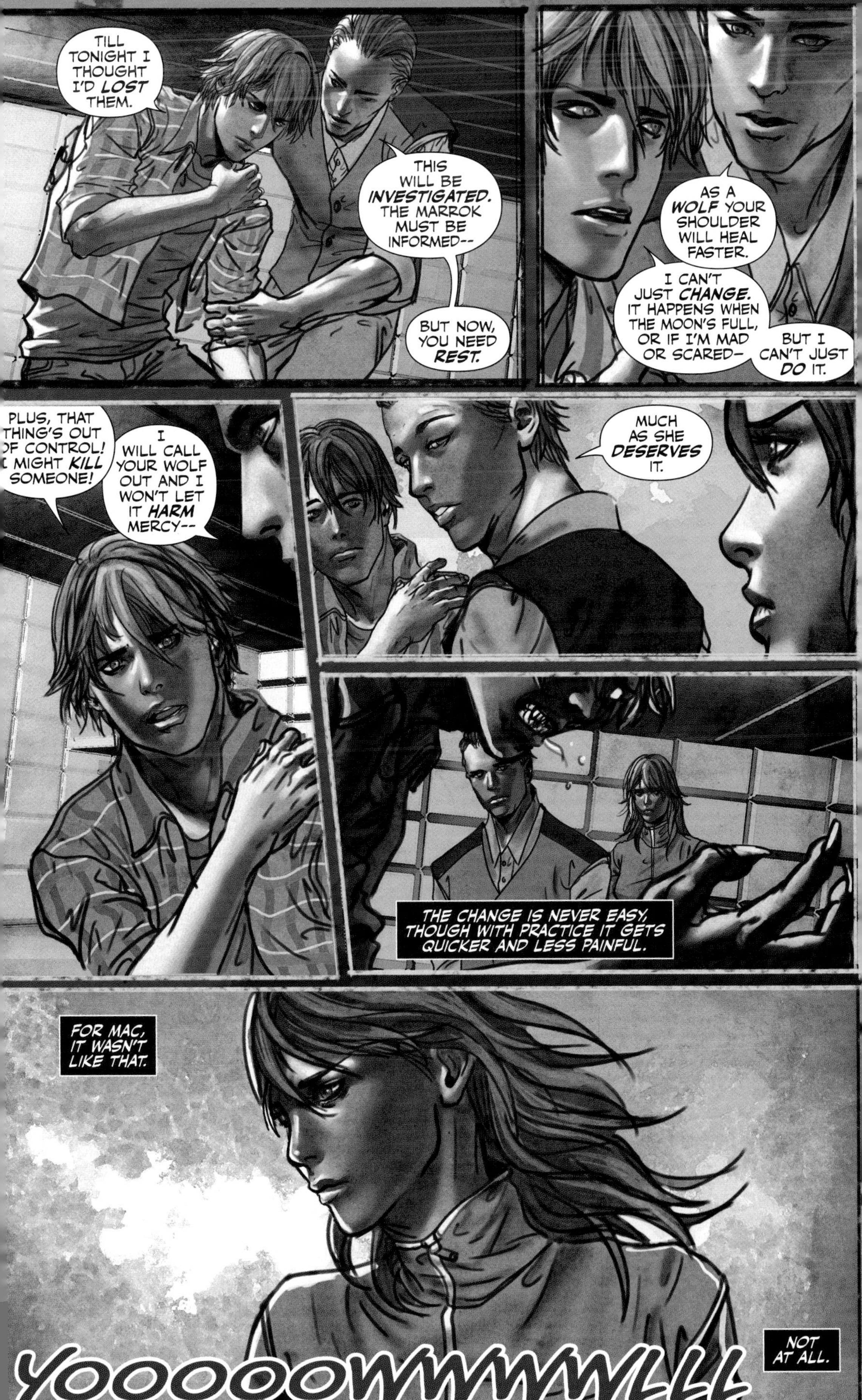
TILL TONIGHT I THOUGHT I'D LOST THEM.
THIS WILL BE INVESTIGATED. THE MARROK MUST BE INFORMED--
BUT NOW, YOU NEED REST.
AS A WOLF YOUR SHOULDER WILL HEAL FASTER.
I CAN'T JUST CHANGE. IT HAPPENS WHEN THE MOON'S FULL, OR IF I'M MAD OR SCARED-
BUT I CAN'T JUST DO IT.
PLUS, THAT THING'S OUT F CONTROL! MIGHT KILL SOMEONE!
I WILL CALL YOUR WOLF OUT AND I WON'T LET IT HARM MERCY--
MUCH AS SHE DESERVES IT.
THE CHANGE IS NEVER EASY, THOUGH WITH PRACTICE IT GETS QUICKER AND LESS PAINFUL.
FOR MAC, IT WASN'T LIKE THAT.
YOOOOOWWWWLLL
NOT AT ALL.

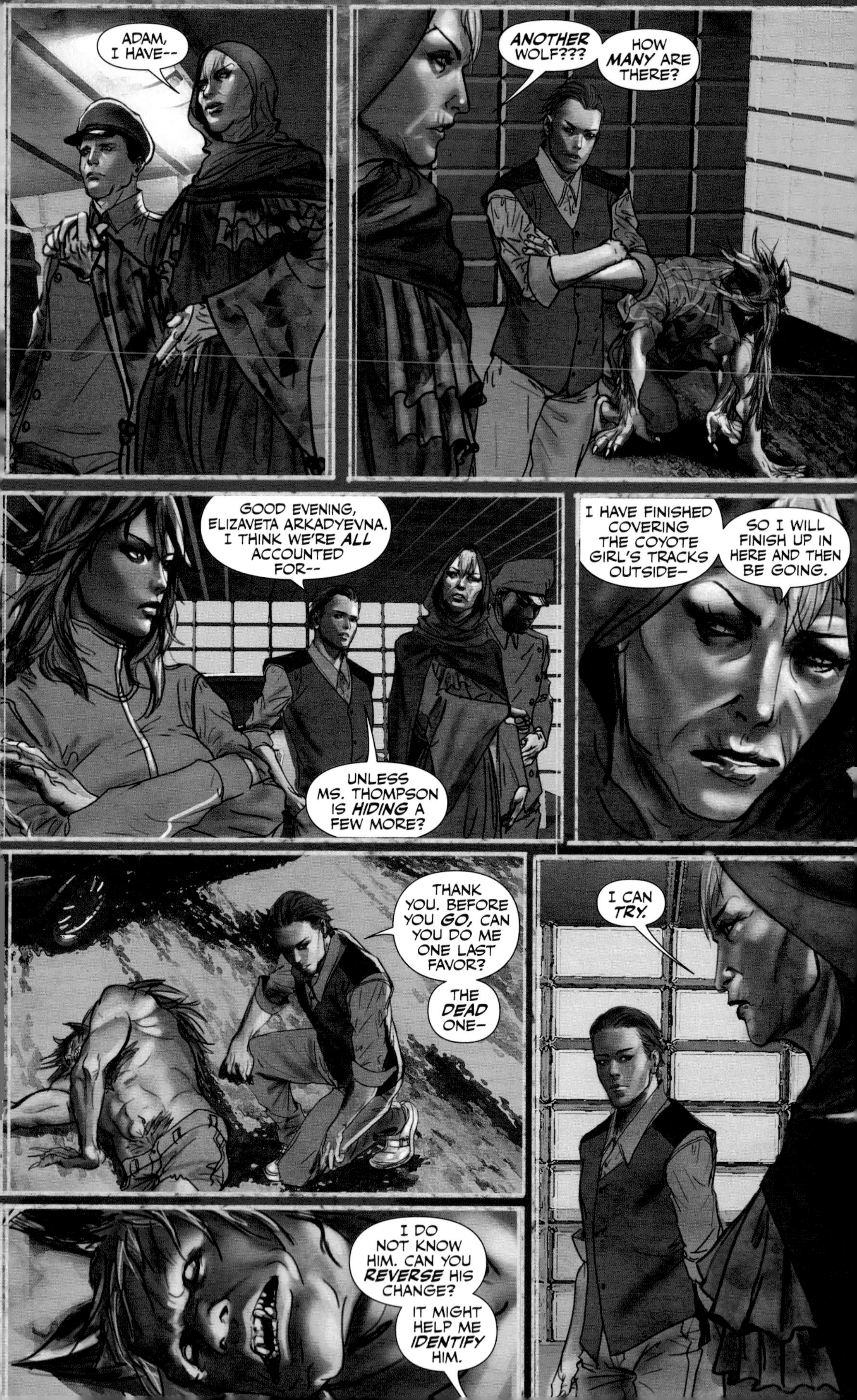
ADAM, I HAVE--
ANOTHER WOLF???
HOW MANY ARE THERE?
GOOD EVENING, ELIZAVETA ARKADYEVNA. I THINK WE'RE ALL ACCOUNTED FOR--
UNLESS MS. THOMPSON IS HIDING A FEW MORE?
I HAVE FINISHED COVERING THE COYOTE GIRL'S TRACKS OUTSIDE–
SO I WILL FINISH UP IN HERE AND THEN BE GOING.
THANK YOU. BEFORE YOU GO, CAN YOU DO ME ONE LAST FAVOR?
THE DEAD ONE–
I DO NOT KNOW HIM. CAN YOU REVERSE HIS CHANGE?
IT MIGHT HELP ME IDENTIFY HIM.
I CAN TRY.

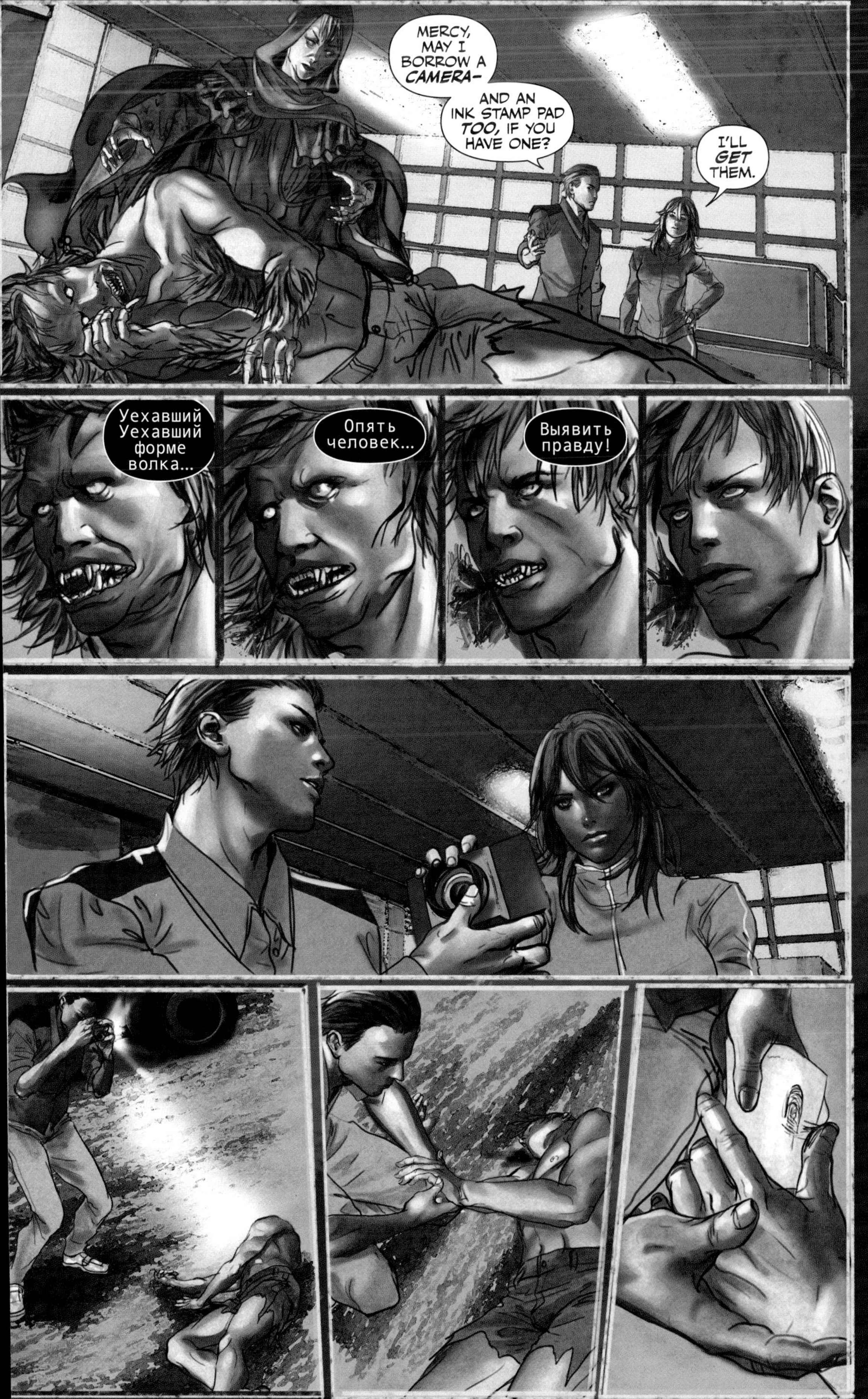
MERCY, MAY I BORROW A CAMERA–
AND AN INK STAMP PAD TOO, IF YOU HAVE ONE?
I'LL GET THEM.
Уехавший Уехавший форме волка...
Опять человек...
Выявить правду!

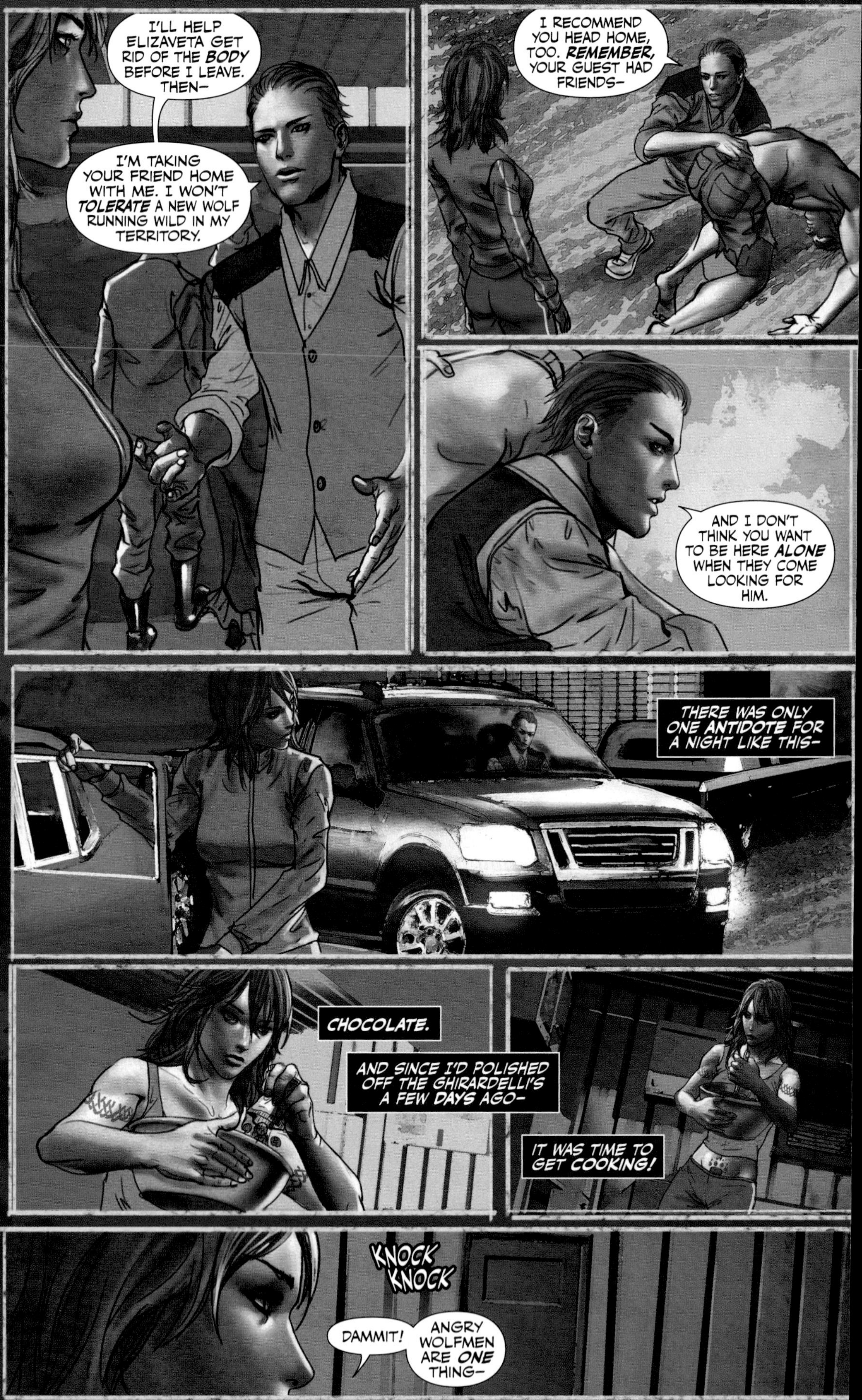
I'LL HELP ELIZAVETA GET RID OF THE *BODY* BEFORE I LEAVE. THEN–
I'M TAKING YOUR FRIEND HOME WITH ME. I WON'T *TOLERATE* A NEW WOLF RUNNING WILD IN MY TERRITORY.
I RECOMMEND YOU HEAD HOME, TOO. *REMEMBER,* YOUR GUEST HAD FRIENDS–
AND I DON'T THINK YOU WANT TO BE HERE *ALONE* WHEN THEY COME LOOKING FOR HIM.
THERE WAS ONLY ONE *ANTIDOTE* FOR A NIGHT LIKE THIS–
CHOCOLATE.
AND SINCE I'D POLISHED OFF THE GHIRARDELLI'S A FEW *DAYS* AGO–
IT WAS TIME TO GET *COOKING!*
KNOCK KNOCK
DAMMIT!
ANGRY WOLFMEN ARE *ONE* THING–

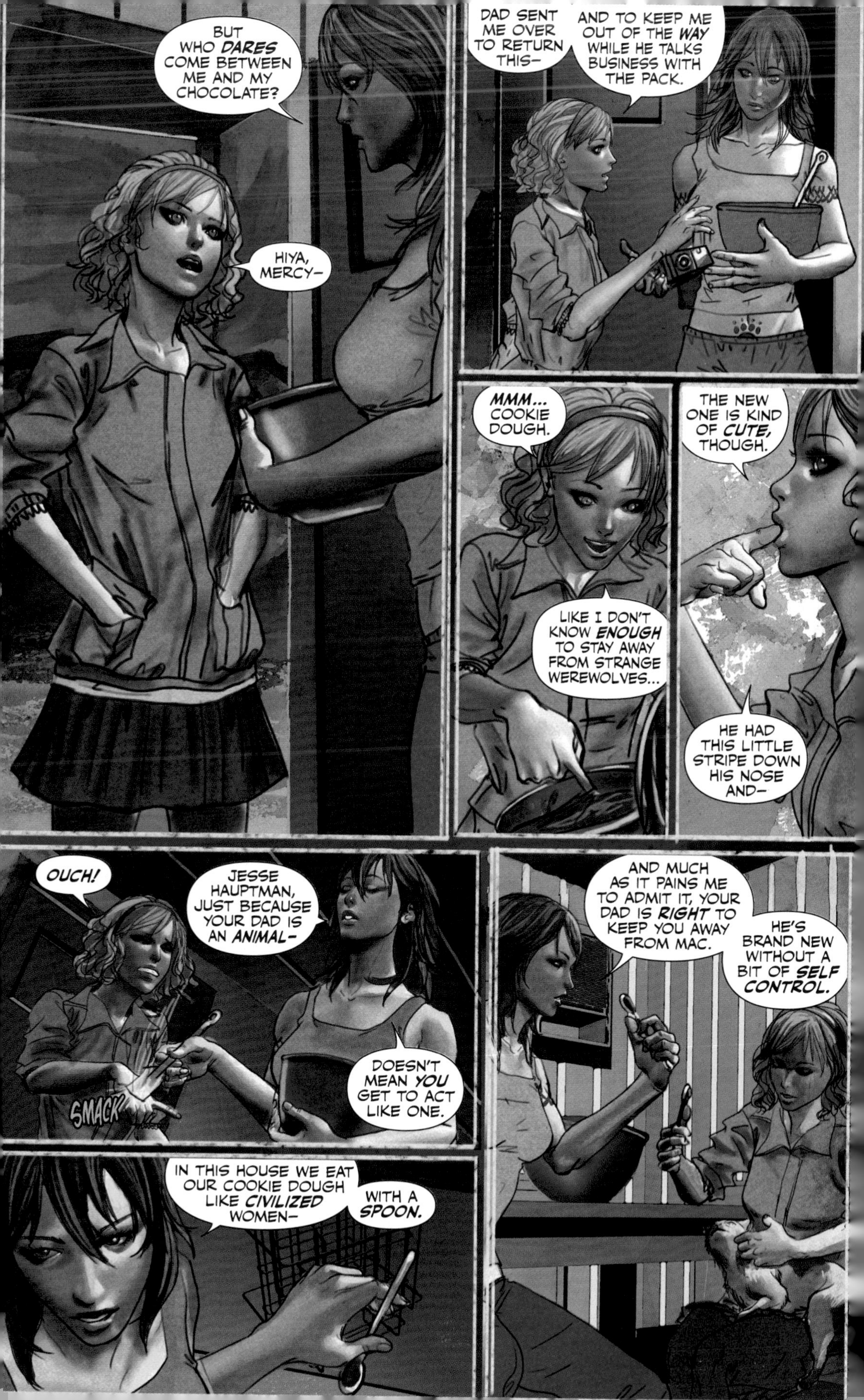
BUT WHO DARES COME BETWEEN ME AND MY CHOCOLATE?
HIYA, MERCY-
DAD SENT ME OVER TO RETURN THIS-
AND TO KEEP ME OUT OF THE WAY WHILE HE TALKS BUSINESS WITH THE PACK.
MMM... COOKIE DOUGH.
THE NEW ONE IS KIND OF CUTE, THOUGH.
LIKE I DON'T KNOW ENOUGH TO STAY AWAY FROM STRANGE WEREWOLVES...
HE HAD THIS LITTLE STRIPE DOWN HIS NOSE AND-
OUCH!
JESSE HAUPTMAN, JUST BECAUSE YOUR DAD IS AN ANIMAL-
DOESN'T MEAN YOU GET TO ACT LIKE ONE.
SMACK
IN THIS HOUSE WE EAT OUR COOKIE DOUGH LIKE CIVILIZED WOMEN-
WITH A SPOON.
AND MUCH AS IT PAINS ME TO ADMIT IT, YOUR DAD IS RIGHT TO KEEP YOU AWAY FROM MAC.
HE'S BRAND NEW WITHOUT A BIT OF SELF CONTROL.

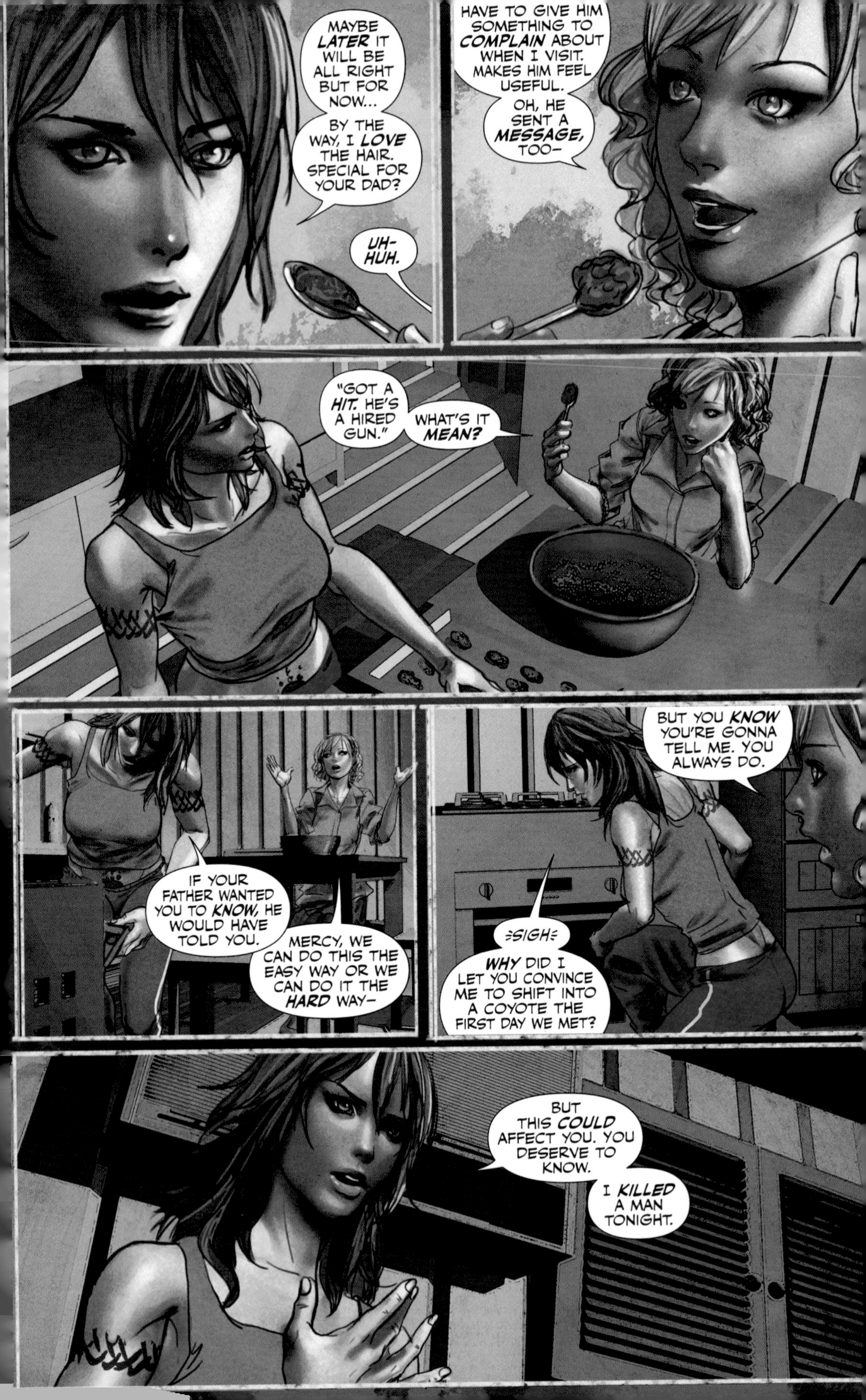
MAYBE LATER IT WILL BE ALL RIGHT BUT FOR NOW...
BY THE WAY, I LOVE THE HAIR. SPECIAL FOR YOUR DAD?
UH-HUH.
HAVE TO GIVE HIM SOMETHING TO COMPLAIN ABOUT WHEN I VISIT. MAKES HIM FEEL USEFUL.
OH, HE SENT A MESSAGE, TOO--
"GOT A HIT. HE'S A HIRED GUN."
WHAT'S IT MEAN?
IF YOUR FATHER WANTED YOU TO KNOW, HE WOULD HAVE TOLD YOU.
MERCY, WE CAN DO THIS THE EASY WAY OR WE CAN DO IT THE HARD WAY--
BUT YOU KNOW YOU'RE GONNA TELL ME. YOU ALWAYS DO.
SIGH
WHY DID I LET YOU CONVINCE ME TO SHIFT INTO A COYOTE THE FIRST DAY WE MET?
BUT THIS COULD AFFECT YOU. YOU DESERVE TO KNOW.
I KILLED A MAN TONIGHT.

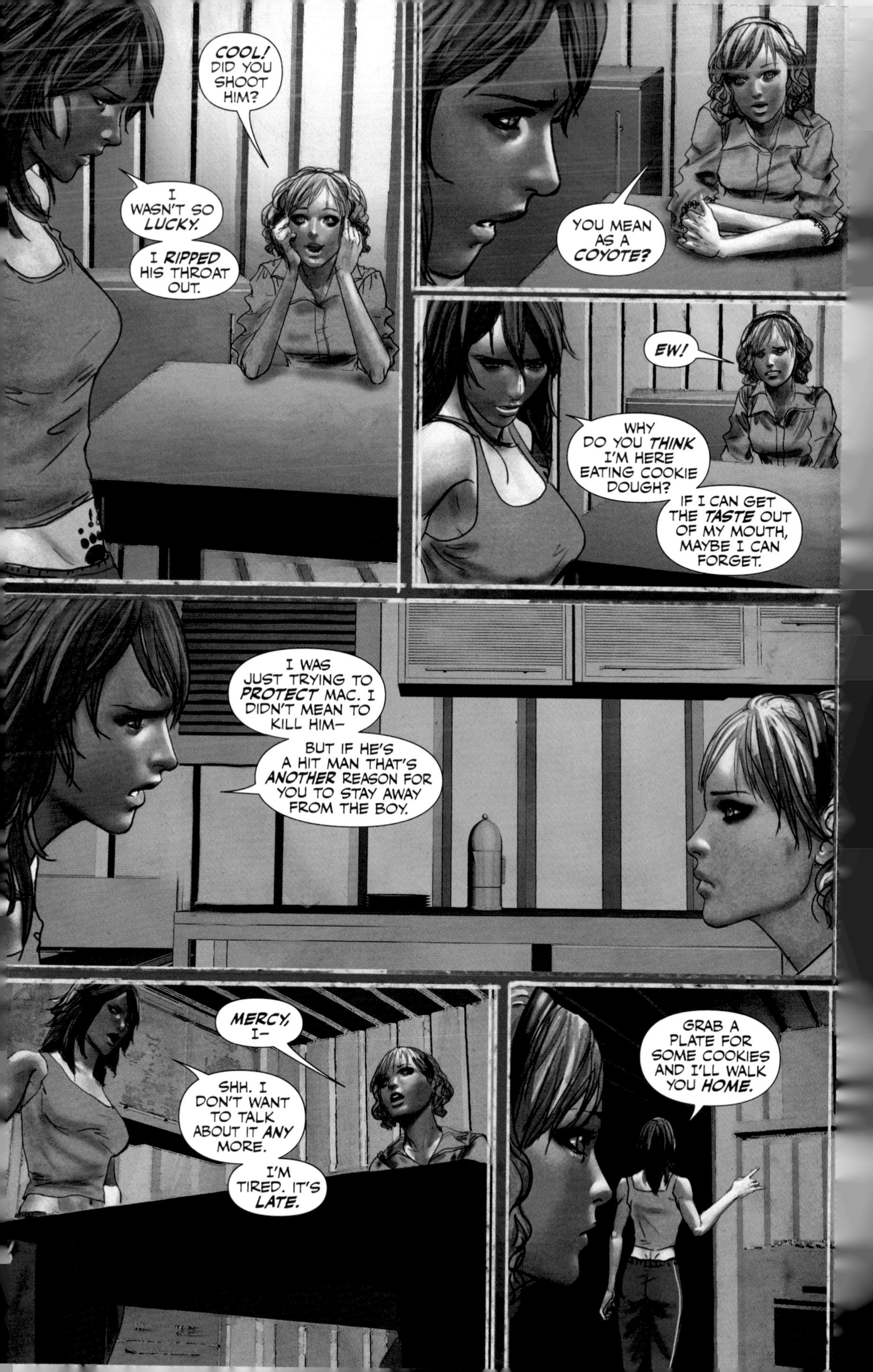
COOL! DID YOU SHOOT HIM?
I WASN'T SO LUCKY.
I RIPPED HIS THROAT OUT.
YOU MEAN AS A COYOTE?
EW!
WHY DO YOU THINK I'M HERE EATING COOKIE DOUGH?
IF I CAN GET THE TASTE OUT OF MY MOUTH, MAYBE I CAN FORGET.
I WAS JUST TRYING TO PROTECT MAC. I DIDN'T MEAN TO KILL HIM–
BUT IF HE'S A HIT MAN THAT'S ANOTHER REASON FOR YOU TO STAY AWAY FROM THE BOY.
MERCY, I–
SHH. I DON'T WANT TO TALK ABOUT IT ANY MORE.
I'M TIRED. IT'S LATE.
GRAB A PLATE FOR SOME COOKIES AND I'LL WALK YOU HOME.

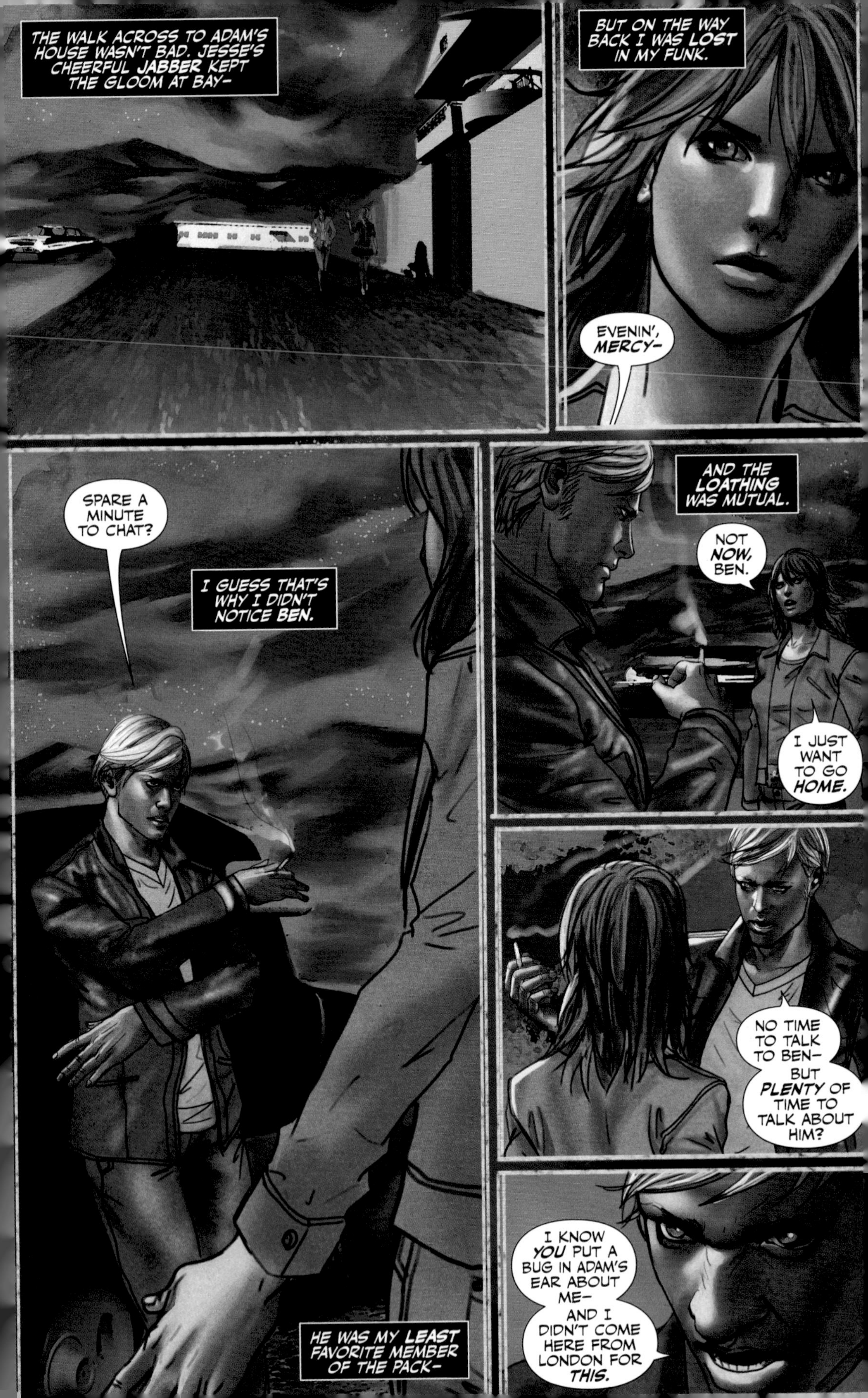
THE WALK ACROSS TO ADAM'S HOUSE WASN'T BAD. JESSE'S CHEERFUL JABBER KEPT THE GLOOM AT BAY–
BUT ON THE WAY BACK I WAS LOST IN MY FUNK.
EVENIN', MERCY–
SPARE A MINUTE TO CHAT?
I GUESS THAT'S WHY I DIDN'T NOTICE BEN.
HE WAS MY LEAST FAVORITE MEMBER OF THE PACK–
AND THE LOATHING WAS MUTUAL.
NOT NOW, BEN.
I JUST WANT TO GO HOME.
NO TIME TO TALK TO BEN–
BUT PLENTY OF TIME TO TALK ABOUT HIM?
I KNOW YOU PUT A BUG IN ADAM'S EAR ABOUT ME–
AND I DIDN'T COME HERE FROM LONDON FOR THIS.

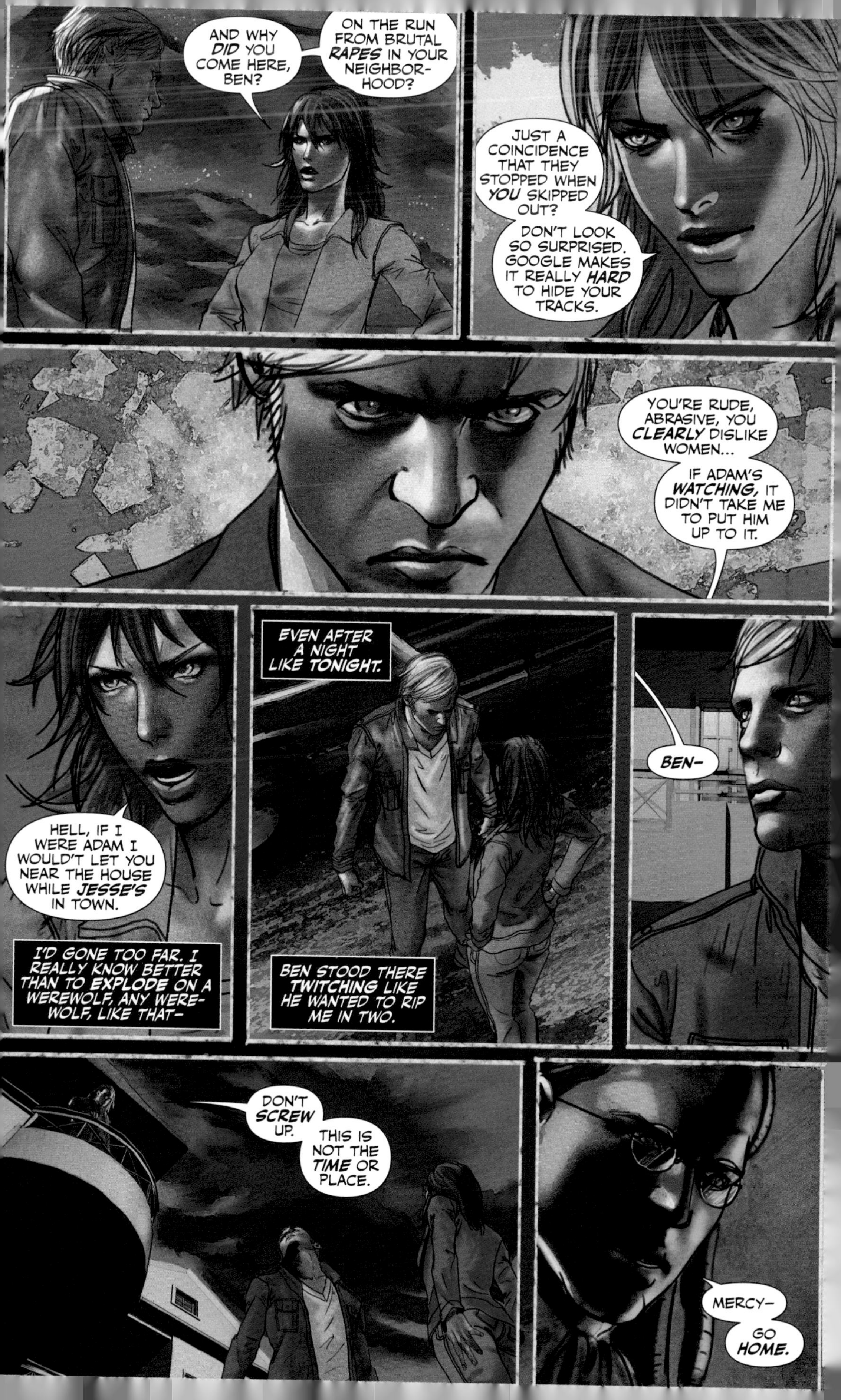
AND WHY *DID* YOU COME HERE, BEN?
ON THE RUN FROM BRUTAL *RAPES* IN YOUR NEIGHBOR-HOOD?
JUST A COINCIDENCE THAT THEY STOPPED WHEN *YOU* SKIPPED OUT?
DON'T LOOK SO SURPRISED. GOOGLE MAKES IT REALLY *HARD* TO HIDE YOUR TRACKS.
YOU'RE RUDE, ABRASIVE, YOU *CLEARLY* DISLIKE WOMEN...
IF ADAM'S *WATCHING,* IT DIDN'T TAKE ME TO PUT HIM UP TO IT.
HELL, IF I WERE ADAM I WOULD'T LET YOU NEAR THE HOUSE WHILE *JESSE'S* IN TOWN.
I'D GONE TOO FAR. I REALLY KNOW BETTER THAN TO *EXPLODE* ON A WEREWOLF, ANY WERE-WOLF, LIKE THAT-
EVEN AFTER A NIGHT LIKE *TONIGHT.*
BEN STOOD THERE *TWITCHING* LIKE HE WANTED TO RIP ME IN TWO.
BEN-
DON'T *SCREW* UP.
THIS IS NOT THE *TIME* OR PLACE.
MERCY-
GO *HOME.*

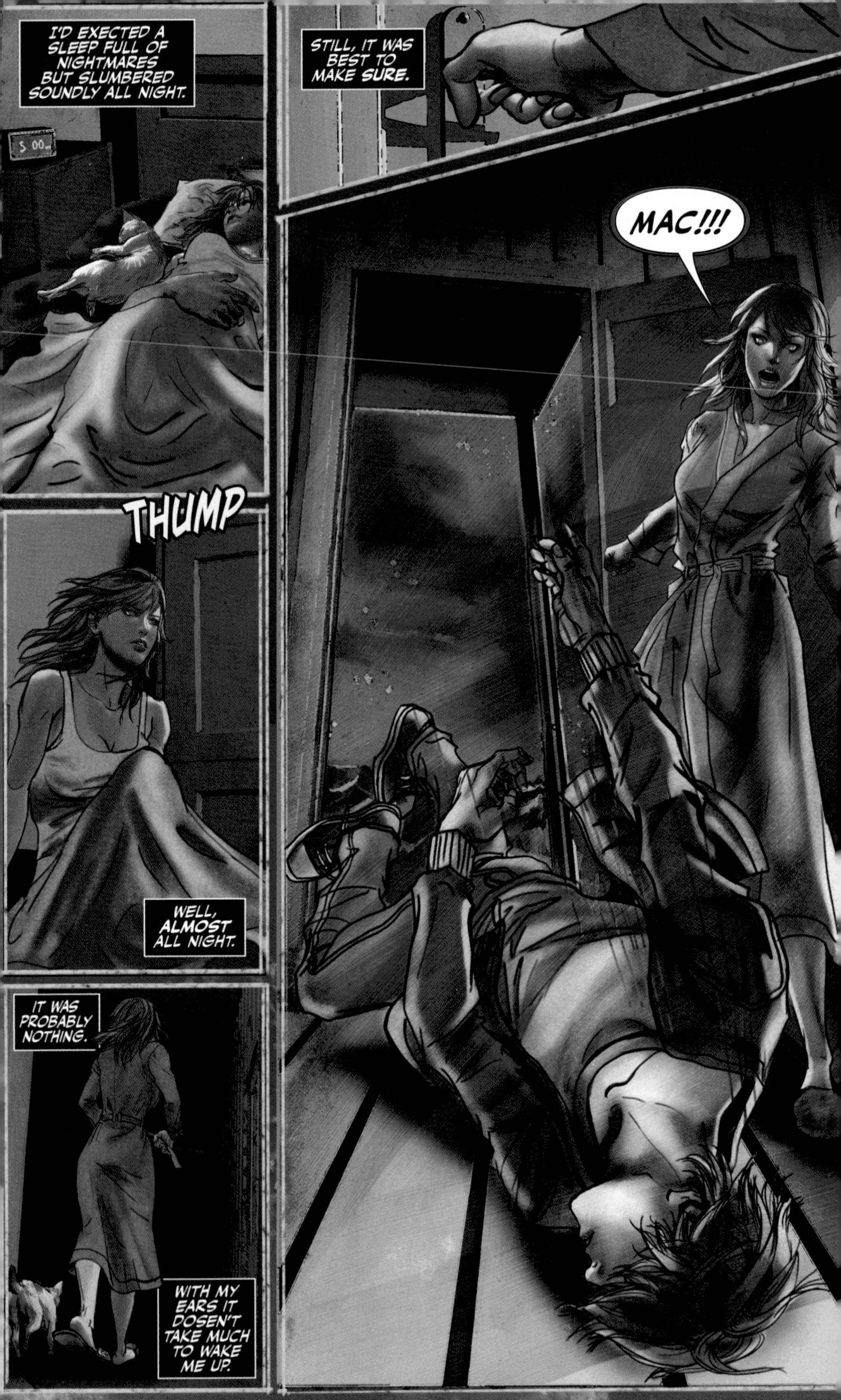
I'D EXECTED A SLEEP FULL OF NIGHTMARES BUT SLUMBERED SOUNDLY ALL NIGHT.
THUMP
WELL, ALMOST ALL NIGHT.
IT WAS PROBABLY NOTHING.
WITH MY EARS IT DOSEN'T TAKE MUCH TO WAKE ME UP.
STILL, IT WAS BEST TO MAKE SURE.
MAC!!!

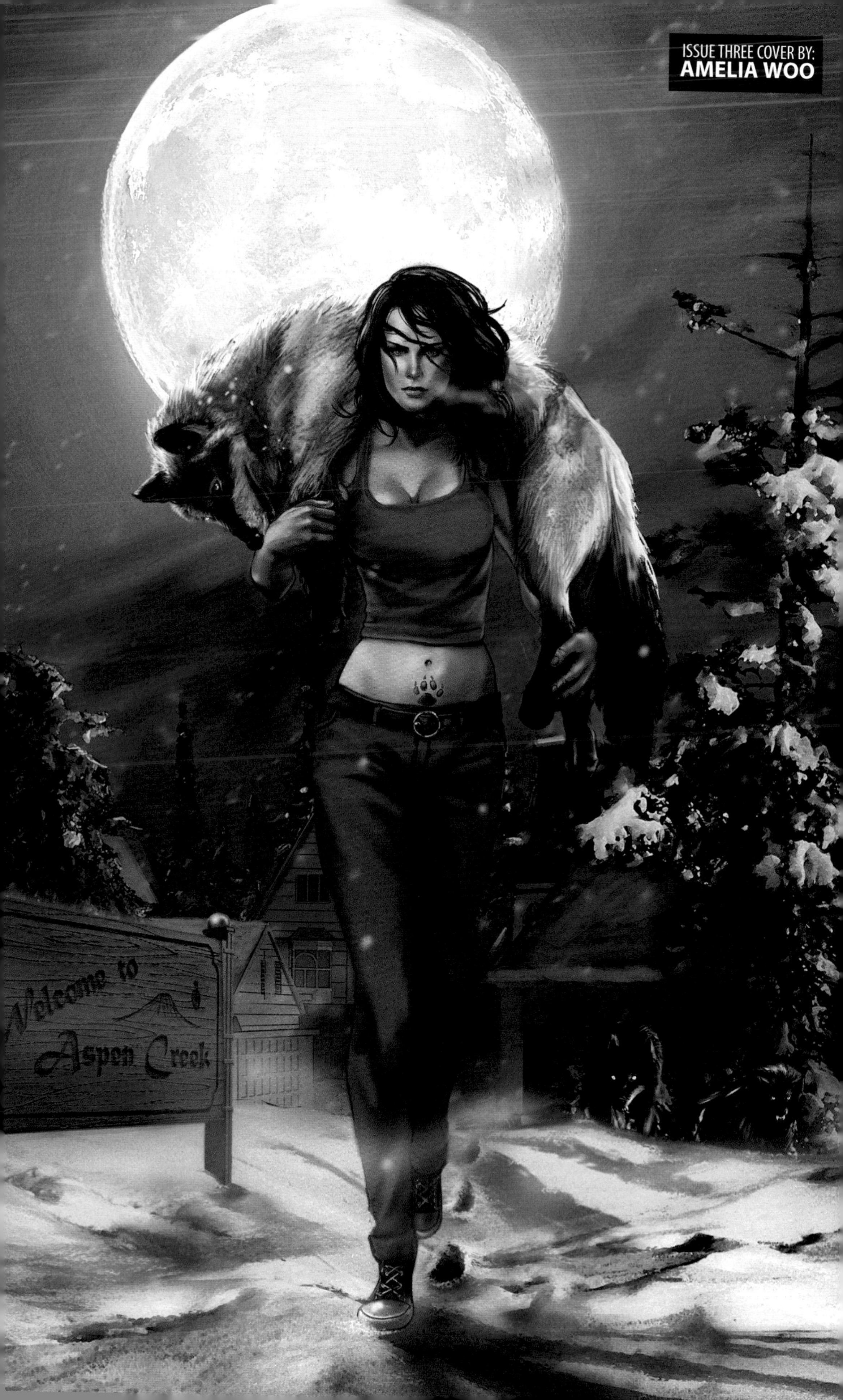

Welcome to
Aspen Creek

ISSUE THREE COVER BY:
AMELIA WOO

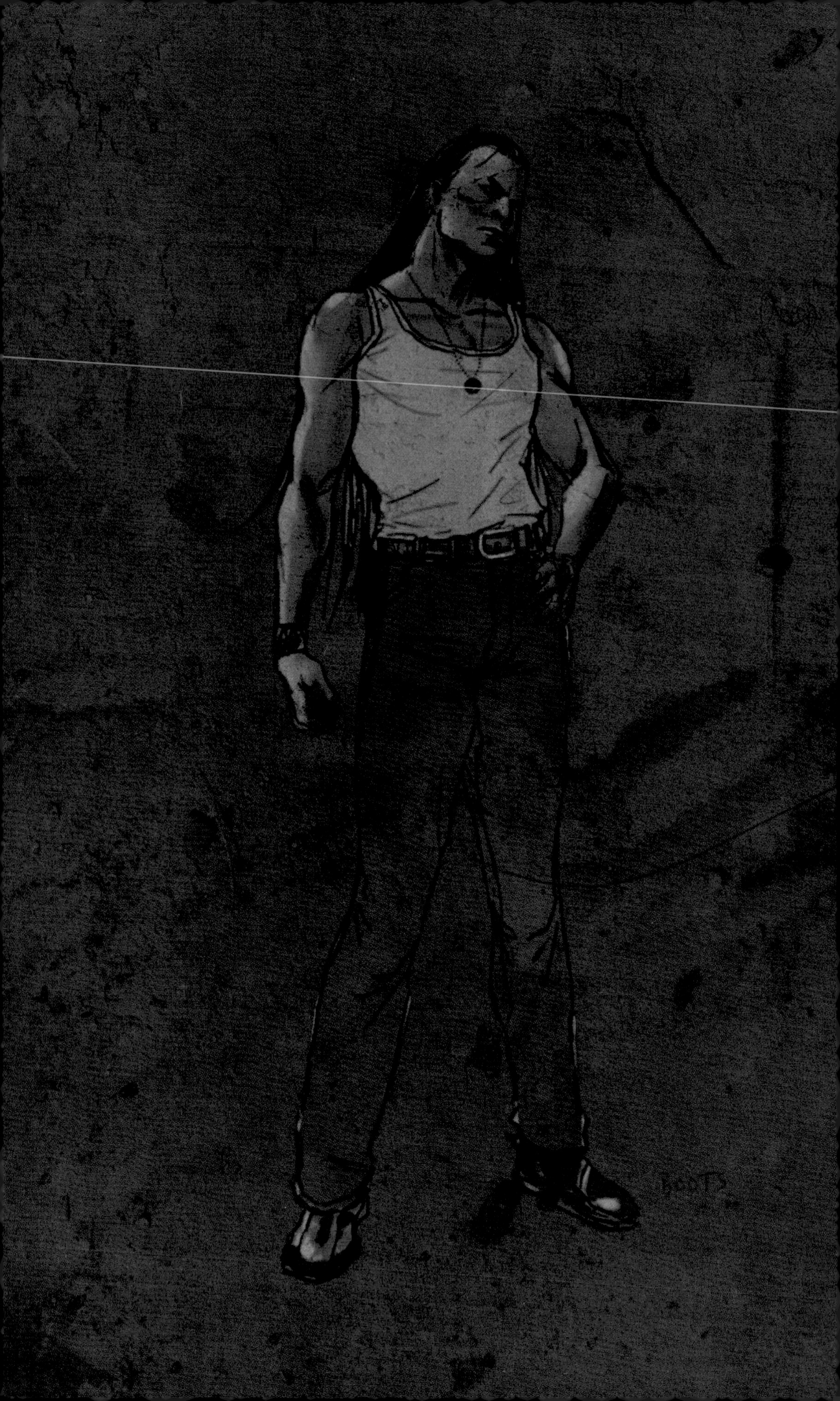

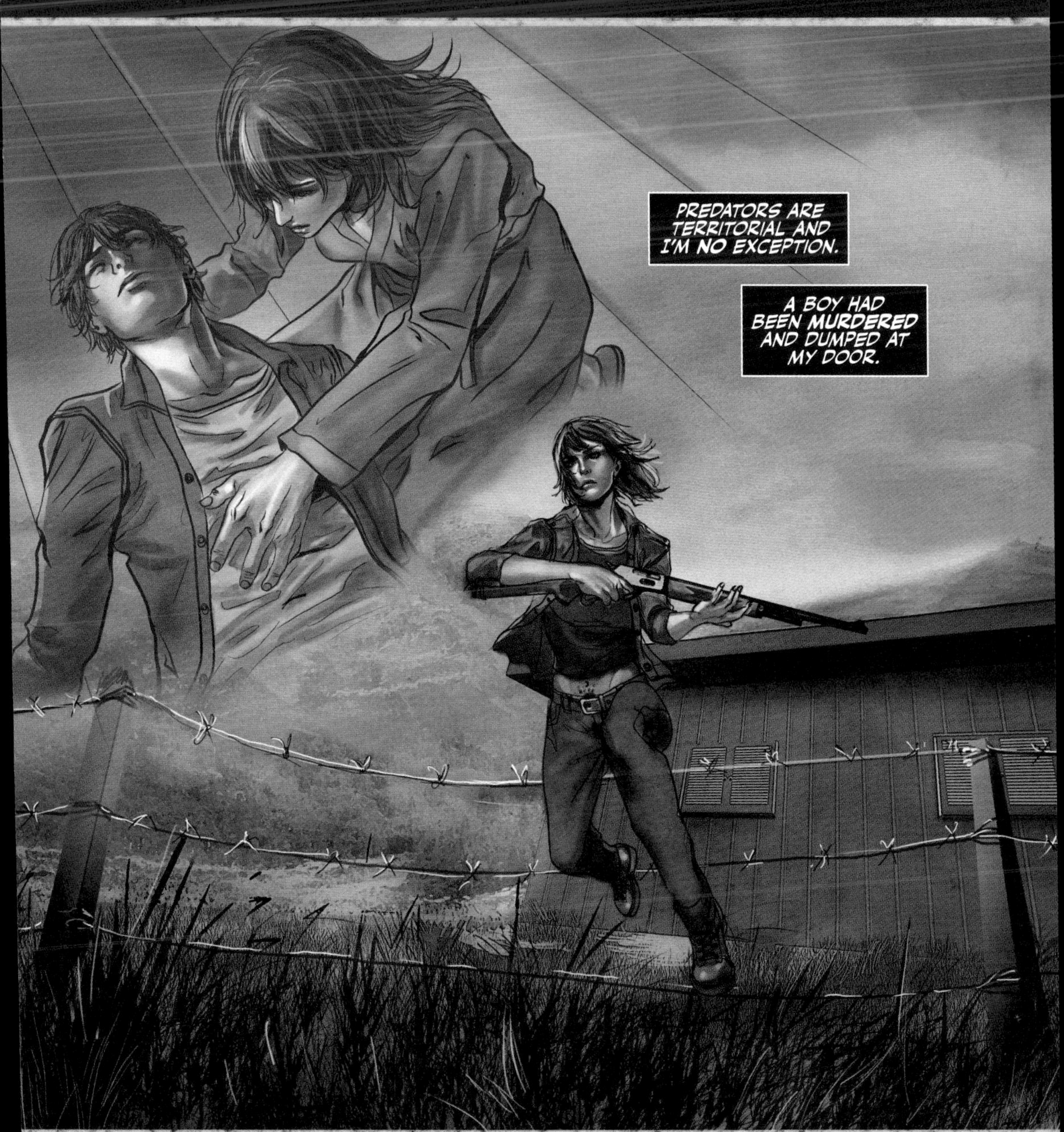
PREDATORS ARE TERRITORIAL AND I'M NO EXCEPTION.
A BOY HAD BEEN MURDERED AND DUMPED AT MY DOOR.

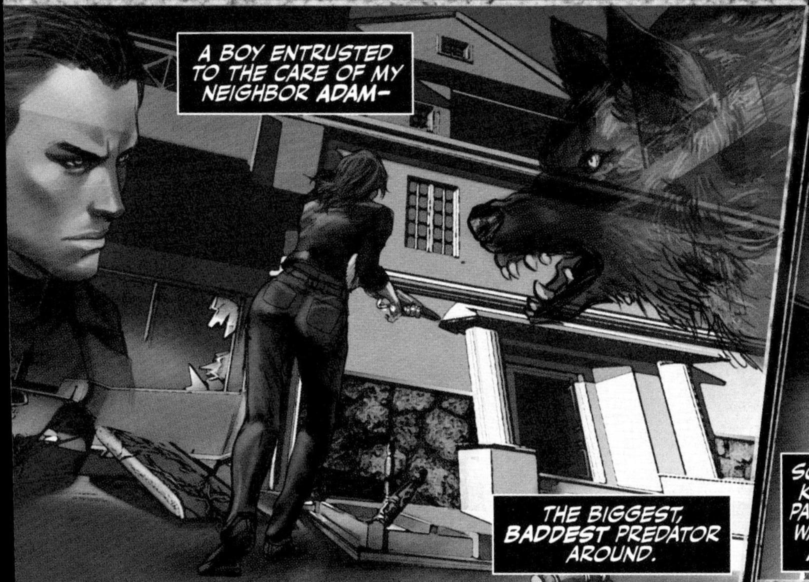
A BOY ENTRUSTED TO THE CARE OF MY NEIGHBOR ADAM–
THE BIGGEST, BADDEST PREDATOR AROUND.

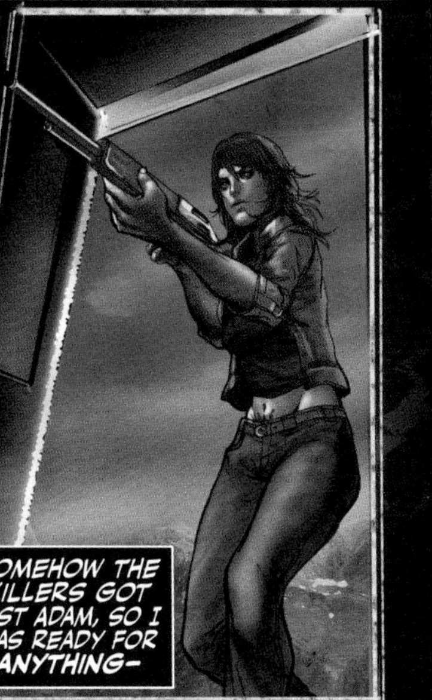
SOMEHOW THE KILLERS GOT PAST ADAM, SO I WAS READY FOR ANYTHING–

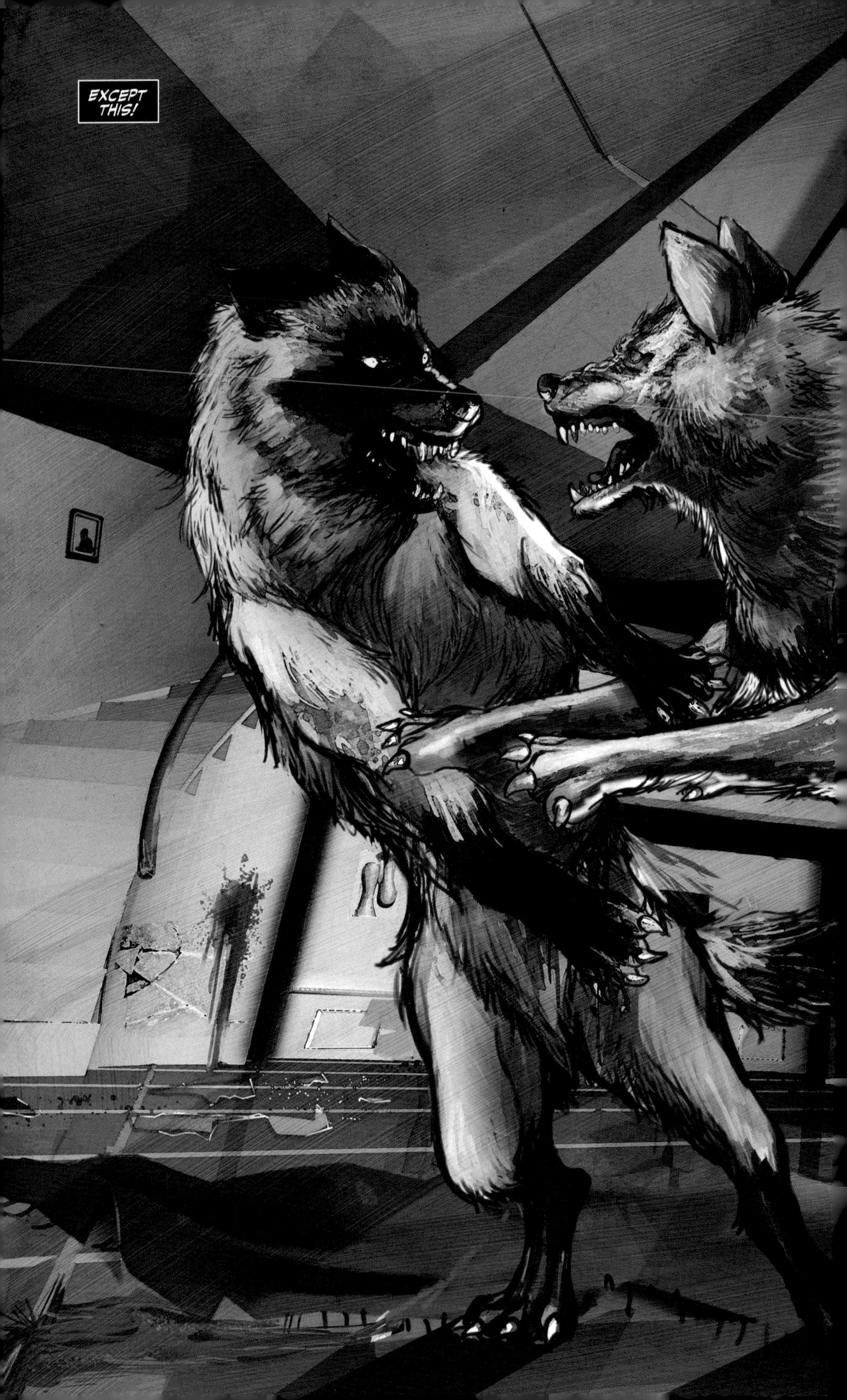
EXCEPT THIS!

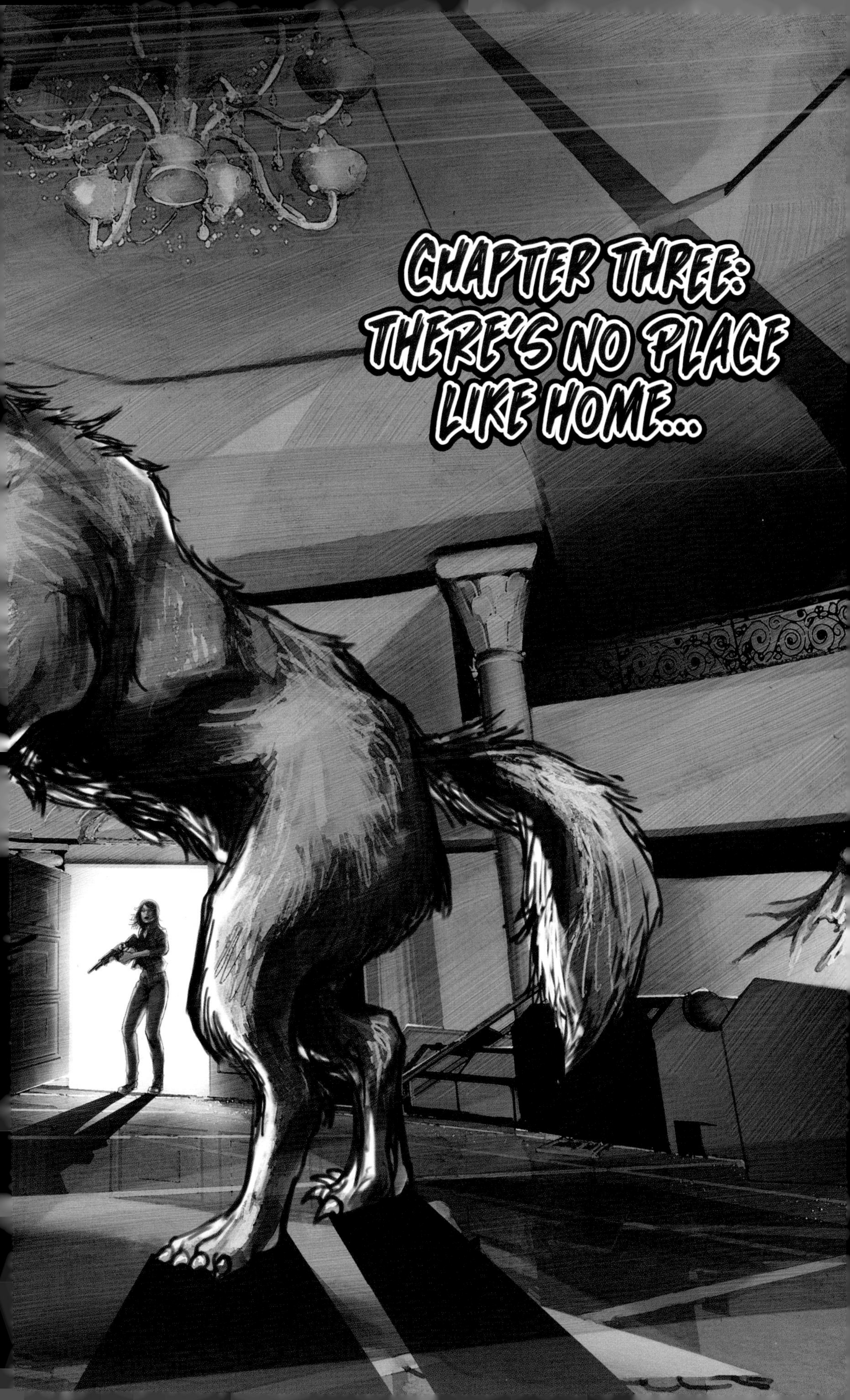
CHAPTER THREE:
THERE'S NO PLACE
LIKE HOME...

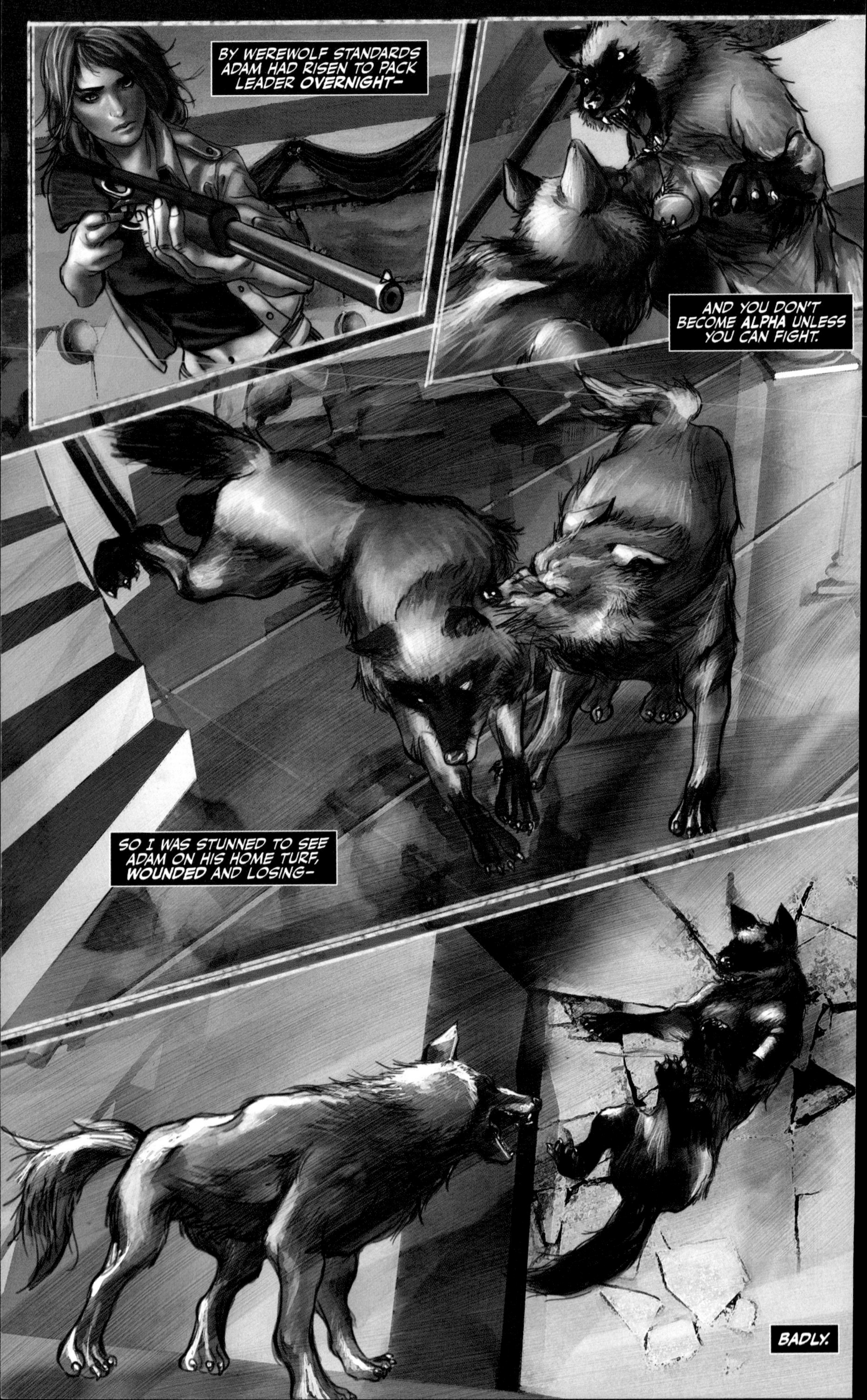
BY WEREWOLF STANDARDS ADAM HAD RISEN TO PACK LEADER OVERNIGHT-
AND YOU DON'T BECOME ALPHA UNLESS YOU CAN FIGHT.
SO I WAS STUNNED TO SEE ADAM ON HIS HOME TURF, WOUNDED AND LOSING-
BADLY.

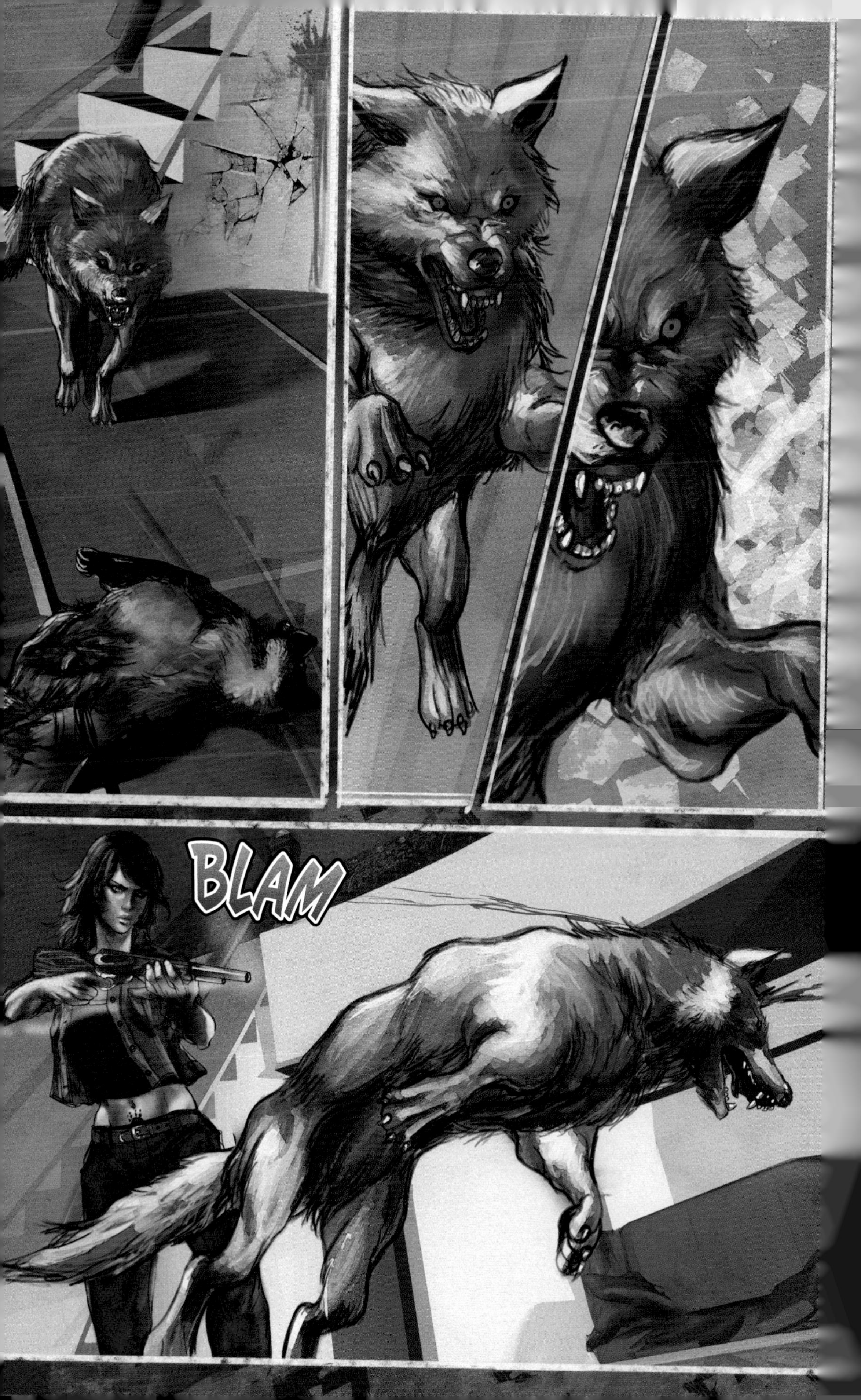
BLAM

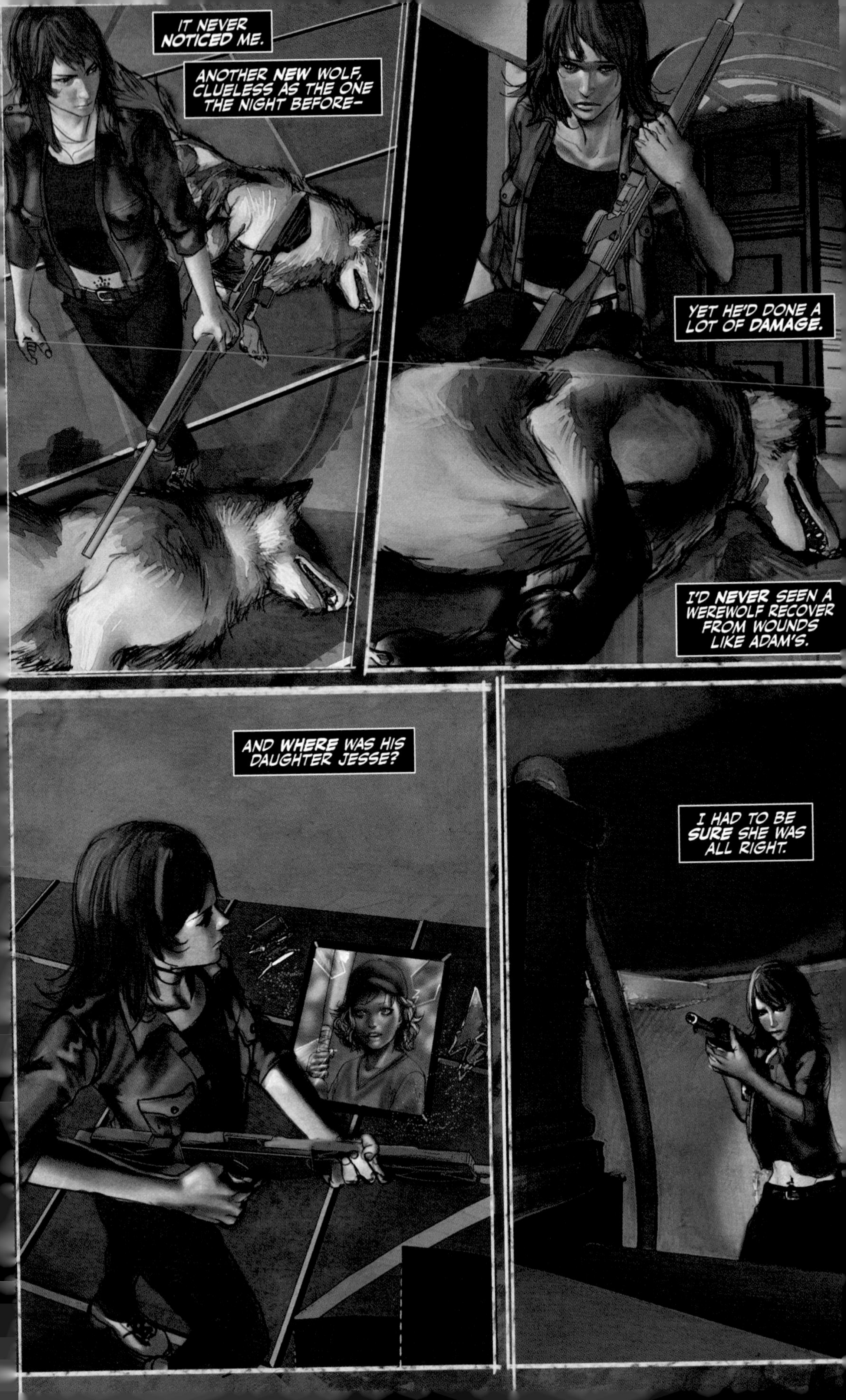
IT NEVER NOTICED ME.
ANOTHER NEW WOLF, CLUELESS AS THE ONE THE NIGHT BEFORE–
YET HE'D DONE A LOT OF DAMAGE.
I'D NEVER SEEN A WEREWOLF RECOVER FROM WOUNDS LIKE ADAM'S.
AND WHERE WAS HIS DAUGHTER JESSE?
I HAD TO BE SURE SHE WAS ALL RIGHT.

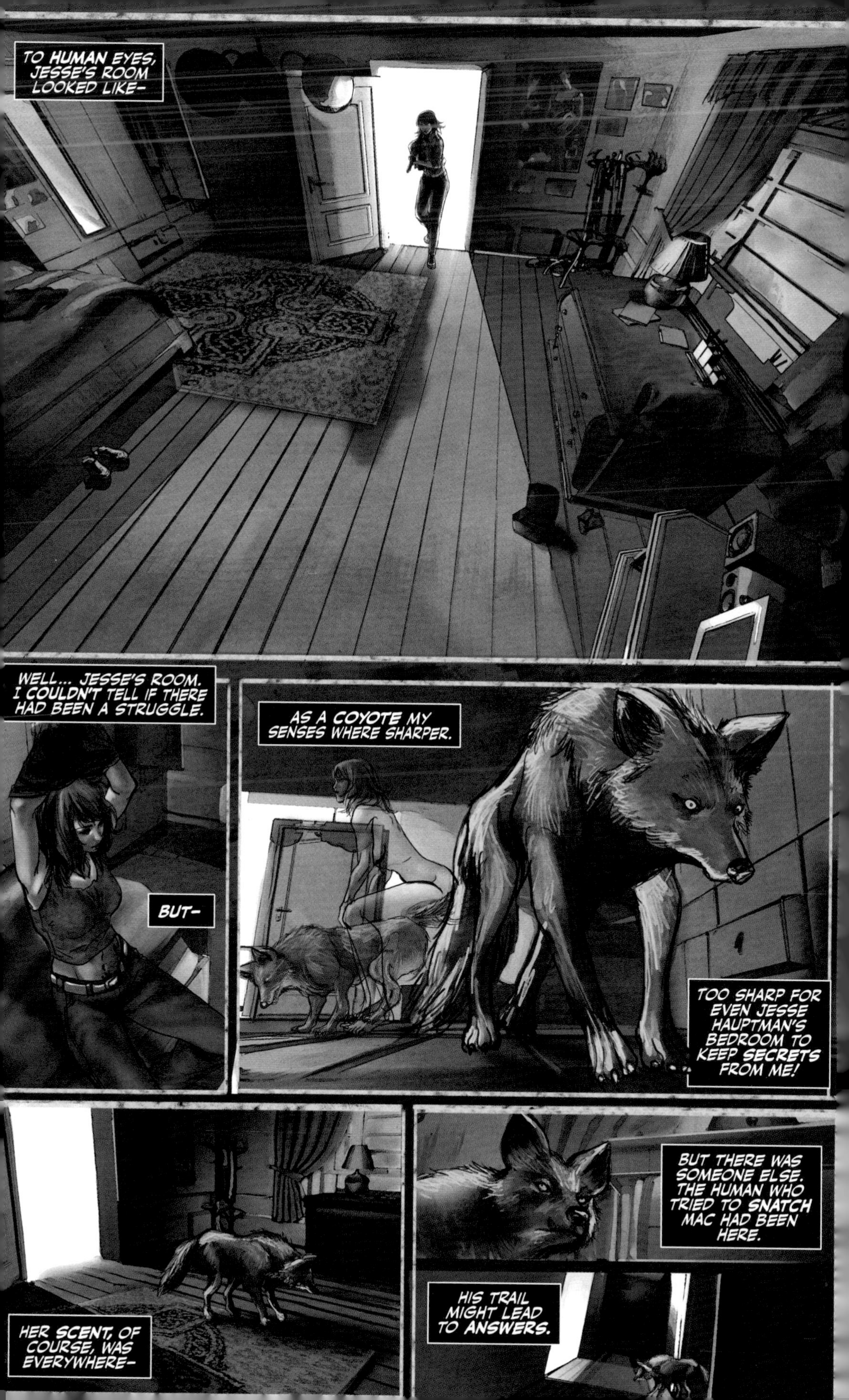
TO HUMAN EYES, JESSE'S ROOM LOOKED LIKE-
WELL... JESSE'S ROOM. I COULDN'T TELL IF THERE HAD BEEN A STRUGGLE.
BUT-
AS A COYOTE MY SENSES WHERE SHARPER.
TOO SHARP FOR EVEN JESSE HAUPTMAN'S BEDROOM TO KEEP SECRETS FROM ME!
HER SCENT, OF COURSE, WAS EVERYWHERE-
BUT THERE WAS SOMEONE ELSE. THE HUMAN WHO TRIED TO SNATCH MAC HAD BEEN HERE.
HIS TRAIL MIGHT LEAD TO ANSWERS.

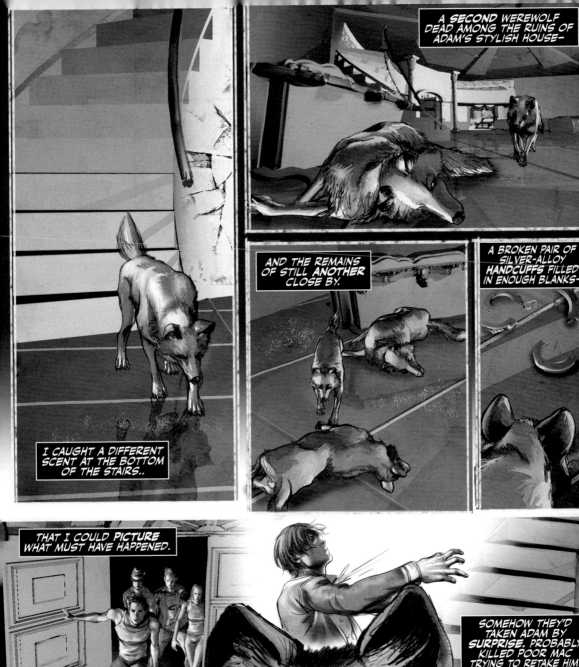

A SECOND WEREWOLF DEAD AMONG THE RUINS OF ADAM'S STYLISH HOUSE—

AND THE REMAINS OF STILL ANOTHER CLOSE BY.

A BROKEN PAIR OF SILVER-ALLOY HANDCUFFS FILLED IN ENOUGH BLANKS—

I CAUGHT A DIFFERENT SCENT AT THE BOTTOM OF THE STAIRS..

THAT I COULD PICTURE WHAT MUST HAVE HAPPENED.

SOMEHOW THEY'D TAKEN ADAM BY SURPRISE. PROBABLY KILLED POOR MAC TRYING TO RETAKE HIM.

THEY FORCED ADAM TO SURRENDER...

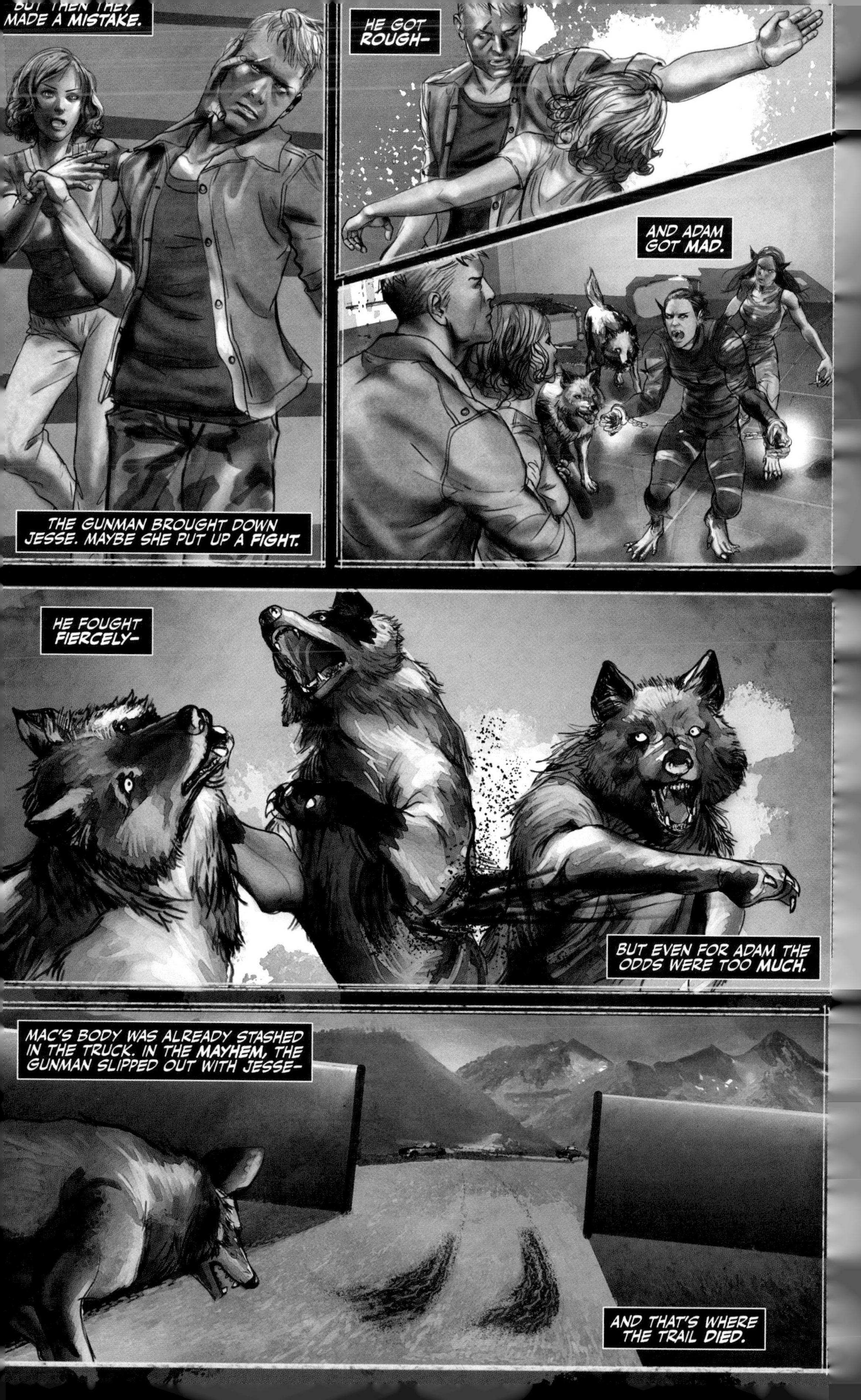
MADE A MISTAKE.
THE GUNMAN BROUGHT DOWN JESSE. MAYBE SHE PUT UP A FIGHT.
HE GOT ROUGH-
AND ADAM GOT MAD.
HE FOUGHT FIERCELY-
BUT EVEN FOR ADAM THE ODDS WERE TOO MUCH.
MAC'S BODY WAS ALREADY STASHED IN THE TRUCK. IN THE MAYHEM, THE GUNMAN SLIPPED OUT WITH JESSE-
AND THAT'S WHERE THE TRAIL DIED.

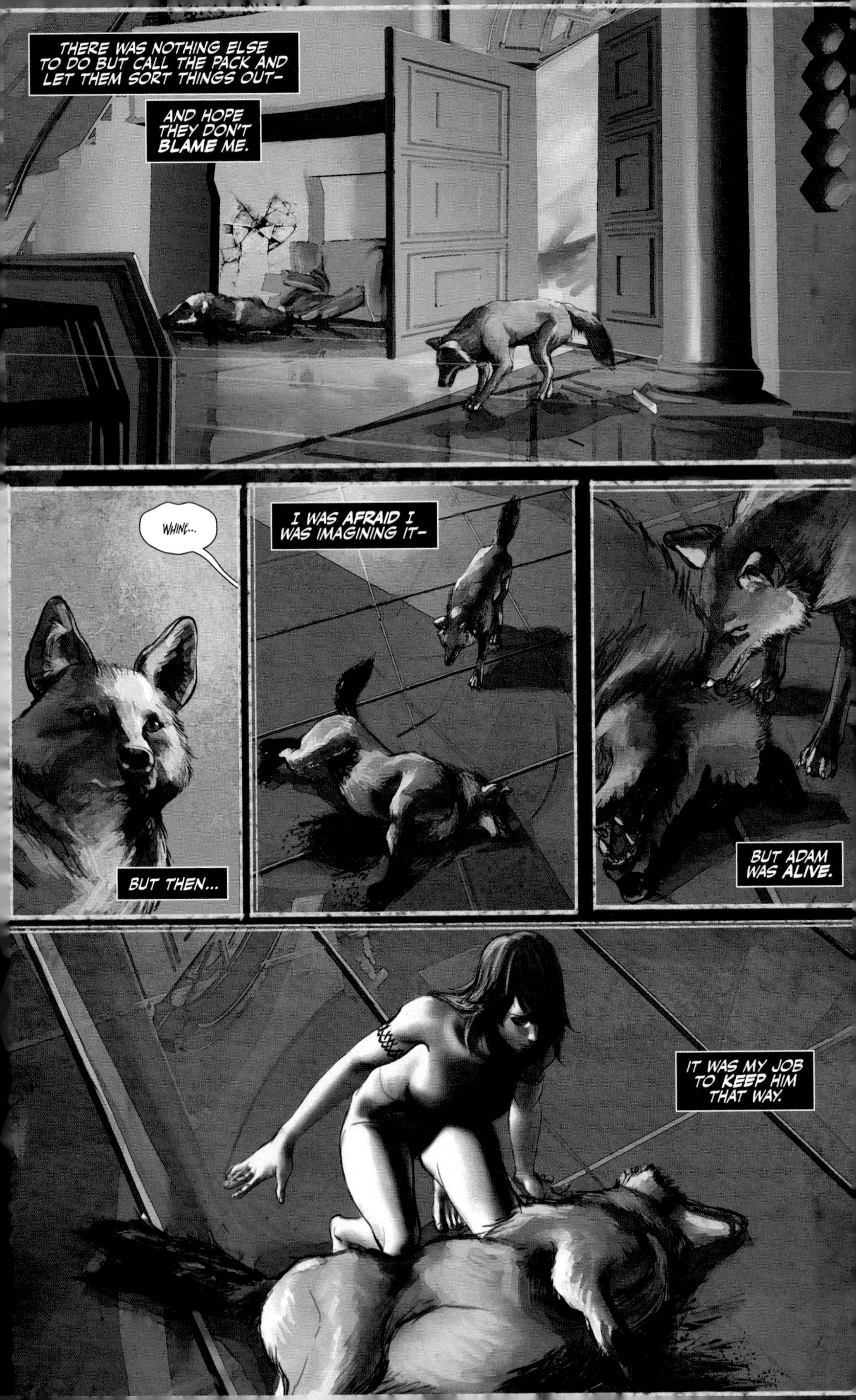
THERE WAS NOTHING ELSE TO DO BUT CALL THE PACK AND LET THEM SORT THINGS OUT-
AND HOPE THEY DON'T BLAME ME.
WHINE...
BUT THEN...
I WAS AFRAID I WAS IMAGINING IT-
BUT ADAM WAS ALIVE.
IT WAS MY JOB TO KEEP HIM THAT WAY.

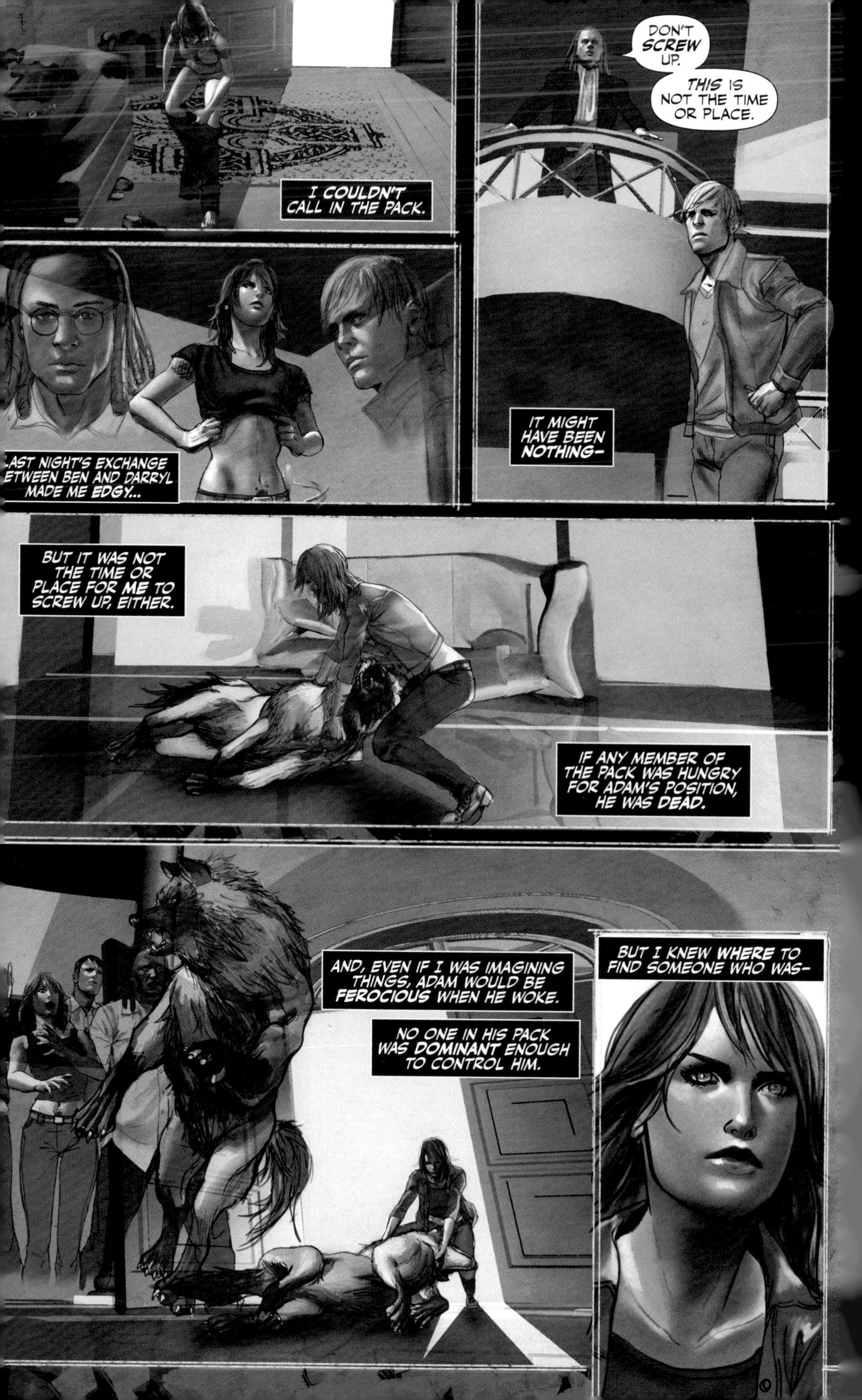

I COULDN'T CALL IN THE PACK.
DON'T SCREW UP.
THIS IS NOT THE TIME OR PLACE.
AST NIGHT'S EXCHANGE ETWEEN BEN AND DARRYL MADE ME EDGY...
IT MIGHT HAVE BEEN NOTHING-
BUT IT WAS NOT THE TIME OR PLACE FOR ME TO SCREW UP, EITHER.
IF ANY MEMBER OF THE PACK WAS HUNGRY FOR ADAM'S POSITION, HE WAS DEAD.
AND, EVEN IF I WAS IMAGINING THINGS, ADAM WOULD BE FEROCIOUS WHEN HE WOKE.
NO ONE IN HIS PACK WAS DOMINANT ENOUGH TO CONTROL HIM.
BUT I KNEW WHERE TO FIND SOMEONE WHO WAS-

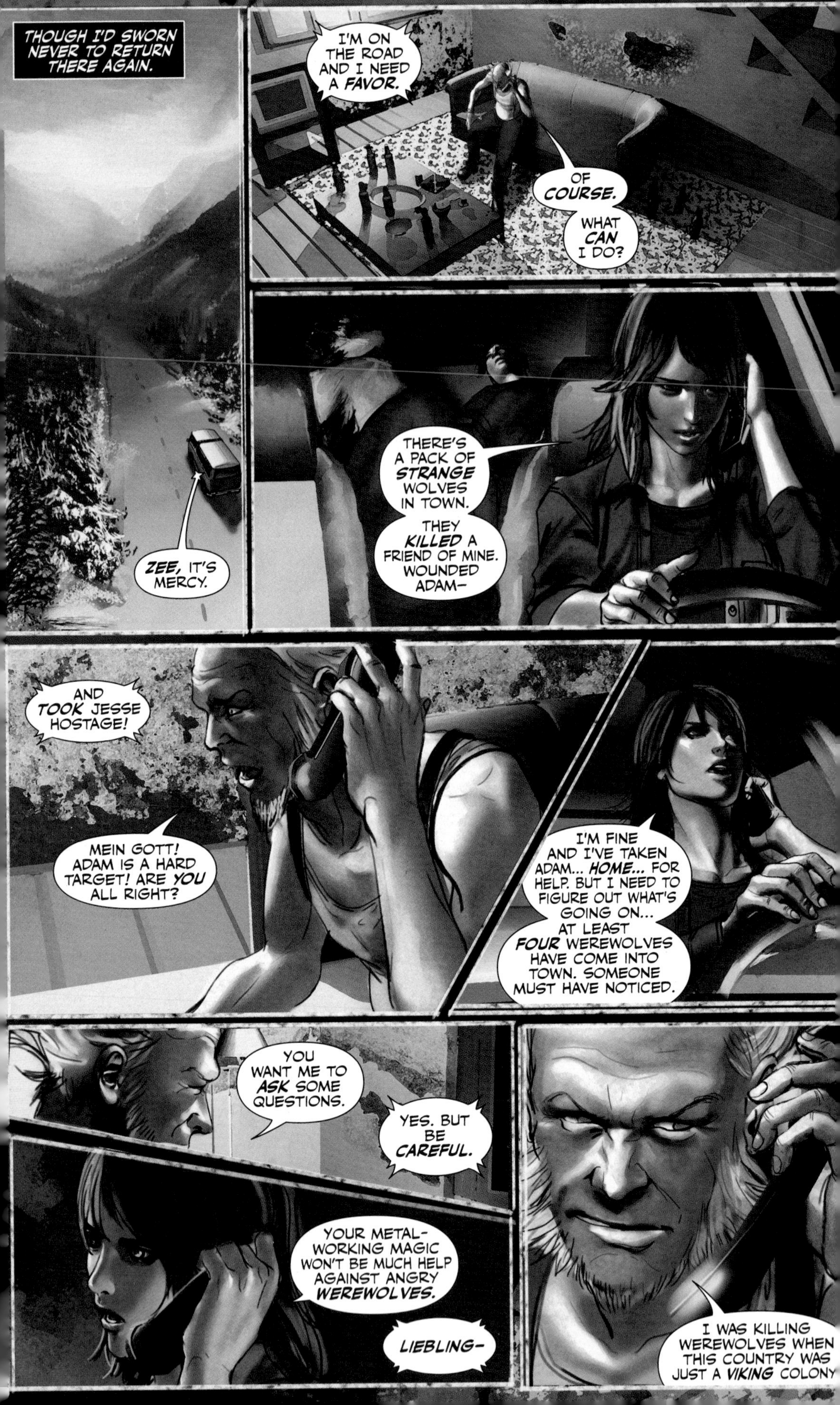
THOUGH I'D SWORN NEVER TO RETURN THERE AGAIN.
ZEE, IT'S MERCY.
I'M ON THE ROAD AND I NEED A FAVOR.
OF COURSE.
WHAT CAN I DO?
THERE'S A PACK OF STRANGE WOLVES IN TOWN.
THEY KILLED A FRIEND OF MINE. WOUNDED ADAM–
AND TOOK JESSE HOSTAGE!
MEIN GOTT! ADAM IS A HARD TARGET! ARE YOU ALL RIGHT?
I'M FINE AND I'VE TAKEN ADAM... HOME... FOR HELP. BUT I NEED TO FIGURE OUT WHAT'S GOING ON... AT LEAST FOUR WEREWOLVES HAVE COME INTO TOWN. SOMEONE MUST HAVE NOTICED.
YOU WANT ME TO ASK SOME QUESTIONS.
YES. BUT BE CAREFUL.
YOUR METAL-WORKING MAGIC WON'T BE MUCH HELP AGAINST ANGRY WEREWOLVES.
LIEBLING–
I WAS KILLING WEREWOLVES WHEN THIS COUNTRY WAS JUST A VIKING COLONY

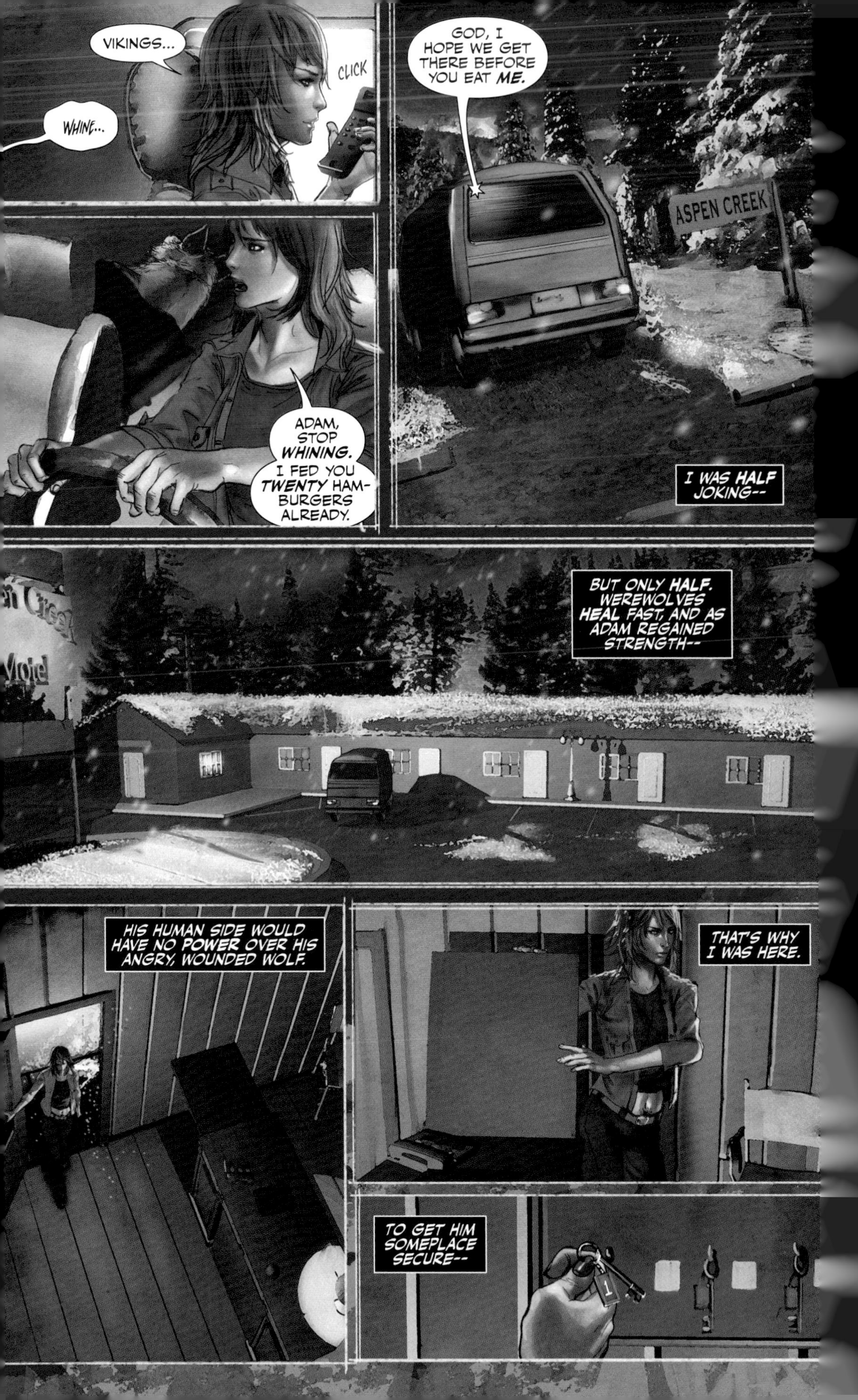
VIKINGS...
CLICK
WHINE...
ADAM, STOP WHINING. I FED YOU TWENTY HAMBURGERS ALREADY.
GOD, I HOPE WE GET THERE BEFORE YOU EAT ME.
ASPEN CREEK
I WAS HALF JOKING--
BUT ONLY HALF. WEREWOLVES HEAL FAST, AND AS ADAM REGAINED STRENGTH--
HIS HUMAN SIDE WOULD HAVE NO POWER OVER HIS ANGRY, WOUNDED WOLF.
THAT'S WHY I WAS HERE.
TO GET HIM SOMEPLACE SECURE--

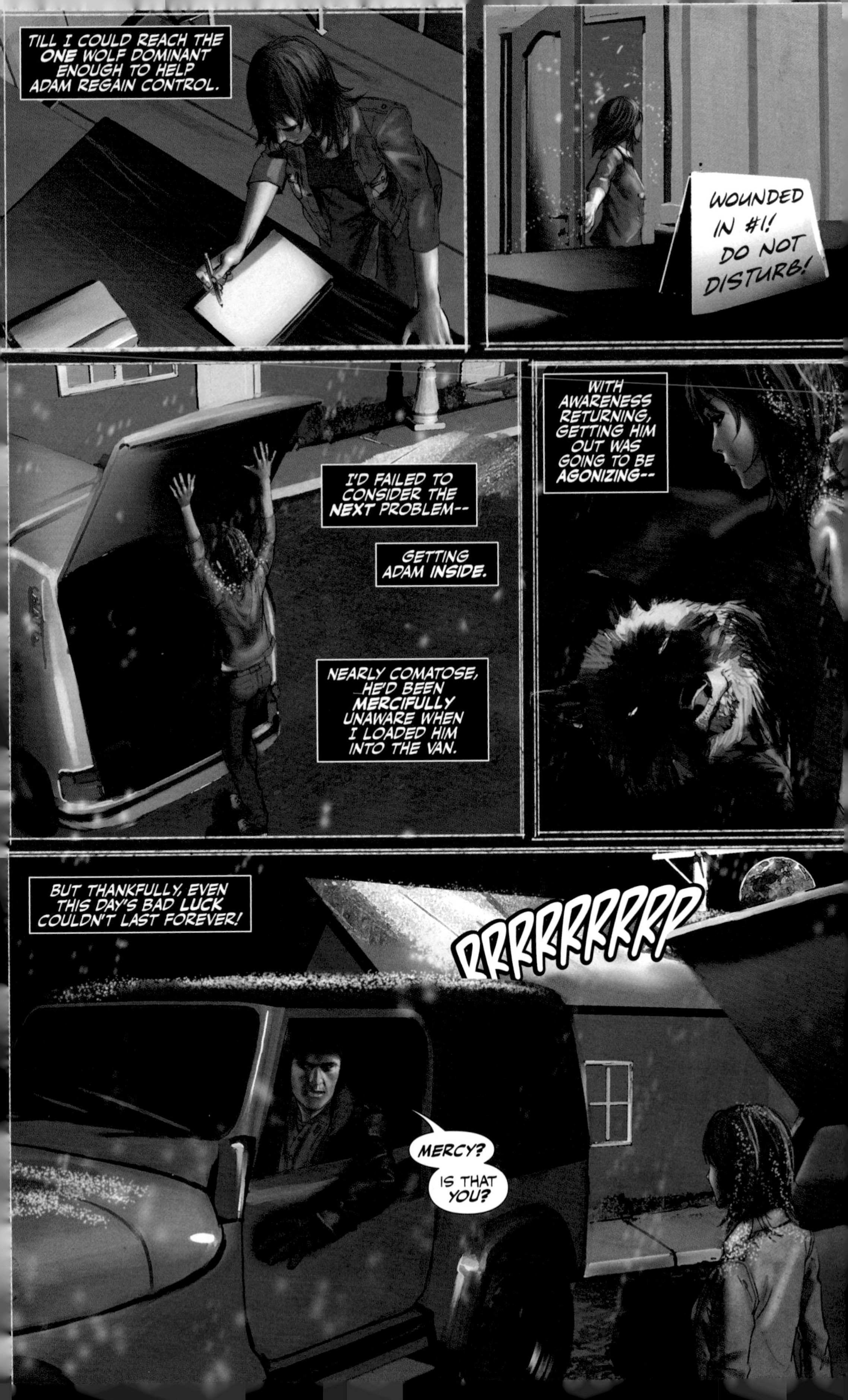
TILL I COULD REACH THE ONE WOLF DOMINANT ENOUGH TO HELP ADAM REGAIN CONTROL.
WOUNDED IN #1! DO NOT DISTURB!
I'D FAILED TO CONSIDER THE NEXT PROBLEM--
GETTING ADAM INSIDE.
NEARLY COMATOSE, HE'D BEEN MERCIFULLY UNAWARE WHEN I LOADED HIM INTO THE VAN.
WITH AWARENESS RETURNING, GETTING HIM OUT WAS GOING TO BE AGONIZING--
BUT THANKFULLY, EVEN THIS DAY'S BAD LUCK COULDN'T LAST FOREVER!
RRRRRRRRP
MERCY?
IS THAT YOU?

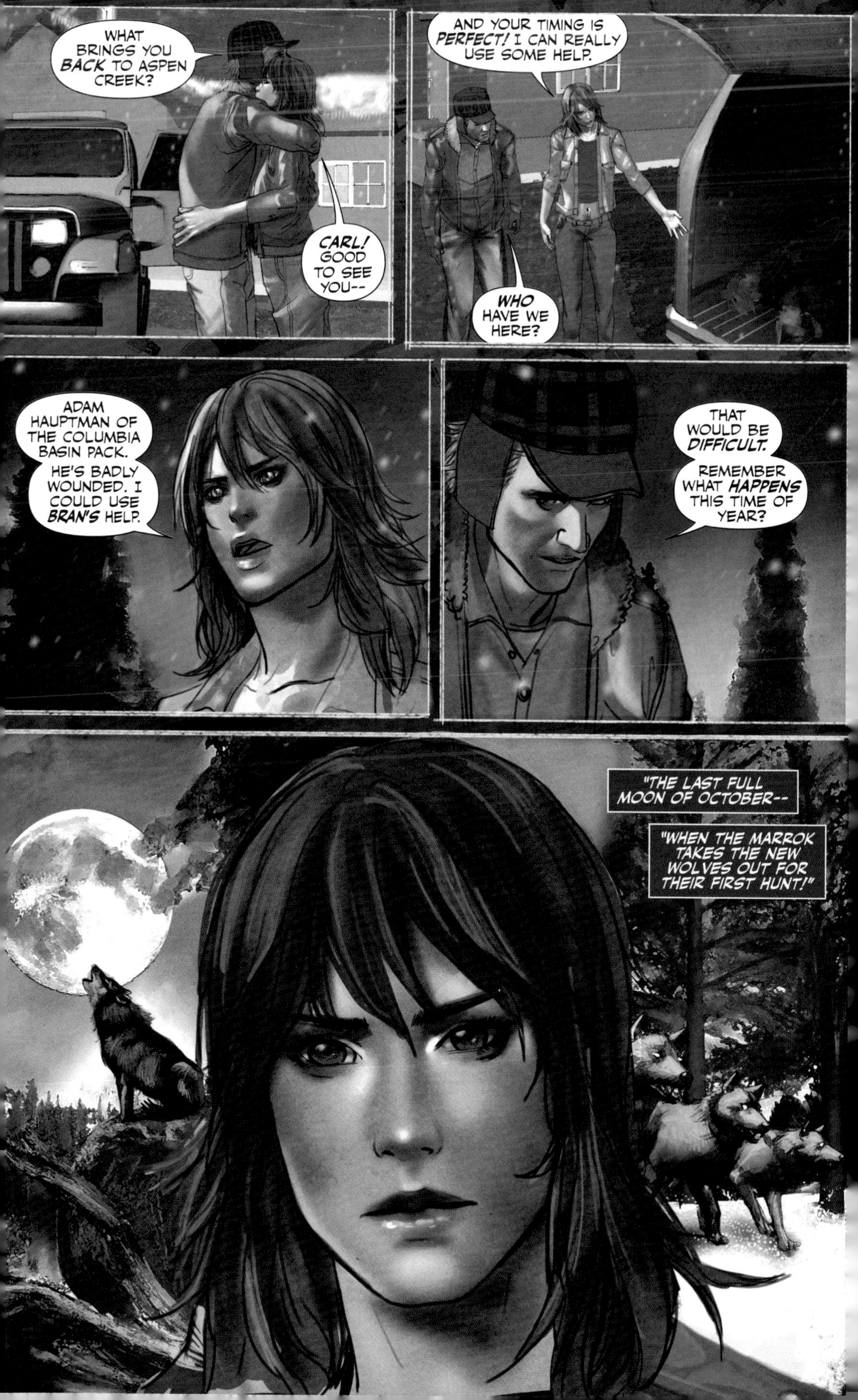
WHAT BRINGS YOU BACK TO ASPEN CREEK?
CARL! GOOD TO SEE YOU--
AND YOUR TIMING IS PERFECT! I CAN REALLY USE SOME HELP.
WHO HAVE WE HERE?
ADAM HAUPTMAN OF THE COLUMBIA BASIN PACK.
HE'S BADLY WOUNDED. I COULD USE BRAN'S HELP.
THAT WOULD BE DIFFICULT.
REMEMBER WHAT HAPPENS THIS TIME OF YEAR?
"THE LAST FULL MOON OF OCTOBER--
"WHEN THE MARROK TAKES THE NEW WOLVES OUT FOR THEIR FIRST HUNT!"

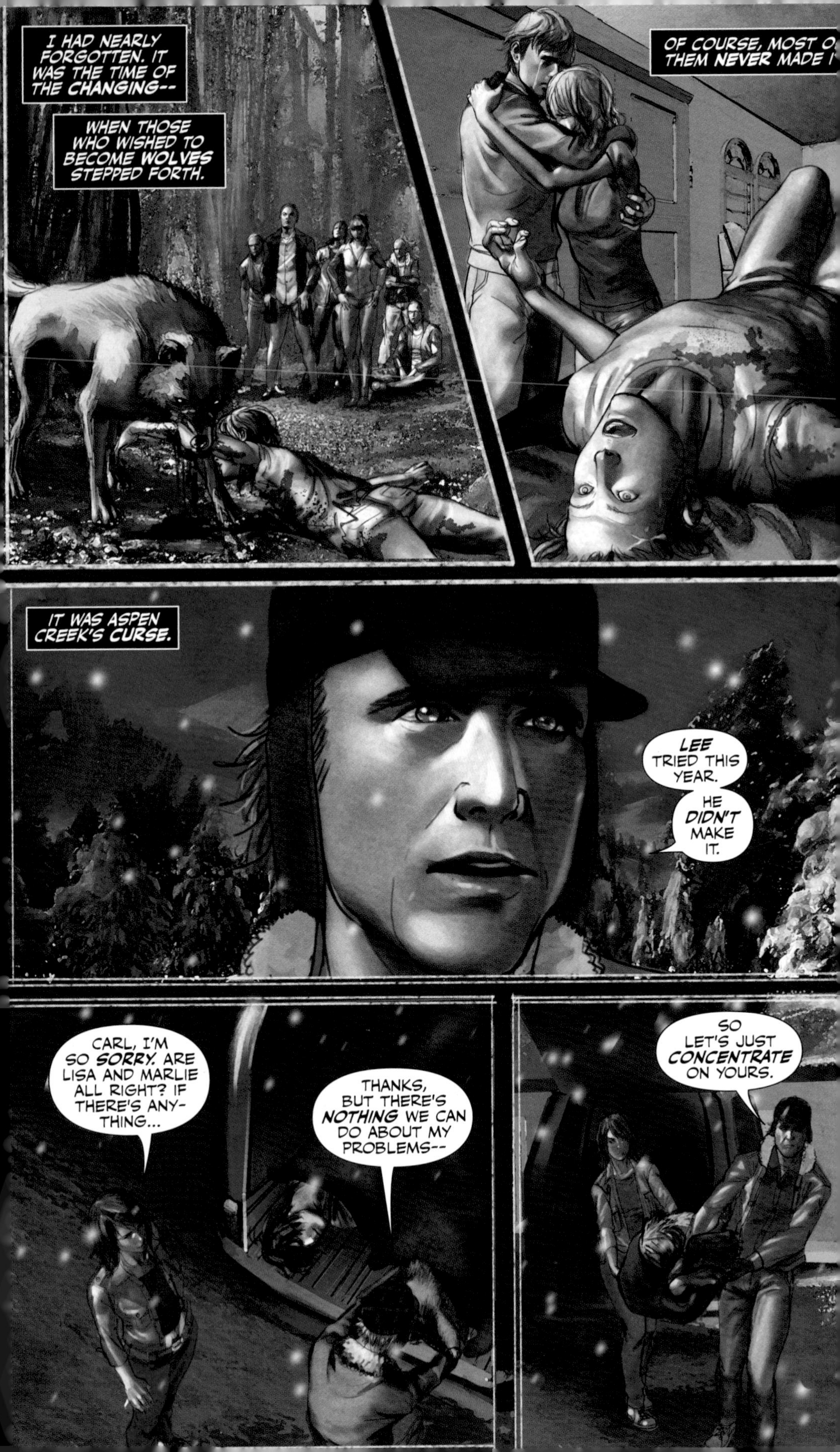
I HAD NEARLY FORGOTTEN. IT WAS THE TIME OF THE CHANGING--
WHEN THOSE WHO WISHED TO BECOME WOLVES STEPPED FORTH.
OF COURSE, MOST O
THEM NEVER MADE I
IT WAS ASPEN CREEK'S CURSE.
LEE TRIED THIS YEAR.
HE DIDN'T MAKE IT.
CARL, I'M SO SORRY. ARE LISA AND MARLIE ALL RIGHT? IF THERE'S ANY-THING...
THANKS, BUT THERE'S NOTHING WE CAN DO ABOUT MY PROBLEMS--
SO LET'S JUST CONCENTRATE ON YOURS.

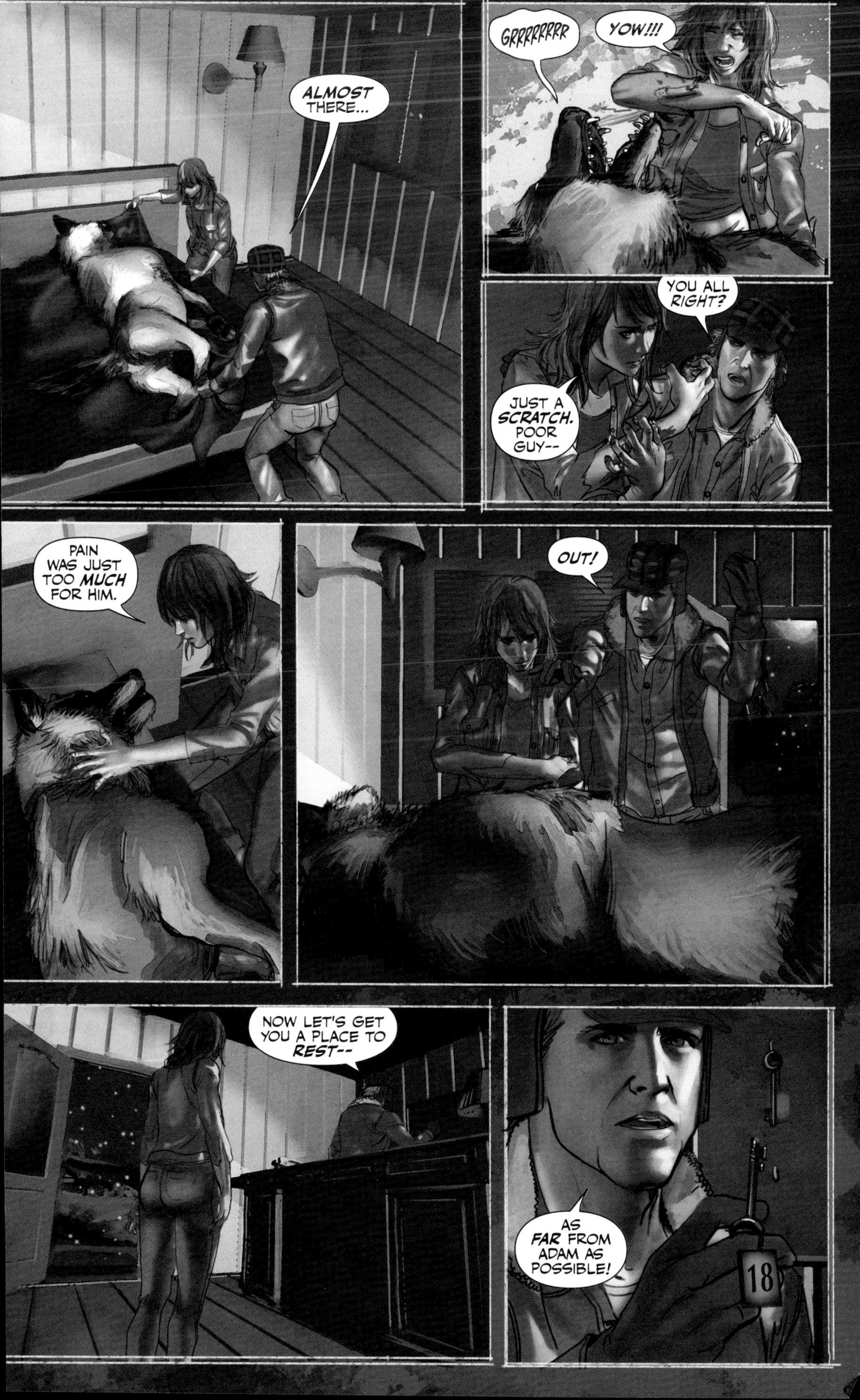
ALMOST THERE...
GRRRRRRRR
YOW!!!
YOU ALL RIGHT?
JUST A SCRATCH. POOR GUY--
PAIN WAS JUST TOO MUCH FOR HIM.
OUT!
NOW LET'S GET YOU A PLACE TO REST--
AS FAR FROM ADAM AS POSSIBLE!
18

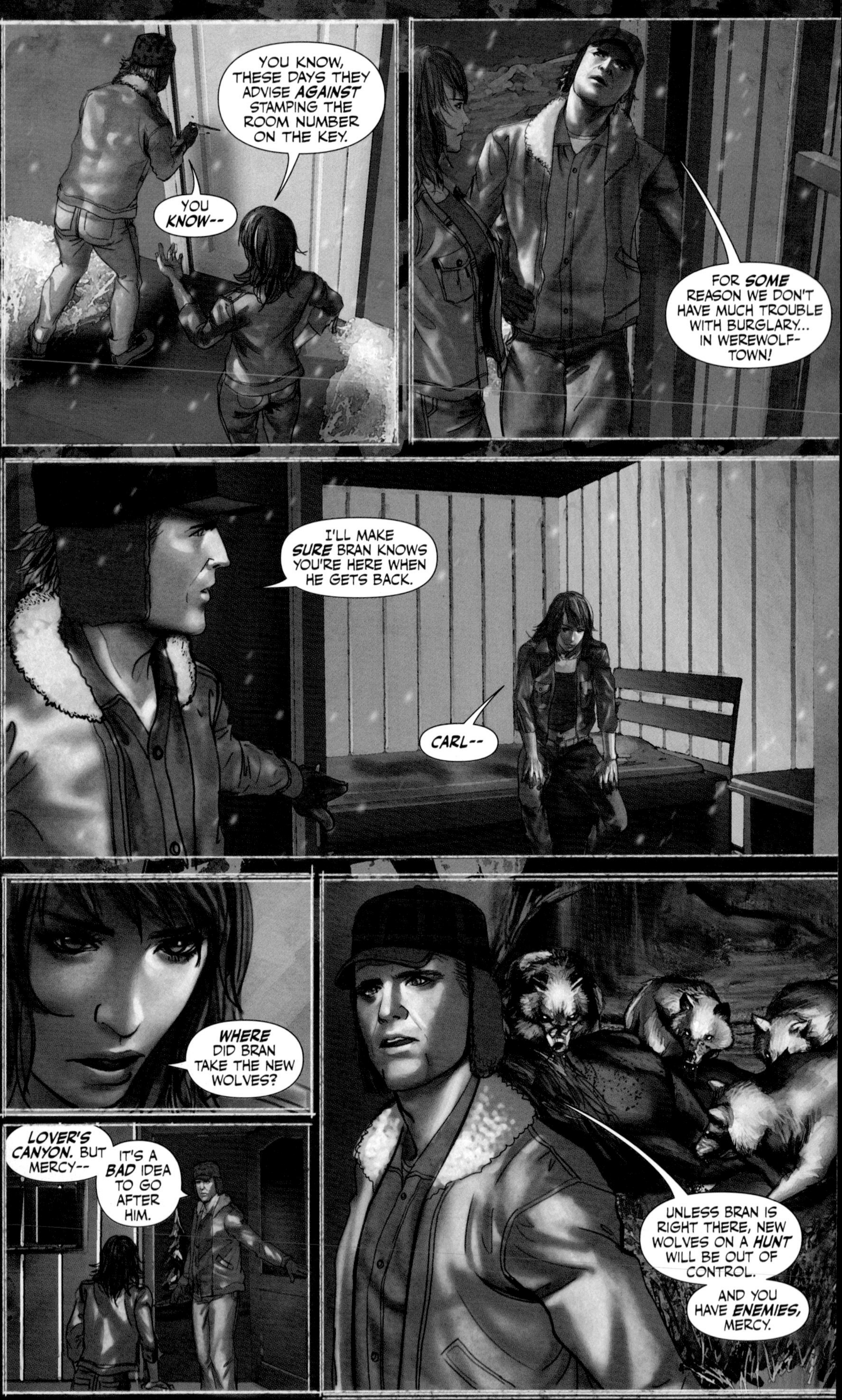

YOU KNOW,
THESE DAYS THEY ADVISE AGAINST STAMPING THE ROOM NUMBER ON THE KEY.
YOU KNOW--
FOR SOME REASON WE DON'T HAVE MUCH TROUBLE WITH BURGLARY... IN WEREWOLF-TOWN!
I'LL MAKE SURE BRAN KNOWS YOU'RE HERE WHEN HE GETS BACK.
CARL--
WHERE DID BRAN TAKE THE NEW WOLVES?
LOVER'S CANYON. BUT MERCY--
IT'S A BAD IDEA TO GO AFTER HIM.
UNLESS BRAN IS RIGHT THERE, NEW WOLVES ON A HUNT WILL BE OUT OF CONTROL.
AND YOU HAVE ENEMIES, MERCY.

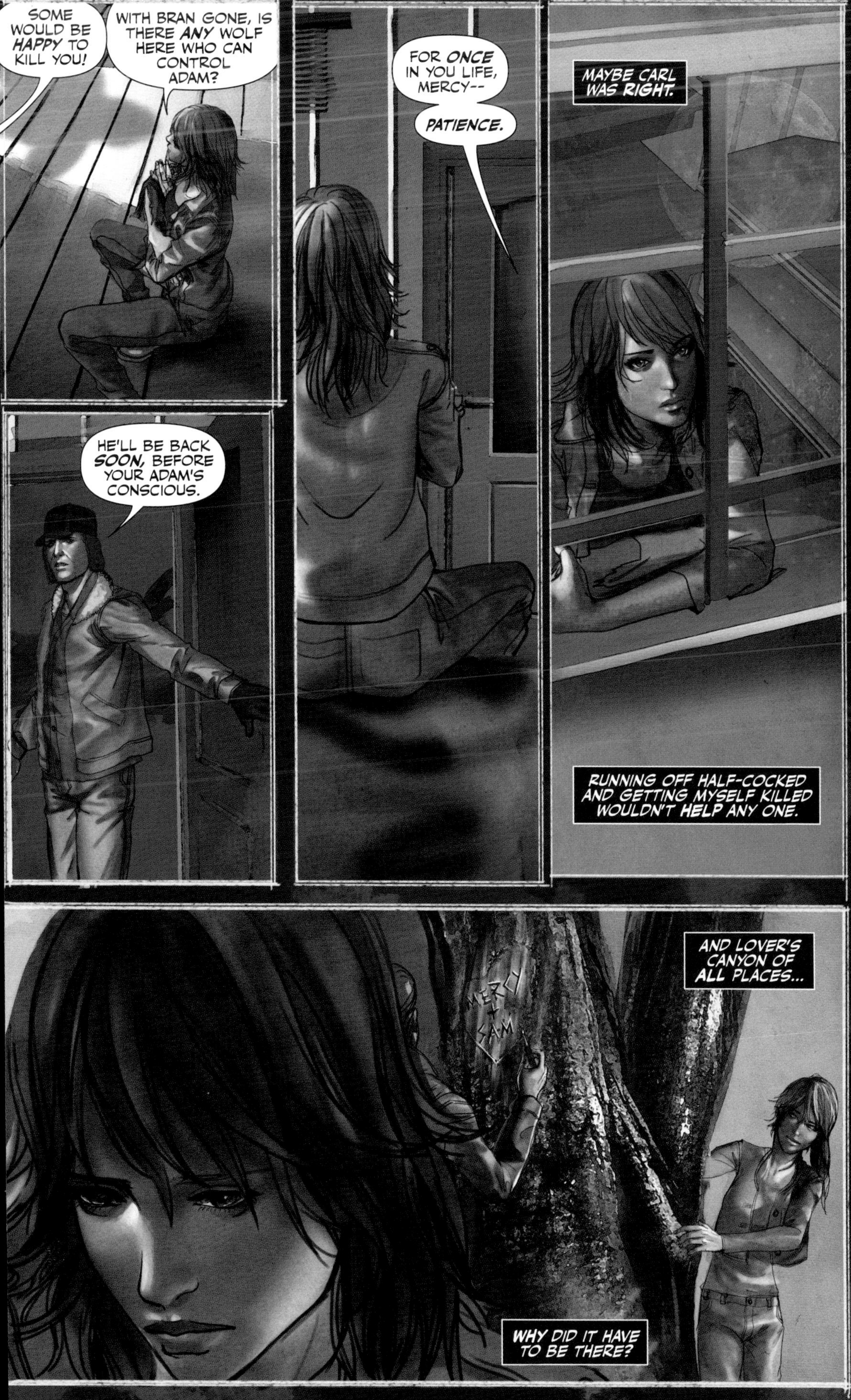
SOME WOULD BE HAPPY TO KILL YOU!
WITH BRAN GONE, IS THERE ANY WOLF HERE WHO CAN CONTROL ADAM?
HE'LL BE BACK SOON, BEFORE YOUR ADAM'S CONSCIOUS.
FOR ONCE IN YOU LIFE, MERCY--
PATIENCE.
MAYBE CARL WAS RIGHT.
RUNNING OFF HALF-COCKED AND GETTING MYSELF KILLED WOULDN'T HELP ANY ONE.
AND LOVER'S CANYON OF ALL PLACES...
MERCY + SAM
WHY DID IT HAVE TO BE THERE?

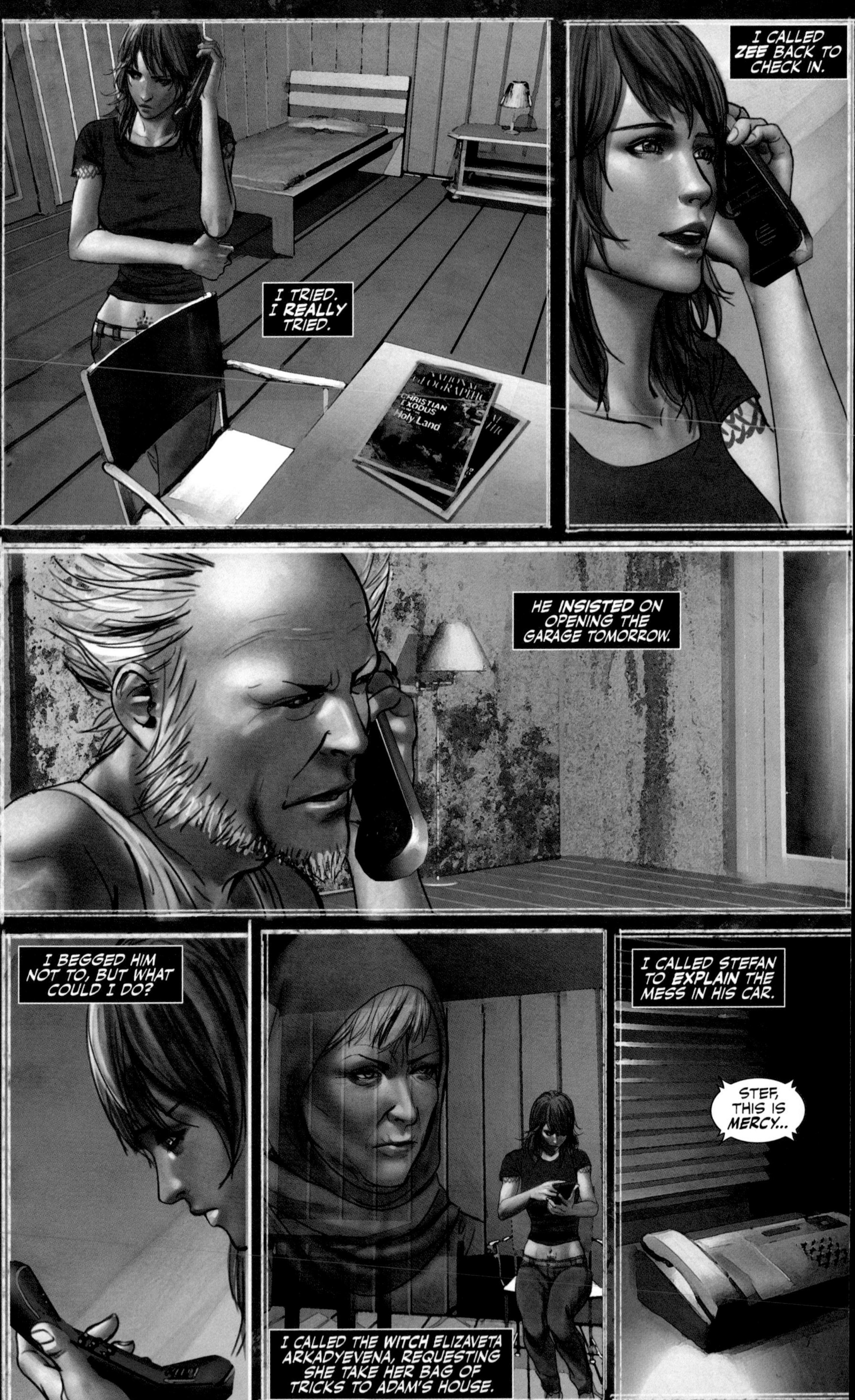
I TRIED. I REALLY TRIED.
NATIONAL GEOGRAPHIC
CHRISTIAN EXODUS
Holy Land
I CALLED ZEE BACK TO CHECK IN.
HE INSISTED ON OPENING THE GARAGE TOMORROW.
I BEGGED HIM NOT TO, BUT WHAT COULD I DO?
I CALLED THE WITCH ELIZAVETA ARKADYEVENA, REQUESTING SHE TAKE HER BAG OF TRICKS TO ADAM'S HOUSE.
I CALLED STEFAN TO EXPLAIN THE MESS IN HIS CAR.
STEF, THIS IS MERCY...

I FRETTED FOR ADAM.

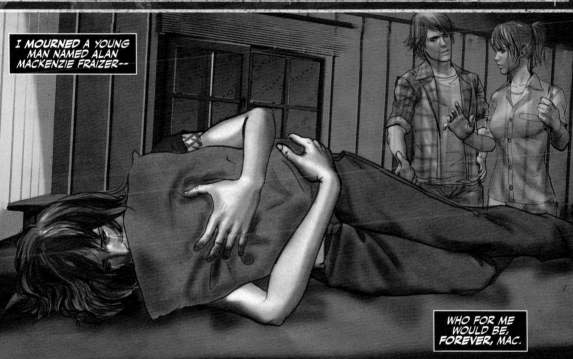

I MOURNED A YOUNG MAN NAMED ALAN MACKENZIE FRAIZER--

WHO FOR ME WOULD BE, FOREVER, MAC.

AND THEN--

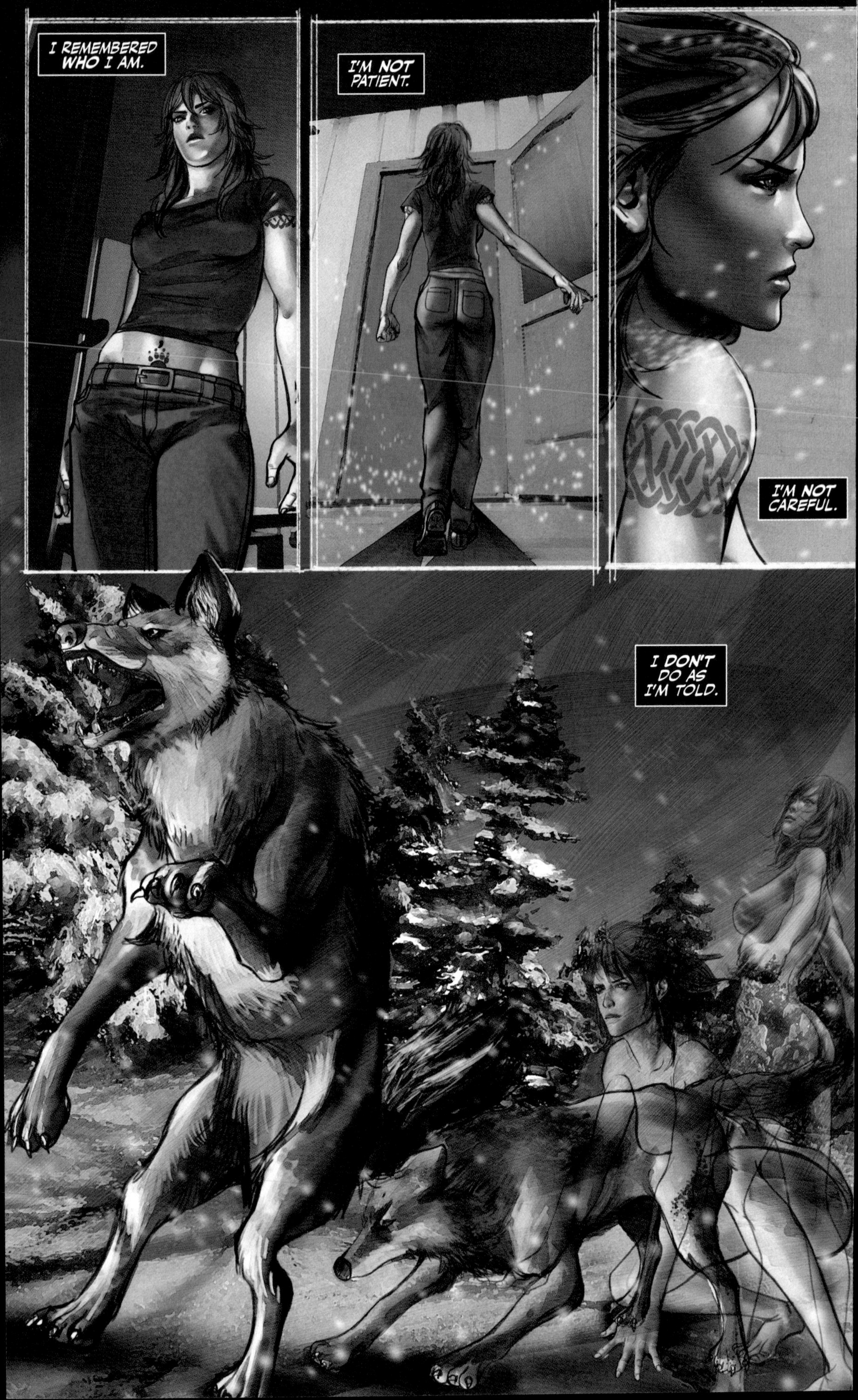
I REMEMBERED WHO I AM.
I'M NOT PATIENT.
I'M NOT CAREFUL.
I DON'T DO AS I'M TOLD.

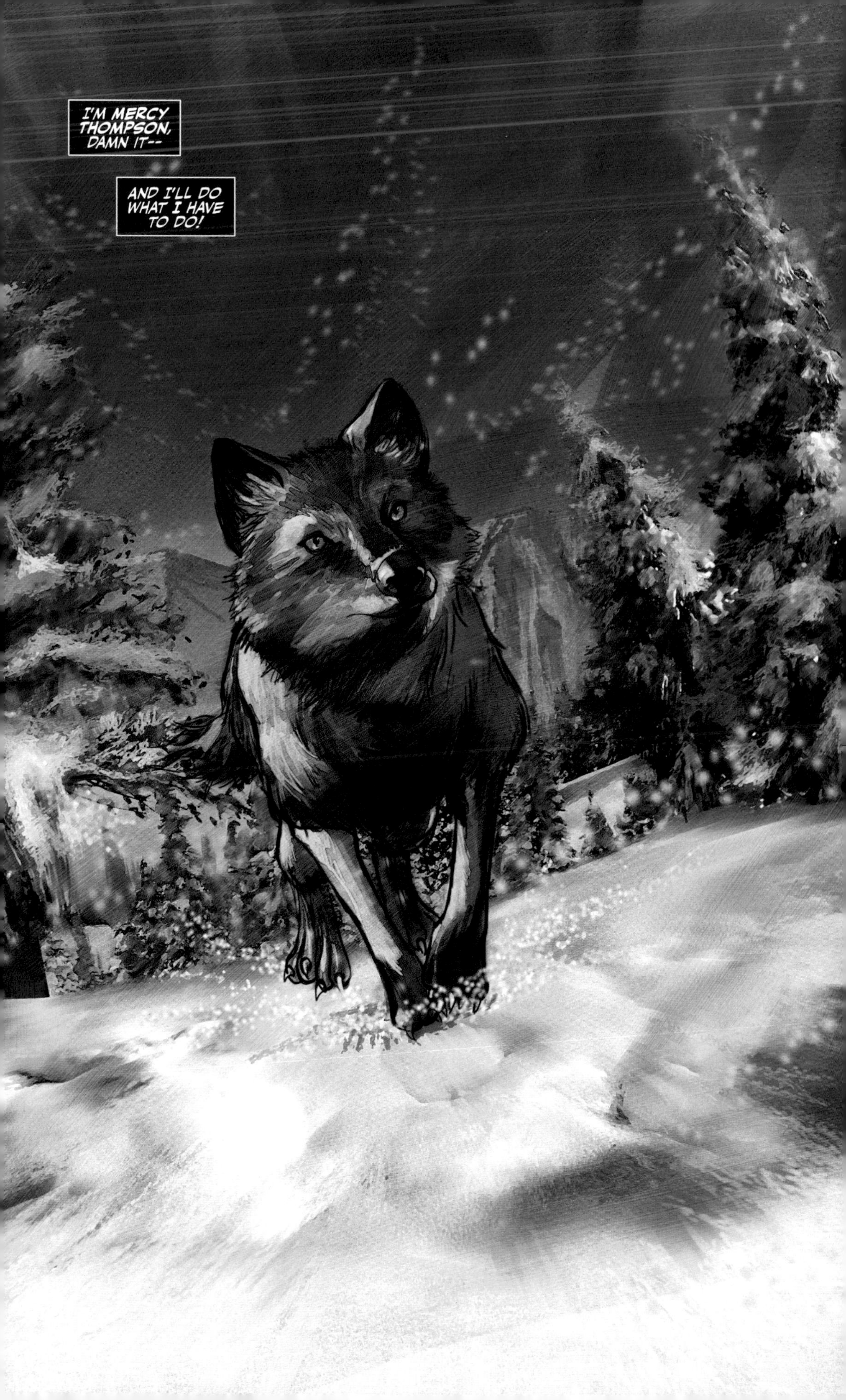
I'M MERCY THOMPSON, DAMN IT--
AND I'LL DO WHAT I HAVE TO DO!

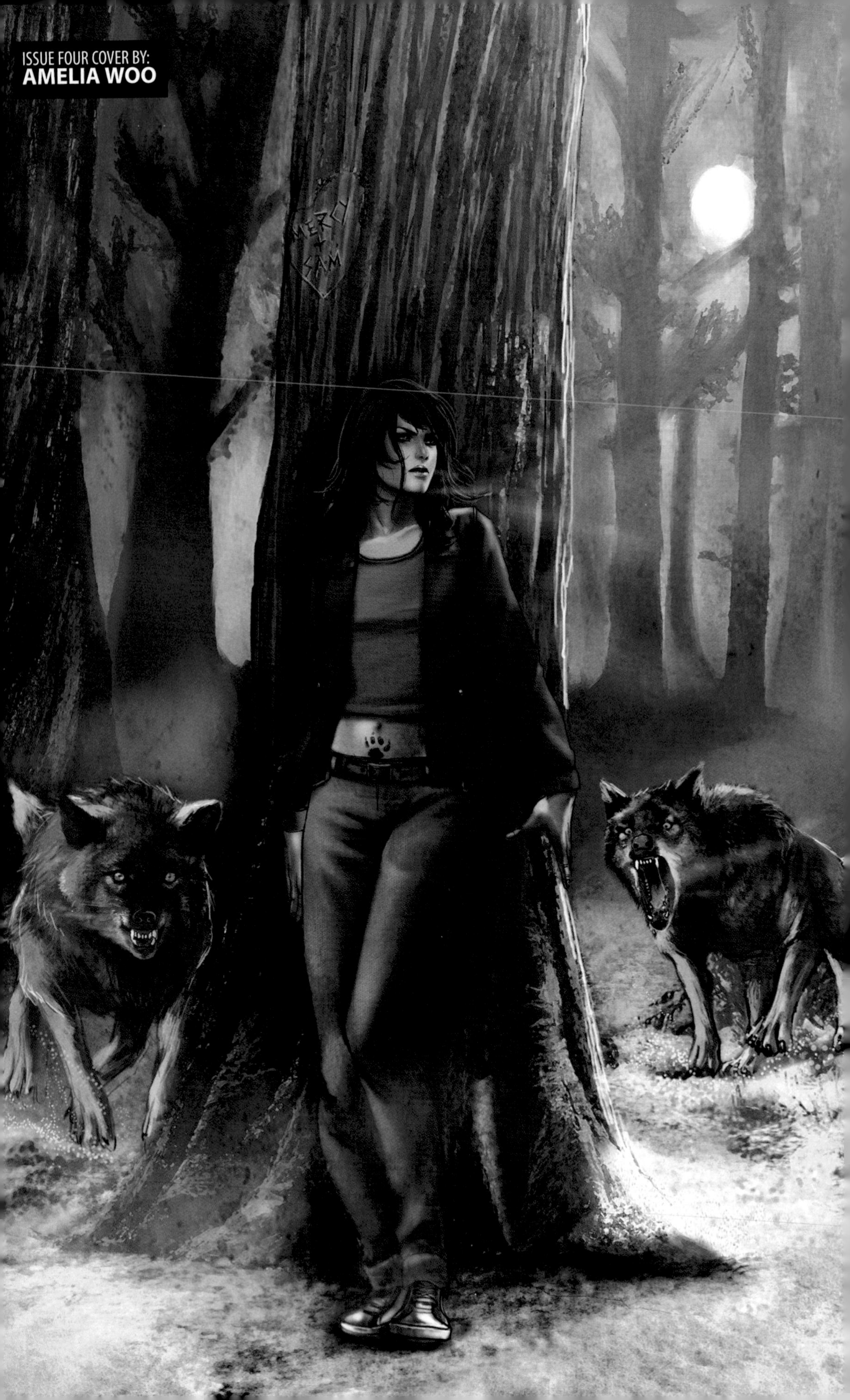
MERCY
+
SAM

ISSUE FOUR COVER BY:
AMELIA WOO

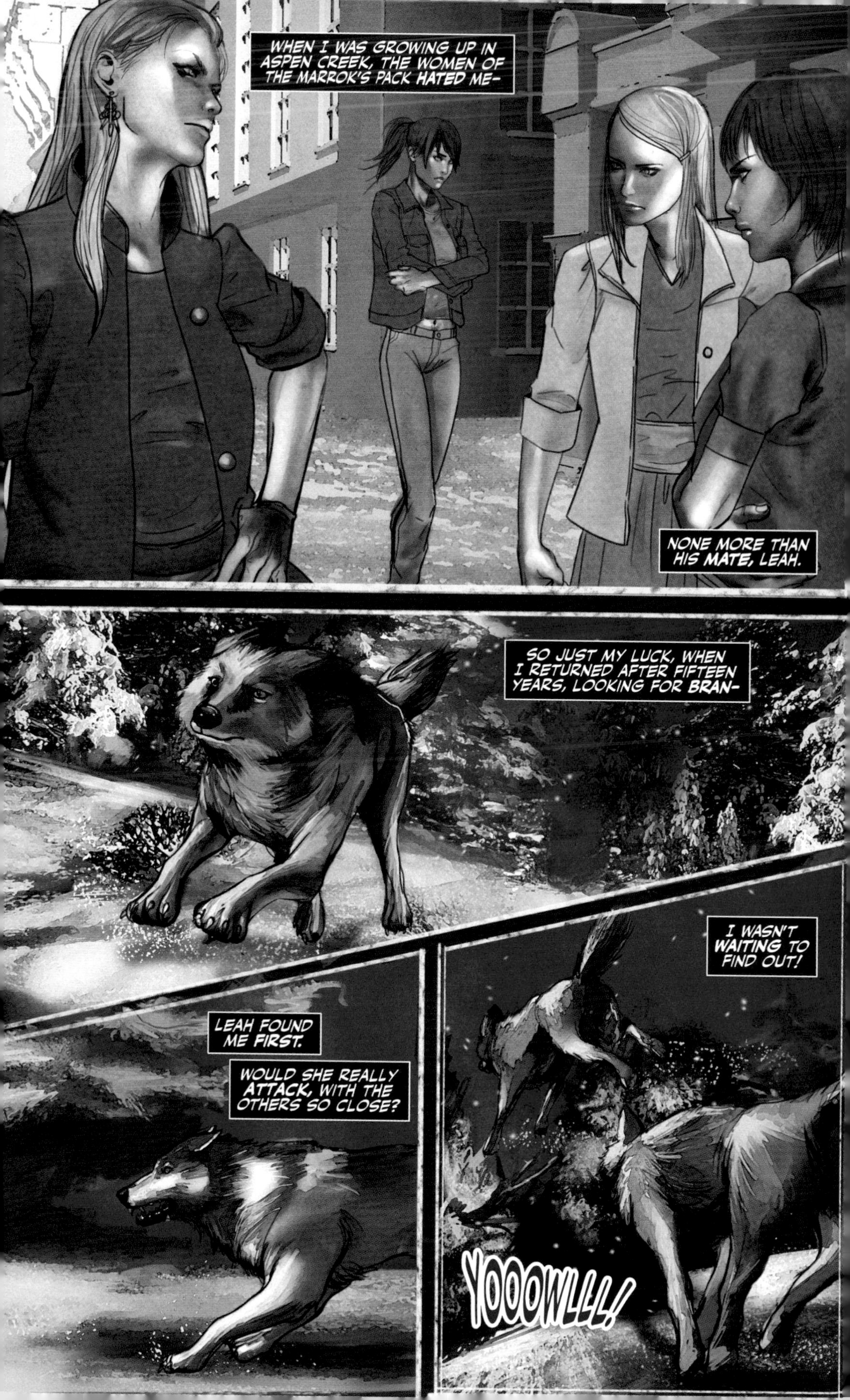
WHEN I WAS GROWING UP IN ASPEN CREEK, THE WOMEN OF THE MARROK'S PACK HATED ME-
NONE MORE THAN HIS MATE, LEAH.
SO JUST MY LUCK, WHEN I RETURNED AFTER FIFTEEN YEARS, LOOKING FOR BRAN-
LEAH FOUND ME FIRST.
WOULD SHE REALLY ATTACK, WITH THE OTHERS SO CLOSE?
I WASN'T WAITING TO FIND OUT!
YOOOWLLL!

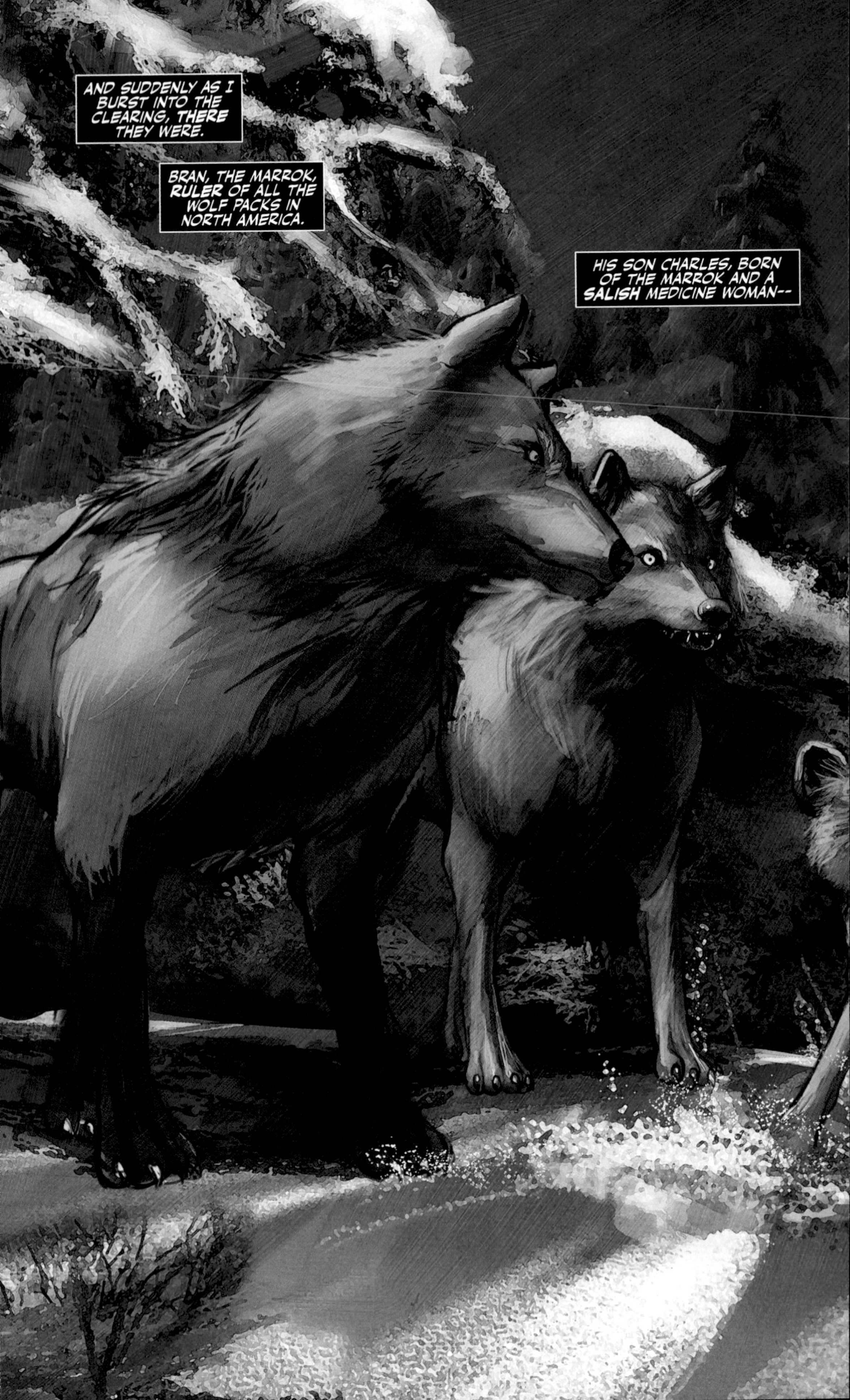
AND SUDDENLY AS I BURST INTO THE CLEARING, THERE THEY WERE.
BRAN, THE MARROK, RULER OF ALL THE WOLF PACKS IN NORTH AMERICA.
HIS SON CHARLES, BORN OF THE MARROK AND A SALISH MEDICINE WOMAN--

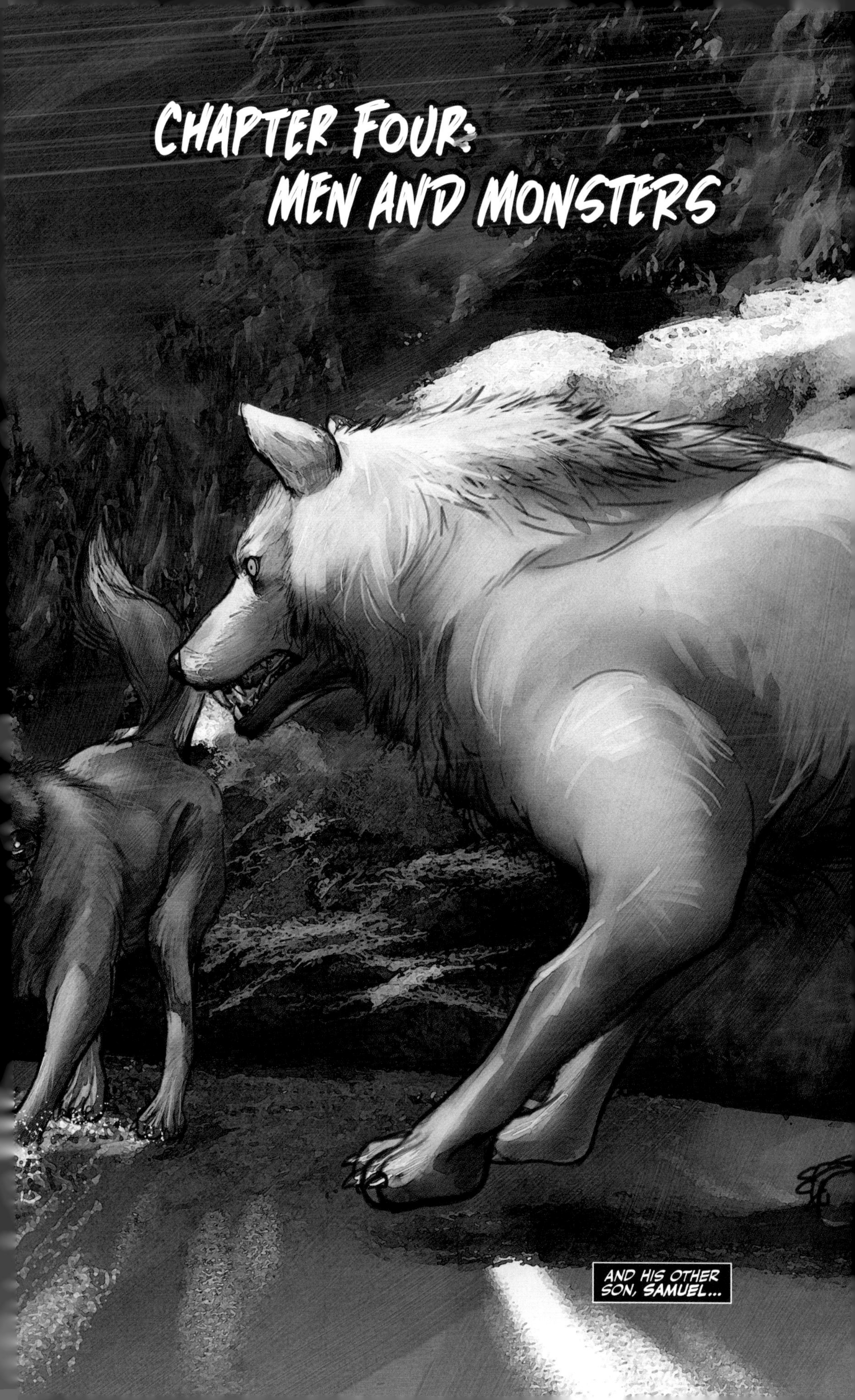
CHAPTER FOUR:
MEN AND MONSTERS
AND HIS OTHER SON, SAMUEL...

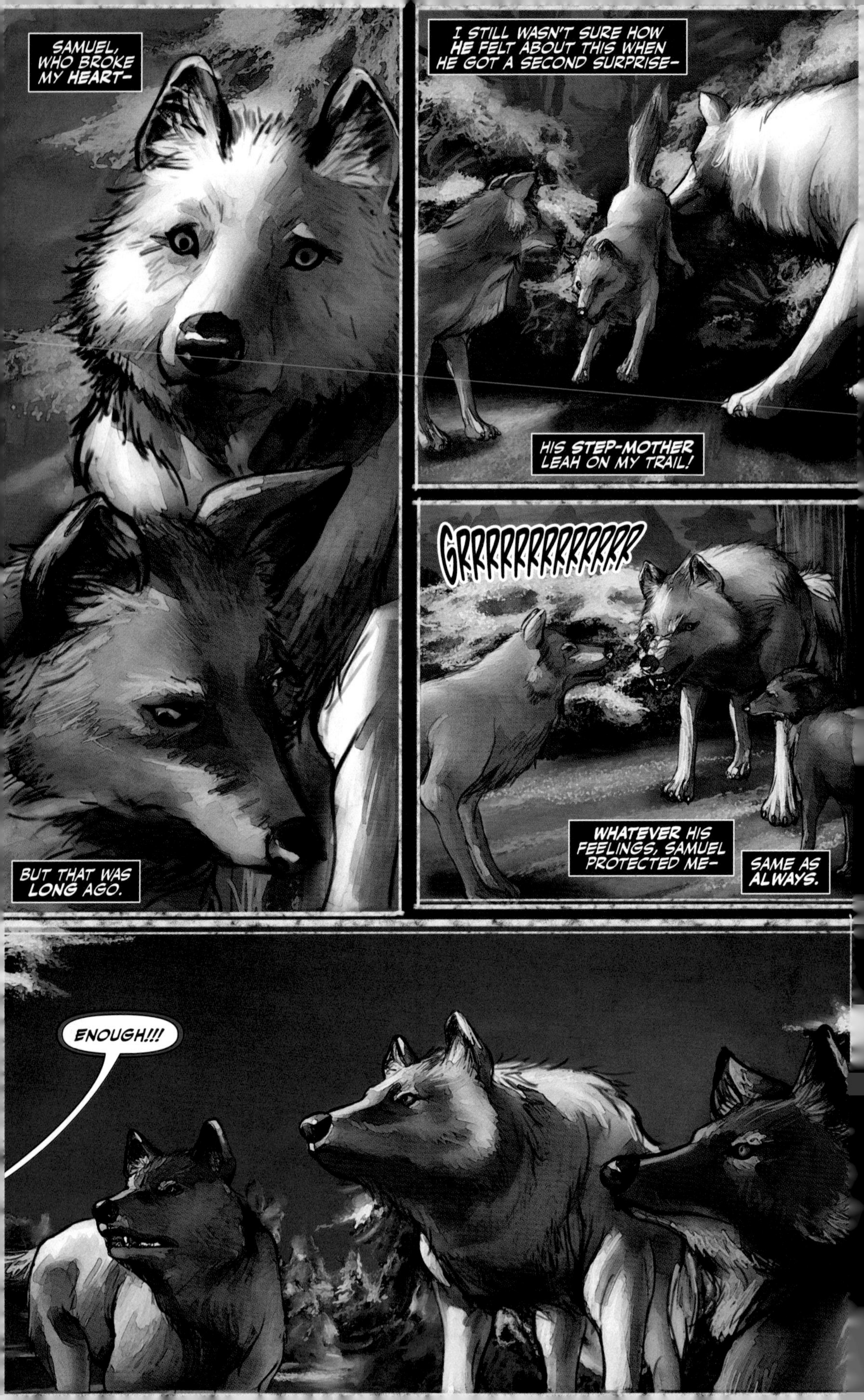

SAMUEL, WHO BROKE MY HEART-
BUT THAT WAS LONG AGO.
I STILL WASN'T SURE HOW HE FELT ABOUT THIS WHEN HE GOT A SECOND SURPRISE-
HIS STEP-MOTHER LEAH ON MY TRAIL!
GRRRRRRRRRRRRR
WHATEVER HIS FEELINGS, SAMUEL PROTECTED ME-
SAME AS ALWAYS.
ENOUGH!!!

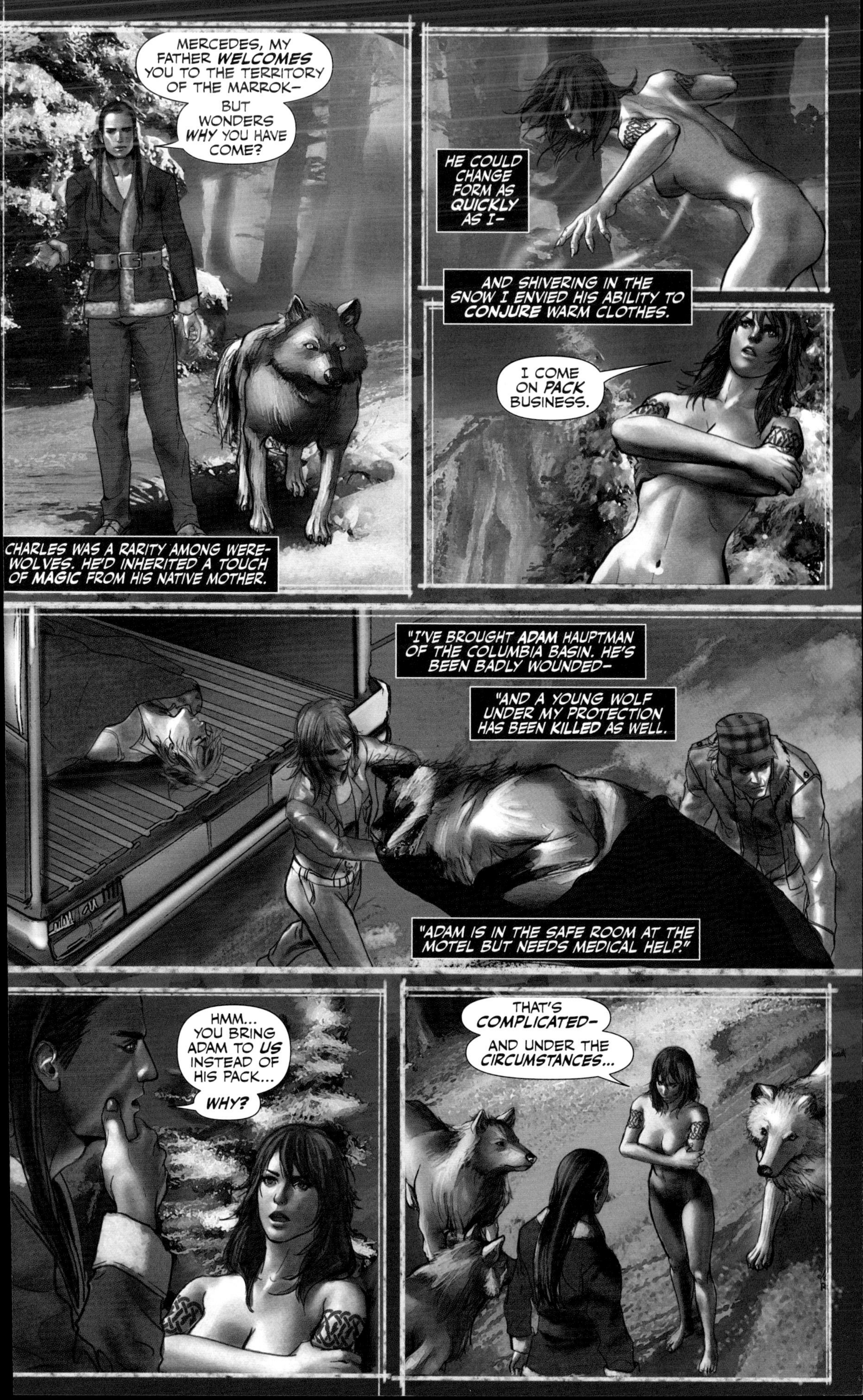
MERCEDES, MY FATHER WELCOMES YOU TO THE TERRITORY OF THE MARROK-
BUT WONDERS WHY YOU HAVE COME?
CHARLES WAS A RARITY AMONG WERE-WOLVES. HE'D INHERITED A TOUCH OF MAGIC FROM HIS NATIVE MOTHER.
HE COULD CHANGE FORM AS QUICKLY AS I-
AND SHIVERING IN THE SNOW I ENVIED HIS ABILITY TO CONJURE WARM CLOTHES.
I COME ON PACK BUSINESS.
"I'VE BROUGHT ADAM HAUPTMAN OF THE COLUMBIA BASIN. HE'S BEEN BADLY WOUNDED-
"AND A YOUNG WOLF UNDER MY PROTECTION HAS BEEN KILLED AS WELL.
"ADAM IS IN THE SAFE ROOM AT THE MOTEL BUT NEEDS MEDICAL HELP."
HMM... YOU BRING ADAM TO US INSTEAD OF HIS PACK...
WHY?
THAT'S COMPLICATED-
AND UNDER THE CIRCUMSTANCES...

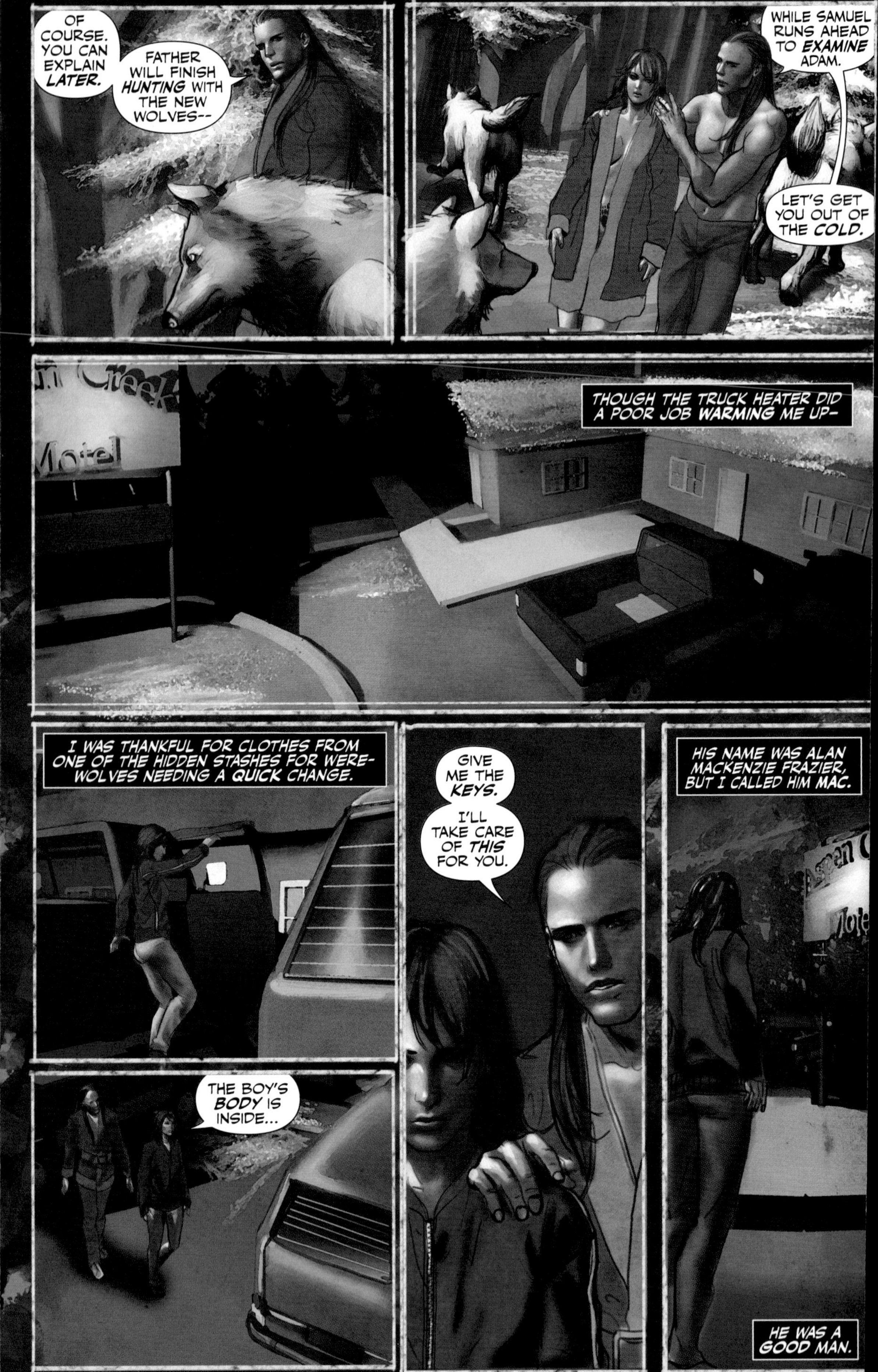

OF COURSE. YOU CAN EXPLAIN LATER.
FATHER WILL FINISH HUNTING WITH THE NEW WOLVES--
WHILE SAMUEL RUNS AHEAD TO EXAMINE ADAM.
LET'S GET YOU OUT OF THE COLD.
THOUGH THE TRUCK HEATER DID A POOR JOB WARMING ME UP-
Motel
I WAS THANKFUL FOR CLOTHES FROM ONE OF THE HIDDEN STASHES FOR WERE-WOLVES NEEDING A QUICK CHANGE.
THE BOY'S BODY IS INSIDE...
GIVE ME THE KEYS.
I'LL TAKE CARE OF THIS FOR YOU.
HIS NAME WAS ALAN MACKENZIE FRAZIER, BUT I CALLED HIM MAC.
HE WAS A GOOD MAN.

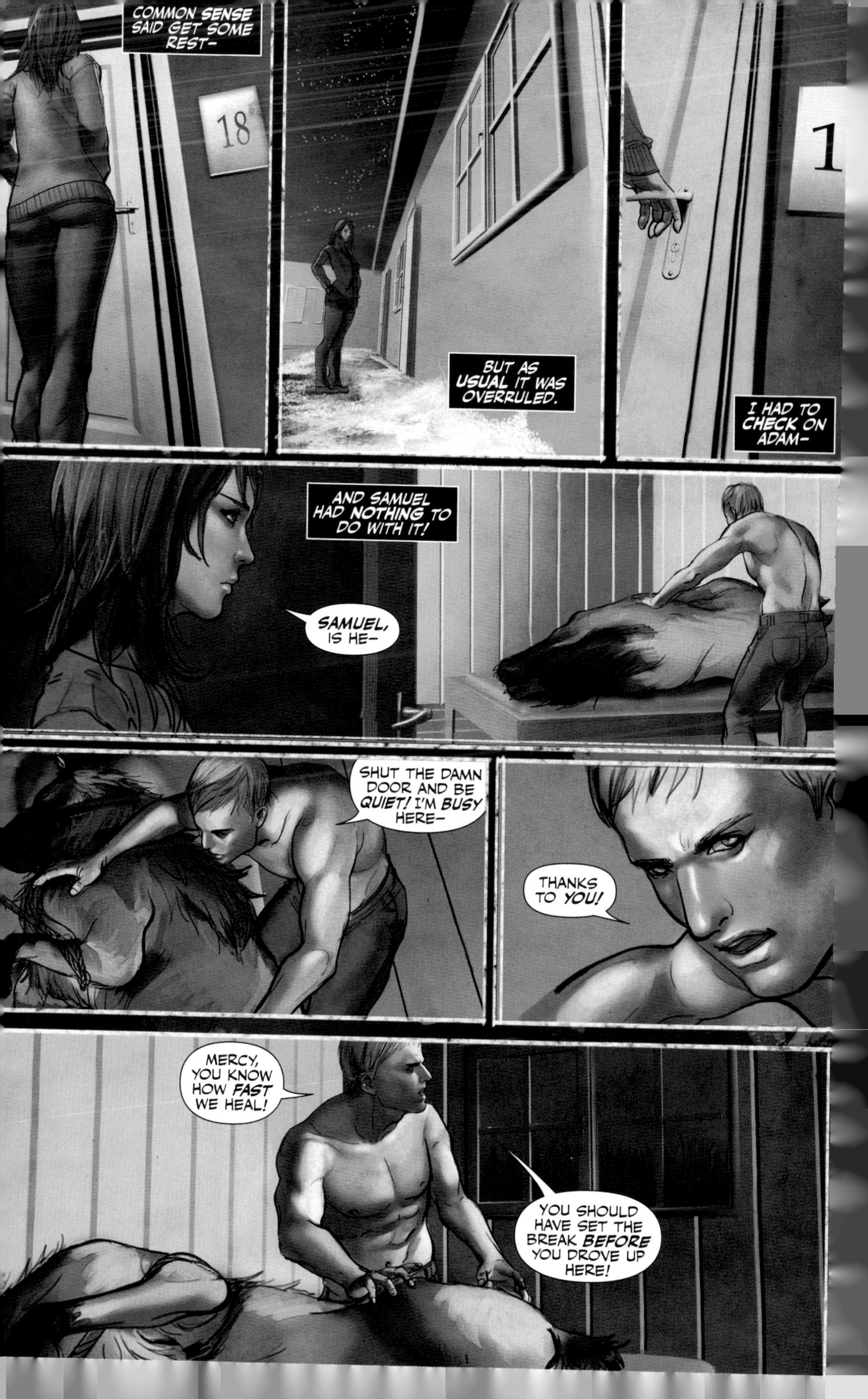
COMMON SENSE SAID GET SOME REST-
18
BUT AS USUAL IT WAS OVERRULED.
I HAD TO CHECK ON ADAM-
AND SAMUEL HAD NOTHING TO DO WITH IT!
SAMUEL, IS HE-
SHUT THE DAMN DOOR AND BE QUIET! I'M BUSY HERE-
THANKS TO YOU!
MERCY, YOU KNOW HOW FAST WE HEAL!
YOU SHOULD HAVE SET THE BREAK BEFORE YOU DROVE UP HERE!

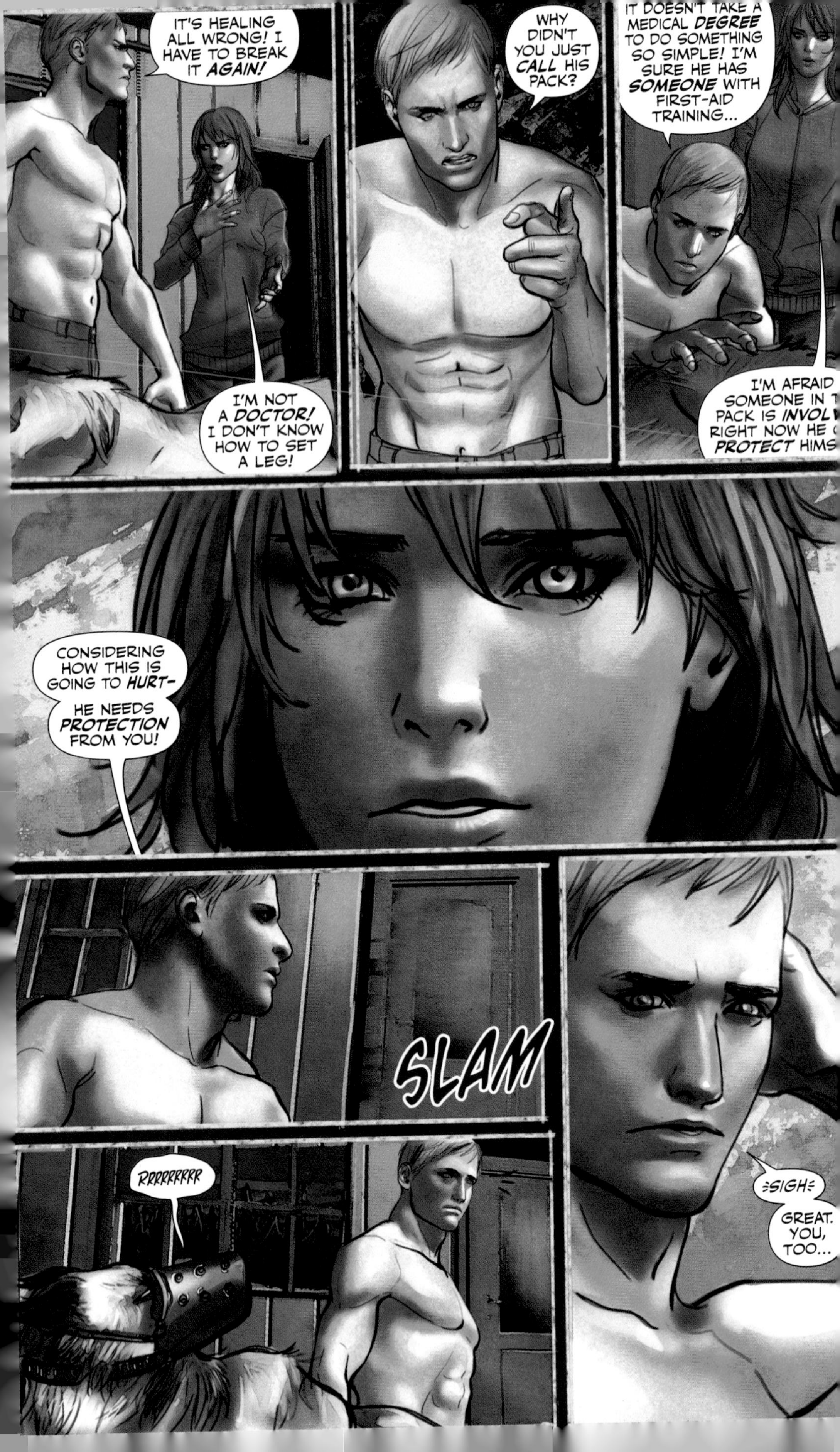
IT'S HEALING ALL WRONG! I HAVE TO BREAK IT AGAIN!
I'M NOT A DOCTOR! I DON'T KNOW HOW TO SET A LEG!
WHY DIDN'T YOU JUST CALL HIS PACK?
IT DOESN'T TAKE A MEDICAL DEGREE TO DO SOMETHING SO SIMPLE! I'M SURE HE HAS SOMEONE WITH FIRST-AID TRAINING...
I'M AFRAID SOMEONE IN T PACK IS INVOLV RIGHT NOW HE PROTECT HIMS
CONSIDERING HOW THIS IS GOING TO HURT-
HE NEEDS PROTECTION FROM YOU!
SLAM
RRRRRRRR
SIGH
GREAT. YOU, TOO...

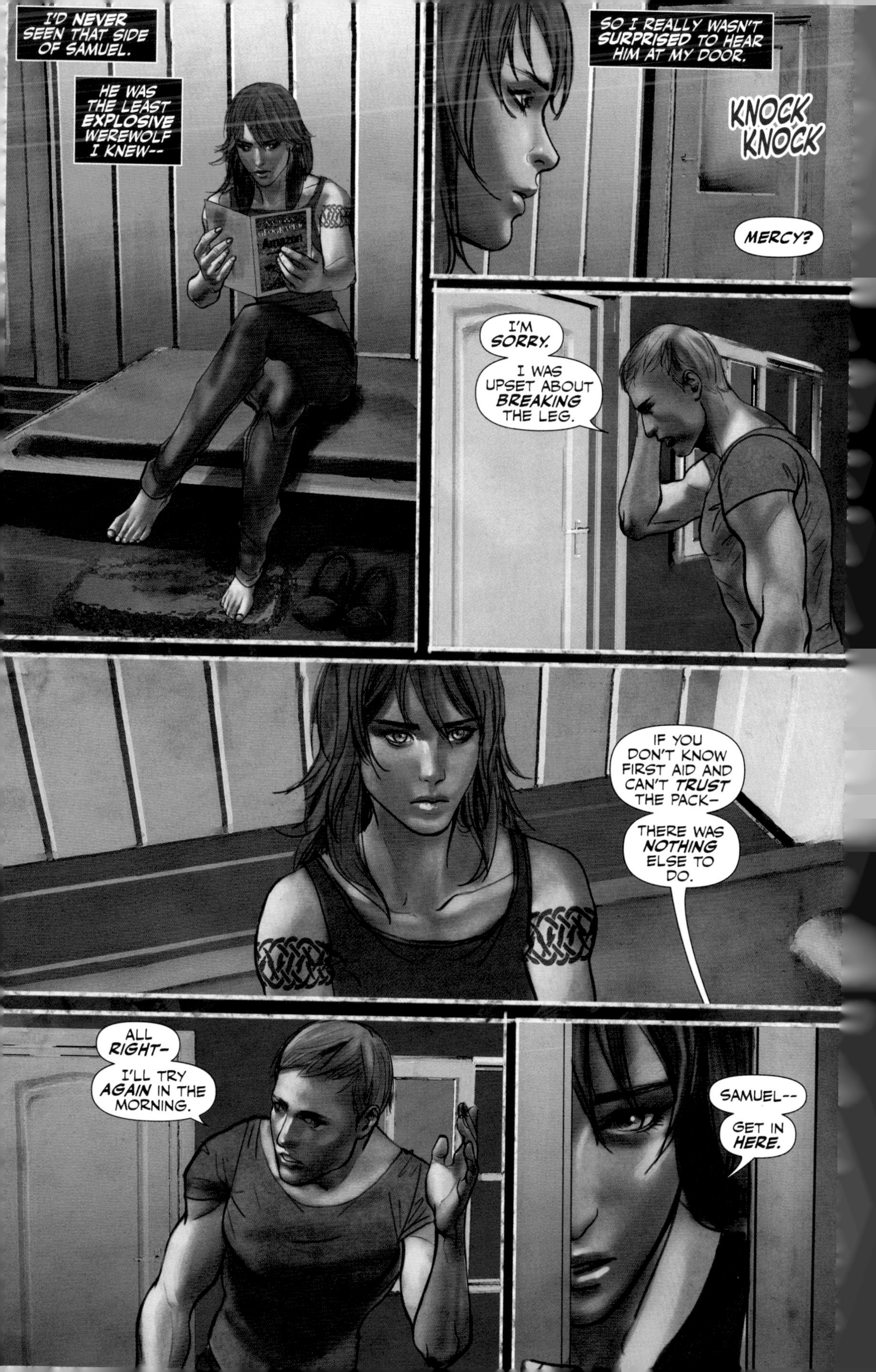
I'D NEVER SEEN THAT SIDE OF SAMUEL.
HE WAS THE LEAST EXPLOSIVE WEREWOLF I KNEW--
SO I REALLY WASN'T SURPRISED TO HEAR HIM AT MY DOOR.
KNOCK KNOCK
MERCY?
I'M SORRY.
I WAS UPSET ABOUT BREAKING THE LEG.
IF YOU DON'T KNOW FIRST AID AND CAN'T TRUST THE PACK-
THERE WAS NOTHING ELSE TO DO.
ALL RIGHT-
I'LL TRY AGAIN IN THE MORNING.
SAMUEL--
GET IN HERE.

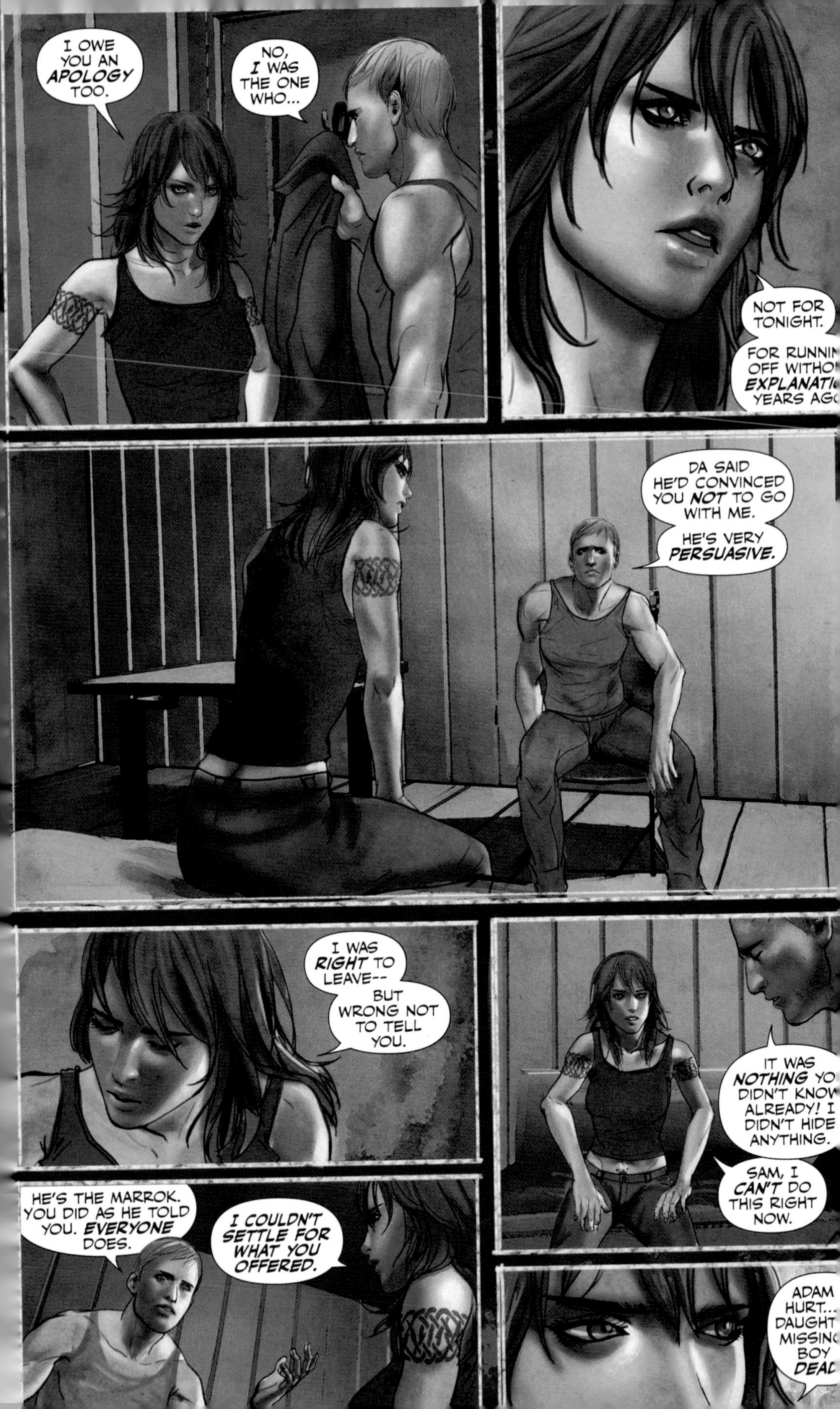
I OWE YOU AN APOLOGY TOO.
NO, I WAS THE ONE WHO...
NOT FOR TONIGHT.
FOR RUNNIN OFF WITHO EXPLANATI YEARS AG
DA SAID HE'D CONVINCED YOU NOT TO GO WITH ME.
HE'S VERY PERSUASIVE.
I WAS RIGHT TO LEAVE--
BUT WRONG NOT TO TELL YOU.
IT WAS NOTHING YO DIDN'T KNOW ALREADY! I DIDN'T HIDE ANYTHING.
SAM, I CAN'T DO THIS RIGHT NOW.
HE'S THE MARROK. YOU DID AS HE TOLD YOU. EVERYONE DOES.
I COULDN'T SETTLE FOR WHAT YOU OFFERED.
ADAM HURT... DAUGHT MISSIN BOY DEAD

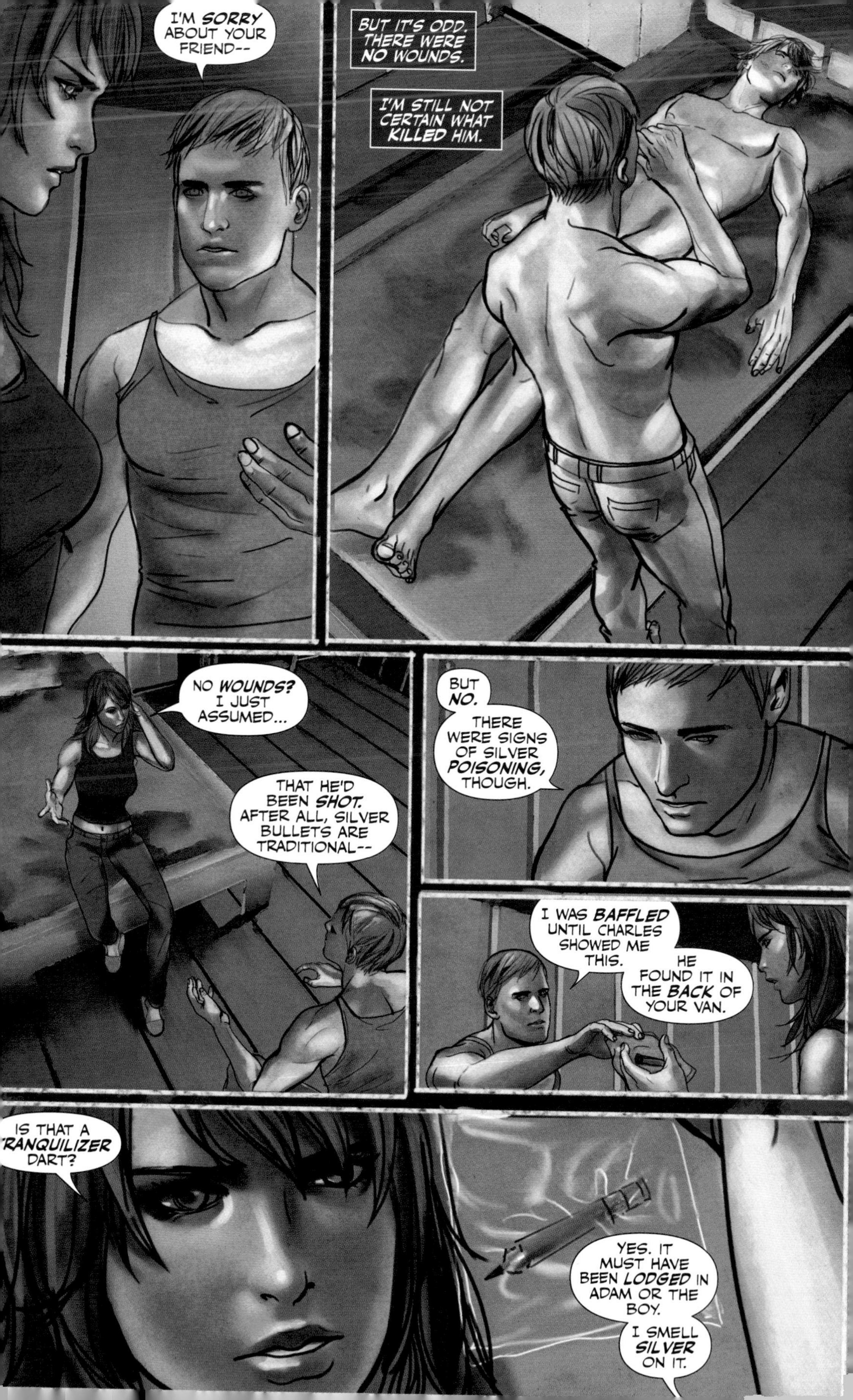
I'M SORRY ABOUT YOUR FRIEND--
BUT IT'S ODD. THERE WERE NO WOUNDS.
I'M STILL NOT CERTAIN WHAT KILLED HIM.
NO WOUNDS? I JUST ASSUMED...
THAT HE'D BEEN SHOT. AFTER ALL, SILVER BULLETS ARE TRADITIONAL--
BUT NO.
THERE WERE SIGNS OF SILVER POISONING, THOUGH.
I WAS BAFFLED UNTIL CHARLES SHOWED ME THIS.
HE FOUND IT IN THE BACK OF YOUR VAN.
IS THAT A TRANQUILIZER DART?
YES. IT MUST HAVE BEEN LODGED IN ADAM OR THE BOY.
I SMELL SILVER ON IT.

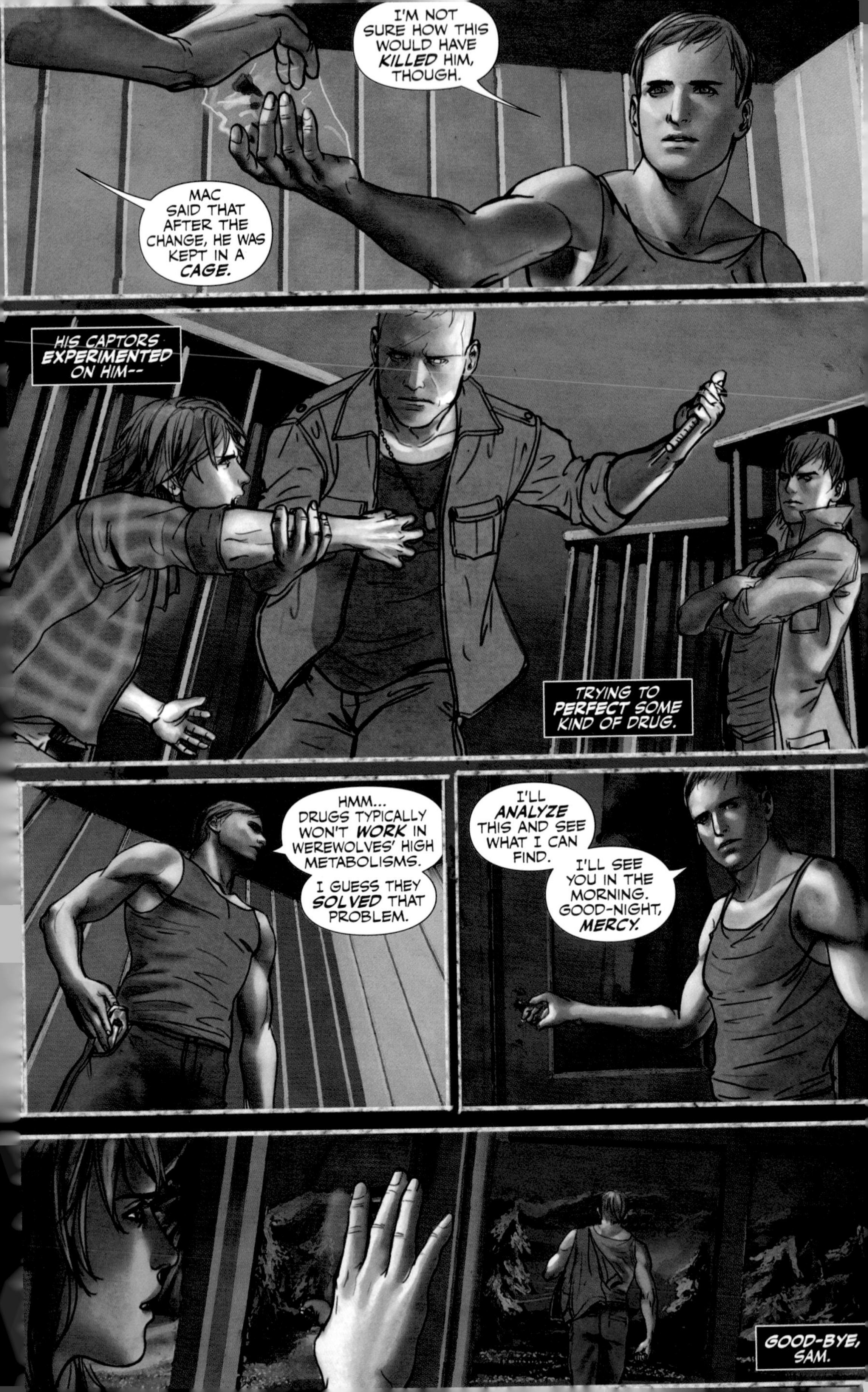

I'M NOT SURE HOW THIS WOULD HAVE KILLED HIM, THOUGH.
MAC SAID THAT AFTER THE CHANGE, HE WAS KEPT IN A CAGE.
HIS CAPTORS EXPERIMENTED ON HIM--
TRYING TO PERFECT SOME KIND OF DRUG.
HMM... DRUGS TYPICALLY WON'T WORK IN WEREWOLVES' HIGH METABOLISMS.
I GUESS THEY SOLVED THAT PROBLEM.
I'LL ANALYZE THIS AND SEE WHAT I CAN FIND.
I'LL SEE YOU IN THE MORNING. GOOD-NIGHT, MERCY.
GOOD-BYE, SAM.

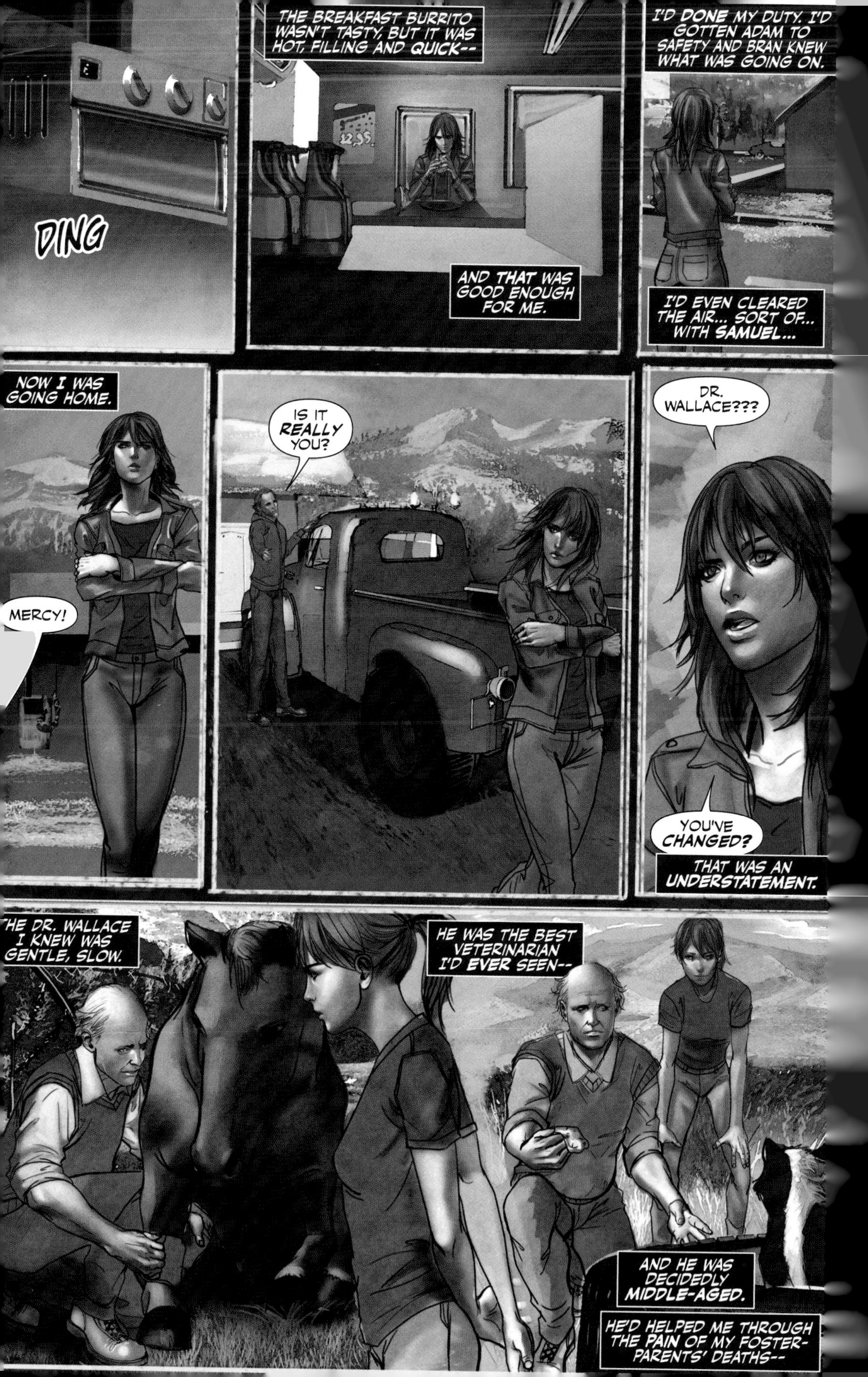
DING
THE BREAKFAST BURRITO WASN'T TASTY, BUT IT WAS HOT, FILLING AND QUICK--
AND THAT WAS GOOD ENOUGH FOR ME.
I'D DONE MY DUTY. I'D GOTTEN ADAM TO SAFETY AND BRAN KNEW WHAT WAS GOING ON.
I'D EVEN CLEARED THE AIR... SORT OF... WITH SAMUEL...
NOW I WAS GOING HOME.
MERCY!
IS IT REALLY YOU?
DR. WALLACE???
YOU'VE CHANGED?
THAT WAS AN UNDERSTATEMENT.
THE DR. WALLACE I KNEW WAS GENTLE, SLOW.
HE WAS THE BEST VETERINARIAN I'D EVER SEEN--
AND HE WAS DECIDEDLY MIDDLE-AGED.
HE'D HELPED ME THROUGH THE PAIN OF MY FOSTER-PARENTS' DEATHS--

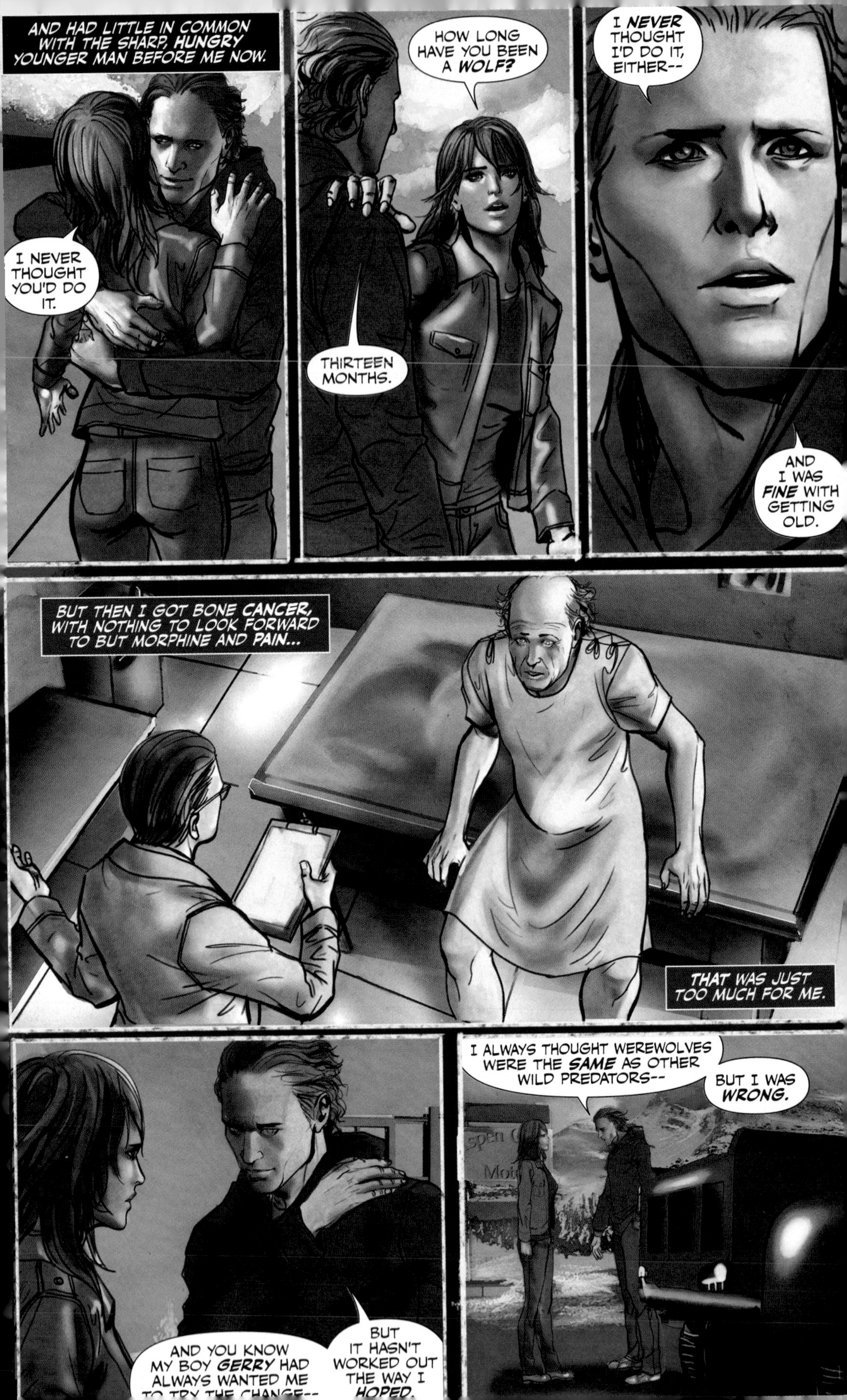
AND HAD LITTLE IN COMMON WITH THE SHARP, HUNGRY YOUNGER MAN BEFORE ME NOW.
I NEVER THOUGHT YOU'D DO IT.
HOW LONG HAVE YOU BEEN A WOLF?
THIRTEEN MONTHS.
I NEVER THOUGHT I'D DO IT, EITHER--
AND I WAS FINE WITH GETTING OLD.
BUT THEN I GOT BONE CANCER, WITH NOTHING TO LOOK FORWARD TO BUT MORPHINE AND PAIN...
THAT WAS JUST TOO MUCH FOR ME.
AND YOU KNOW MY BOY GERRY HAD ALWAYS WANTED ME TO TRY THE CHANGE--
BUT IT HASN'T WORKED OUT THE WAY I HOPED.
I ALWAYS THOUGHT WEREWOLVES WERE THE SAME AS OTHER WILD PREDATORS--
BUT I WAS WRONG.

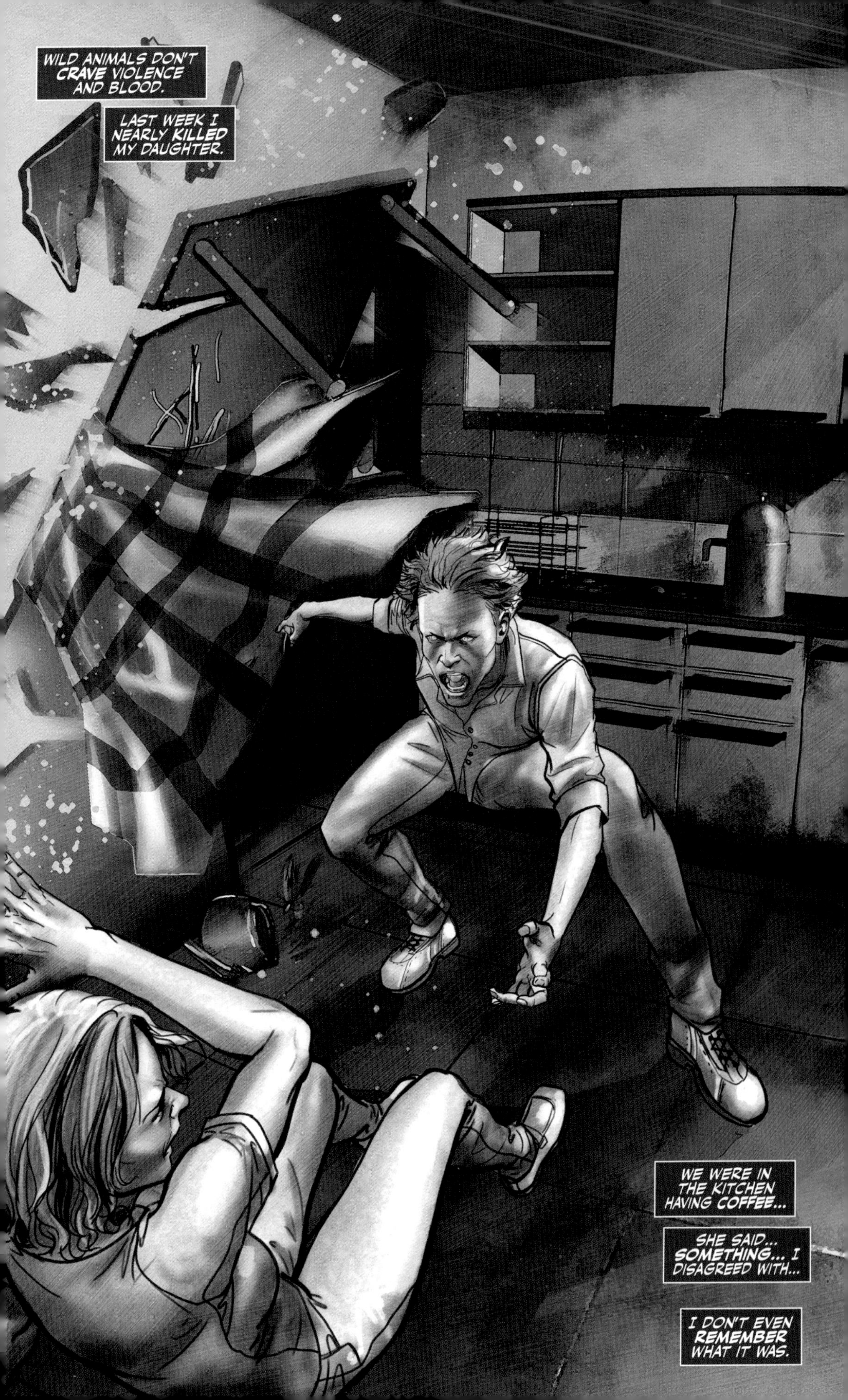

WILD ANIMALS DON'T CRAVE VIOLENCE AND BLOOD.
LAST WEEK I NEARLY KILLED MY DAUGHTER.
WE WERE IN THE KITCHEN HAVING COFFEE...
SHE SAID... SOMETHING... I DISAGREED WITH...
I DON'T EVEN REMEMBER WHAT IT WAS.

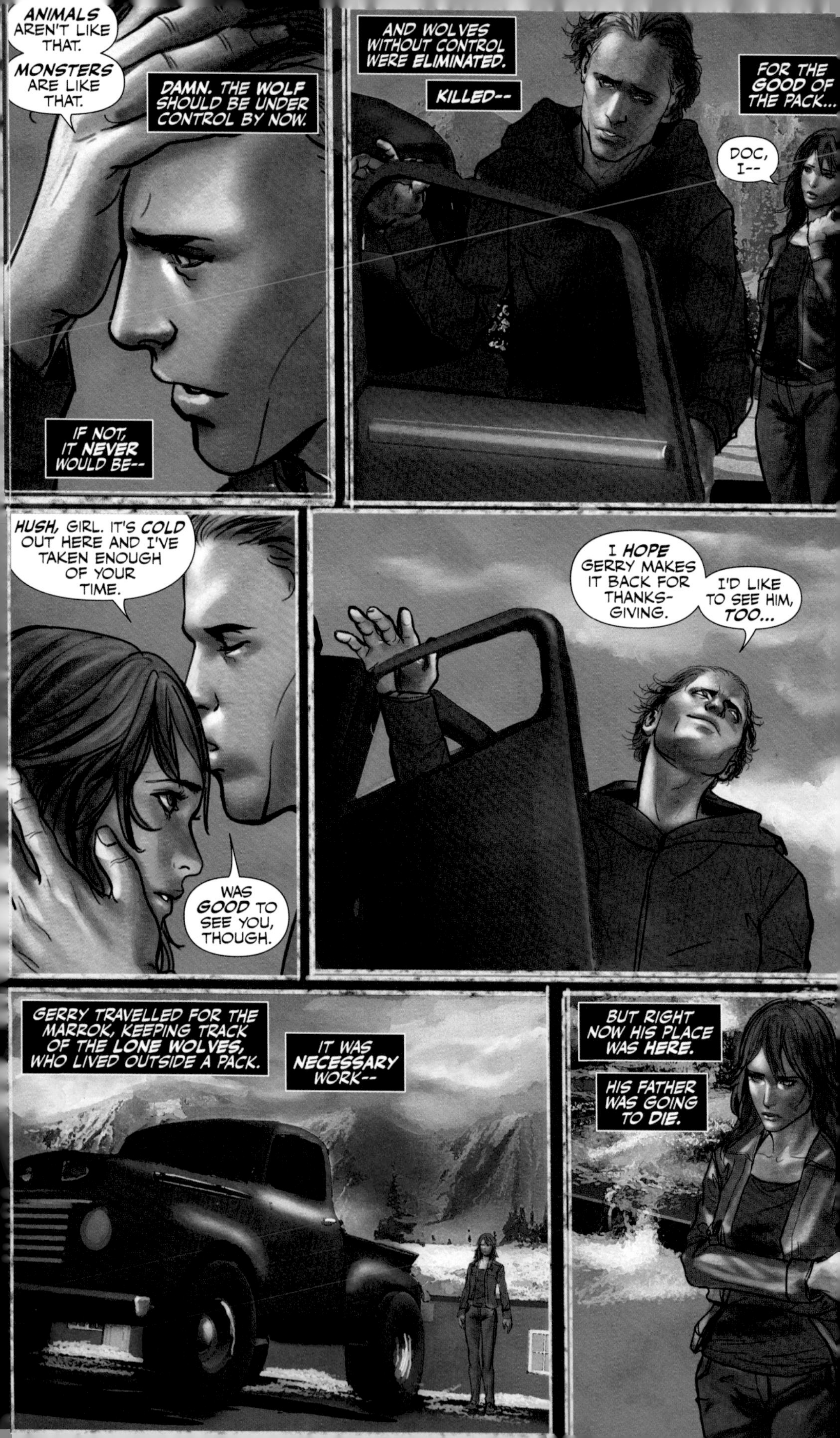
ANIMALS AREN'T LIKE THAT.
MONSTERS ARE LIKE THAT.
DAMN. THE WOLF SHOULD BE UNDER CONTROL BY NOW.
IF NOT, IT NEVER WOULD BE--
AND WOLVES WITHOUT CONTROL WERE ELIMINATED.
KILLED--
FOR THE GOOD OF THE PACK...
DOC, I--
HUSH, GIRL. IT'S COLD OUT HERE AND I'VE TAKEN ENOUGH OF YOUR TIME.
WAS GOOD TO SEE YOU, THOUGH.
I HOPE GERRY MAKES IT BACK FOR THANKS-GIVING.
I'D LIKE TO SEE HIM, TOO...
GERRY TRAVELLED FOR THE MARROK, KEEPING TRACK OF THE LONE WOLVES, WHO LIVED OUTSIDE A PACK.
IT WAS NECESSARY WORK--
BUT RIGHT NOW HIS PLACE WAS HERE.
HIS FATHER WAS GOING TO DIE.

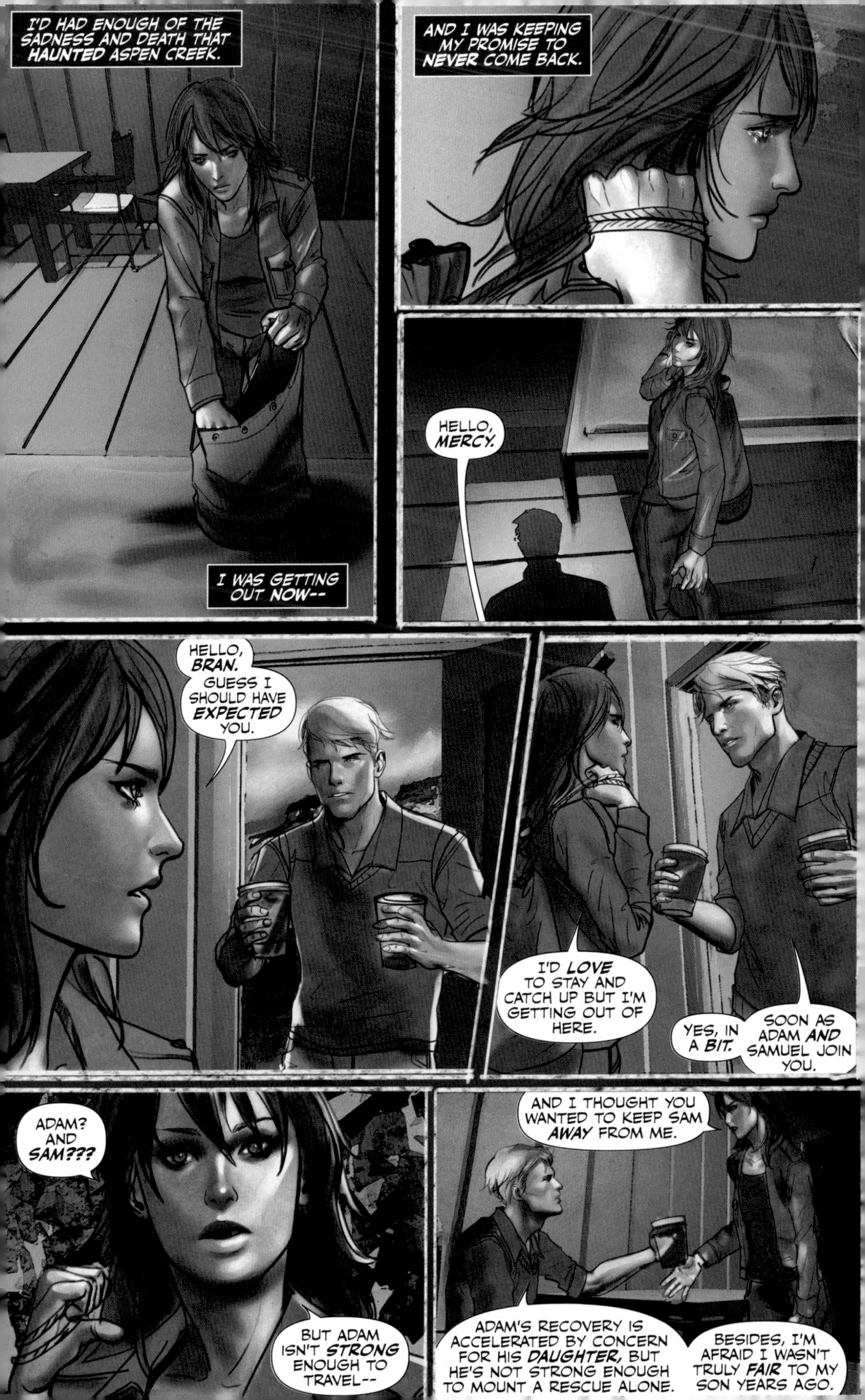
I'D HAD ENOUGH OF THE SADNESS AND DEATH THAT HAUNTED ASPEN CREEK.
I WAS GETTING OUT NOW--
AND I WAS KEEPING MY PROMISE TO NEVER COME BACK.
HELLO, MERCY.
HELLO, BRAN. GUESS I SHOULD HAVE EXPECTED YOU.
I'D LOVE TO STAY AND CATCH UP BUT I'M GETTING OUT OF HERE.
YES, IN A BIT.
SOON AS ADAM AND SAMUEL JOIN YOU.
ADAM? AND SAM???
BUT ADAM ISN'T STRONG ENOUGH TO TRAVEL--
AND I THOUGHT YOU WANTED TO KEEP SAM AWAY FROM ME.
ADAM'S RECOVERY IS ACCELERATED BY CONCERN FOR HIS DAUGHTER, BUT HE'S NOT STRONG ENOUGH TO MOUNT A RESCUE ALONE.
BESIDES, I'M AFRAID I WASN'T TRULY FAIR TO MY SON YEARS AGO.

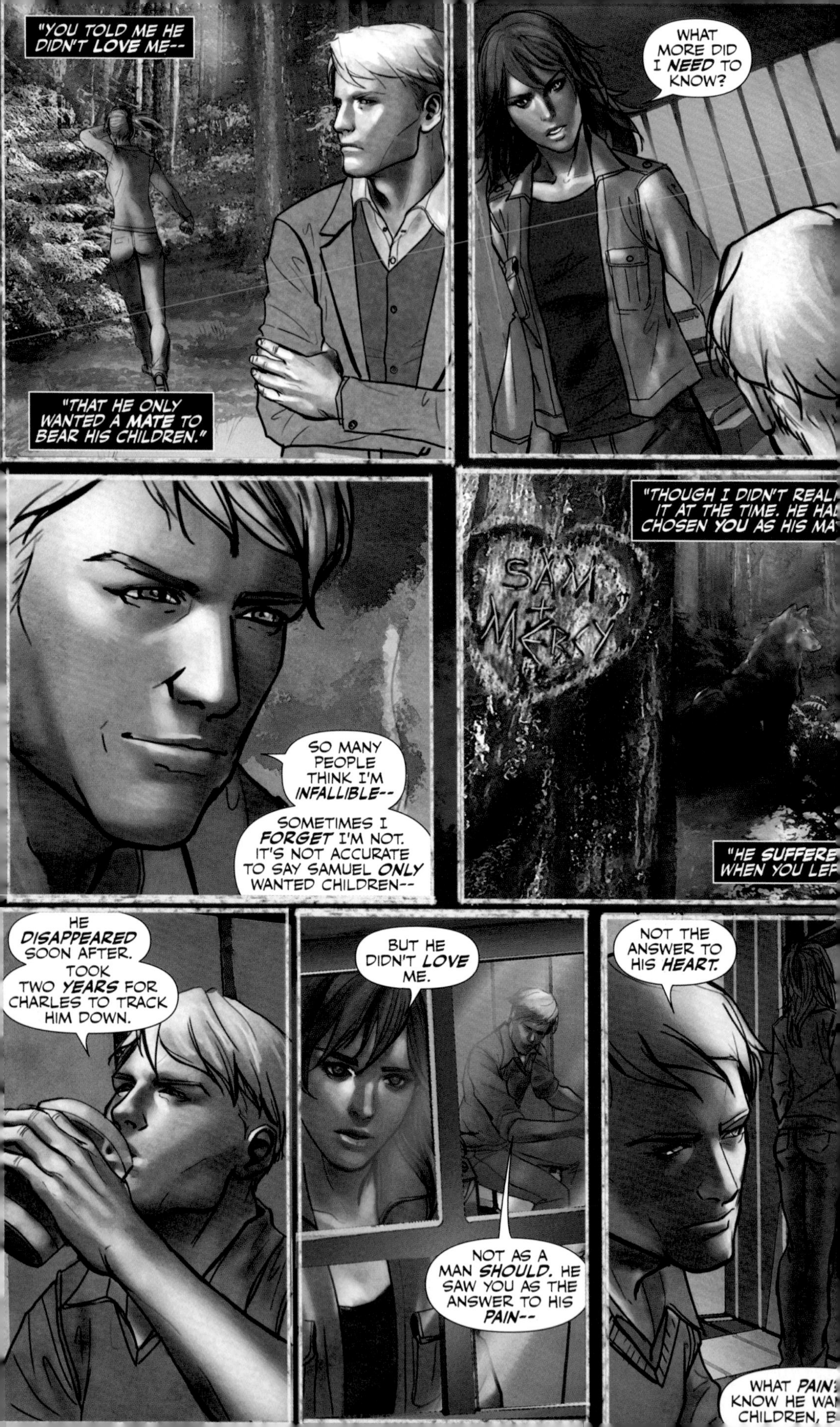

"YOU TOLD ME HE DIDN'T LOVE ME--
"THAT HE ONLY WANTED A MATE TO BEAR HIS CHILDREN."
WHAT MORE DID I NEED TO KNOW?
SO MANY PEOPLE THINK I'M INFALLIBLE--
SOMETIMES I FORGET I'M NOT. IT'S NOT ACCURATE TO SAY SAMUEL ONLY WANTED CHILDREN--
"THOUGH I DIDN'T REAL
IT AT THE TIME. HE HA
CHOSEN YOU AS HIS MA
SAM + MERCY
"HE SUFFERE
WHEN YOU LEF
HE DISAPPEARED SOON AFTER.
TOOK TWO YEARS FOR CHARLES TO TRACK HIM DOWN.
BUT HE DIDN'T LOVE ME.
NOT AS A MAN SHOULD. HE SAW YOU AS THE ANSWER TO HIS PAIN--
NOT THE ANSWER TO HIS HEART.
WHAT PAIN
KNOW HE WA
CHILDREN, B

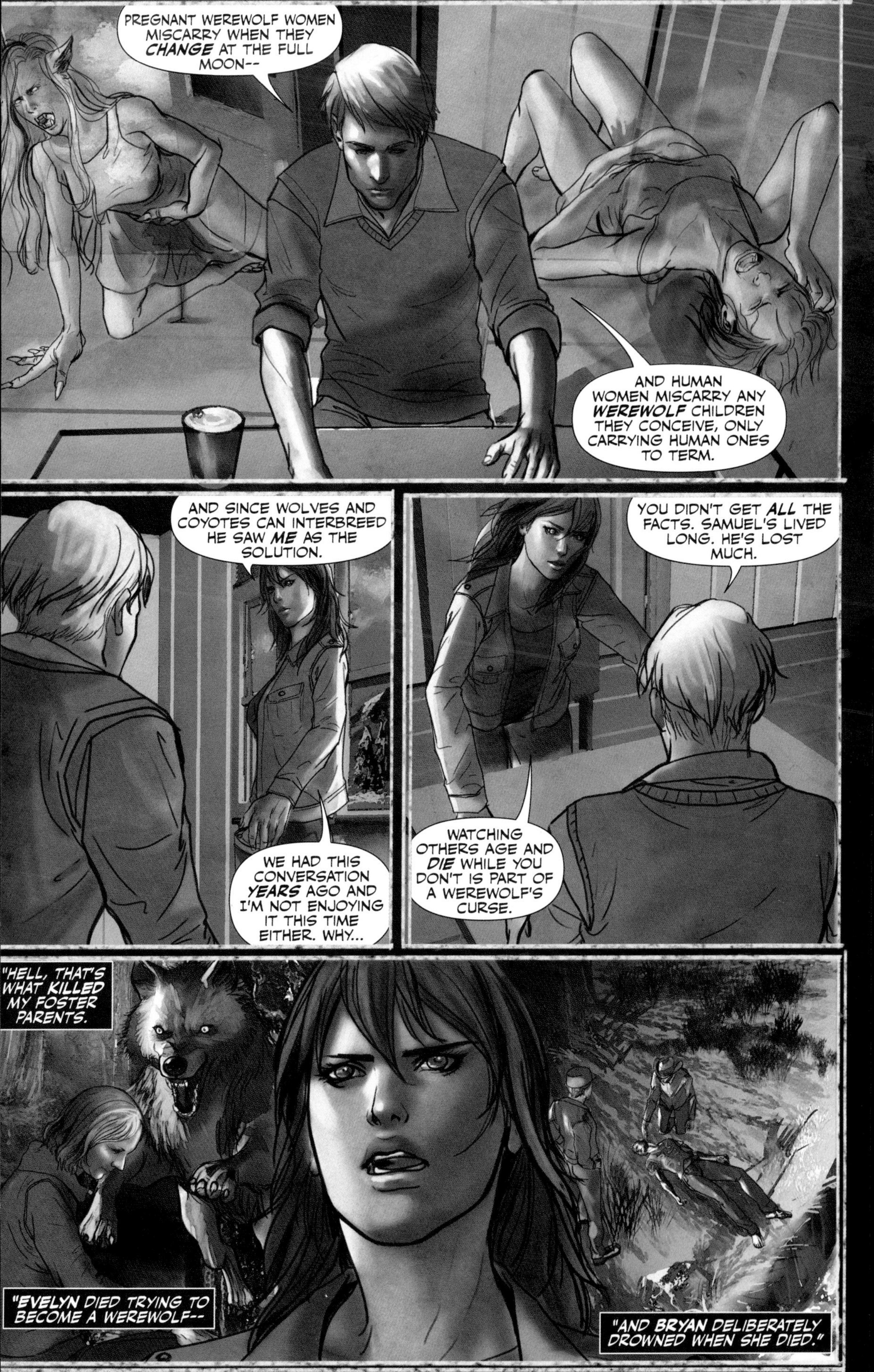
PREGNANT WEREWOLF WOMEN MISCARRY WHEN THEY CHANGE AT THE FULL MOON--
AND HUMAN WOMEN MISCARRY ANY WEREWOLF CHILDREN THEY CONCEIVE, ONLY CARRYING HUMAN ONES TO TERM.
AND SINCE WOLVES AND COYOTES CAN INTERBREED HE SAW ME AS THE SOLUTION.
WE HAD THIS CONVERSATION YEARS AGO AND I'M NOT ENJOYING IT THIS TIME EITHER. WHY...
YOU DIDN'T GET ALL THE FACTS. SAMUEL'S LIVED LONG. HE'S LOST MUCH.
WATCHING OTHERS AGE AND DIE WHILE YOU DON'T IS PART OF A WEREWOLF'S CURSE.
"HELL, THAT'S WHAT KILLED MY FOSTER PARENTS.
"EVELYN DIED TRYING TO BECOME A WEREWOLF--
"AND BRYAN DELIBERATELY DROWNED WHEN SHE DIED."

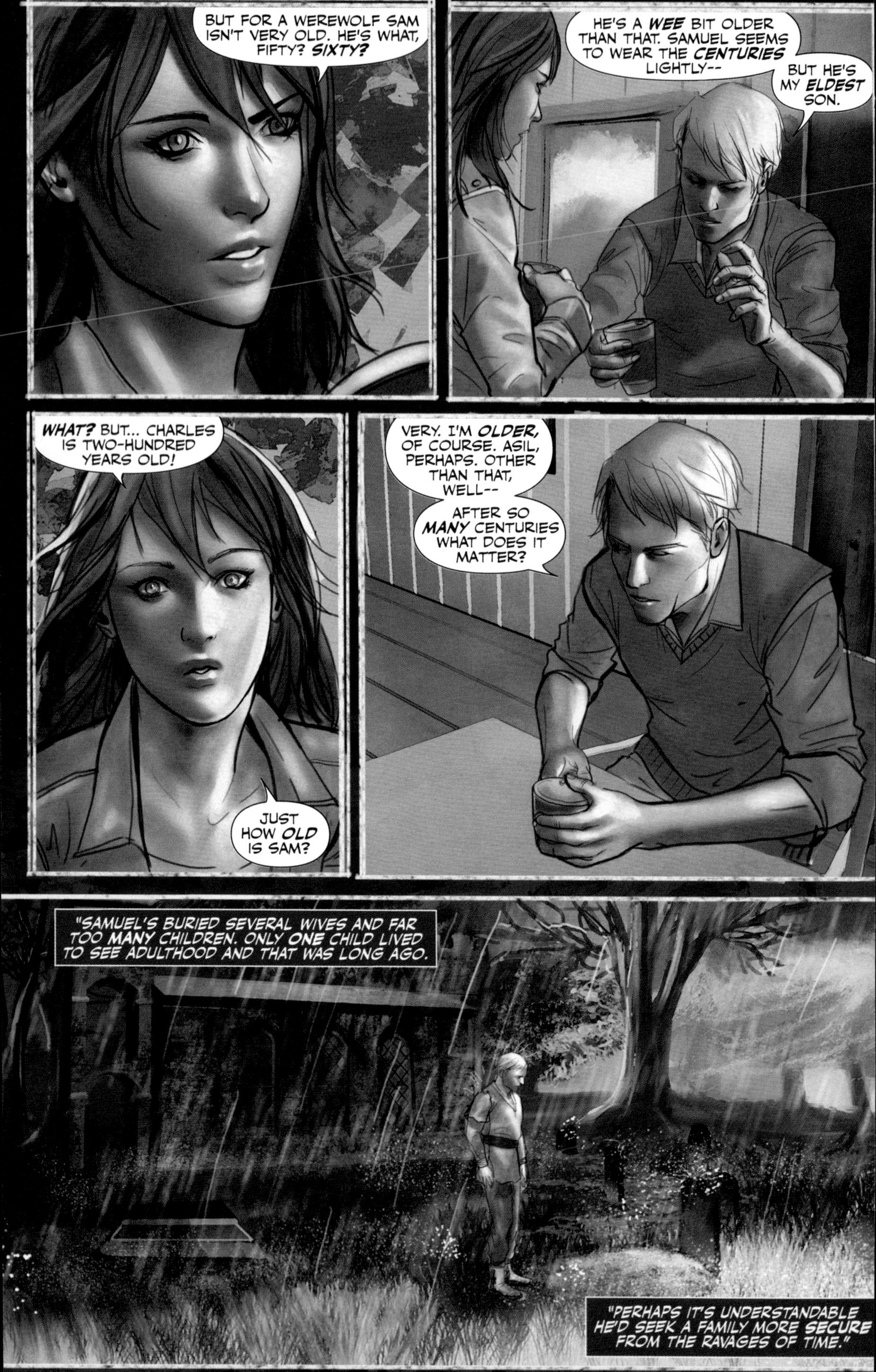
BUT FOR A WEREWOLF SAM ISN'T VERY OLD. HE'S WHAT, FIFTY? SIXTY?
HE'S A WEE BIT OLDER THAN THAT. SAMUEL SEEMS TO WEAR THE CENTURIES LIGHTLY--
BUT HE'S MY ELDEST SON.
WHAT? BUT... CHARLES IS TWO-HUNDRED YEARS OLD!
JUST HOW OLD IS SAM?
VERY. I'M OLDER, OF COURSE. ASIL, PERHAPS. OTHER THAN THAT, WELL--
AFTER SO MANY CENTURIES WHAT DOES IT MATTER?
"SAMUEL'S BURIED SEVERAL WIVES AND FAR TOO MANY CHILDREN. ONLY ONE CHILD LIVED TO SEE ADULTHOOD AND THAT WAS LONG AGO.
"PERHAPS IT'S UNDERSTANDABLE HE'D SEEK A FAMILY MORE SECURE FROM THE RAVAGES OF TIME."

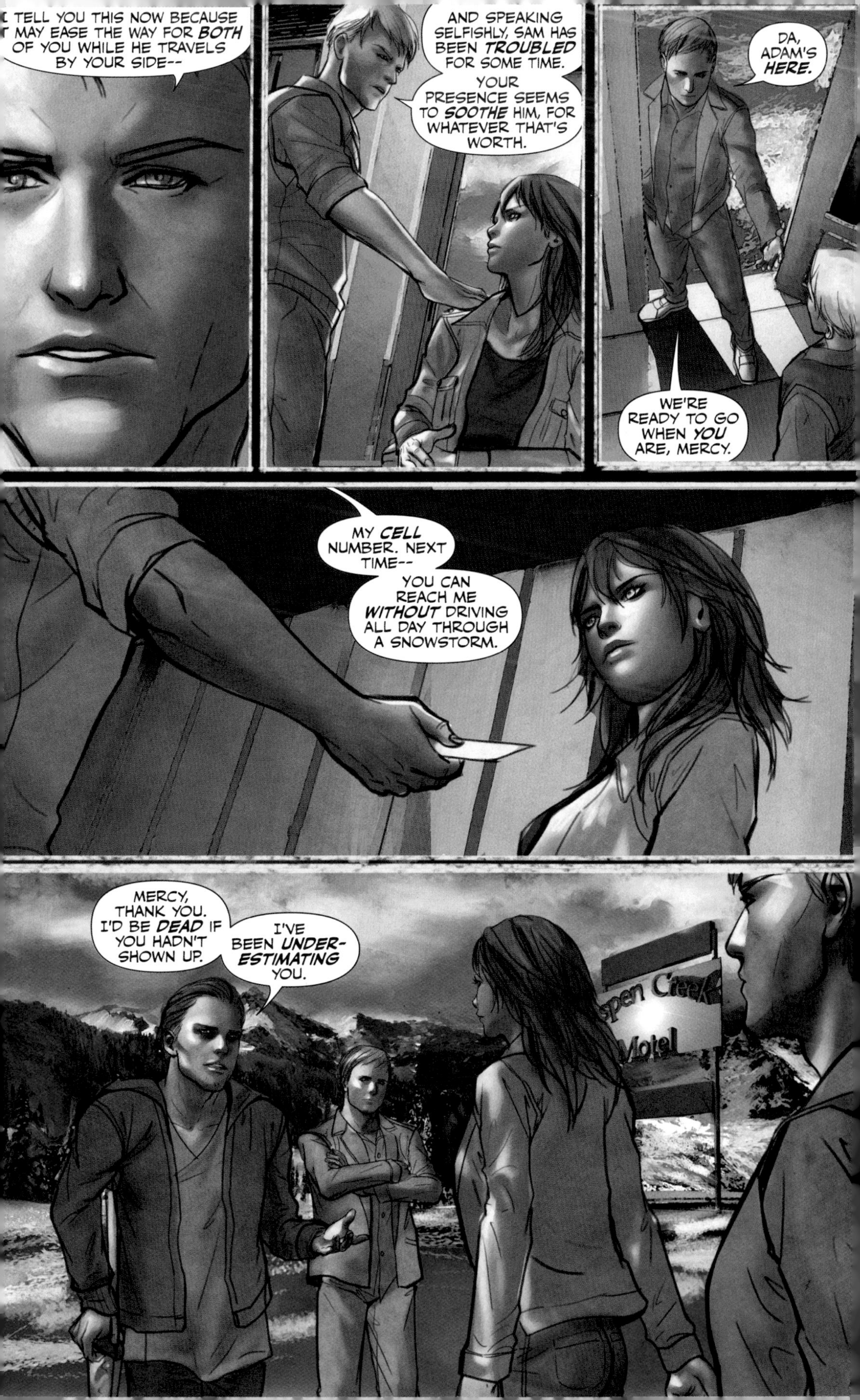
I TELL YOU THIS NOW BECAUSE IT MAY EASE THE WAY FOR BOTH OF YOU WHILE HE TRAVELS BY YOUR SIDE--
AND SPEAKING SELFISHLY, SAM HAS BEEN TROUBLED FOR SOME TIME.
YOUR PRESENCE SEEMS TO SOOTHE HIM, FOR WHATEVER THAT'S WORTH.
DA, ADAM'S HERE.
WE'RE READY TO GO WHEN YOU ARE, MERCY.
MY CELL NUMBER. NEXT TIME--
YOU CAN REACH ME WITHOUT DRIVING ALL DAY THROUGH A SNOWSTORM.
MERCY, THANK YOU. I'D BE DEAD IF YOU HADN'T SHOWN UP.
I'VE BEEN UNDER-ESTIMATING YOU.
Motel

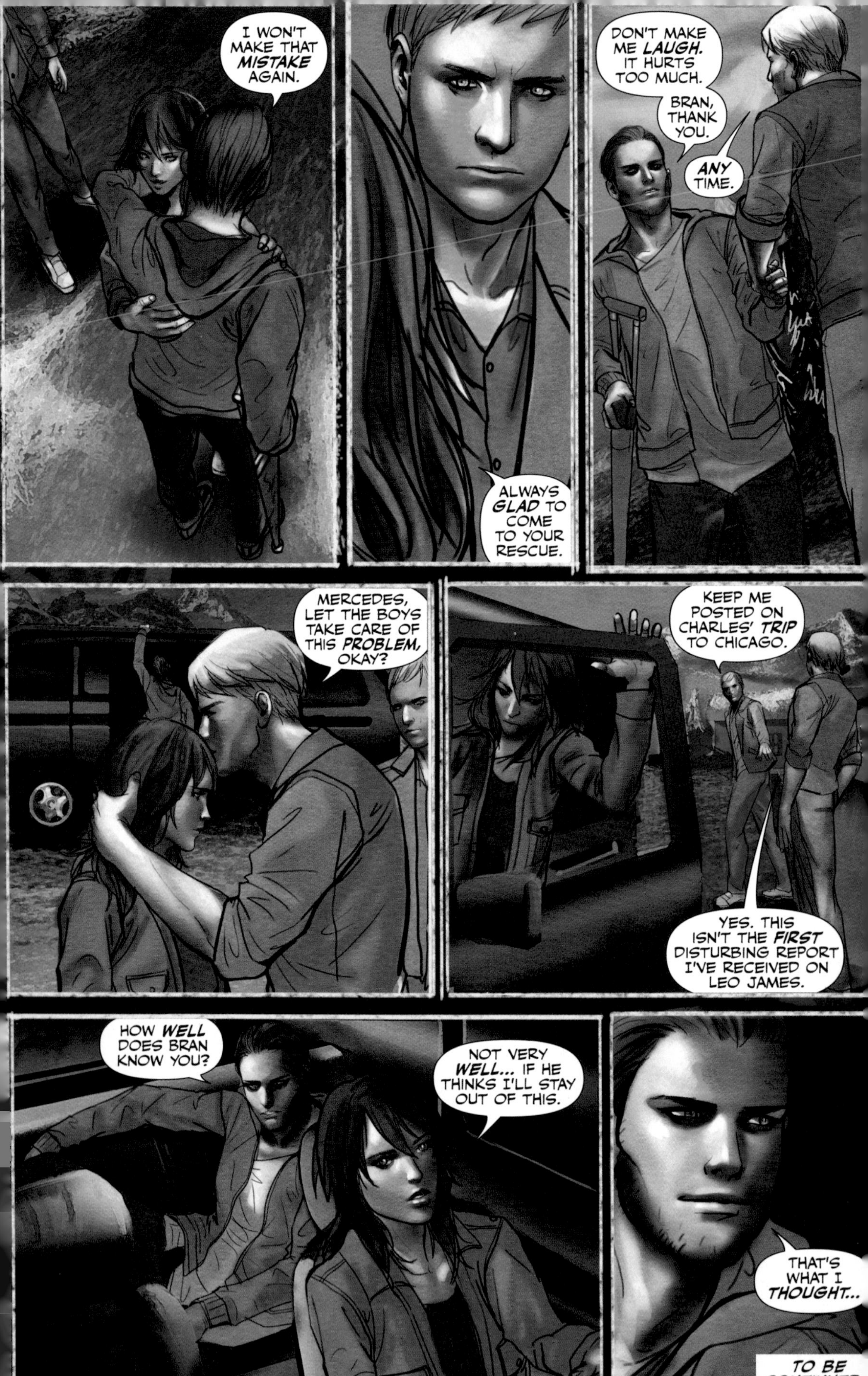
I WON'T MAKE THAT MISTAKE AGAIN.
ALWAYS GLAD TO COME TO YOUR RESCUE.
DON'T MAKE ME LAUGH. IT HURTS TOO MUCH.
BRAN, THANK YOU.
ANY TIME.
MERCEDES, LET THE BOYS TAKE CARE OF THIS PROBLEM, OKAY?
KEEP ME POSTED ON CHARLES' TRIP TO CHICAGO.
YES. THIS ISN'T THE FIRST DISTURBING REPORT I'VE RECEIVED ON LEO JAMES.
HOW WELL DOES BRAN KNOW YOU?
NOT VERY WELL... IF HE THINKS I'LL STAY OUT OF THIS.
THAT'S WHAT I THOUGHT...
TO BE CONTINUED

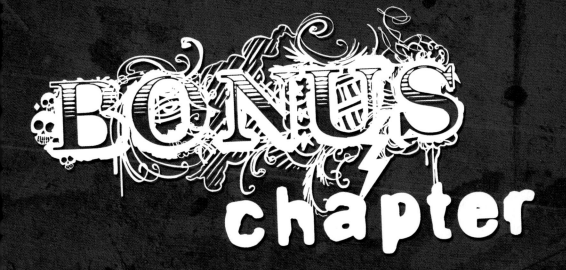

BONUS chapter

WRITTEN BY:
DAVID LAWRENCE

ARTWORK BY:
TODD HERMAN

COLORS BY:
MOHAN

LETTERS BY:
ZACH MATHENY

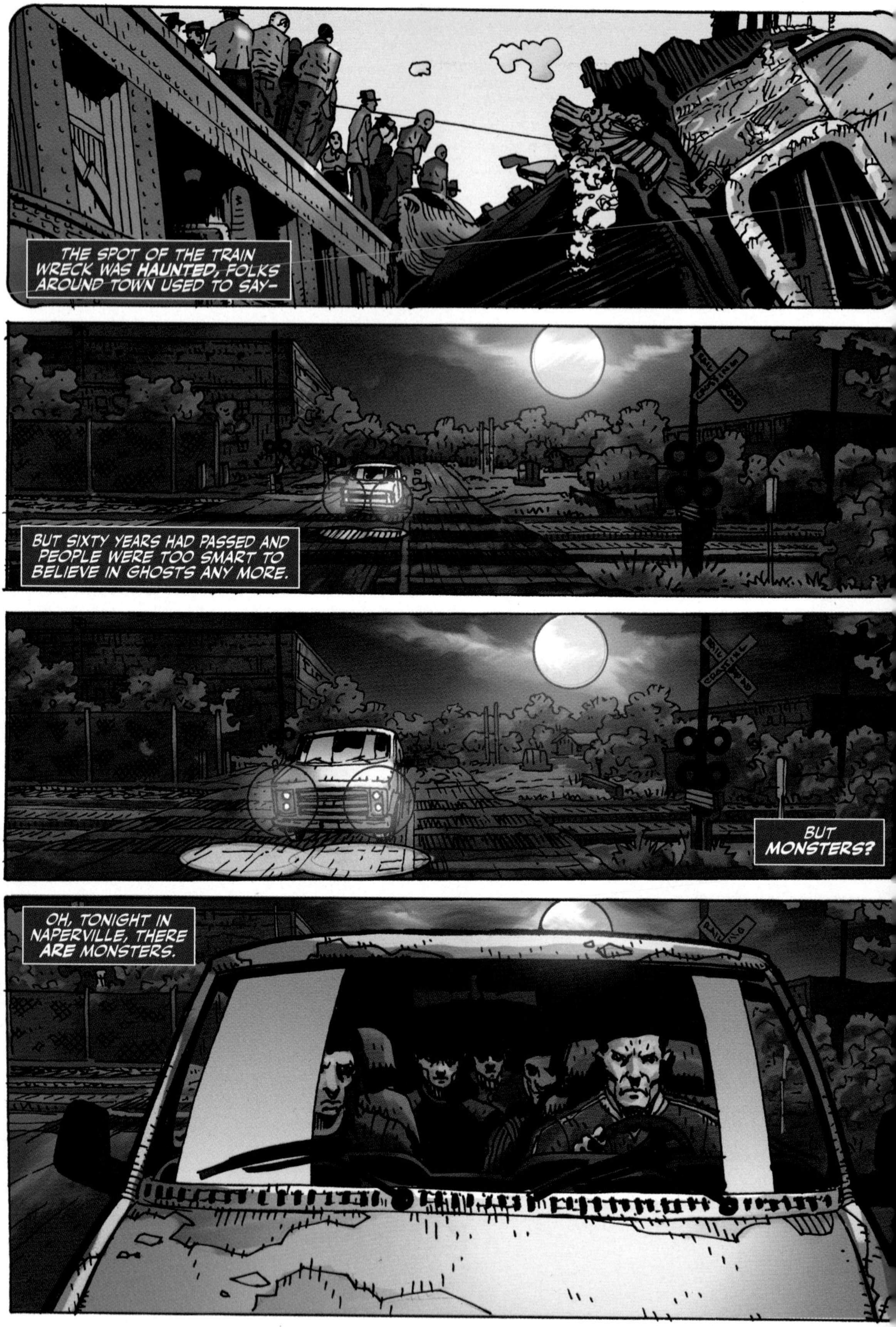
THE SPOT OF THE TRAIN WRECK WAS HAUNTED, FOLKS AROUND TOWN USED TO SAY–
BUT SIXTY YEARS HAD PASSED AND PEOPLE WERE TOO SMART TO BELIEVE IN GHOSTS ANY MORE.
BUT MONSTERS?
OH, TONIGHT IN NAPERVILLE, THERE ARE MONSTERS.

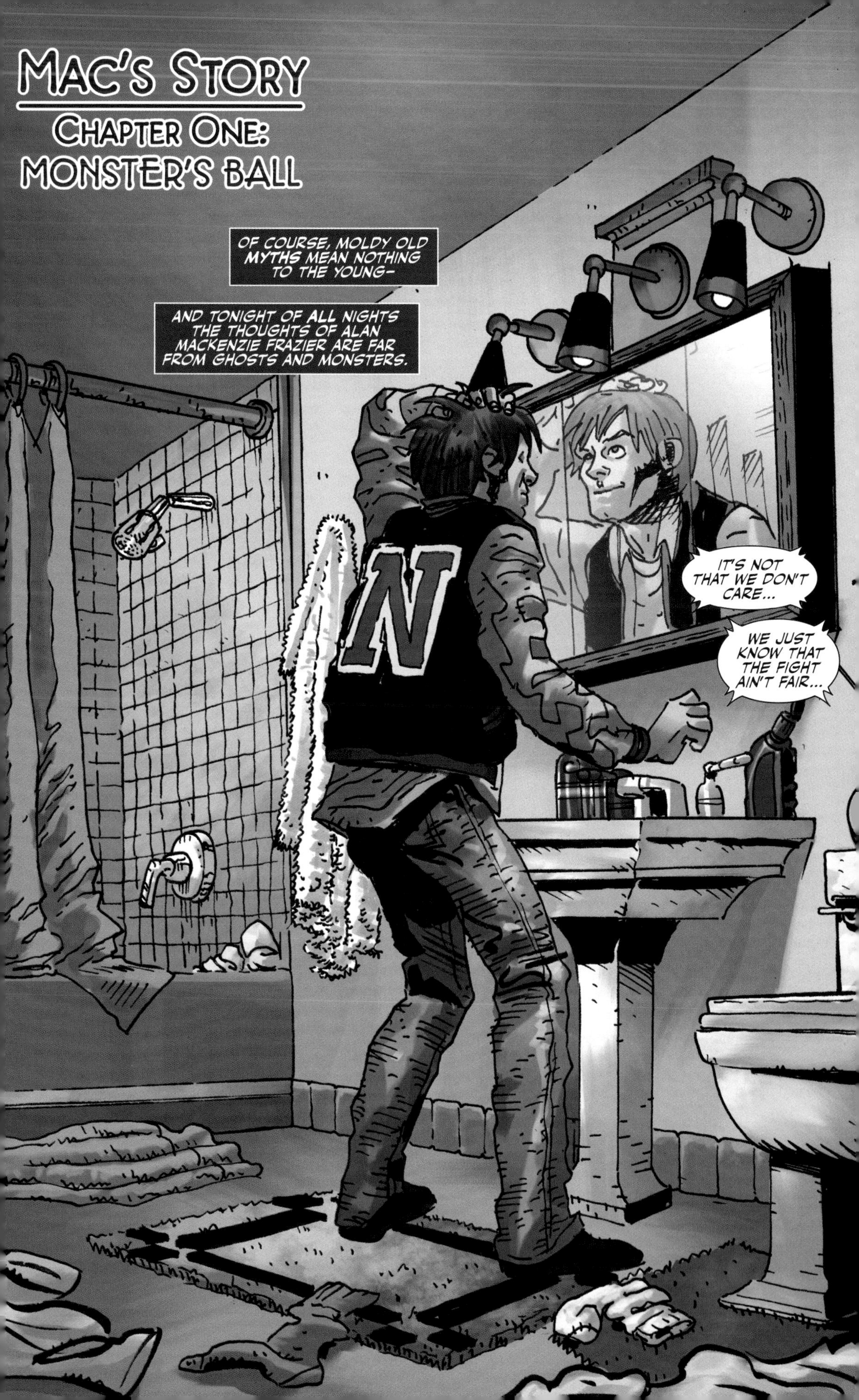
MAC'S STORY
CHAPTER ONE:
MONSTER'S BALL
OF COURSE, MOLDY OLD MYTHS MEAN NOTHING TO THE YOUNG-
AND TONIGHT OF ALL NIGHTS THE THOUGHTS OF ALAN MACKENZIE FRAZIER ARE FAR FROM GHOSTS AND MONSTERS.
IT'S NOT THAT WE DON'T CARE...
WE JUST KNOW THAT THE FIGHT AIN'T FAIR...

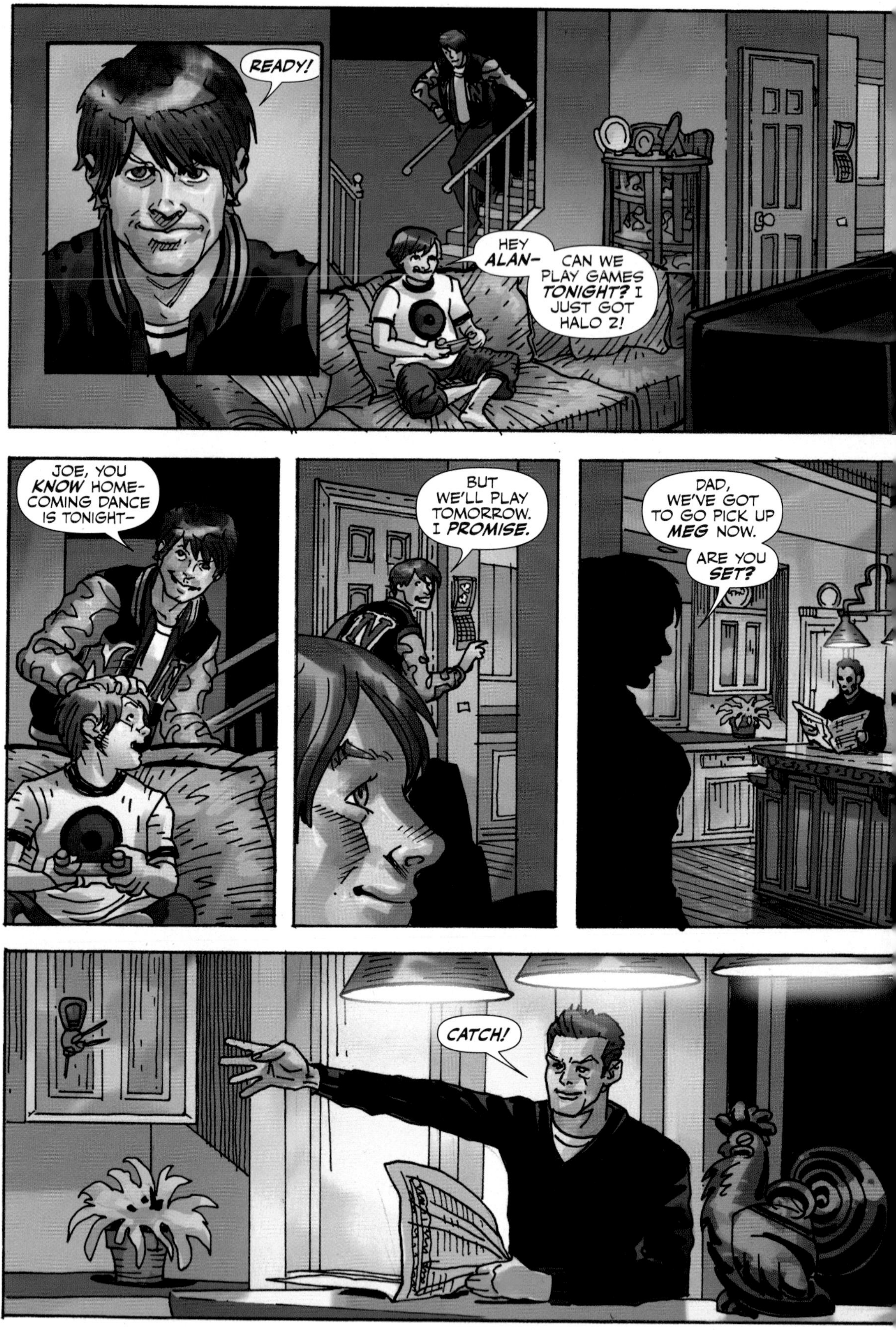
READY!
HEY ALAN-
CAN WE PLAY GAMES TONIGHT? I JUST GOT HALO 2!
JOE, YOU KNOW HOME-COMING DANCE IS TONIGHT-
BUT WE'LL PLAY TOMORROW. I PROMISE.
DAD, WE'VE GOT TO GO PICK UP MEG NOW.
ARE YOU SET?
CATCH!

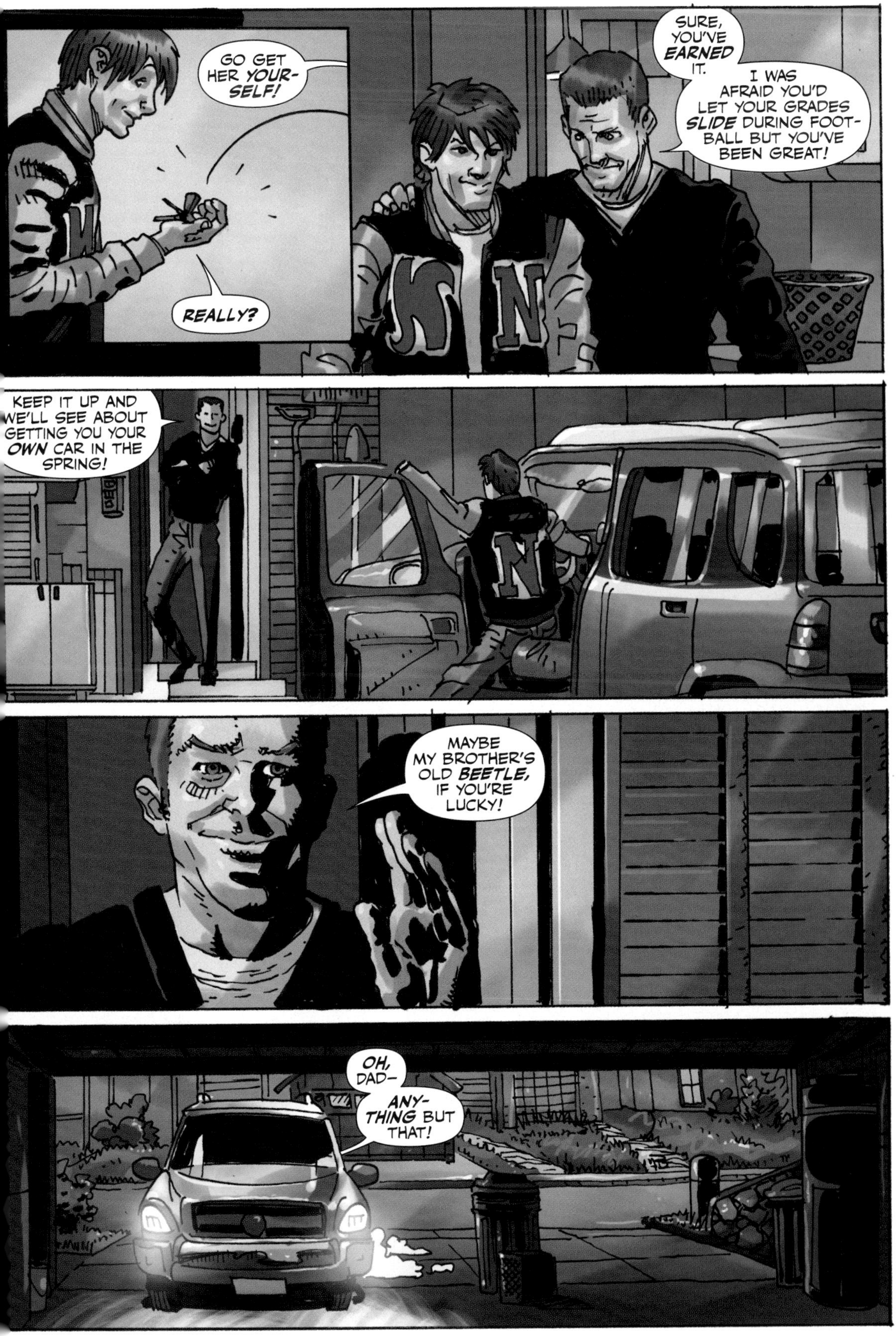
GO GET HER YOURSELF!
REALLY?
SURE, YOU'VE EARNED IT.
I WAS AFRAID YOU'D LET YOUR GRADES SLIDE DURING FOOTBALL BUT YOU'VE BEEN GREAT!
KEEP IT UP AND WE'LL SEE ABOUT GETTING YOU YOUR OWN CAR IN THE SPRING!
MAYBE MY BROTHER'S OLD BEETLE, IF YOU'RE LUCKY!
OH, DAD--
ANYTHING BUT THAT!

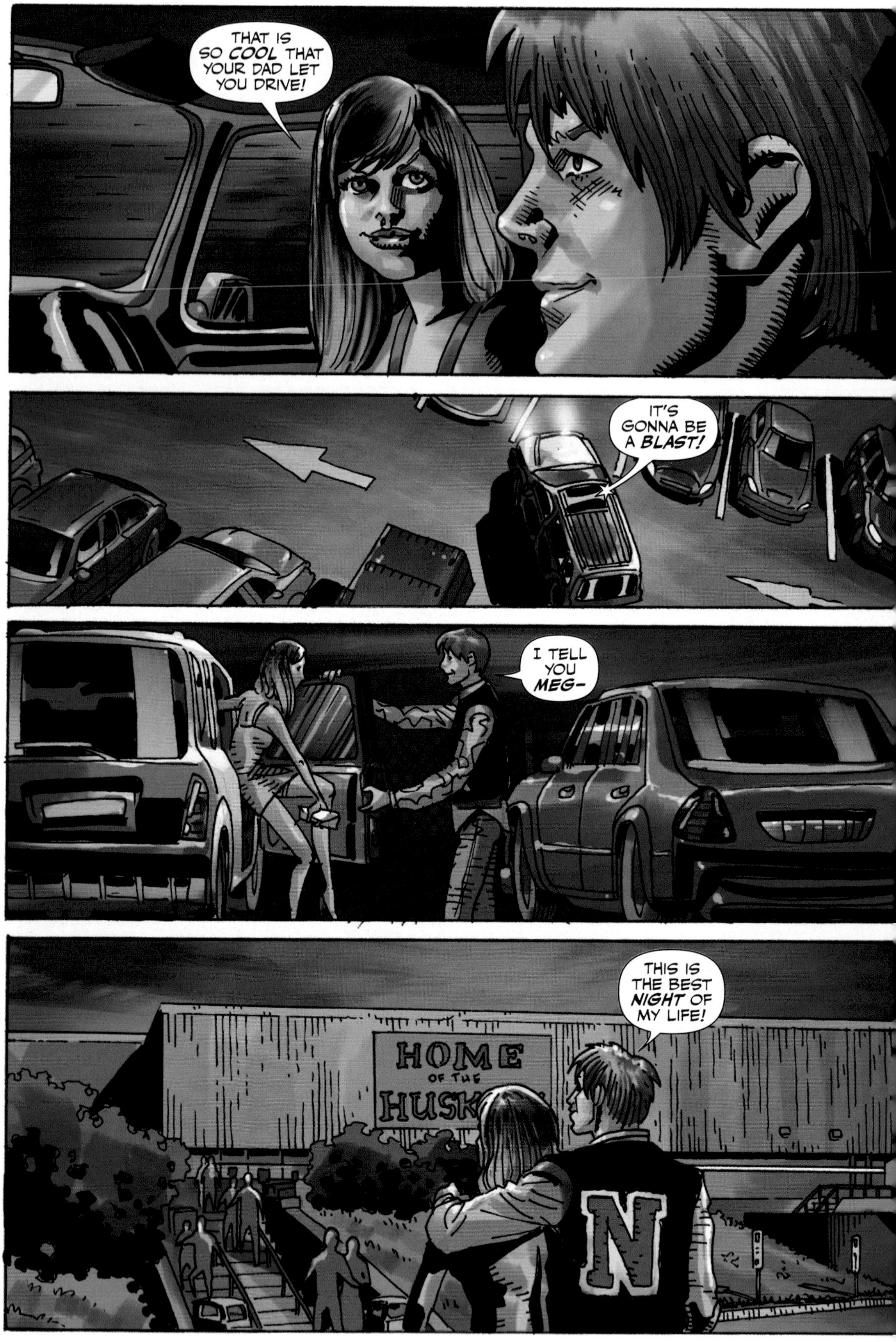
THAT IS SO COOL THAT YOUR DAD LET YOU DRIVE!
IT'S GONNA BE A BLAST!
I TELL YOU MEG–
THIS IS THE BEST NIGHT OF MY LIFE!
HOME
OF THE

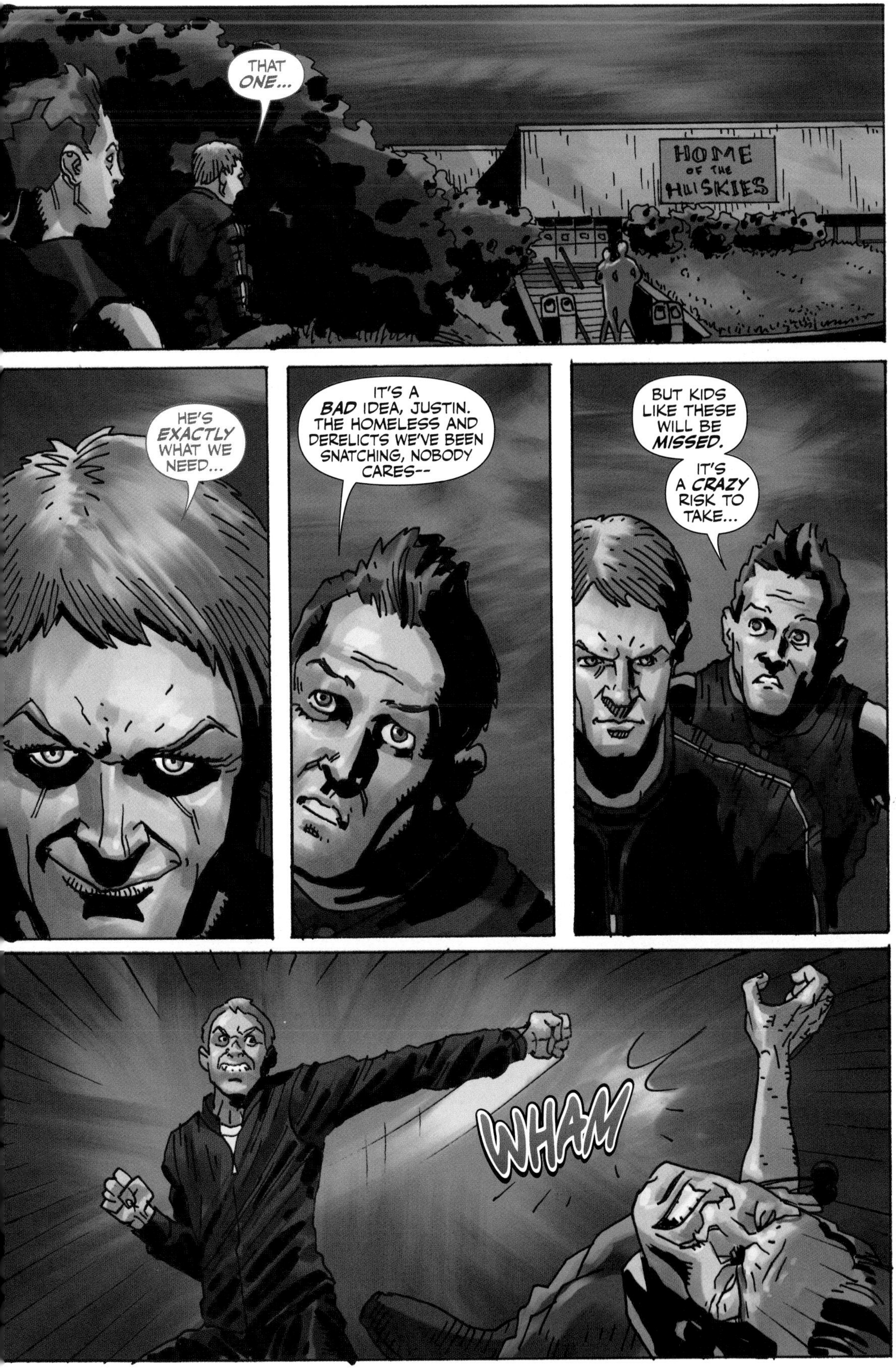
THAT ONE...
HOME OF THE HUSKIES
HE'S EXACTLY WHAT WE NEED...
IT'S A BAD IDEA, JUSTIN. THE HOMELESS AND DERELICTS WE'VE BEEN SNATCHING, NOBODY CARES--
BUT KIDS LIKE THESE WILL BE MISSED.
IT'S A CRAZY RISK TO TAKE...
WHAM

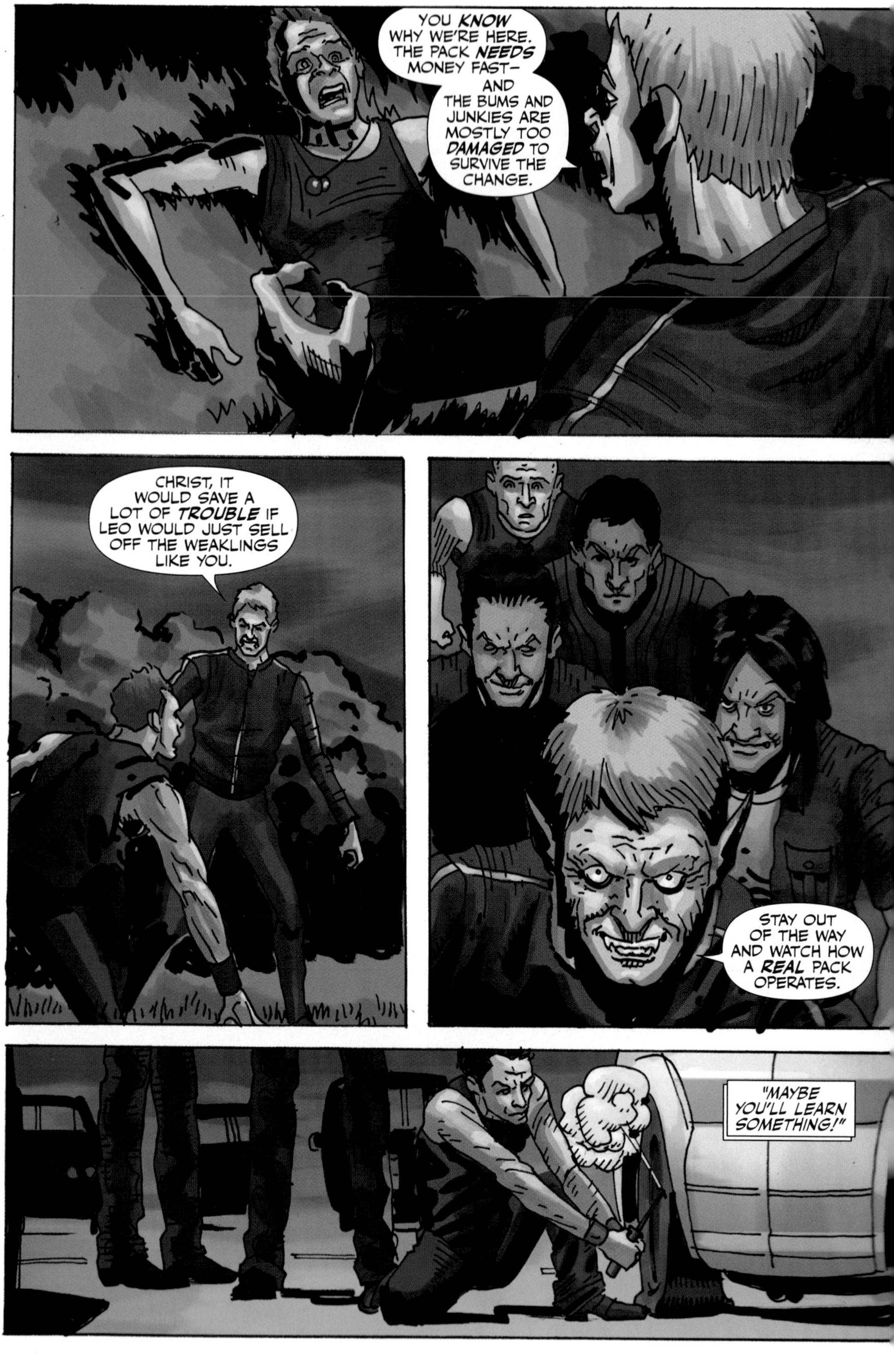
YOU KNOW WHY WE'RE HERE. THE PACK NEEDS MONEY FAST–
AND THE BUMS AND JUNKIES ARE MOSTLY TOO DAMAGED TO SURVIVE THE CHANGE.
CHRIST, IT WOULD SAVE A LOT OF TROUBLE IF LEO WOULD JUST SELL OFF THE WEAKLINGS LIKE YOU.
STAY OUT OF THE WAY AND WATCH HOW A REAL PACK OPERATES.
"MAYBE YOU'LL LEARN SOMETHING!"

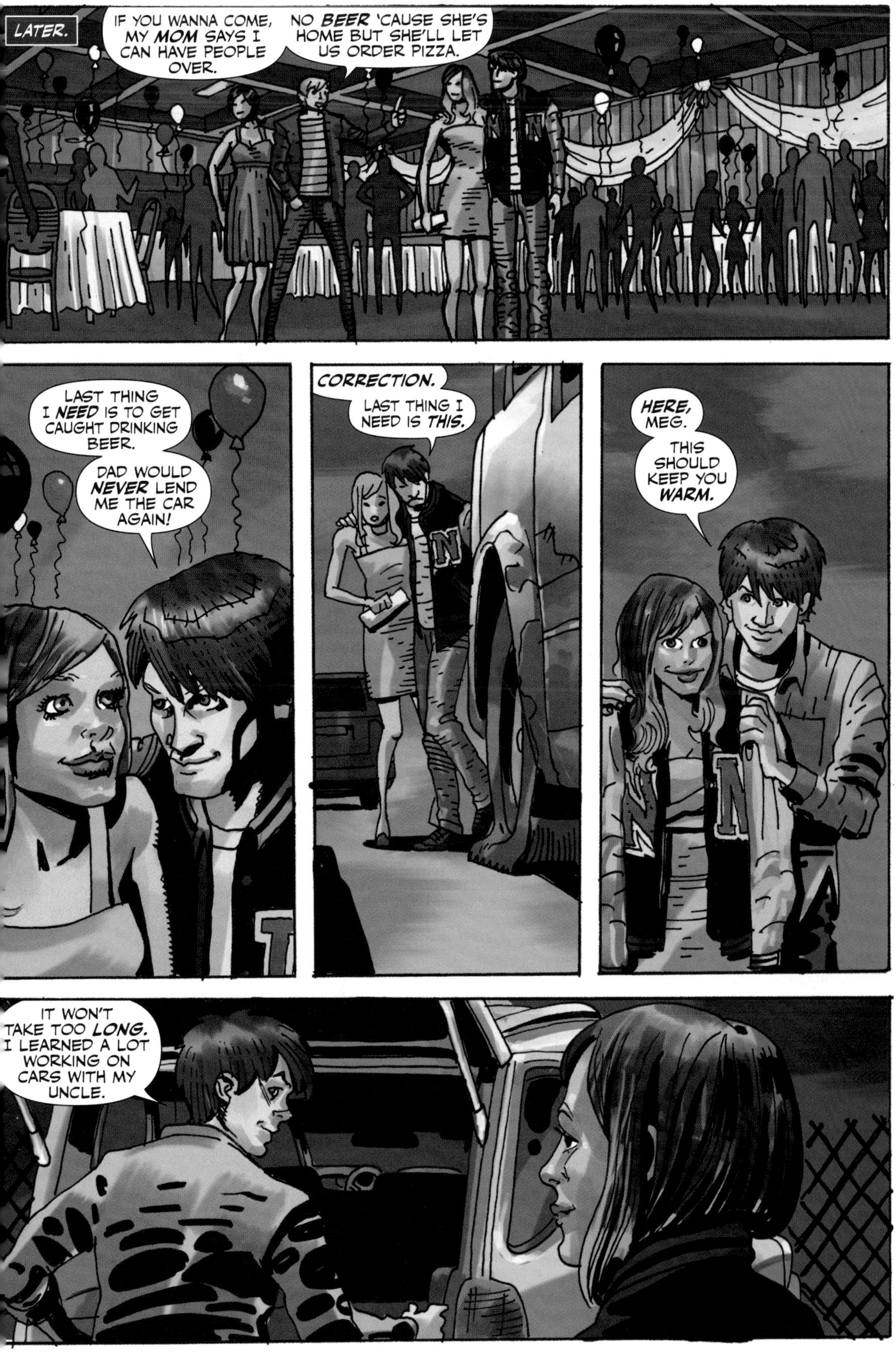
LATER.
IF YOU WANNA COME, MY MOM SAYS I CAN HAVE PEOPLE OVER.
NO BEER 'CAUSE SHE'S HOME BUT SHE'LL LET US ORDER PIZZA.
LAST THING I NEED IS TO GET CAUGHT DRINKING BEER.
DAD WOULD NEVER LEND ME THE CAR AGAIN!
CORRECTION.
LAST THING I NEED IS THIS.
HERE, MEG.
THIS SHOULD KEEP YOU WARM.
IT WON'T TAKE TOO LONG. I LEARNED A LOT WORKING ON CARS WITH MY UNCLE.

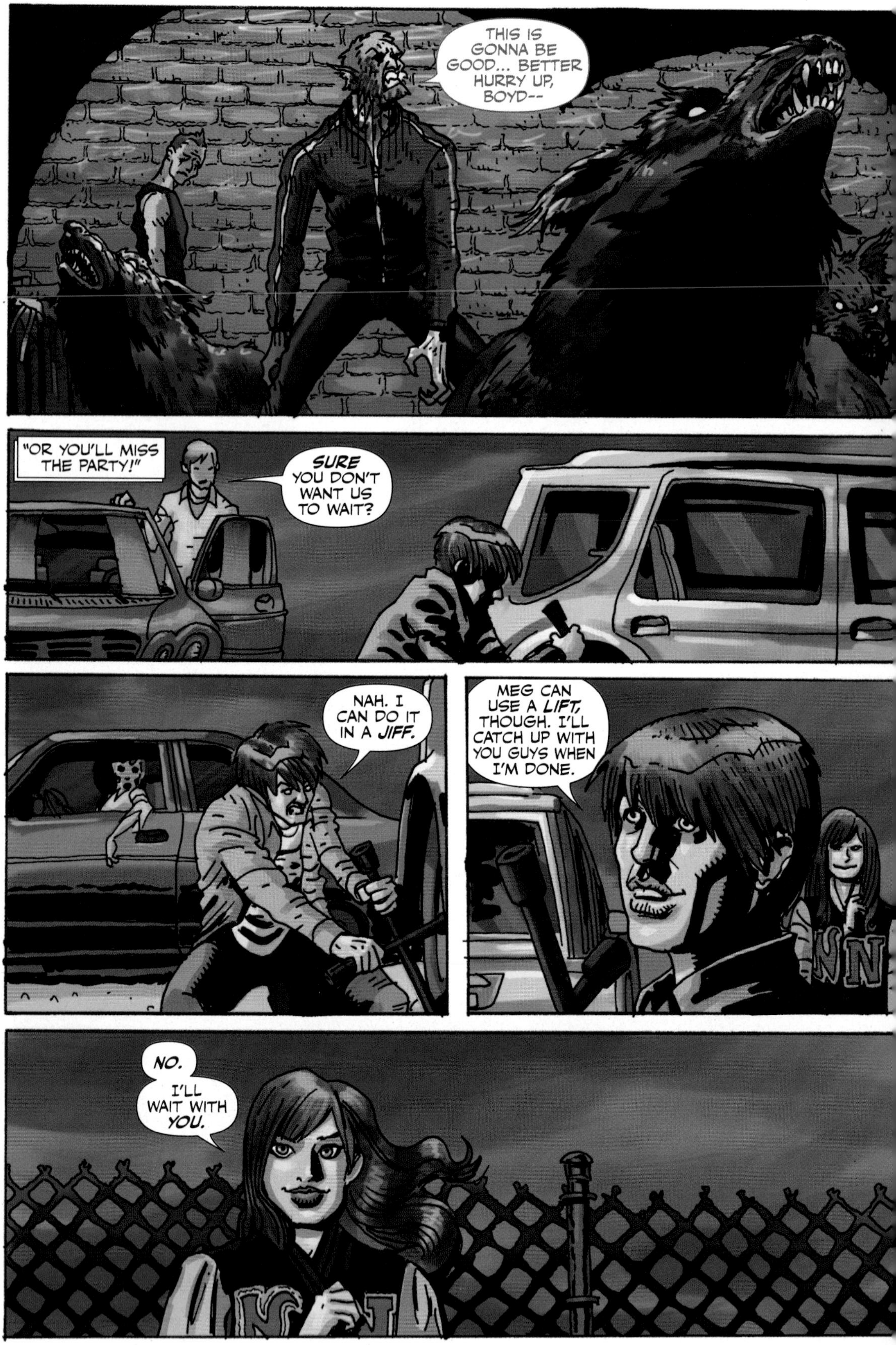
THIS IS GONNA BE GOOD... BETTER HURRY UP, BOYD--
"OR YOU'LL MISS THE PARTY!"
SURE YOU DON'T WANT US TO WAIT?
NAH. I CAN DO IT IN A JIFF.
MEG CAN USE A LIFT, THOUGH. I'LL CATCH UP WITH YOU GUYS WHEN I'M DONE.
NO.
I'LL WAIT WITH YOU.

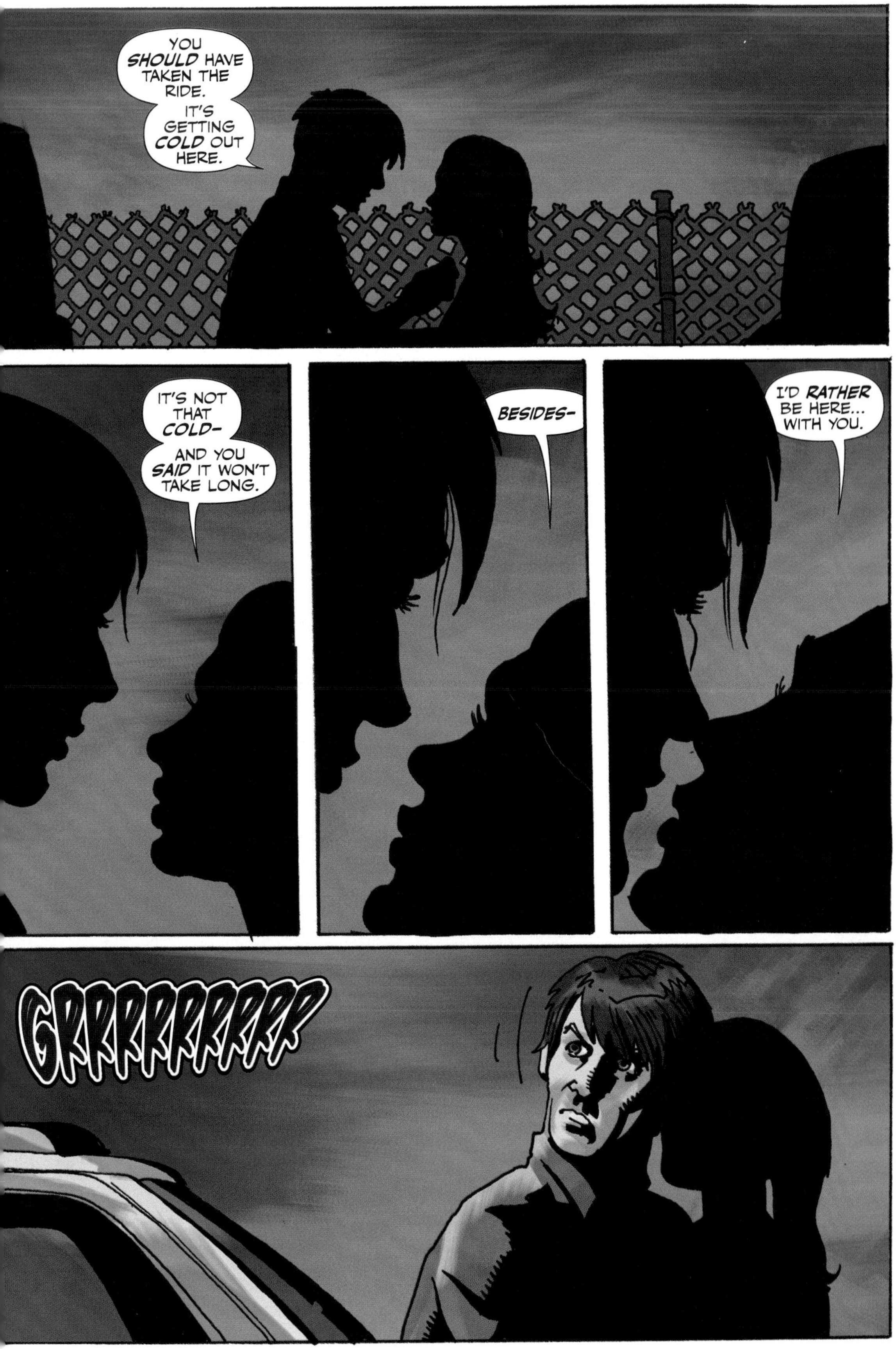
YOU *SHOULD* HAVE TAKEN THE RIDE.
IT'S GETTING *COLD* OUT HERE.
IT'S NOT THAT *COLD*-
AND YOU *SAID* IT WON'T TAKE LONG.
BESIDES-
I'D *RATHER* BE HERE... WITH YOU.
GRRRRRRRRR

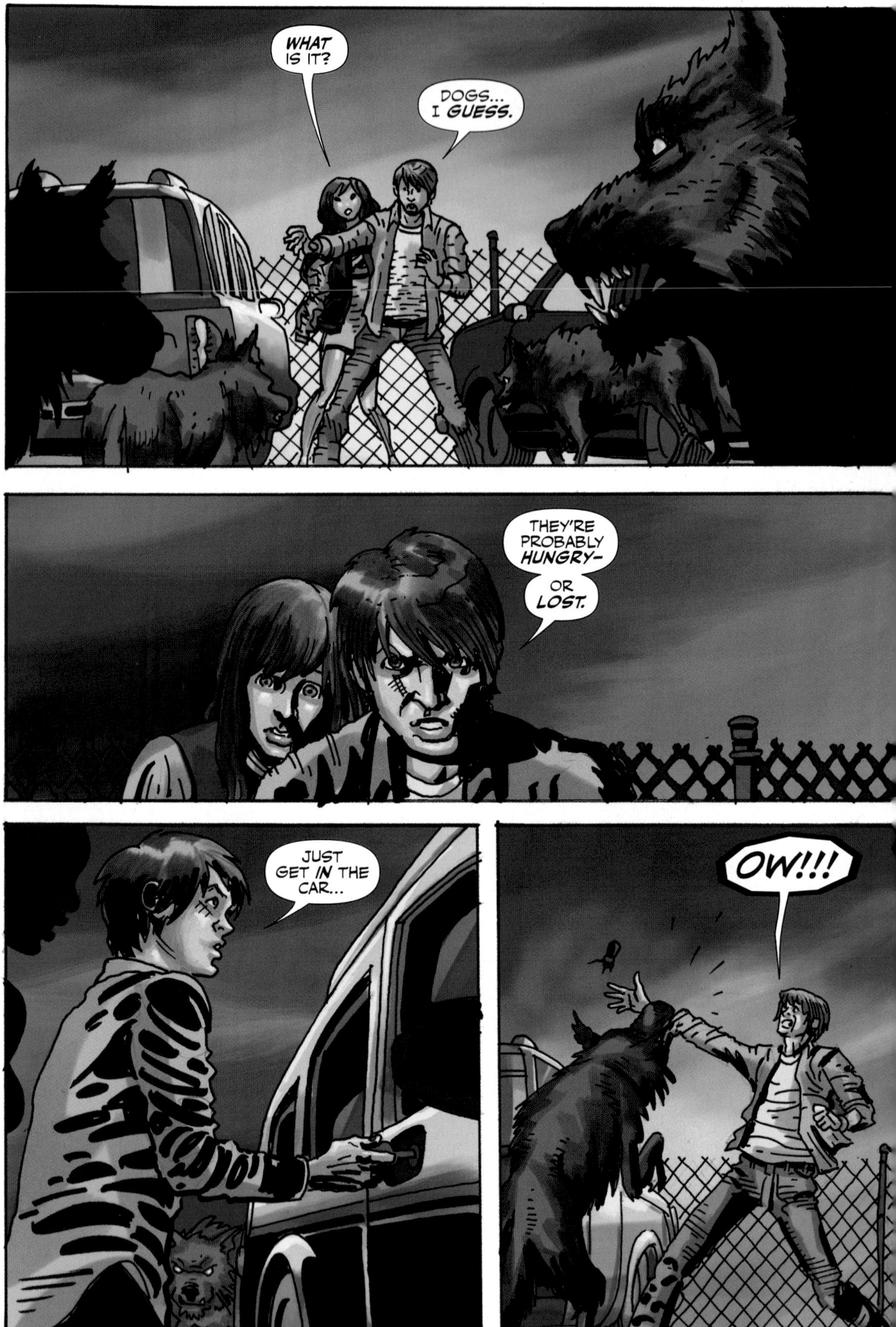
WHAT IS IT?
DOGS... I GUESS.
THEY'RE PROBABLY HUNGRY-
OR LOST.
JUST GET IN THE CAR...
OW!!!

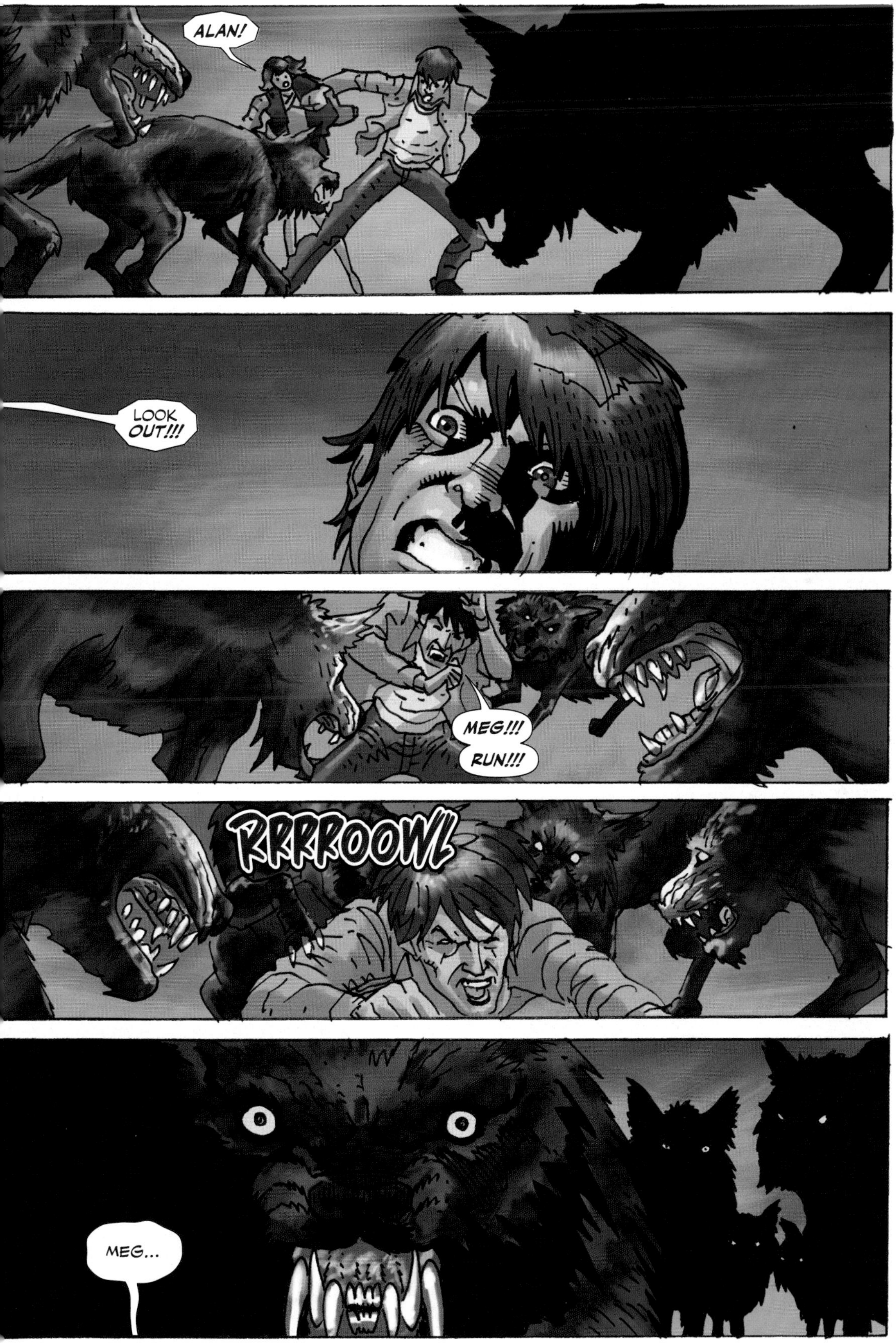
ALAN!
LOOK OUT!!!
MEG!!!
RUN!!!
RRRROOWL
MEG...

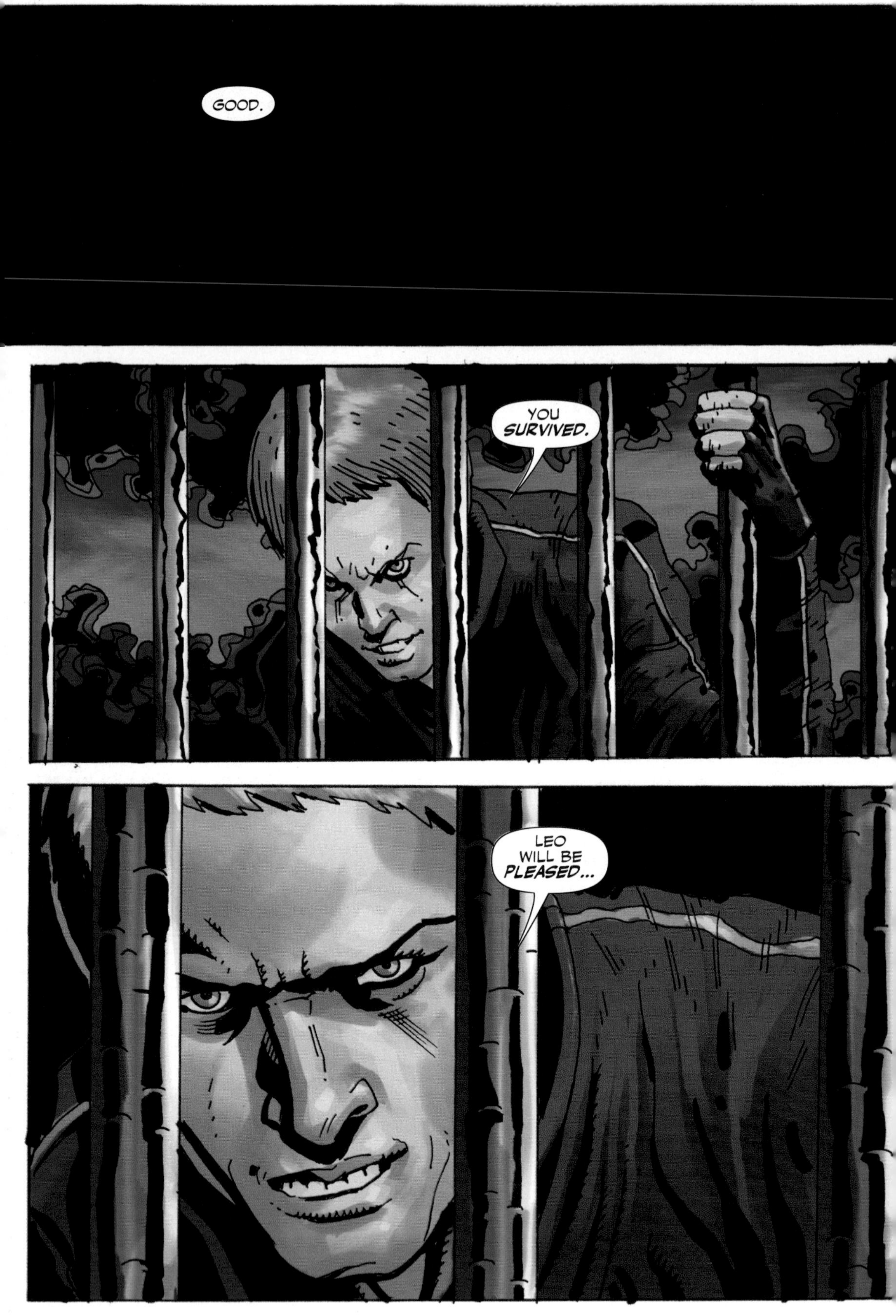
GOOD.
YOU SURVIVED.
LEO WILL BE PLEASED...

Afterword
with
David Lawrence

"You do what?"

That, more or less, is the standard response when I tell someone what I do. "I'm adapting a book as a graphic novel" is confusing to the uninitiated. And quite possibly to the initiated as well.

If I told them I was writing a book they would probably understand. And even if I told them I was writing comic books they would most likely get it.

But adapting? What is this thing? And graphic novel? What does that mean?

Of course, since you are holding this book (and for whatever reason are actually taking the time to read an essay from the adapter) you've most likely already got a grasp of all that. But you might still be wondering…just what do I do?

A friend of mine who'd done this sort of thing in years past (adapting, among others, Terry Pratchett) said the best you can hope is you don't screw things up too badly. Every time you make a cut…and no matter how many pages you have you're going to make cuts…you're leaving out somebody's favorite part of the book. And they are not going to forgive you.

So, with fingers crossed that I haven't spent the last six months of my life ruining your favorite novel, let's see if we can unravel the mystery of…what exactly I do.

First and foremost, I try to find the best way to tell somebody else's story. No matter how attached I might get to the characters, no matter how much I might enjoy working with them, no matter how cool I think it would be if Mercy could fly…they are not my characters…this is not my story!

My job is to stay true to the vision of the author while using the tools of my medium to tell her tale. Patty doesn't need my help to tell a story or create a compelling character. She does both damn well. Mostly what I do is think in pictures, and about how to use pictures instead of words to tell a story.

Even under the best of circumstances, in this medium, the writer is a supporting character. Sure, there's the odd Alan Moore here or there, but for the most part the star level creators in comics and graphic novels are artists, or writer/artists. Which is fair, because this is a visual medium. If my words were all that pretty I would have been a poet.

(Hungry and poor probably, but a poet.)

Writers provide the super-structure, the steel skeleton, the foundation that helps the artist shine. You might sometime have picked up a comic or graphic novel and said "This art is great but this story sucks!" But I'll bet you never said "This is a great script but the artist ruined it." Nope, you just said "This sucks."

And here, adapting the work of another author, I'm working even further in the background. It might even be, ideally, that you should read this book with no idea I am here. A good adapter might just be an invisible adapter. Got to check the ego at the door.

One of the first and most basic choices an adapter makes is what to leave out. That is probably counter-intuitive, the reverse of what most people would expect. In fact "So, you just pick out the best parts and leave those in?" is something, more or less, I've heard more than one person say.

Umm…no.

See, I don't pick what is in. As I start work, everything is in. It's all there, in the book in front of me. But even with 180 or so pages, we can't fit in every last bit of a 280 page novel. So no ifs or maybes, some things have got to go.

Case in point is the very first chapter of Moon Called…the novel, not the comic. It is twenty or so wonderful pages introducing Mercy and Mac and her world. It includes a wonderful scene at a church that I was just dying to work in…

Yet in the end that scene, and a lot of that chapter, had to go.

My solution, I think, was creative. Or at least, like Kirk's solution to the Kobayashi Maru, it had the benefit of not being tried before.

I tried to set the stage and capture the essence of Mercy's world in one page, a few words, and some eye-catching images so we could then just dive right into her story. Some folks liked it, some didn't. But as I said, even at its best an adaptation is a condensation.

And here, a condensation in a different medium, with different needs. We tell stories with pictures. That means, simply, that something has to happen. There has to be action, or at least activity, on a lot of the pages. 22 pages of talking heads isn't a comic book, or a graphic novel. It's a monologue, or a dialogue. Maybe it's a very good dialogue.

But it's not what this medium is built for.

So that's my job: respecting Patty's vision while retelling her story through pictures.

Oh, and one more detail: it has to be entertaining.

It may sound simple but it needs saying. It is painfully easy to be a bad adapter…and easily painful to read a bad adaptation. How many bad movie adaptions have you read? Everything was in there…but it was all blah. Or perhaps a better comparison, the old Gilberton Classics Illustrated, with their snooze inducing versions of hundreds of literary classics?

It's easy to recognize a bad adaptation, but how do we define a good one?

It should be as exciting as an original while remaining true to the author's (in this case Patty's) vision. It should tell the story through sensational pictures that add an extra dimension without obscuring the source. It should be embraced by old fans while winning new ones.

"You do what???"

Well hopefully, all that.

But enough of my philosophic waxing. The following pages, if you are still awake, will give you some further idea of the nuts and bolts of what I do. Enlightenment awaits within!

But before I shut up (finally!!!) a few brief words of acknowledgment:

I'd like to thank Patty Briggs for generously letting me play in her sandbox and supporting all I do, as well as thanking Patty and her husband Mike for just generally being great people. I'd like to thank Linda Campbell and Deb Lentz for giving generously of their time and encyclopedic knowledge to keep the facts of Mercy's world accurate as possible. I'd like to thank the wonderfully talented Amelia Woo, who not only provides beautiful art but uncomplainingly satisfies every single request to redraw or reconsider or retry. I could not ask for a better collaborator; she makes me look better than I am.

And I would like to thank Danny Lawrence, who made me what I am (whatever that is) today…and who I very much wish were here to hold this book in his hands today. Miss ya, Big Daddy!

David Lawrence

January 6, 2011

PAGE ONE

Panel one:
An establishing shot of the WALLA WALLA FAE RESERVATION. Here's
a photo to base the shot on:
http://www.colorado.gov/dpa/doit/archives/wwcod/granada.htm
But instead of the long barracks you see in the photo break them
up into long rows of small, identical houses, with small identical, individual yards, packed tightly into grids. The reservation is surrounded by a tall cinder-block wall with razor wire
on the top and a guardhouse at the gate. A red and yellow sun-
set fills the sky.

1 CAPTION:
The Walla Walla Fae Reservation holds the largest concentration
of magical beings on the West Coast.

Panel two:
Here's another photo to base panel two on:
http://farrit.lili.org/node/94
but instead of Asians the internees are sprites and elves and
such. Similar to humans, but different. Some might have oversized eyes or big heads or pointed ears. Perhaps one or two have
wings. The large figure, in the foreground, should sort of
resemble a shar-pei dog. (In case you don't know, a shar-pei
looks like this: http://canined.com/dogs/category/chinese-shar-
pei/)

To be clear, don't give him a dog's head, but kind of base the
features on this. Deep wrinkles, kind of droopy, big brown eyes,
an oversized head.

2 CAPTION:
The Gray Lords, rulers of the fae, saw the time of hiding was
past. Human science would soon uncover their presence, so they
forced their subjects to unmask.

3 CAPTION:
Unfortunately they failed to anticipate humanity's reaction.

Panel three:
Inside one of the small reservation house Mercy's friend ZEE (see
reference) peeks out his window into the common yard, a serious
look on his face.

4 CAPTION:
Or perhaps, as some suspected—

5 CAPTION:
It was just the first step in the Gray Lords larger plan…

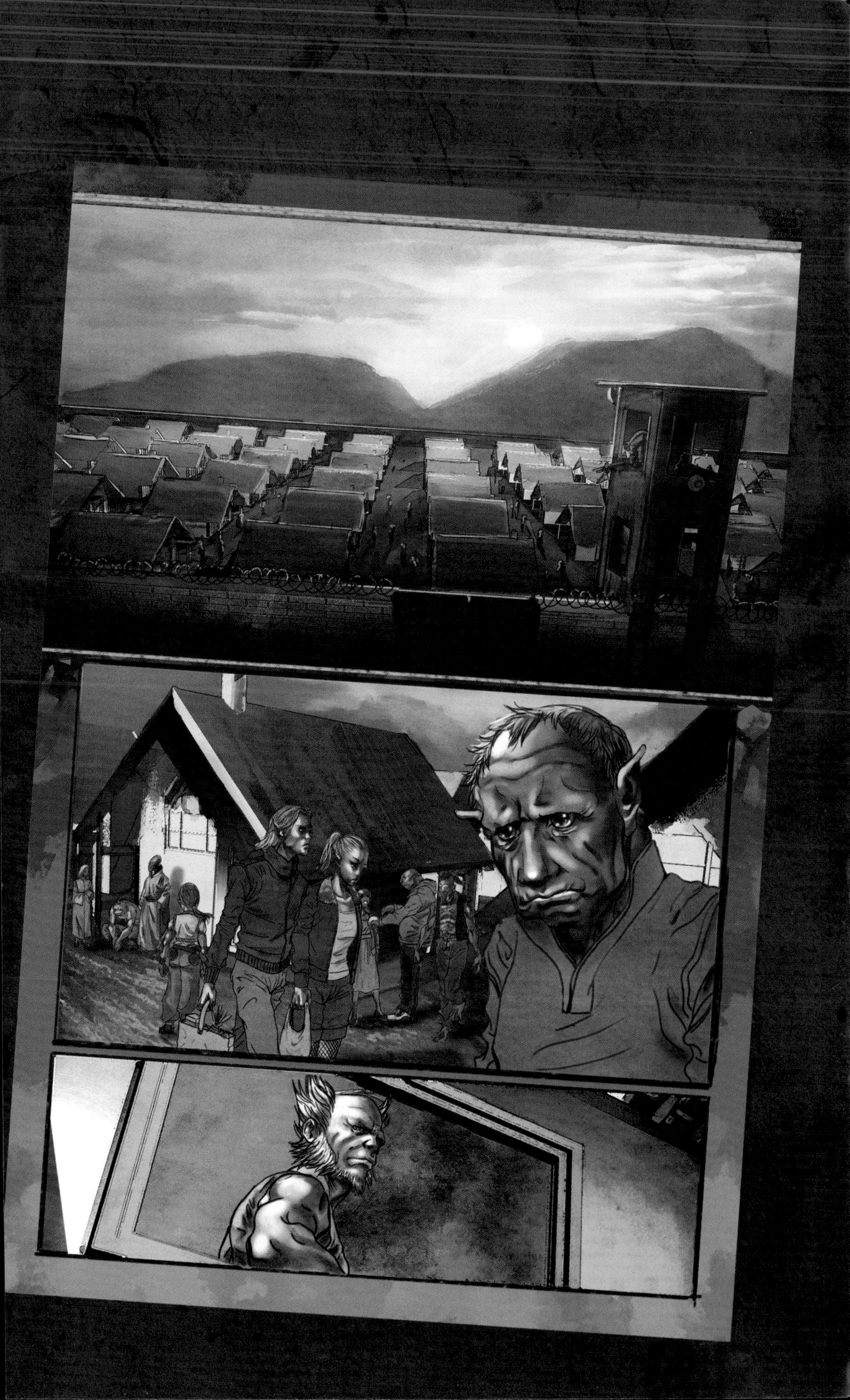

PAGE TWO

Panel one:
Long panel. Night. A half moon hangs in the sky. An establishing shot of Mercy's garage and lot, at a bit of a distance and from a little above. A tall sign at the edge of the lot says "VW REPAIR", using the VW logo. A few scattered cars are parked on the lot, mostly VWs. A van is parked in front of the door. The van is painted to look like the Mystery Machine in Scooby Doo.

1 CAPTION:
I work in Kennewick, one of the Tri-Cities in Washington. It's about 40 miles away--

2 CAPTION:
But we have no shortage of things that go bump in the night.

Panel two
MERCY THOMPSON comes out of the front door, dressed in sweats with a jacket, purse over her shoulder and keys in her hand. There are people on the other side of the van, though neither Mercy nor we can see them.

3 BALLOON (from off panel):
I'm packing silver bullets.

Panel three:
Reaction shot. Tight close-up on Mercy's eyes, one eyebrow raised in surprise.

4 BALLOON (from off panel):
Get in the car, kid--

Panel four:
Mercy starts to slip out of her clothes.

5 BALLOON (from off panel):
Or you're dead.

Panel five:
Big panel. Multiple figure transformation sequence. We have Mercy in her human guise, now naked, standing erect, then Mercy hunched forward, then Mercy in coyote form, and finally coyote Mercy leaps into the air toward the top of the van. The first three figures are translucent, with the first one the faintest, each succeeding figure a little more solid. Only the last figure, the leaping coyote, is completely solid.

6 CAPTION:
My name is Mercy Thompson. I'm not fae, strictly speaking, and free from the whims of the Gray Lords--

7 CAPTION:
Though I have magic of my own.

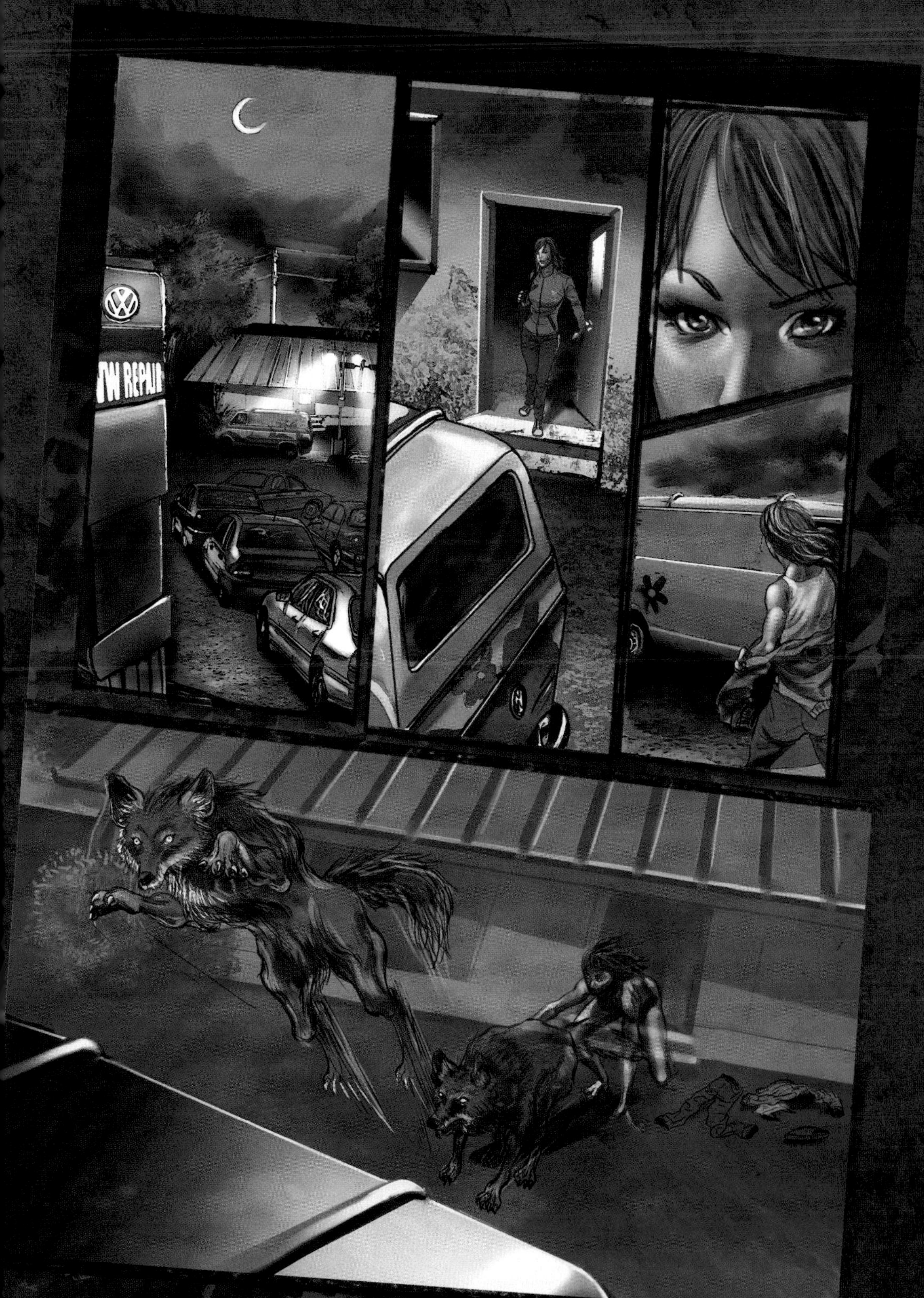

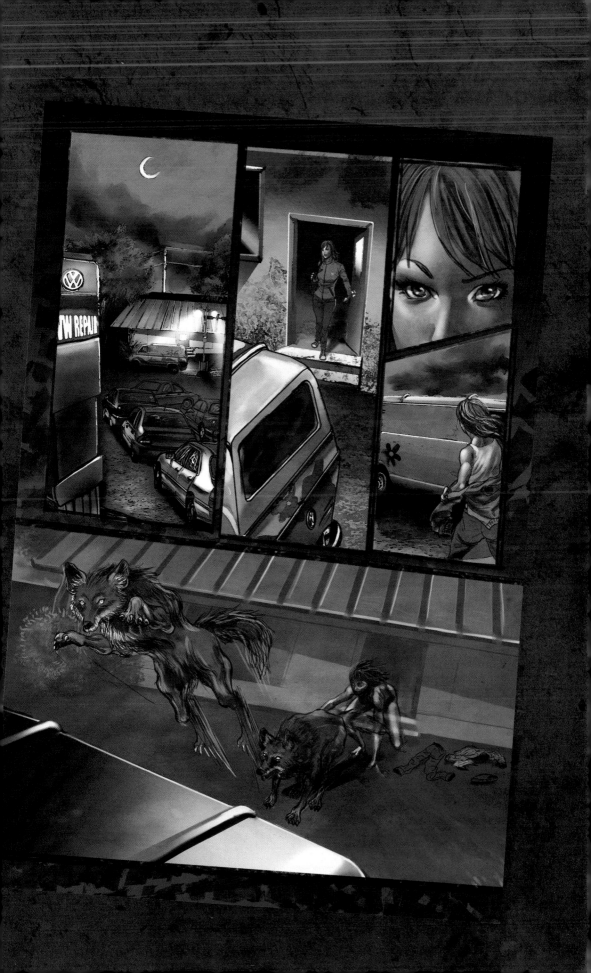

PAGE THREE

Panel one:
Full page splash. Coyote Mercy stands atop the van, looking down on the scene.

Below Mercy two hard looking men are holding a boy at gunpoint. The boy is Mac, a 15 or 16 year old runaway. He is gaunt with chestnut hair, tall for his age with big hands and shoulders wide but bony. He's got chestnut colored hair and brown eyes. He wears ratty jeans and a worn flannel shirt. His back is to the van and Mercy. He is frightened, arms and legs spread, knees bent, looking for a chance to make a break for it. The man closer to Mac, who we will simply call Man #1, points a big, black automatic handgun at him. He wears his hair in a close-cropped crew-cut. A larger man, with longer hair, stands a couple of steps back; we'll call him Man #2. Both stand very erect, with military posture. They face in Mercy's direction though they are too intent on the boy to see her. Behind men is a big, black Hummer, with the lights on and the engine running.

1 MAC:
And if I get in I'm <u>dead</u> anyway--

2 MAC:
Just like Meg and the poor people you kept in the <u>cages</u>.

3 CAPTION:
<u>Cages???</u>

4 CAPTION:
Maybe this <u>was</u> too big for me.

5 CAPTION:
Maybe I should have gone to <u>Adam</u>.

6 TITLE:

Chapter One:
FIRST BLOOD

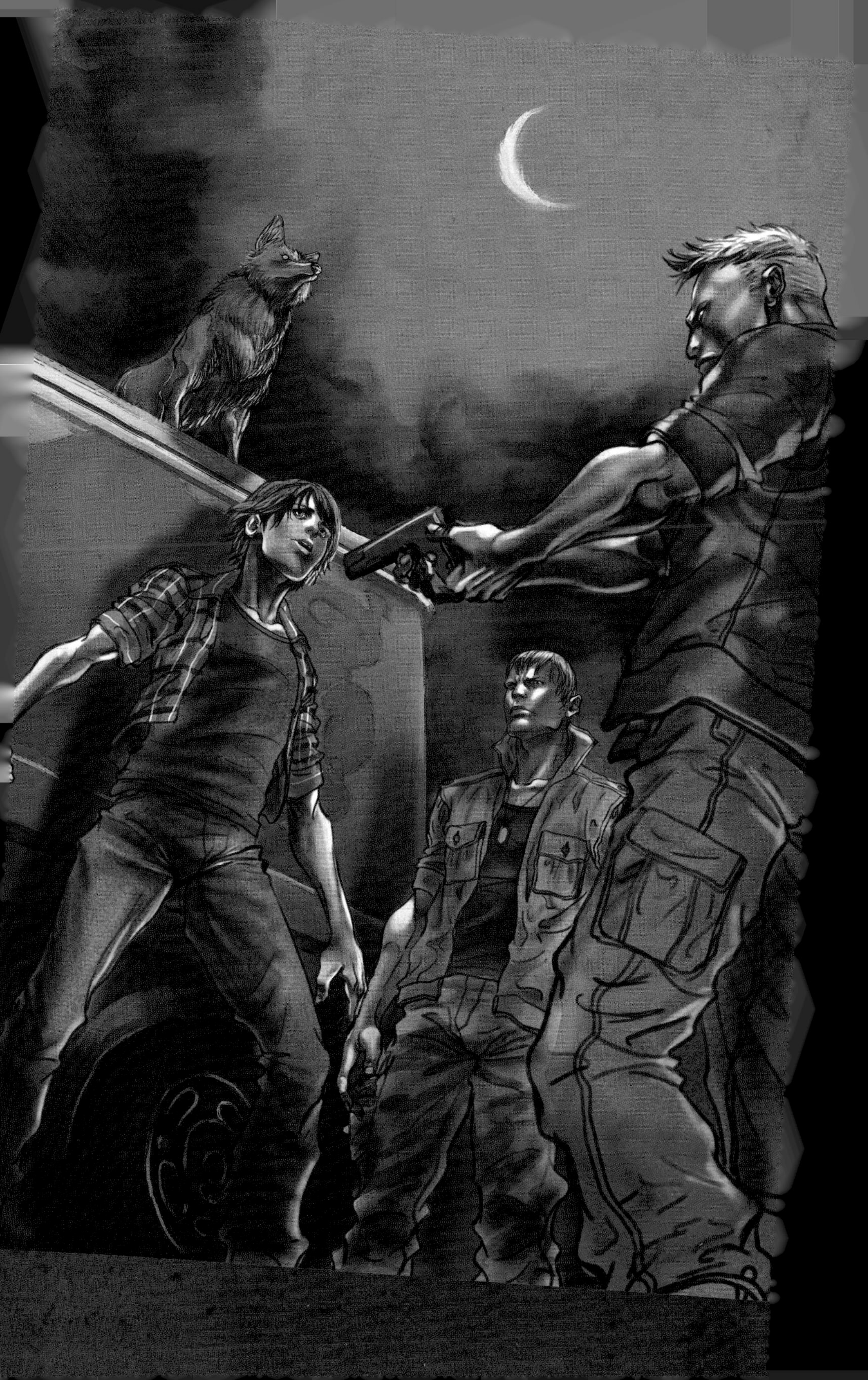

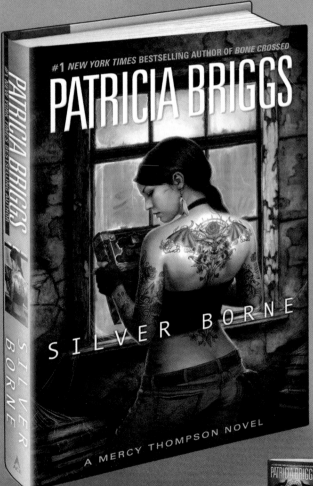